Hamish MacDonald was born in Helensburgh in 1958 and raised in Clydebank. He worked as an engineer before turning full-time to writing and production of drama, previously writing comedy, plays and poems in his spare time, with comedy contributions to BBC TV and Radio. He wrote *Redcoats: A Folktale for the Twenty-First Century* (Highland Festival '98), then *The Captain's Collection* (Highland Festival '99), which he adapted into an international award winning four-part drama-documentary for BBC Radio Scotland (Celtic Film and TV 2000). This was followed by *The Strathspey King* which collected first prize for BBC Radio Scotland at Celtic Film and TV 2001. *The Gravy Star* is his first novel. He lives in Inverness with Kim and their daughter Kenna.

The Gravy Star

www.11-9.co.uk

The Gravy Star

Hamish MacDonald

First published by

303a The Pentagon Centre
36 Washington Street
GLASGOW
G3 8AZ

Tel: 0141 204 1109
Fax: 0141 221 5363

E-mail: info@nwp.sol.co.uk
www.11-9.co.uk

A catalogue record for this book is available from the British Library

11:9 is funded by the Scottish Arts Council National Lottery Fund

ISBN 1 903238 26 9

Typeset in Utopia
11:9 series designed by Mark Blackadder

Printed in Finland by WS Bookwell

For Kim and Kenna

Thank you to Donald and Grace MacDonald

Many thanks to James Robertson and his Kettilonia Press for active support and encouragement from the early days

The author wishes to acknowledge the support of the Scottish Arts Council for the purpose of writing this book

★	channels	1
★★	annals	139
★★★	daniels	269

channels

I have to shut it all out. Somebody's out there with a channel-clicker. Surfing through me and my head just flashes from one thing to the next. Maybe God with His remote-control. I manage to stop the pictures but He keeps teasing me. Twiddling a tuner along the air waves so's I can hear things. Best to switch off altogether if you can. Unplug yourself at the mains. Blackness.

At last a distant glow. I'm walking through a spent intestine in the corpse of an ancient industrial giant. Through the old railway tunnel towards a tiny eye of light that waxes into a white star with each advancing step. Eyeflash. Floaters crawling across my vision and now I'm squinting into the brightness of the twenty-first century. A blinding hemisphere of light streaming through iron palings that bar the tunnel mouth. Razorwire curling round the bars like thorns. Yawoo. A formidable portcullis. Glowering out into the silent gully. Only bush and tree out there now no train rumble here for plenty years.

Leaves gone dark green hang heavy out in the stillness of the cut. Drowsy from sap on account of the summer drouth. Windless out there too. Edgy kind of. I bide inside the dark and watch clouds pass across the sun. Looks like trouble. The day holding its breath. Cowering from the threat of the storm like a dog waiting to be kicked. In the sky above clouds draw together then spew out a lightning bolt and let go with a blast of thunder. A forked tongue and a roar. Stillness. Now rain. A heavy lump thuds then another then a steady beat on the parched embankment rises to a frenzied drum solo on leaves and pathways and soon. Puddles. A great hissing pissing deluge. Bastardo! Shopping expedition? No way MacNab. Out of the question.

Out beyond the park is the boulevard and I'm hearing traffic drone and the wash of wheels on flooded tarmac. Regular like waves on a shore. Mhm Yes Siree-Oh. Just stand awhile looking out. Dropping the jangle of keys I've held in palm-clutch for the last fifty paces back into a deep pocket of the trusty langcoat. Then guddle among the gallery of inside pockets for the smoke tackle rolling up a thin-ee with a liquorice paper and a crumb of dry baccy from a corner of the tin. Jesus Sliced. The supplies are low. When I go reach in for the tinder my arm releases a pocket of stale air from the left oxter so's I get a smell of me for a moment. Whoof. Howlin. Gad. I'm needing a bath. Bad style aye mister a big hot soaking steaming bath. Maybe even two. The rain really dinging it now and for a sec I'm considering getting raw bollock nae-kit and going out into it for a shower a richt good soak. Na. Joke. I'd prob'ly end up with the heeb-jeebs or the flumonia or the dreaded lergy. Probably the prile. That's the deal I would get. Fate's hand. A prile of diseases. Just smoke the rollie fag then head back uptunnel. Back up north tunnel to the doss. The auberge.

I let go a plume of rollie smoke that curls into the light as another thunder-blast ripples across the sky. I only allow the outside light to caress me from the knees down keeping my body in the upper darkness. Keeping the Camp Secret. Careless moves cost abodes. Three steps back would erase me. Twenty paces takes me down into The Silence. The tomb. The womb. That's all it takes. The thin-ee's well smoked so take the last sook and flick it down then start the uptunnel hike. But don't dilly dally on the way. Because The Silence is. Well. Not really a silence. Not if you stay among it too long not if you've spent the time in it I have no sir no sir I've heard it all down here. The screams of a new-born bairn. The long lost shouts of distant friends. The wind. And the girl who cries goodbye. Surge of a river swear I can hear the river sometimes clear as you like as though I'm walking along the bank and it's right there next to me in the darkness flowing along chattering. Then I hold on to my ears in case there's a drowning man in there and he's calling for me to help so I start running a bit to reach the light at the other end then maybe I'll go sideways and hit the tunnel wall and give myself a dunt. Hey Mac. Plod on. For to dwell on such things is not healthy. I say. Sir. It's not healthy.

Waiting for the light of the vent. Be a whilie yet. Through black air and soil above is the Botanic Gardens. Manicured lawns. Giant ferns and palms drooping fronds in the sweating heat of glass arcades. There's a smell in there. A thick muggy mulchy smell. Like a Victorian lady's crotchpiece. *Are you wise? Give it a rest.* Well. What of it? Gladstone and Disraeli both gave speeches in there you know. Empire City and all that. O*oh! Well Ya-Boh! Ya-Boh! Invooboo! Pass me the rifle whilst I don the kilt and pith helmet Corporal MacNab. And we'll go and pick off a few fuzzies for the greater glory of Scotland.* Yes! Ya-Boh! Let's hear it for Baden-Powell and the Scout's War Cry! Een-Gonyama Een-Gonyama! Ya-Boh! Ya-Boh! Invooboo! Zing-a-Zing! Bom Bom! He is a lion! No! He is better than a lion! He is a hippopotamus!

Up there under a glass dome pale statues surround the fish-pond. Eve. The Elf. King Robert of Sicily. Cain. The Nubian Slave. Looking down with benign marble gaze on giant orange and creamy carp that glide round and round and round the ornamental pond. As I'm pacing up the tunnel I'd say at this very moment that two lovers are sitting on the wall of the pond. Sheltering from the rain that thrums against the glass and laughing at the world. Then making a wish with a coin that disperses the fish with a jolt and rocks down to settle in the silt as the shoal regathers to begin their weary lap again. Yes. True lovers. In the light of that wishful moment conspiring to some bright invincible future. Now here's your urban troglodyte shambling blind along the burrow below. But tell me this. Who else could boast of such beauty on the roof of their world?

My legs are weak yet my step is assured. I said. My step is assured. If I keep to a steady pace the ancient ballast stones of the extinct Caledonian Railway carry no stumble-threat settled under the weight of a hundred and thirty years. Loose rocks bottles cans all have been heaved aside by your man MacNab. Yours truly the Patron Saint of Stench. I'm wishing I hadnae smelled my oxter back there. The memory of it's lingering in my neb.

Pacing up the curve of blackness. Measured to a step. A hundred and twenty-five. Twenty-six. Twenty-seven. Darkness. There's a density to it like you're pushing against something. Like it's trying to repel you a firm hand against your breast. Warning. This is down Hell's garden path. This is up Auld Nick's close. Chap the door and run away. Do you mind that when you were a bairn? In the distant days we used to call it Wee White Horse. On a dark night a crowd of you would sneak up to the door of the fiercest auld geezer in town. Some lonesome misery-chops with a cupboard full of burst baws that had found their unfortunate way into his tattie-rigs. Then somebody would rap the door. Everybody running away laughing and shouting A Wee White Horse! Don't ask why the white horse. Don't think I'd like to chap any imaginary doors down in this dark place. No way Farchar MacNab. Easy the Fachie boy. Steady steps. Breaths. Hold it together. A hundred and eighty-eight. Eighty-nine. Ninety. No need to think about The Shimmer either. The Brocken Spectre. It wasn't on me on the way down.

Two four one. Easy. Two four two. Easy. Three. Look straight ahead and soon see the glow of the vent and the station. In this season an island of weeds nourished by the shaft of light that reaches down into it. There she is. Botanic Station. Heel ya ho boys. Three hundred and fifty-four. Sailing homeward. To Chez MacNab.

Light increasing. Tunnel pressure easing. High on the walls foxgloves sprout from fractured bricks holding their bonny blue cups to the sky. Rain's pouring down into the vent so I jouk on to the platform where it's dry. Graffiti Central. Tall painted letters on smoke-blacked walls. JAZZA. YOUNG HEADS # 1. VIPER. RIZLA. ACID-BOY. There's an edge of terror to it. Hech! Prob'ly just some young 'uns having a bit of a crack with a tin of emulsion blagged out the hall press. *Hey! Agnes! C'mere! Did you shift that bloody…?* As for the fading felt-marker messages on the old station wall tiles. Well. Depravity or whit? Most of the messages've been obscured by green ooze that's leached out the moss between the tiles. No bad thing. Check this. *Mary Kellys Fannies Goupin*. Or how about over here? *Minnie The Wife Pumper*. I've had visions of this guy. A kind of cartoon character. A white-socked sleazeball in a cheap suit cruising downtown lounge bars in search of extramarital sex. Only underneath the suit trousers he's got a bicycle pump for a penis. He woos a fair maiden then they adjourn to a crumbling wall in a back pend off the Saltmarket to begin their knee-trembling congress. Minnie's pumping away like fury. Then the woman begins to inflate and it all goes a bit Tex Avery after that with her all pumped-up towering over the buildings. Anyways. All this graffiti business. It's at least circa late-Eighties so there's no worries. No entry to the tunnel these days except for yours truly The Bold Keeper of the Station. Grip the side of the langcoat. Give it a wee shake to hear those keys jingle.

The rain's eased a touch but still clatters on to the platform. Spraying down off foliage that deeks over the top of the vent. There's been a bit of a flood on The Cross up there I can hear traffic ploughing through it.

My very own tract of sky above is a triangle of light. A grey lid over the vent. If I go to the far end of the platform and shimmy up the ancient signal pylon I can see the roof of the hotel on the other side of the boulevard. A fancy parapet on it with a balustrade. Best of all I can see into the top decks of the buses. Yawoo. When there's a red light at Botanic Cross you can get a good look at the passengers. Facing forward. Not knowing. The I-can-see-you-but-you-can't-see-me kind of thing. But I'd never do this in the daytime oh no cause you never know somebody might look down into the dim and see me seeing them and a secret's a secret eh no? I mean. Here it is. The most secure abode in the city outside of the jail. Beats the jail so it does. Beats freezin your erse off in some freezin Gallowgate pend too. And no rents. No fuel bills. No mortgage and no exorbitant council taxes getting hounded out of you by government lick-arses and their bloodsucking henchmen. No polis around to do a sweep-up either. So have to be on guard now yes sir yes sir yes siree. I walk to the edge of the south tunnel. Peer into the black then throw down a couple of rocks. Dull thuds. Fire down a few stones. Swifties. Throw them side arm and about testicle-high. All clear Roger Dodger. Pretty safe actually. Down yonder the south tunnel entrance has been shuttered off with solid steel plate and welded fast so the only way in here now is by oxy-acetylene or abseil. Or you could jemmy the locks and shackles on the north mouth. I did once.

The story goes. The story goes that the tunnels lay open to the four winds and the graffiti merchants. Until the City Parliament got word of some big weekend scene in a tunnel under Gibson Street. Half a mile down under the Grove in the bowels of dark Atlantis. Supposed to be all wheesht-wheesht but what's the chances of keeping a rave Masonic? Flocking punters and vans going down the darkness under the park. Lights. Music. Drink. Substances. I wasn't there myself so I can't vouch for what it was like. Anyroads. Word got back to the longbeards in the citadel. The Ancient Faithers. They summoned themselves together in the cedar-panelled gloom of a chamber deep within the city.

Days of civic festivity had long passed. Once a Phoenix had risen from the ashes of industrial ruin with a Rembrandt in her beak and a garden trowel gripped in her talons. For two glorious years her gigantic shape had circled city skies screaming out a piercing cry of triumph. Gardening and Art were the new salvation of Atlantis. We celebrated. The Ancient Faithers glowed with satisfaction and lured tourists to a hedonistic paradise with the promise of the 2 am pint. Festivals and exhibitions. And oh how we all looked skywards and flourished our trumpets as the great bird swooped and cast her shadow across us. We had culture. We were the best. We could drink after midnight. We swaggered. We were the Chest-Beating Capital of the World.

When the Phoenix's wings inevitably turned to dust she fell from the sky and her carcass lay smouldering on a ridge of hills to the south of the city. The smoke from the wreckage cast a choking fug over Atlantis and things returned to normal as the city became veiled once again in the gloom cast by the five hundred year old shadow of Knox's beard.

The visitors were no sooner on to the stairheid and the door slammed behind them when the good china was locked back into the press. It was back to the cracked mugs. People had stayed out late. Things had got out of hand. So the Faithers furrowed their brows and clicked their great eyebrows together like knitting needles. And from the balls of wool in their heads they stitched together a great baggy straitjacket of social prohibition to contain the hysteria of the citizenry in their charge. Early pub closing. Midnight curfews. Drinking out of doors whilst inhaling God's air became a punishable offence. When news of the pagan ceilidhs under city cobbles swirled into the whorls of the elders ancient hairy ears their eyebrows shot upwards into exclamation marks!! Party time below the weel-kempt cobbles? Those noble shining cobbles. On wet nights their greasy sheen reflected more than just the dull orange glare of the streetlights. They were a memorial. Reflecting back a century and more when foundries cast their fiery halos into a night sky and streets echoed to the clink of the hammer. When dark figures of work-bent men passed wearily to and fro casting thin shadows. The Work. Sleep. The Work. A dram. Sleep. The Kirk. The Work. There was a rhythm to it. Purpose and certainty. Now only the cobbles remained. Complete with their inlaid smooth stone tracks to steady the passage of carts drawn by ghosts of horses.

Forbye the tunnel dancers represented an untapped commercial resource for the knuckle-crunching proprieters of clubland. And so an army of spike-carrying men was mobilised and advanced to bar up the tunnel mouths. Then razorwire was curled around the palings. Nightmare quality. Jarring awake the mud-entombed corpses under the Western Front. Visiting their sleep with images of rotting limbs suspended on fang-like barbs. Curiously. Curiously down in north mouth Botanic a gate was inserted in the middle and fitted up with locks and shackles. Removable of course just hope nobody else gets the same idea No No No.

For along came a man with some snips and a bar. Some snips and a bar ha HA.

Clipping out just enough of the deadly r-wire to huddle-in huddle-out. Changing the locks. Nyahah! And then there's this theory about south mouth being sealed off and north mouth being shackled up to make a cosy wee fallout bothy for The Faithers and Co in the event of a nuclear attack. I've news for you. If these civic dignifieds turn up in their Gucci suits jangling the wrong set of keys during a plutonium downpour. Nae joke. They can make dae with their fuckin golf brollies. Hech! Hech hech hech! HECH HECH HECH HEE – EEEEECH!

The sky lightens. The rain eases. Somehow this makes the sound of traffic washing through the flood up on The Cross louder. Walk down platform.

ADVANCE to arched doorway in tiled wall. Scabby tiles. Feech feech. Such feculence.

SLIDE BACK rusted corrugated iron.

APPLY SHOULDER to rotted wooden door. And in.

It's a right fine pile rug I have in the lobby here. A right fine pile of pigeon shite. They're roosting on the riveted beam in the dark up there. Fuckers. Still going on about Peru. Or maybe it's Scoobie Doo or Doctor Who or Irn Bru some fuckin thing who knows but it sounds like Peru to me. Anyway just wish the bastard eejits would take wing and migrate there I swear one day I'll brick every last one of them. Na. Shame. Wouldnae do that. I'd napalm the little coo-cooing feathery fuckers. Whah! Get that Nissen sheet back into position. Remember. Keep the Camp Secret. Cover your tracks. Baden-Powell. Scouting For Boys. Freudian or whit? Surely not. No Baden. *Scouting For Boys – A Handbook For Instruction In Good Citizenship. Rovering To Success – A Book Of Lifesport For Young Men.* Some valuable anti-wanking advice. Scoutmaster Baden-Powell versus Scout Masturbation-Pull. Antithesis of the latter-day scud-mag. Back when the old wrist industry was in its infancy and plump corseted ladies would pose with their favourite horse. First-Baron BP was concerned that the vice of stroking the pudding was more likely to assail a lad than tobacco or alcohol. And no small wonder it is to me that the Chancellor hasn't put a tax on it. Revenue by the bucket load. But Master Baden's concerns were for the welfare of the nation. He reckoned it could bring on idiotcy and lunacy. He was worried too about preserving a man's seed and about how pulling the woggle might bring about the degeneration of the Anglo-Saxon race. Thus the need *to keep the racial organ clean* and bathe it in cold water every day. Rich foods. Soft beds.

Smutty talk. Constipation. These were all symptoms which could bring it on and it had to be met with a steely determination. You had to exercise the top half of the body. Boxing exercises or maybe a spot of Indian-club swinging. To draw away the blood. The reward for keeping a cork on the juice of your manhood was that one day you could meet and marry a Girl Guide. Start a wholesome family. Ain't masturbatin. I'm savin all my love for you. Thanks for that Baden. I always wondered where I went wrong.

There's a trickle of light here from a hole in the wall up there so's I can see to guddle the keys out the langcoat pocket and get the right one to unlock ye ancient creaky gate at the stair foot. Original article the gate here. Hinges took some work a few skooshes of the old WD-40 but it got there. Still some bonny tiles on the wall there and the old iron handrail. If I win The Lottery I'll splash out and get a cigarette-machine mounted here maybe one for Cadbury's chocolate as well yum dee fuckin dum. Shackle back up ye ancient creaky. That seals it. There used to be a building up there but it got demolished yonks ago then they concreted over it. There was one time I was in the hotel bar over the road. And there it was. An old photo on the wall. The surface building. The station. An elegant gadget it was with slender twin clock towers at either end with kind of onion shaped domes. Kind of Eastern like. Minarets. And there's this horse-drawn tram going past and a gentleman and a gentlewifie in the foreground dressed to the nines. Him in the dark suit and the bowler. She's in a farthingale dress and carrying a parasol. I can mind on having a wee smile at it and wondering if they were making their way across to the station to catch a Snorting Billy. A locomotive out to some quiet country spot just to get away from the clamour and smog who can say? Picnic under a hawthorn tree and whispering their love. So. This is where it gets black. Pitch. Eleven steps to the landing so. Hup we go hand on the rail. Simpson. Gemmell. McCreadie. Greig. McKinnon. Baxter. Wallace Bremner McAlliog Law and Len HUPYA Bastard! Forgot there was a bit of a gouge in Lennox. Funny how we still go on about that one. Some mediocre scoreline at Wembley. We only beat the Saxon 3-2 but they say we ripped the pish. A glorious summer Saturday in '67. Big Baxter. Just after they'd won the World Cup too. Ancient history. Now. Ten paces across to the wall. Here goes. Good King Bi-lly Had A Ten Foot Wi-lly. Got it. There's a candle on the old ticket kiosk if I shuffle along the wall here we go strike a light for auld Scotia and yes! The Enlightenment! Charred wick flares up a bit so shadows dance before it settles I'll spark up the Tilly lamp now in the Waiting Room. Excuse me. The *living-room*. Yee! I saw the light! Praise be. Hose Anna. And Hal E. Lou Yah. Disco Mama. Let there be love.

* * * * * * * * * * * * * * * *

Primus stove roars on to the base of a blackened kettle. Sending yellow tongues of flame searing up the sides. Water in the kettle creaks and groans readying itself for the boil. The tea score's almost as bad as the baccy I'll have to do something about this. A cupped palmful of tea hits babbling bubbles to send up a rich steamy aroma. Ah! Elixir. Oracle juice and nectar. Into the old tin mug with it. Just one stale biscuit left and it's a meagre spot of tiffin for the Fach. Shimmy arse on to the bench. I must do something about this. Really.

I dunk the biscy in and out the tea to give it a bit softness and flavour lowering my mouth on to it in case the end plops off down into the shadowy dust at my feet. I once heard about this place down in the city centre aye right down below it. A street covered over. Who knows how old from moons and moons and multiple moons ago. Medieval maybe. But the thing is they sealed this street over and put buildings and roads and the Central Station on top of it and it's still intact down there can you beat that? With all the closes and winding stairs and wee rooms and windaes the whole caboodle. There's supposed to be a secret way down into it who knows maybe a manhole or something. But the thing is this right. I could start a community down there. A sort of rent-free Trolls

Housing Co-op or something. All we'd need is an air vent and we could dig up a spring for water and all live down there and tell them to stick their inflated rents and mortgages and extortionate council taxes right up their arses and what could they do about it? Then the council'd put a tax on us for having the air vent intruding on their air up there and they'd need to charge us Ventilation Tax. Then they'd prob'ly claim ownership of all the air in the city and levy the people with Air Tax and it would start a riot. Then all us trolls we'd emerge from our burrow with banners and trumpets and go on this great victory march around the town and folk would say. There go the champions! That's the ones that stuffed it right up the arse of the government!

It's always in candlelight when I'm writing I notice how grubby the fingernails are. It glows right through the tops of my fingers when I hold a thin-ee up to the candle for a light. Gad I'm needing that bath. Got a gig tonight too. There's a bowf on me that would knock you dizzy. I should really do a vocal warm-up some scales and fa la la's and da dee doo daws's and the like but then again. Priority Number One. A richt guid scrubbin. I've still two buckets of water I got from the spigot behind the orchid house. Should be dark outside now the park'll be shut yeah safe enough to light a fire. The smoke always finds its way up the lum out through cracks in the concrete. I'll kindle a blaze in the old Waiting Room grate that warmed all those respectable Victorian shins away back in the freeze-fog of distant time. Aye. Should be okay. The wee man in the lodge house the Parkie Supreme should be settling down to some TV by now with the pooch slumming it on the sofa beside him. I reckon he knows anyway caught me in his torch beam one night at the spigot filling the buckets. WOOF. *Quiet.* Nightlight reflecting on his specs. Kept the torch on me for a bit. Didn't say anything but he was taking a lot in. You know the way. I just walked off down the park with the buckets towards the gully at the far end where the north tunnel mouth is. I doubt he bothered following. But when he comes out at night there must be times he can smell the smoke the lodge house isn't a kick in the chops away. Still. Live and let live.

That's the impression I got anyway.

Now there's a bonny blaze. Home is where the hearth is. I can heat up a whole galvy bucket of water on that. Start washing with the one then up on to the flames with the other for rinsing while I'm dooshing away with the soap and the brush. At least there's a decent block of soap left I won't have to do anything about that for a while. Good wood supply there too. From down the river bank where the park boys were cutting back the trees. It's off with the woolly jersey baggy breeks and long johns and down to raw bollock nae-kit for a good rub a dub scrub all over. Now. Hold on. I wonder if I was to kind of lower myself down on to that bucket of water squat-fashion would I actually be able to steep the boaby and the scrotum in the soapy hot? Oop. Wait. Oop. Oah! Yes siree! Ah Oh Mhmm. Oracle juice and nectar of the ablutionary kind is that good or what? I'll undulate myself up and down to enjoy the sensation on a repetitive basis yes mister that is good. It's like the way I was dunking that stale biscuit in and out the tea earlier on only up and down goes my big moon arse in and out the bucket in and out the bucket. I'll get the soap in about there now and give it a right good wash. Whew. There's a strange-smelling smoke off that wood. Sap smoke green kind of. Breathe in too much of that I'll end up with a tree growing out of each nostril. Potent. Be good that though. Good for the ecosystem if everybody had them. Think I'd like a set of rowans to keep the demons out my head. Imagine. Birds roosting right in front of your face. Shoot the pigeons right enough. Squirrels stuffing your ears with nuts in the autumn. Snobby gits with their nose trees all pruned up posh like. Whole fashion concept there. Or you see somebody walking down the road with a bairn in a pram and there's these two little saplings jutting out the hood. It's as hard as nails that brush but at least I've given the bollock cleft a right good dicht to get the smell out. It was bad before kind of smelt like a kebab somehow. Oh the water. Oh-oh the water. Oh the water. Let it run all over me. Gad. Praise the Laird in his Holy Estate. It's time I got out of this. I mean. Nose trees. Enough's enough.

Cool air in the vent's put a nice chill into my wet shorn head. The storm's washed the dirt out the atmosphere and I'm in harmony with it. I've covered my tracks shackling the ancient creaky and sliding back the corry now stand on the platform to roll me the very last thin-ee from the final dusty fragments of the tin. Yawoo. Think of those great Snorting Billies. Grinding impatiently at the rails. Chuffing great steamclouds up the vent into the trees and out over the road. Waiting for the release of the brake to go shrieking down the tunnel there like a mad banshee from its lair. Out the city and beyond. Aye. To the lands beyond.

Above streetlights dull the clarity of the night sky. A veil of orange vapour across a fifty mile urban sprawl. When was the last time I saw a star? Can't honestly say. Must've been away back in my Strath days. Up at the Haven. Late Autumn. Before the mists came. That winter with all the mist and fuck-all stars. Christ. Stars in the Strath. You could see thousands of them. We stood on top of Meikle Carnock and looked out into a clear cosmic distance. We picked out a burning blue coal. Gazing back a thousand years at some long-gone planet that had self-detonated into a billion splinters in a final act of glory. Still shining at us in starlike perfection. The star had ceased to exist back in the days when the tribal clan still roamed Scotia and Viking galleys came plundering from the seas. We looked at it a thousand years ago and it winked back a thousand years on. Ola. My Ola. Enough. Enough Haven now. A burning emptiness comes into the pit of the gut. My mouth fills with saliva and there's a flash of heat across the brow. My legs shaking a wee bit so I walk to the edge of the platform and gob out saliva to stop the boak then take a clear breath.

Stick the unlit rollie behind the ear then climb the rungs of the old signal pylon to sit on the crow's nest. Shift myself along the seized signal arm it makes a good perch. Leg dangle. Reach into the langcoat pocket gallery for the tinder. Careful how I spark this thin-ee or the flame'll shoot up one side the baccy dust'll end up down in the weeds and that'll be that. *Game's a bogey the man in the lobby done a wee jobby.* Yes indeed. The fellow in the vestibule shall have deposited a minute amount of his excrement therein. *Jeez. Give it a rest.* A good even light for the dust-filled snout no danger. Good timing too here's a double-decker stopped at the traffic light. I like this. The passengers looking dead ahead held in my frame of vision. Hech! Voyeuristic encounters. Without the suggestion of sex of course. No sex please I'm Brittle. No need for the upper arm or boxing exercises either. Wonder if I took a drag off the smoke if somebody'd look down off the bus into the dark hole and see a pinprick of orange light. Or a floating head flashing on and off if the fag glow was strong enough na I'd need to roll a right big thick-ee for that. Imagine though. Him up there with the newspaper. *Nyargh! Whit's that doon that hole? Big neep lantern flashin oan an aff whit the?* Prob'ly dismiss it as a brief hallucination. A mote in the eye an optical delusion. Phantom heid? I see no phantom heid. Freaksville Caledonia think about something else quick skim through the newspaper fitba weather Queen Maw racing-page TV cartoons Page 3 Diddy-Wummin half-finished crossword and the price of halibut per box in the far off fishing port of Fraserburgh. Anything to distract you from the phantom heid.

The bloke up there in the tammy. Three from the back. Shift worker. Fidgety looks like he might get off at the next stop. Bit of a boozer's neb on him. Straight home to supper or stop off for a cool beer in Trotsky's? I heard somebody got chibbed across the back of the head in there. That's taking a theme bar to its ultimate conclusion. There's some good quarry up on the bus though. Like that wizened crone in the fake fur. There's enough compact trowelled into that face of hers to smother Barbara Cartland. And beJaz even under all that you can still detect a corrugated complexion that would carry away first prize at the World Face-Like-A-Fossilised-Prune Championship. The Elephant's Knob Trophy. Big bulgy eyes on her. Sticking out her heid like donkeys' hard-ons. Lipstick. Makes her gob look like two deflated tomatoes. Poor wee dog hanging off her arm there poor wee pooch one of those wiry trembly skittish efforts looks like a depressed glove puppet. Maybe a mutated extension of yon coat sleeve. Dog's eyes must be stinging from that cigarette she's holding under it. Supposed to be banned the smoking on the buses some of the auld yins have nae respect. I can even spy from away down here half the filter's caked thick with cherry lipstick. If some dosser picks up one of her fag dowts and takes a puff he'll walk into the hostel later on to some fairly funny looks. *Ooh. Ah like yer lipstick ther Charlie. Hiv ye been doon tae the beauty parlour for a makeover?* The more I look at that wee dog the more I'm convinced it's a puppet. Would it not be the bees-knees if the wifie took a drag off the fag and blew smoke out the dog's nostrils then leered down into the vent giving a wee wave? That would be something.

But the best thing to do with the passengers is to give them characters and destinations. Unwitting players in the drama of Farchar's psyche. Take old Mrs Marasmus there. The dog lady. I'd say she just ain't what she seems. And who's that schmuck three seats behind her in the felt hat? Johnnie da Homburg dat's who. I'd say he's tailin her. Maybe she knows but they ain't givin any games away. Johnnie the Homburg. Suave chap. Epitome of respectability maybe from some semi-detached out on The Switchback. Retired. Works manager maybe or production planner. Fifty years in the same shop working his way up from grubby apprentice. Workshop memories. Hung from a jib twenty feet from the floor with the old bawz greased up to celebrate end of apprenticeship. The unexploded Luftwaffe landmine stuck in the yard embankment. A dying breed a lingering shadow. Yeah. Sure. Good cover Johnnie. I *know* what you are you crafty sonofabitch. You're a goddamn cop that's what you are. Taggin Mrs Marasmus. She'll step down offa that bus and you'll go after her. Hangin back. Followin to a dimly lit rail bridge. She'll look back with a sly smirk and see you approachin through an aurora of headlights as chip shop steam blows across the sidewalk. Then she'll give you a knowing nod. Reeling you in like a helpless saithe. High priestess of the criminal underworld and you've only gone and fallen in love with her ya lousy sap. Now she's got you stitchin up cops the length and breadth of the city. Dancing to her tune. And you wanna know why? Cause you're cute Johnnie that's why. But who's that wise guy on the bus behind *you* Johnnie? Shift-workin Tammy-Man that's who. Bevvyhead. I'd say he's on to you both. Undercover who would think it? What a nose. A prize strawberry. Little bunches of inflated veins on it like electrified elvers. Mrs Marasmus Johnnie the Homburg Tammy-Man all lurch forward as the bus takes off then ease back into their seats as the driver finds second gear and their window-framed portraits go drifting out of sight past the vent. I climb down the rungs back to the platform. A quartet of geese goes bugling over. Jazz. Contemporary. Night fliers in late summer? Park dwellers I'd wager from the pond down The Grove with the skootery fountain. Sophisticated city birds. Eclectic. Fellini movies and a discerning taste in coffee. Insincere trumpeting that for a goose I'd say. Not like I once knew them in the wilds of The Strath. Out yonder in late October when winter's breath chilled twilight skies to an endless blue. Circling out of the north they would come. A distant call and then look up to a thousand wild cries. Thrusting wings. Sighting Loch Mhor far below pale yellow cradled in dark mountains. Filling the skies with their strange Arctic song that told of earth and ice and stars.

The thin-ee's reduced to a papery roach I throw it spinning down into a puddle. It lands in the water with the faintest siss. A midge's fart. It's time to bale out of here and hit the dim city lights. A draught of air fills the langcoat with a *shoomf* as I leap off the platform. It's into the north tunnel with me. Glow into darkness. Street sounds into silence. But you know all about The Silence. Don't you?

Hell. Fuck hell. Fuckin hell it's on me again. Only fifty paces down into the blackness and it's started again. The silver glow. Shining out of me. This Brocken Spectre thing it scares me shitless. Fuck off ya bastard! I spin an arm round fast like a propeller but the light birls round with it. Break into a run it follows. I stop. It stops. No one'll be able to see it out in the street or in the pub but they can *sense* there's something about you. The way they look. Wary. Fear maybe. But they keep a distance that's what I'm saying. It's a triple glow that's on me now. One for each soul. Get off me ya fuckers! Leave me alone. Charge down the tunnel full steam like a Snorting Billy. But it is on me. This light. This energy. Maybe I can beat it this time not let it get to me ignore it. No. No more. But it is on me. Run run run. Out of the blackness and out of this soot-coated grotto. Portcullis ahead in the gleam. Full steam stoker. Full steam.

Brocken slides off in dim north mouth glow. A brief look out to make sure no one's around. You never know there's been a few empties out on the embankment recently. Alcopops and Bucky mostly the bairns havin a wee swally. What the fuck would they think if they saw me emerge? I stoop under the r-wire and shackle up. Bolt lock with double throw and snap up the two invincible looking padlocks on their heavy chains. Just the job. Air. There's a fresh smell around now that the embankment's been quenched by the storm. Take a deep draught of it. It throws up a wild woodland smell in spite of the city location. For a moment it reminds me of the Strath. Damp earth and oaks in a gorge where the black swirling Caldon slips secretly from its cover of trees into grazing parks to meet the broad flow of the Finglas. Each draught of the smell triggers the mind-eye into a series of images that flash through me like a slide-show. Gilquhan Tower's crumbling spires clad in ivy rise above the gorge. Dunreoch's pinnacle rising abruptly from the floor of the Strath with trees clinging to its ledges and fissures then bare rock at the top where mist pours through a splintered crag. Long hills with a river whose source splits into the hills in five silver strands. There's a village in the fold of the hills there. My mind-eye soars up like a falcon then drops looking down over its winding streets and slate roofs then sweeps away eastward to a glen that cuts deep into the hills. A loch with a blackened ruin by the shore. The charred remains of the cabin. No I say No No! I shake my head around and expel breath with a gasp to purge my mind and deny it Strath visions. No more no more. Then was then. Now is now. There was there here is here. I take a spring into the brambles and nettles then breenge up the gully to the top. Shimmy the tree beside the townhouse wall reach up and pull on the rusty iron bracket. Throw a leg up then hoist myself belly over the wall to dreep down into the garden. Keeping to the side shadows under the trees until I get to where I can jouk through the fence into the street then down the public steps to the boulevard.

Striding along by the Botanic railings. Just before The Cross is a chainlink fence with a wall behind where the vent drops down to Chez MacNab. The pavement's still wet and I'm hitting a good stride the langcoat spreading out with the draught. It's good. Bounding along in the billowing togs. You can't beat Shanks's Locomotion. Striding forth on my great long legs the gangle-hoppers man. There was a time when I would have walked twenty miles in a day and just for the hell of it.

Yonder on the other side of the Cross there's a row of shops with folk to-ing and fro-ing. Tube-lit signs cast rainbow reflections on the pavement. Pizza. Massage. Budweiser. Trotsky's. And yonder is the twenty-four hour fruit shop! Those decadent vitamin noshers! There's a brood of them. Anarcho-veggies milling around outside with the standard-issue dreadlocks and knee-length jerseys garment of eco-consciousness if ever there was one. Yawoo! Full steam. Stand aside ye tofu warriors. Here comes Farchar MacNab. I am The Fach. I AM THE GLOWING MAN.

Downhill to the five-way junction. There must have been a time when every busy cross in Atlantis had its own public lavatory. Subterranean shunkies with their rows of gleaming Made In Barrhead piss-pots. All that remains is three decades of litter trapped in a little street-level stockade of flaking palings. A hundred paces beyond the five-ways takes you out of traffic noise into city stillness. Only the occasional car. Drones past then fades to a roadway distance.

Maybe I'm like a ghost drifting along here in the langcoat. Streets with no purpose branch off into nowhere with pot-holed roads and cracked pavements terminating in mounds of rubble. No standing thing to echo the memory of the dockside siren that roused people to their daily toil. Back at the five-ways are a few remnants. The Blue Whale. Regency Bingo. The Dragonchurch with its façade still bearing the stains of the Smog Age where four wild-eyed dragons snarl out from the lower corners of a squat steeple. Clouds of little black screaming birds pour like smoke in and out of broken windows. Congregating inside on rain-rotted pews and screeching from a shit-encrusted pulpit. Ammonia stench of starling pish drifting over the street.

Funny. I'd always thought the place was totally condemned and hadn't paid much attention to the smaller building joined on at the back. A kind of one-storey church hall affair. Then one Saturday morning last summer when I was passing by there was this coach parked outside and a door open in the building. I was a tad curious and hung back for a spell to see what would happen. I can tell you I was both flabbered and gasted to see a number of crimson blobs in electric blue trousers emerging with a number of unwieldy items. Loading them into the coach. On closer inspection these turned out to be drums and accordions being carried by gentlemen members of the Order of the Orange. Obviously preparing for a folk-pageant in some distant burgh to display their devotion to the values of Christian love. I poised to marvel at their regalia. Tunics were ornamented with shiny buttons and epaulettes. Those electric blue strides with the crimson piping. Man. Trumpton on bad acid. They were only loading up the bus and you could still feel the hate vibe. Tasselled blue bunnets cocked at a jaunty angle brought into sharp relief the life-chiselled features of these part-time soldiers of Christ. God's Territorial Army. Out on weekend manouevres defending the boundaries of Scripture with flute notes and drumbeats as angry as whistling shells and gunfire. I thought I'd seen it all when out stepped the Majorettes from Hell. Young women with faces that could split kindling. They appeared in shiny silver suits with red cuffs that flashed up sleeves like bursts of flame. The coach was filled then off they went with a song on their lips.

* * * * * * * * * * * * * * *

Upstream of the riveted iron bridge river surge is amplified in night air. Streetlamp reflection dragged in the flow gets spun in tiny whirlpools until the river spills over the weir of the old flint mill into the shadow of giant willows. Downstream waters run deep. Channelled by high concrete walls. A mountain of scrap cars poised over like an avalanche waiting to crash down into the channel. Open jaws hang silent on the end of a long steel boom. A giant Meccano dinosaur frozen in mid-bite.

I put Shanks's Locomotive on steady steam and stride on. The road stretches towards the twin black monoliths of the derelict riverside granaries. Where pigeons glide on the updraught of a brickwork precipice as dark soaring Vs. I pass under the railway through the arch with its single glowing bulb as a train goes over thuds booms. Wheels grind and screak as it rolls down the incline to the three-mile tunnel that passes under the city centre.

Now I can see it. There it is. The Coffin! Ghost ship on a lonely sea dark isle in a foggy minch. The tenement above's been pulled away leaving this squat box shining through condensation-soaked windows. The outside's been painted pitch black with the exception of the garish white sepulchral urns kind of half 3D'd out the wall. Aye. The Coffin. Ales and spirits. More of a mausoleum than a coffin I'd say. Like one of those right Jim Dandy tombs that some of the wealthy merchants had built for themselves up yonder on Necropolis Hill. In fact. Etched on doorway glass as you enter the bar is the legend: Welcome To The City Of The Dead. The Faithers must have been choking on their Prozacs when the licensing went through for this one.

Swing in doors to foggy light. Some heads turn. The Living mostly I'd say although there's one or two vampires in with dummy blood dribbling down their chins aye The Undead can be a real hoot. There's a number of balding pony-tailed hippies lounging on the leather settees with their bottles of Fraoch. I reckon maybe there's a science fiction thing on upstairs with these guys around. But for me it's the special hooly in the cellar. The upstair Coff's got a great wailing wall of a bookcase that somebody's stuffed with tattered old Sci-Fi paperbacks from Azimov to Zebrowski so the place has become a bit of a church for the science fiction community. An inferno of candles burns fiercely reflected in the great arched mirror. On a platform high over the gantry life-size figures of Burke and Hare ride in a cart heaving on a wild snorting horse. The cart pitches up at a dangerous angle and somebody's stuck one of those joke severed arms out the back. I head down the stair into Golgotha's Vaults where the cabaret's to be to see Maggie. She's behind the bar getting the till ready then swings around with gob agape after Sound Andy's spotted me and given her the nudge that I'm on my way over. She lets out the customary Maggie shriek.

Fachie! Ya big Hielan jobbie!

Marguerita! Gie us a ki-mmpwah!

Ya big numptie ye! So how's it gaun? Ya big shite! Are ye here tae play for us or whit? Coupla songs? Naw? Ye just in for a swally?

I'll play a few tunes if ye like. I was driftin round the West End and saw your poster for tonight. For the Birthday Party eh? Is there a spare guitar around?

You bet there will be. Aw. So how have ye been? Ye look like a big daud o shite as usual. Nyeee! Naw. Ye don't. No really. Ye look gorgeous so ye do. Din't he Andy? In't he no jist fuckin gorgeous?

Pwuh! Cheers ya big smelly cow!

Eeeeeeee!

So how's business Maggie? Don't say it. Dead.

Dead? Fuckin maggot-ridden. Na. It's no. No really. It's gaun fine. So it is.

That's grand Maggie I'm glad it's workin out for you.

Aye. But honestly. How are ye big man? We've no seen ye for yonketty's.

So we're having the crack and a hoot when suddenly Mags goes all quiet and starts looking at me a bit strange like. Surely she can't actually see the Brocken Spectre glowing out of me not in this light surely. Na. But what a ticket she is. What can you say about the woman that's opened Scotland's first and I'd venture only Death theme bar? She's also given the OAPs the cheapest and longest happy hour within the walls of the citadel. No sooner was the tariff on the wall when the drums rumbled and the ancients came drifting across the wasteground from their various howffs on the promise of the ninety pence nip. Coffin-fodder she'd called them and they'd wheezed into their drams. And there was her behind the bar in the vampire outfit. From 11 am the long and the short and the tall of the seniority were dim ghosts within clouds of grey smoke. Tilted whiskies glinted like gold nuggets shining in a lucky cave. This being The Coffin and in recognition of their own waning mortality the auld yins called it The Last Gasp Saloon. At 8 pm Maggie regulated the tariff back to normal and they drifted out into the dim streetlamp glow and back to wherever it was whence. I like the auld yins. You can spend a better crack of a day with them than half of the jabbery twats that cruise in here looking for some kind of alternative culture. Striking up half-arsed rhetorical arguments and flexing their imaginary intellectual biceps. No such blabber the ould folk. Yawoo. No sir-ee.

Maggie heads off round the empty tables to place the complimentary party-porcupines on the tables. Half-apples speared with cocktail sticks with wee squares of cheddar cheese and pickled onions impaled on them. So I drag a bar stool over for a perch stuffing the langcoat down into the spars. Leg dangle. It's up with the baggy woolly sleeves to get tucked in about a beer and a nice big thick-ee from the new liquorice papers and crop of baccy. BE PREPARED. Yes. An appropriate thing to be here in Empire City. The great Scoutmaster Baden-Powell once took a grip of his quill and began flexing his wrist to shoot a few words on the origins of the word *Empire*. What came spurting out was that it derived from the old Roman word *Imperium* meaning well-ordered rule.Then he explained how the title of the word *Emperor* came from *Im* and *Parere* which means *To Prepare For*. Yes. To BE PREPARED. He wrote that an Emperor had to BE PREPARED to face any danger that might threaten his country. And so Scouts must BE PREPARED in case their country was in difficulty or danger. This would leave us standing cocksure and upright behind our King. GOD SAVE THE KING. I raise up the Guinness to toast all the kings and rulers of Empires that lie mouldering in their worm-crawling lairs. Oracle smoke and nectar! First drink in a while. Champion-ee. Just sit supping for a bit studying the hundreds of skulls that sit head-to-head on the shelves around Golgotha's Vaults.

The place is filling up to a healthy babble and there's a good wee atmosphere building. Home is where the crack is. Aye if only. Anyway. Every table's got a lit candle melted into a bottle that's clotted in coloured tallows. I look up the room with my eyes narrowed to make a mini-galaxy of the candlelight. A few folk catch me looking in their direction so turn away or reach for a cigarette or draw a finger-picture with spilt beer anything but look at the glowing man. I scud back a couple of drams then sluice them down with a Guinness. I go a wee tad nervy and a shiver goes through me then I relax and get another Guinness to sip back nice and slow to chill out. Yeah that's good the place has filled right up now and. Wahay! Ya hup! Here we go! Mags is on the mike.

Wwh! One TWO. Wwh! Is that okay? TWO. ANDY! Yeah? ALRIGHT! WHOO! HOW IS EVERYBODY THE NIGHT? ALRIGHT?

Yay…

FOR FUCK'S SAKE. IS THAT IT? HOW…IS…EVERYBODY...TO-NITE?

YAY!

AYE THAT'S MORE LIKE IT YA CUNTS! ANEEEWAY! WELCOME MY DECOMPOSED CHUMMIES WELCOME! WELCOME TO OUR VERY FIRST ANNIVERSARY HERE AT THE COFFIN BAR THEE BEST PUB IN TOWN AND FUCK THE REST A THEM!

Yo!

EXACTLY MISTER. SO WELCOME TO OUR VERY SPECIAL PARTY. WE'RE ONE YEAR OLD TODAY SO IT MUST BE THE RIGOR-MORTIS ANNIVERSARY OR SOMETHIN LIKE THAT. AND WHAT A LINE UP WE'VE GOT. WE'VE GOT SOME GREAT ENTERTAINMENT FOR YE THE NIGHT. WE'VE GOT. POETRY FROM KELVIN O'CONNOR…

YAY!

AND WE'VE GOT COMEDY. FROM THE ONE AND ONLY. ERCHIE SHANKS!…

YAY!

MAYBE A SONG OR TWO FROM FACHIE MACNAB…

YAY!

A TOUCH OF MAGIC FROM MYSTIC MARTIN!…

WOOOOOOOOO!

SO PREPARE YOURSELF FOR THE WONDERS OF HIS HAUNTED CROTCHPIECE! WELL THAT'S WHAT HE TELLS ME ANYWAY. AND RIGHT NOW WE'VE GOT SOME MUSIC…

YO!

FANFUCKINTABULOUS MUSIC!…

WWAY!

NOW EVERYBODY. STAMP YOUR HANDS AND CLAP YOUR FEET FOR A VERY… SPECIAL… APPEARANCE. IT'S SCOTLAND'S MENTALLEST ROCK BAND. IT'S REEZ!

YAAAY! YAAY!

Rumble of feet. Drumming of tables. I'm into another dram a double this time necking it seeing REEZ take the stage through one eye and a tilting ebb of gold warmth that goes down my throat. Guts. Hunger. Deep burning hunger. Yeah yeah yeah.

SO WHERE HAS ALL THE STARLIGHT GONE? EH? WHERE IS IT? Just a big ugly ceiling on the world *EH? HERE GOOSIE GOOSIE!* Ya snobby goose cunts. Hide in the hogweed ya. Geese. Why's there nae starlight shinin on the river? Cause it's the Kelvin. There's nae starlight that's how. Nae real fuckin stars anyway. *Where's the fuckin stars then*? Poor ducks are skittering off in shock I should *SHUT THE FUCK UP EH?* There's some steps over the bridge if I can just swing over the gate hee-re oh ho who is it locks these fuckin gates then *EH?* Wisnae me. No this time. *IT WISNAE ME MISTER! HONEST IT WISNAE!* Must've been Parkie eh? Steps here bring ye in at the cactus joint. Mexico. Fuckin Mexico. Mexico in a greenhoose. In West Central Scotland. Down South of the Borde-eeer. Down Mexico Way. Aye aye aye aye! *AH DINNAE FUCKIN THINK SO NEE-BUR!* Fu-cken wrap *it EAST COAST CUNT*. Hey! Have ye heard the story about East Fist and West Fist? *HECH!* Robert Mitchum. Right hand left hand. Scotland. East fist west fist. Bang fuckin *BANG!* Take that on the puss ya Glesca cunt. Here's wan oan the moosh ya big Embra shite. *Bump Bump fuckin Bump*. Aye yooo. Here till I slap ye on the dish wi ma fuckin civic award ya poof. Ma art gallery's better than your art gallery any day ya fuckin tossbag. *HEY! WHERE IS THE STARS? EH? STARS! ECHO! FUCKIN ECHO ECHO ECHO! WHERE'S THE heaven fuckinly CHOIR THEN?*

> *UGGY UGGY UGGY!*
> *AYE AYE AYE!*
> *UGGY UGGY UGGY!*
> *AYE AYE ECHO!*
> *ECHO FOREVER AND EVER AND EVER AND EVER.*
> *HA HA HAAAA! HECH! HECH HECH HEEE-EECH!*
> *HEY!*
> *PARKIE!*
> *THERE'S A MALARKEY*
> *IN THE PARKIE!*
>
> *PARKIE PARKIE PARKIE!*
> *AYE AYE AYE!*

PARKIE PARKIE PARKIE!
AYE AYE AYE!
HARKIE!
PARKIE!
MALARKEY!
PARKIE!
PARKIE PARKIE PARKIE!
NYEET NYEET NYEEEET!

HEY! PARKIE SUPREME! IN YER wee but an *BEN* wi yer bonnie wee *HEN! HEN! AH SAID FUCKIN HE-EEEN! BWAAWK BWAAWK BWAAWK BWAAWK!* Oh ya fu'n bastard right on MA PUS who put that there? Right on ma. *Ya fuhin shrub man. Ya SHRUB! AWOOOOO! AWOOOOO!* Shut up. You stupid fool. Parkie'll bring the roof in. Set fire roond aboot smoke ye oot Sawney Bain doon the drain. Now wheesht. *Shoosht.* Get down that gully that old Railway Glen. Go home ya hun go home. Down go oh fuck down go ya down ya breenger ha *HA!* Aw fuckin soakin still so it is and all brambly. Langcoat'll be in tatterdom. Darkest tatterdom. Toom Tabard ya fuckin bawjawin cunt. It's thorny biscuits. Awoo. Cheemie Logan. Thorny biscuits. Thorny thorny biscuits. Wet smell whit is that smell? Oniony. Wild garlic. Mind of it from the distant days in the Strath. *Bonnie bonnie Strath.* Oniony ya hun ye. Path. Path of sorts. Leading to the port. Much Buckie drinking here amongst the branches Farchar sahib. Young fellows on the Sidney Devine. Beware of bottle trip ya ya nettle knuckle ya bass. *BASS!* Too dark down here to find a docken that does the trick mister rub away the white sting lumps soothing. Down the slope here *AYAH* spin tumble branches spin in the sky. Round on to my. Back. Orange glimmer up above. Peaceful here. Glimmer glimmer in the sky. Shine your glow and tell me why. Tell me why-aye. I was lying in a burned out basement. Na na showin your old hippy age aye but not total hippy. Na na. Stiff Tour put paid tae yon musty auld nonsense. Nineteen Seventy when? History. Still. Like old Neil Young right enough good harmonica takes you away somewhere nostalgia kind of thing. Hey I could sleep here it's not bad at all.

Mother Earth won't swallow me. Mother Earth's a soggy auld mattress. Slept on worse in the Great Festerin Hotel. Pish-mingin mattresses. Shitey memories man. Shitey Gallowgate memories. Give me the Earth not hell on it. Earth. Hello Mammy. How are you ya auld? Element. Aye. It's youse elements that get us all in the end eh Mammy? Water drowns. Fire cremates. Earth. Thumps down on the coffin. Air. Okay so it gives life but it creeps in at the end and decays us to the mouldering pile of maggot fodder that's been waiting to happen from the day we were born. *HECH!* Yeah yeah yeah my friend we're all elemental victims one way or another. When the auld referee wi the scythe blaws the final whistle. Then we join you Earth. Zashes to zashes. Rust to rust. HEY how long have I been stretched out in this fuckin place? Better arise Sir Fach yer bloody knees are caked wi glaur GET UP YA SAD MAN hey for pity's sake stay on yer feet. Stepping through the nettles here like a Highland country dancer. Hee – ooch! Wo steady hey. WEEBLES WOBBLE BUT THEY DON'T FALL DOWN! *I SAID WEEBLES!* Weebles. *WOBBLE!* Wobble. Weeble wobbles won't. Fall. Hup. Damn langcoat. Good bramble protection. BAD trip hazard. Razorwire at twelve o'clock Biggles. Roger Algie. Stiffen the shanks man and nae wobblin or you'll be 'anging on the ould barbed wire. Steady steady pull it together sober up. Can't face this tunnel. It'll be ok when I get to the gaff but the tunnel's driving me. This is mental. Easy. Reach for the keys. What kind of a crank designs this stuff? Entrepreneurs. Brits I'll wager. In respectable stripy shirts and ties at some Belgian arms fair enthusing to potential punters about the slash factor what an existence man fuckin even worse than mine. Lucrative no doubt so big bendy on the conscience. But I'll get through. Giant steps and baby steps. Ye cannae slash me for a wee bawbee. It's all in the stoop that's the secret. Fastening the shackles in the dim north mouth glow. Got to fasten the shackles before the next stage.

Tunnel tunnel in the park. I've a potion for the dark. For antidote to darkness dispense with contents of whisky bottle in three swift swigs. Go. Little bubbles shoot up the liquid kedunk kedunk

kedunk into the air pocket at the upturned base. Misty this when I close my eyes. *There was three kings unto the east. Three kings both great and high. And they hae sworn a solemn oath. John Barleycorn will* DIE! Ah ONE! Warm toxic golden breath go for the second swig. *His colour sickened more and more. He faded into age. And then his enemies began. To show their deadly* RAGE! Ah TWO! Nearly there. Foamy eyes ha ha! Foamy eyes? For fuck's sake. Three. Go. *John Barleycorn was a hero bold. Of noble enterprise. For if you do but taste his blood. He'll make your courage rise* and THREE-AH! Crash splinter glass sparks a buzzbomb right off the fuckin tunnel wall. Kamikaze Grouse. Dark swaying towards me. Into it. Deeper.

YAH! It's now I see me from twenty feet outside of myself. Run run running up that tunnel. Drawn out from myself I go. OUT OUT OUT from myself. My body leaving me and running ahead. Seeing myself fleeing uptunnel like I'm watching some terror stricken deer in a wood following it at a fixed distance. Uptunnel I go shaking shoulders and aiming forearm smashes into the air as I run to try and shake off the Brocken. The Aura. Running Running. Roaring some mad Gaelic war cry in defiance of this thing. This light. This energy. Staggering on ancient cinders and boulders in the blackness rolling to the ground knees ripped. Tears in my eyes and wet blood on stinging palms skin flapping and then. Seeing the light. The dull glow of the vent. Running towards it reaching out to it. Make the platform and lie there gasping for breath. I close in on myself still keeping ten feet distant. I'm up then crumpling going down on the bad knee buckling but somehow hirpling along the platform to the corrugated iron. Then I'm just above myself. Seeing my hands fumbling with the shackles then hauling on the iron handrail up the Wembley eleven. Get to the kiosk. Make a torch from a twisted-up *Herald* then stagger toward the bedroom with a flaming light. I feel myself being drawn in to my body then I'm back inside with a jolt. Stagger forward with the force of it seeing the Waiting Room from behind my eyes tilt towards me lit by the flaming *Herald*. Stagger to the bedroll then fall down on to it flakes of burning newsprint scattering around as I drop. The flakes descend. Spent fireflies. Newsprint embers gutter and crinkle sending out wisps of smoke then no light at all. The Statue of Liberty has fallen. Into a blackness you couldn't imagine.

In blackness bedroll's all twisted up among my legs. Sweat chills. There are two gremlins inside my head. One behind each eye. Both've got a Black and Decker with a 1mm drill bit rotating at 3,500 rpm pushing and gouging to penetrate into the backs of my eyes. Pieces of eye whirl off and splatter their overalls with shiny scales as they laugh and gouge all the harder. The bedroll underneath me soaking with the sweats. Hold arm up at least the Brocken's getting a lot fainter. Almost away.

Good Gad Jesus I can mind chucking up at some point I think over on the woodpile towards the fireplace there. Bile mostly by the taste of it there's a burning rubber sensation in my palate whatever the fuck that's like ask the single malt whisky experts. *Although the nose has hints of diesel this fine malt whisky offers a round turnippy finish with burnt rubber undertones.* Gad. What would it be like going out on the drink with that crew? I roll aside and this noxious fart escapes that would have a shit-scraper in a chicken factory fleeing for mercy my goodness gracious me. There's a dirl in my ears then it gives way to the hissing. Louder and louder a great long breath. The giant serpent down in south tunnel. Maybe the serpent on the ocean floor that Ma used to tell us about. Six hours to breathe in and six to breathe out. The tide rising and ebbing on its breath. I probably disturbed it last night woke it up with yon roaring shenanigans on the way in here. Ach shit. The roaring. Inside the Gardens too I hope Parkie Supreme hasn't put two and two together. But I think I was well away from the house. Over the footbridge and up the back steps came in via Mexico. Fuckin eejit I am roaring and bawling. Maybe he heard it in his bed. It might've leaked into his dreams. Dreaming about werewolves on some dark plain clutching whisky bottles and barking at the moon. Awooo awooo. Gad. Maybe Parkie woke up later and vowed to stay off the late-night curries. Said to the wife. Did you hear anything? *Eh? Go back to sleep.* They settled back into the sheets with buttock pressing reassuring buttock. Jesus I'm hot. I can't move. I'm a big steaming sweating shite lying here shat out the arsehole jaws of Hell. Jeez I'm starving. When was the last time I had a meal?

Aw naw. Here. Yes. Up it comes. Here come the tears and there's nothing I can do about it. It surges up out of me like a spring. If I try to stop it I'll just start convulsing. Like a pump. Where does it come from? I don't will it on that's for sure. It's always when I'm lying here in the black then BANG a bit like the storm kicking in yesterday. Flash of lightning on a distant memory. Then the rain. The tears. It's the good memories that make me cry that's what worries me. I try lying face down in the woolly jersey pillow but soon it's saturated through. Salty. Like lying on your belly with your head in a rock pool. Did you ever do that? As a bairn I mean. To get a better look at the crabs and limpets and things but when you dook your head in it's blurred and your eyesight's all swimmy. A bit like that time trying on Mammy's glasses and stumbling around the room. Ma was down at the shops and Kathy and her pals all fell about laughing at the sight of a six-year-old eejit in giant glasses and then the spare false teeth came out the sideboard drawer and you squeezed them into your mouth. You doddered into furniture not being able to see and Mairead O'Donnel pished herself with hysterics. The tunnel hissing comes and goes. Wave sounds washing up distant memories from the depths of the past. Waves on a shore and me with my face in a rock pool. I lift my head into the air and there's water popping in my ears. My eyes unblur and a rocky coast is all around me. A tiny voice piping on the wind.

Mammy mammy mammy! Fackwer's stuck his face in a sea!

Ma's coming over the rocks towards me. Her hair lifts up on the breeze. An oil tanker on the flat grey horizon. Sea pounding on rocks.

Och my goodness. What are ye playing at wee man?

Cabs mammy! Cabs! In da watter!

Look mammy look! Fackwer's greetin.

Naw ah'm urny!

Neither I was. Just nippy-eyed from the salt that's all. To prove I wasn't I roared out my famous big laugh and everybody else laughed tottering on the rocks trying to keep their balance. I stuck my tongue out as far as it would go and licked round my top lip and chin in a wide circle to taste the sea. I'll try it now. Na. A bit of saltiness from the tears but the skin flavour's mingled with pub smell and bile.

Then back at the house in Clydebank after the day at the sea Ma painted us a picture. There was something childlike about it painted on the back of an old wallpaper roll. A coastline with a couple of squiggly lines in the sky for seagulls. Two matchstick people with round heads were on the shore waving at a boat that was drifting towards the horizon. Over the horizon were black swirls of cloud. She'd painted names under each of the characters. KATHLEEN. FARCHAR. And next to the boat. MAMMY. I looked up at her.

You're no waving back to us Mammy.

What are ye saying?

In the picture. You're no waving back.

Then she looked out the window. There wasn't much to see but she'd taken to staring out the window a lot. Just the tenement across the road and the towering cranes of the Rothesay dock. There was a dusty dockside building that constantly smoked sending flurries of grey snow across the tenements when the wind rose. CALEDONIAN CEMENT.

That was a nonsense picture for Ma. She was an accomplished artist in her own right but I suppose she was already losing it by then. Drifting away from us like the matchstick sailor towards an unreachable horizon. Always looking out. Until the windows lit up on the other side of Glasgow Road and the rows of chimney pots sent lines of grey smoke curling into the night. BeJaz. I've come over all Tenement Tales. I'll be dancing oot the close wi ma Coulter candy in ma hand. A game at peever wi ma cronies. Dodging the razor thrusts of Big Dan Docherty and Bawjaws MacLetchie trying to rip out each other's throats as we skip up and down the chalk-beds toeing the Cherry Blossom tin before us *wanzy-twozy-threezy-fourzy*. Lanny MacKay reeling out of the Iona Vaults having pissed the filched coppers of the neighbourhood menage against Shanks of Barrhead.

Drifting out of tenement land. Tunnel hiss rising. To a surge. Churning and splashing now. Water voices amongst it whispering messages that send the chill-fear through me. I let the river pull me into the flow to escape it. Rising and falling. Down into a deep gorge a roof of trees spinning above as the river swirls then slows. Now I'm out of the water climbing up the side of the gorge. There's a wind blowing among the trees making a wild sough that becomes one with the river. Where does the song of the river end and the song of the wind begin? I've always wanted to find that place. The secret world between the songs. Find the border and a way in. No terrible voices in there. No Book of Revelations or Corinthians gargling and spitting at you. Only good things. The flow of the river and the wind in the trees.

I reach the light at the top of the gorge and I can see over the Strath now. I hold back for a moment. Take a faltering step at first then walk towards it.

The black swirling Caldon roaring far below. Twisting down then slipping out secretly under trees to flow down the grazing parks where it joined the Finglas. It faded quickly into silence as I left it behind then struck the disused embankment of the branch line railway that would take me on to the Finny Viaduct. Over the river's deep waters then up through Drums to the distant village on the hill. There came the rev of an engine. I swung and saw the machine trundling down a park trailing a cutter. Making a broad swath through the crop. A chunky arm hanging from the cabin window bounced with the motion as the machine bore down towards the old railway banking. A scream rose over the engine.

FACH! FACH YA BIG BASTARD!

As he approached the foot of the hill I could see a wide-eyed face beaming through a moving reflection of field tree and hedgerow. The machine began turning on a radius of itself to travel back uphill.

FUCK! AH CANNAE STOP! ARE YE GOIN UP THE BULL?

AYE DEKE! THE BULL!

RIGHT! AH'LL SEE YE UP THE BULL!

Deke gave a big rev on the pedal then continued round and up. I hung around for a moment to see if he would manage to roll the tractor and trailer and wreck the whole gubbins. Man. Deke was an officially declared disaster zone. He'd a history of destroying borrowed cars or waking up with a house blazing round his ears. The age-old fable of the Piss-Head and the Chip-Pan. He managed to shoot a guy in the leg once while explaining the gun's safety catch. Managed to tumble an on-hire JCB down a bank into the depths of the Finny. Mind the time in the Bull? They were talking about Deke's talent for wreckage when somebody came to his defence. *Ach aye. But he's a harmless enough big lad really.* Harmless? Everybody was hooting it and with that the name stuck. Harmless Deke. But me and the Deke we go away way back. Moons and moons and multiple moons ago it was Deke that taught me Barnyard Surfing. We sneaked into Psycho Buchanan's big shed at the back end of a long winter. The shite on the floor was a yard thick. Deke hitched a piece of rope to a cow's tail and held tight then handed me the cattle prod.

Go on Fach. Gie it a dunt.

I gave it a jolt and the poor moo careened up the shed. Deke held on *yahaying* with the green stuff spurting out from under his wellies.

> *EVERYBODY'S GONE SURFIN! SURFIN USA! Hey Fach ye've heard o the Beach Boys eh? Well WE'RE THE FUCKIN KEECH BOYS! YAHOOOOO!*

Walking higher up Drums I could see the village lying on the hill. Early evening fell with a chill on it and gathering clouds. St Ronans chimneys began to unfurl their thin grey banners to the wind sending a tang of woodsmoke through the air. Up there in the centre of the village the great granite obelisk in memory of Mad Sir Duggie the IXth pointed at the scowling sky. Some slate roofs stretched back to the edge of the knowes and that was all there was.

* * * * * * * * * * * * * * * *

My thumb pressed down on a pad that lifted a metal lever out of its catch with a dull clunk then I swung the old creaking door across the flagstones. The place was empty so I went behind the bar to pour myself a Guinness a good slow pour. I put the cash on the gantry then went custom side and rolled up a smoke to accompany the beer. Milk with the honey. I could hear the door through the house opening and soft shuffling footfall. Slippers. Bell emerged.

> *Farchar MacNab! Fachie ma wee pet!*

She was out from behind the bar and giving me a big hug. I could see her putting her tongue under her lit cigarette and rolling it to the corner of her mouth so's not to burn a hole through my cheek in mid-embrace. She took the fag from her mouth and let go a big plume of smoke still half-nelsoning me with the other arm and kissed me on the cheek. We drew apart.

> *So how hev ye been eh? Grand eh? A wee bird telt me*

you wis comin home.

Ah'm fine Bell. It's good being back.

Aw. Great fun eh? My my eh? That's lovely. Aye.

She was back in bar side and pouring me the next Guinness. Bell's era behind the bar in the Bull went back a long way. Some said it had been in her family right away back to the cattle days when Highland drovers had rested their cows on the square. Bell herself had been here so long she could mind on the locomotive men slowing up to throw off coal at the back of the bar. This would be exchanged for inner warmth at a later date. A dram from the gantry or a bottle from the distillery. I caught more crack from Bell then got a fire together for her. There was still some oak out in the backyard left over from a big storm so I kindled a slab of it then laid over a few lumps of coal. Flame scampered up and down lichen leaving brief red galaxies. A sudden low *whump* of backdraught pushed a cloud of smoke into the mouth of the grate then swiftly inhaled it back up the lum sending a blaze dancing across the coals.

Gweed lad Fachie. That's a fine fire son.

Looking out the ingle-side window through dusk to the distance. Gilquhan Tower in the trees above the gorge. All dark shapes and shadows. Shadows cast by the flames of history. Flames that twist between centuries. Flames that had roasted alive Gilquhan's innocent victims. Screams lost among the roar of flame and the crack and spit of their own burning flesh and sinew. It had all begun with an unexplained outburst of fires in the crops around the Strath. Haystacks flaring up of their own accord. Widows and healing-wives had been dragged to the Tower with steel hooks impaled in their cheeks and the fires of a cruel autumn harvest had sent out shadows of terror. Shadows cast by the acrid stench of burning humanity that wafted around the musk-scented capes and powdered wigs of the Gilquhans. Shadows that stretched down the years. Shadows cast by lightning bolts as one mad bad or syphilitic Sir Duggie followed the next on the dynastic hobby-horse of their exotic history. Shadows cast in the flash of electrical experiments. There were still the remains of early generating equipment down there in the gorge. The dammed-up pool. The pipe and turbine.

Their memorials are decaying towers and gazebos. The obelisk. The Institute in the square. Ruins of animal cages and the rusting hulk of the paddle-steamer *Queen Euphemia* by the pier on Loch Mhor. Crumbling Gilquhan Tower smothered in ivy. Clawing its way through holes in the broken roof of the Great Ha. It seemed like the twisting vines were grappling around the place waiting for a sudden issue of strength when one storm-lashed night they would pull it creaking and banging down below the black earth forever. The switchgear house was at the back among overgrown rhododendrons.

As bairns we climbed through there. Into the inner gloom. Great steel black boxes with huge levers. Ampere and voltage dials frozen in a mesh of cobweb where relics of insects hung like fish in a net. We'd heard that they'd carried out their experiments here. On corpses and on beasts from the cages. There were stories of inmates being brought from the district asylum and being mutated with giant lizards. We recreated it. Putting a chill into our souls until the fear-grip would cause somebody to let out a scream and we'd all run laughing from the switchgear house. Crashing through the rhodies a panic scurry of legs and arms till we hit the field of oaks and across the ruined cages of Gilquhan's zoo where tigers had paced to and fro under a dour Scottish sky. There had been wolves and even a giraffe. The chimps enclosure and the aviary. Then there was the mad beast that had trampled the zoo-keeper. The one they'd buried by the burn. Mad screaming elephant.

* * * * * * * * * * * * * * * *

Nnn. OOJHA Fwack. Eh? Jeeza. Big purples and yellows in ma eyes. The lava lamp effect. Rake among the togs for some flame and fire up a candle then the stove. The auld elephant? Fucks sake. Dig into the tin and roll a cigarette to smoke with the tea. Jesus the ticker's going dunt dunt dunt thought the elephant was coming right down on top of me there. Hot sweet tea should ease the rattling heart take a good hard toke on the roll-up. *Whhh. Lord Almighty.* All bones and tusks he was. No skin. Story of my life one big procession of skeletons. He still had his eyes in him. Big reddish eyes. Only a dream let it go. Just mixed-up memories. By fuck ma lad they're coming thick and fast today. I'm practically getting travel-sick here. Could start up a tourist thing though. Filling a coach full of old English crumblies then going for a spin round the landscape of Fachie's memories. Saga Tours eh? Altogether now... *Ten green bottles 'angin on a wall... ten green bottles.* Enough. Gad. Mind you. Hoot toot toot. The old elephant.

Remember it eh? Rain storms and big game hunting? Fuckin long time ago.

It was the year of the flood. Autumn rains falling hard and the gorge twisting and roaring with wall-to-wall spates. The grazing parks of the Strath were like lochs. All you could see was the top of fenceposts with strings of barbed wire. We were all underneath the obelisk. A big crowd of us the air was buzzing. Turk MacGruer was there. Standing in front of the crowd he had darned elbows on his jersey. He flung his arm forward with a loud *come on.* Wellies scuffing and slapping on the backs of legs. Echoing in the winding street as the mob surged forward spilling down the Carnock Lane towards the old railway bank. I ran to the front to find out what was happening.

> *Hiv ye no heard? A dinosaur's been washed oot the bank o the Caldon.*

I stood back for a moment to consider it as the mob filed past. A bunch of smaller kids had joined on at the back.

A dinin-sword! A big monster! Waaaeeeur!

When we reached the Finny Viaduct the crowd had broken into a half-run. At the edge of the wood we looked down. The Caldon spilling out in a brown torrent. At the mouth of the gorge a high bank had been washed away and we saw the gigantic ribcage sticking out the hill down into the flood. Silence. It only lasted a few seconds. Breathing and blowing. Nobody moved. Then a cry and a collective roar as we charged down like Neanderthals at a wounded mammoth.

We carried gigantic bone trophies back to the streets of St Ronans. Laid them against the base of the obelisk then a wild chanting dance went circling round it. Some primitive echo had reached into us. We roared and cried and jousted with giant bone lances until the stars began to peep. The whole village was out to find out what the roaring was all about.

Somebody sent for the Ancient Crawfords then the pair of them came doddering along on their sticks for an inspection of the bones. One of them jabbed a walking-stick towards the pile.

That's yon ephlicant frae the Gilquhan zoo. That beast was a murderer. We were jist lads at the time when it went loco and killed its keeper.

Aye. Yon elephant went pure mad. It smashed through its cage and picked up the keeper then it whirled him aroon in its trunk. It threw him doon and trampled on him. Then it ran aff and swam across the Finny.

The first Crawford jabbed his stick into the air.

Then it cherged up throw the wids and richt up the hill tae St Ronans where it ran amuk. It was in the village. Chergin up and doon the Shannoch Road hootin like a trumpet.

Everybody wis lookin oot frae their windaes petrified. Then somebody says tae me. Run oot the back door and ower the Battle Hill. Don't stoap till ye get tae George Ferguson's.

And I went wi him. Ferguson was the only man we knew whit had a gun. We wis terrified. Rinnin like we hid dynamite stuck up wir arses. Ower the Battle Hill wi this mad beast jist ahent us.

We chapped up Ferguson. He got up on his white horse wi his gun and fired a shot. The elephant took off and he chased it richt up the Strath. He follied it richt tae the very tap o Dunreoch where it panicked and ran ower a cliff and fell doon ontae the Ugly Stanes. It was the Ugly Stanes whit smashed it deid.

Then wid ye believe? The Duggie Go-whans tried to claim compensation aff Ferguson for killin the beast. That beast had killed a man. They took a big kert tae the mountain and hauled it back tae the Tower wi a team o horses.

Then they got a spee-cialist tae skin it. One o them taximadermatists. But he wisnae much o a spee-cialist. He stuffed the elephant's hide wi auld waste cotton oot the Buchanan Mills. Stuffed it tight and sewed it thegither. They stood it in the middle o the Great Ha. But efter a year or two it began tae sag.

Great Uncle John worked up there. He said the poor thing wis aw crinkled and saggy. Like a burst baw. They hidnae buildit it aroon the banes. They should've buildit it usin the banes.

Aye. But they'd buried the banes doon by the burn. Where the bairns foond it the day.

In the mind-eye I can see the high bank where we found the

skeleton of the crazy Jumbo all those moons and moons ago. The bank's all grown in now of course with tussock and whin. It was years later there was one evening I'd cycled away over from Knockhaven. The time me and Ola had decided we'd brew up a few gallons of elderberry wine to last us over the winter months. I stashed the bike and walked to the mouth of the gorge where there were two good elder trees.

Hand reached up among the leaves and pinched a berry rich ruby juice trickled down my thumb so I knew they were right. Placed the old Bergen in the fork of a tree and filled it with cluster after cluster. I stopped to enjoy the moment while I was up there on the tree. The earth-smell was on my hands. Berries were hanging from stems with a claret radiance. The wind blowing in on the fading light of day had a song on it. The song of the land. Music that can never be written down or played it's just there with you for a time then it's gone and that's all there is to it. A presence. Whisper of the boughs. Night winds caressing the earth. Down below me the sough of the black swirling Caldon rose and fell as it passed through the gorge. It was the time of the spawn when the migrating salmon were lying in the dark pools with drowned leaves gliding across their flanks.

The salmon image fades the river picture becoming harder to see breaking into colours and shadows. The hiss gone silent no more serpents or rivers. Douse the candle. Sleep some more now in bedroll blackness. Maybe I have to get back to St Ronans. Ola. The memory felt warm. No tears either. Go back to burnt-out Knockhaven to pull the memories out from the ashes and let them go in the wind. The Haven man. The Haven.

Unshackle. Slide back corrugated iron magnesium light burning into my eyes. Right through the tiny holes where the gremlins've drilled. Into my brain. Lasers. Must be early evening there's a glow high west of the vent. Traffic sounds are coming down into the station instead of up the way towards the sky. Happens sometimes don't ask me why. Atmospheric pressure. Or my fucked-up head. God fuckin help me but I'm going to have to do this tunnel walk I'm starving to death man. Not far from it believe me. Have to do something about it. No procrastinating. One is starvicating. Jesus my knees. Oh Jesus Sliced Almichty. Mammy Daddy my poor fuckin knees. Hirple shuffle stop. Palms are stinging cut and bruised. *Hands out boy. Both of them! Skelp! Skelp! Skelp!* Skelp with the tawse that's what it feels like. What a state. I'm like a dead leaf being nudged along by the wind. One step. Two step. Three four five. I just need that energy to push me through the tunnel. Gad. Give me strength.

I shut the eyelids tight for the tunnel walk just to keep the shiny bogey-man out of sight. As I'm walking on the blackness in front of each eye blackens. Black holes. Everything around the black holes whitens until what I see is the shape of my own skull in front of me. Like one pulled off the shelf of Golgotha's Vaults. The skull floats in front of me as I walk. Then the darkness in the eye sockets eases until a picture appears in each of them. In the left socket is a city. In the right long hills with a river running through. The pictures come and go but I keep the tightness of my eyelids constant to try not to disturb them till the northglow meets me and I open my eyes to the light. I'm starving and I know I have to get to the Gravy Star. I'm too weak to walk it's miles away. Like Gallowgate miles away.

Subway train I'll take a subway to the city centre and hirple the rest. Can't go past Parkie's house I'll have to go round by Mexico and down the steps to the river walkway. I'm feeling a bit uneasy about last night's roaring shenanigans. Guilt. I'm under the shadow of Knox's beard.

It's good to hear the Kelvin. Low summer murmur even though yesterday's storm's lifted it a touch. Rippling. There's still a few folk around looks like it's been a fine day earlier. The usual park types. Runners. Dog-walkers. There's some long-haired eejit out with a set of hand-drums transporting his consciousness all the way to Marrakesh in the slipstream of his bongo vibes. Christ look at this lot here with the bairn. They're giving that squirrel enough scran to bloat it out like a bloody beach ball. Wee silver bushy-tails scamper bounce scamper oooh did ye see that one Kirsty? Did ye? Did ye see it Kirsty? *See it? Of course I saw it dae ye think I'm fuckin blind? I'm four-and-a-half-years old for fuck's sake stop talking to me like I'm thick. See parents? Pure fuckin scunner ye so they do.* Well here's a sight worth seeing. The fitness fanatic the guy that practises his kick-boxing at the swings he's always here. Does he no get bored without an opponent? Even the bairns on the climbing frame have lost interest in him standing there giving it the Jackie Chan.

It's quieter at this end down at the founds of the snuff mill. Hey. Don't like the look of that pair at the lane there with the dog. Are you looking at me oh malignant one? Skulking like hyenas the three of them vibe vibe vibe fuckin Neddy scum I bet they've lashed out a few beatings on unsuspecting citizens in their time. Well they never give it the Queensberry Rules do they? This big neb of mines has been broken twice in the last year and both times I've been legless and not a hundred yards from this spot either. Hey. I wonder. I fuckin wonder. Can't remember any faces I blacked out.

So when did it start? All this. Malice. Loathing. Envy. There's some would tell you it's just the afterglow of the rancid fart that seeped out Demoness Thatcher's crinkled auld anus for eleven stinking years but that's history now. The stench lingers on right enough. Individualism. Society breakdown and all that stuff. Violence and greed reign supreme. And so what? If you read into the chronicles you'll find instances of unwarranted brutality right back to year zero. But what I'm saying is this. And call me a misty-eyed old git who pines back for the sun-drenched days of yore but it's not all that long ago that there was an easier time. When winos and derelicts were ancient men who came wayfaring out from railway arches and lodgings to wend their way among the park benches and soup caravans that were the routine landmarks of their day. The difference is that they were *old.* There were no young men or women out there to champion the Trickledown philosophy with the spare change request. Unwanted germs on the rim of your disinfected lavatory bowl. The sanitised lavatory bowl of your twenty-first century existence. But. But but. *Bwaaaawk!* It's the system what can you do? Zee masheen! Rolling on relentless there's no stopping it's great pounding works. See it! See zee masheen! Gears switches cams crankshafts hammers levers motors flywheels pistons magnets actuators windings valves. Rumbling grinding hissing. DEAFENING! ZEE GREAT MASHEEEN! PUMPING AWAY ON HUMAN LIFE! Go on. Try to stop it. Make a futile gesture. Stick a finger in its works. It'll drag you in make quality mince of you. So genuflect before the machine. The mighty grinding altar of the Global Corporation. Fuel are we. *Bwaaaawk.*

I slip a furtive one over the shoulder to see what the hyenas are up to. Nobody's following. Hey. Maybe it's time for The Fach to feign a bit of drunken staggering along here some moonless night. Brain and body free of the drink and a hefty ballast of meat and tatties in the gut. Hydraulic surge of adrenalin pumping through the sinews of the forty-inch shanks. Clipped to the inside of the langcoat shall be that solid lump of a cudgel that I keep back in the gaff for emergencies fondly known to me as *Uncle Malky*. Kadunka! Quelle surprise mes petits Neds amis. I continue along the walkway of the rippling Kelvin under the big spanning arch of Belmont Brig with the sandstone crown of the church up in the light high above. I can still see the bit of tinsel hanging off a branch where moons and moons ago me and Cammy and Sharleen threw our Christmas Tree over the bridge one January the fifth. It's always a melancholy event that when you take down the old Christmas deccies so we carried the tree out of the flat still with all the floss and tinsel and baubles and the fairy on top on to the brig and heaved it over the parapet. Out it went catching that bit of tinsel on a treetop then spun all the way down spladoosh into the pool. We ran across the road to watch it rocking down the current with most of the kack still on it and the fairy drifting along behind YEEHOO! One day it would be my turn to go off the bridge. I climbed up on the parapet. Kelvin a ribbon of light under the trees. Rippling far below. Out I Went. OUT OUT OUT I went. Made the leap then drifted outside of myself and saw my body fly out over the water. A buzzard off a crag. Out I went. Out out out I went. Still. Hanging on the updraught. Back up I came. Crashing into myself knocking me sprawling down on the pavement. Swear I heard a splash in the pool below. People were passing. Looking. Auldwife with a shopping bag. *Are ye awright there son?* I knelt shaking holding onto the bridge for a time then walked away. There was an east wind blowing. Chills. Cold numbing chills.

Escalator drops down a perspex tube to the subway kiosk. Then another down into the station below the River Kelvin. The lair of the orange worm. The subway train comes roaring in with a warning toot then stops and the doors slide apart. Into the carriage and sit on a long bench with brown tartan fabric as the station slides away. I like the wee subway. The Mini Metro. Sometimes I give the stations Parisian names. Le Pont du Kelvin. La Croix de Saint George. Pays des Vaches. Rue du Buchanan. Cessnoque. Partique. Partique now there's a wholesome burgh for you. Trains going overhead and buses going by the waft of chippies and pub smells. You can get anything you want there. Cheap batteries lightshades reconditioned cookers. Hoovers. TVs. Wallpaper. The kind of district you wouldn't feel out of place walking along the pavement with a roll of linoleum over your shoulder. Subway train roars down the tunnel shrieking when it takes a curve sending me lurching into the aisle but I'm too weak from the hunger to do anything about it. Bouncing around I must look like a puppet being dangled from invisible strings. Puppet master'll have me doing a wee dance up the train for the delight of the passengers next. Fuckin Thunderbirds. That's me folks. Like a puppet on a string. Like a puppet on a. Oompah Oompah. String. Hey. What the fuck is this? What the fuck IS THIS? Just what the fuck IS THIS? There's a. Fuck off. There's a. Fuck off. There's a faint glow coming off of me a strand that's never happened in the light before. Just off the right arm. There's a wee bit on the right thigh too. Gie it a slap. Take that GET YA. It seems to be fading get ya oops. That's attracted a bit of attention a few sideways glances. Specky book-man there with the paperback's looking pretty annoyed WELL EXCUSE ME JOE 90. But it's gone. Good.

Rolling round the old city circuit on the electric toy train. Station to station. There was a time when this must have been the world's only steam-driven subway can you believe it? Not old smoking locos but a coal power-station up there on the surface. Over yonder at Rue d'Ecosse. The steam powered a great drum that would pull miles and miles of cable round the tunnels for the trains to clutch on to. Carrying packed carriages of workers with the oily smell of industry clinging to their jackets and caps. A weary human cargo travelling through the burrow from one side of the river to the other to toil on giant steel hulks. Unlike the thousands who built the great pyramids to Rameses there would be no mighty monuments to gaze across desert sands to at the end of their toil. Instead they watched the fruit of their labours slip fore to the clang of thrashing chains. Towed away by the tugs. Iron giants sailing down the narrow channel to the firth and out into Atlantic waves. Wooden ships too. Away down at Dumbarton. Masterpieces in varnished timber to ferry opulent whites down African deltas. In Scotland's semi-darkness weary human cargo emerged at surface stations and made their way towards crumbling tenements. Washing off the smell of graft with hard brush and carbolic in the jawbox sink. Gazing through a cracked window pane into a back court of rubble and giant puddles and overflowing middens.

Dark Atlantis. Under a dank sea of perpetual drizzle that seeps into your bones and into your soul. Clouding the present. Drifting vapours shift apart to reveal old shadows. Replacing a hollow world of exclusive river-front hotels and grinding motorways with a procession of towering cranes and the burr of industry that reaches all the way to the heather hills of the Firth. Clinging to the past. Hanging on to ghosts of memories and old songs until they become distorted into comic-hall parodies. Some bow-leggit shilpit wee gallus man in a tartan bunnet leads off the singing. The wafts of steam from his comic fish supper are clouds of laughing gas that drift over the stalls and work the crowd into hysterics until they roll in the aisles. Hoots and we're off into the sunset glory of the past. Marching out of the theatre en masse on the road to the Isles and keeping right on to the end of it. Into a world of winding hill tracks and lochs and but n' bens. Returning home via Grannie's hoose on the brae to find that forty long years have passed and the only boat that's sailin doon the watter is the Sewage Ship *Dalmarnock* wi its great big cargo o shite.

* * * * * * * * * * * * * * * *

I'm relying on the forty-inch shanks to get me the weary quarter mile to the Gravy Star but the thought of the food's enough to carry me. The café sends steam and a weary glow out into the shadows below the metal bridge that once carried trains east and south. Past the Tolbooth. Unicorn high on a blackened stone pillar. Coughing on fumes of passing traffic. Reaching behind the heraldic shield for a lung-saving skoosh from his inhaler. The Gravy Star's busy and I can sense one or two raised eyebrows as I go in the glass door. Glancing up from their fish teas. No worries I've been in here many times and the wifie behind the counter always treats me with courtesy like a real regular yes mister. I order me up a right good scran. Broth. Liver and tatties. An egg on the side. Steak pie. Two plates of bread and butter. A big glass of milk to come over with the meal. I ask for a couple of Cocas then go across to a table sliding up the formica to get myself installed. I'm needing the sugar from the Cola to give me a bit of equilibrium and it works a treat. The broth comes over and I take a cagey sup in case I want to heave it back up again in a big bile fountain but it goes down easy. Over it goes. A few more spoonfuls. No problem. A few more. A glow spreading across the gut now with the warmth of it. Nosh into it now. Scrumptious. Scrump-diddley-tumptious. Guid wholesome soup ambrosian Gallowgate mama in your flowery apron give me your broth. Now as I swallow each spoonful the mind-eye conjures up a picture of rolling fields of golden barley and mile upon mile of lush tattie-rigs under an endless summer sky. The soup's done and now the main event's over and my arm's working away like a mechanical lever regularly forking mouthfuls of steaming goodness from plate to gob. Yes sir. Oracle oracle oracle. A mouthful of fresh cold milk lights up a vision of cows grazing in a buttercup pasture. Top it all with a steaming mug of strong sweet tea and a thick-ee. Peace. Guidwull tae aw. Yeah. Zooba Zooba Zooba!

I suppose I could manage a drink now that the grub is sitting snug in the gut. The knees've stiffened up a bit not so sore if I start walking again soon. Palms are stinging like hell. *Hands out boy*! *Both of them*! Skelp! Skelp! Skelp! that's what it feels like. Some grim reaper of a schoolmaster. Long black cloak and a tawse curving under its own weight into the shape of a scythe. Skull smiling with S&M satisfaction. Satisfied at my remorse. That I've carried my stinging palms well into adult life. *Look at you MacNab. I always knew you would end up in the gutter you useless tramp*. Why did these knob-ends so much want us to fail? I suppose it's just the way the system was. They'd sift off the Uni material then try to drill a hardness into the rest of us in preparation for life in the mills. Some chance. Buchanan's cotton mill of Balshannoch had hung on to the last days of its life like an old veteran. Powered by the water tunnel that surged under it from the fast-flowing Finny. An artery that fed life into the swinging and oscillating machines until the whole place would shake and rattle and creak. A century and a half of dust clung to the windows and the top storey offered a view down the Strath through a grimy lens. Anyone could see the Balshie Mill was breathing its last. It was a tired old man. Comforted only by old anecdotes and memories of former glories.

There were only a handful left in the Mill but the school was talking to us like it was still in full swing. *You're crap at Maths MacNab. And Grammar isn't your strong point either eh? It appears your grasp of French is appalling. And you've not shown much aptitude on the football field. Never mind MacNab. There's always the mills. Aye sonny. There's always the mills.* Even a be-plooked youth of my own tender years could see that there wouldn't always be the mills. You could smell the decay of the place. And so at Balshie Academy I was relegated to the lower orders. To the mill stream. *Hech hech!* The Academy meant little to the likes of us. Fach MacNab. Harmless Deke. Turk MacGruer. Cammy. Sharleen. Doober. Craw. Big Sally of the Songs. Herry Merry. School hours were a hindrance until the dark fell and our mad cries echoed through the back-wynds of St Ronans and out over the knowes. Yawoo. The auld days. Wee White Horse. Torching the bins. Tippling Buckfast among the ancient lichened tombstones. Heading down The Close to wind up the minky MacDougalls. Yawoo! Lead us in Turk! Shanny Aggro! YAWOO YAWOO YAWOO!

Maybe it's no bad thing Uncle Duncan treated me like I was invisible. It gave me the freedom of Saints. In the cold sandstone mansion Baden and Edith had to be sitting at their easel desks by 6:05 pm Monday till Saturday. Sunday was Worship. And so with the exception of the outdoor camping trips to the Shannoch Woods I was spared Uncle Duncan's educational regime and allowed to roam the wynds. Up at Shannoch he taught us How To Walk and How To Sit. How To Breathe and How To Hoist Britain's Flag The Right Way Up. He was a disciple of Baden-Powell. An elder in the kirk. Secret Knight of the Sacred Temple of Roan. Yes mister. Man of secrets. Dark whispered secrets. Duncan MacNab. Deceased. May you Rest in Pish. You may have got to Baden and Edith. But you never got to me.

By Jaz I could do with that drink. The scran's nestling snug in the gut but I'm still feeling a bit doomed-up. Guilt. Knox's beard. Don't know where to begin with Maggie. I reckon I blew it big-style last night. In The Coffin. There's mind-pictures flashing through me. Paranoia-vision. Downstairs in Golgotha's I'm swinging at somebody and roaring. I'm seeing Maggie in the middle of it Jesus don't tell me I clattered her by mistake hell hell hell put a lid on it I'll find out the truth later anyway. Trying to fill in the blanks that's the worst bit. I think my songs went down fine too I was only half pished at that point. Jeez it was a great night and I had to blow it. Maggie was up there introducing the first act.

> *NOW EVERYBODY. STAMP YOUR HANDS AND CLAP YOUR FEET FOR A VERY…SPECIAL…APPEARANCE. IT'S SCOTLAND'S MENTALLEST ROCK BAND. IT'S REEZ!*

Much thundering and cheering. I was seeing Reez take the stage through one eye and a tilting ebb of golden warmth. Two oiled-up near-naked blokes in leather mini-skirts wheeled this giant gong onto the stage. Then they began banging it with big gong-hammers like the intro to the old J Arthur Rank movies. They speed up on each hit until they're swinging these gong-hammers and it's sounding like a speeding train. Skinny-B climbs into the drum kit and starts rolling the sticks round the kit and it's building into a frenzy. Reez herself walks onstage and straps into the telecaster whacking out these wild fuckers of metallic notes and screeches of feedback that blend with the drumbeat into a perfect symphony of chaos. She slaps the guitar to the gong rhythm then slowing it down slowing it down. The whole fuckin Golgotha's Vaults is clapping to that beat. A few folk are out of their chairs clapping and stamping. All we need is the skulls along the walls to start screaming. Reez plays a riff down the fretboard then starts singing in her inimitable staccato scream with its nightmarish beauty.

YOU SAID. YOU WANTED MY HEAD.
TO BORROW MY HEART.
TO BLEED ME DEAD.

Some people went down the front and began dancing awkwardly to it. Limbs moving slowly and deliberately. REEZ played half an hour then headed off to a gig in Edinburgh it was a nice gesture to Maggie. Then it was Kelvin O'Connor's poetry. Some lengthy epic to do with spirals containing the essence of life. It all began with whorled shells then somehow wound up inside intestines and all these spirally bits to do with anatomy. Somewhere around verse a million his mate accompanied him on the sax. Fur fack's sake Kelvin. Go back to the attic. Just as well he was in The Coffin. Best place to be when you die a death harumph guffaw. Erchie Shanks came on next. If there's ever a pogrom organised against our overpopulated community of stand-up comedians then Erchie should be at the front of the queue. He runs onstage in this idiotic turquoise anorak the lights glinting in his stupid big glasses.

> *HALLO THER YA BASTARTS! YES! AH'M ERCHIE SHANKS! RHYMES WITH? ANYWAY. AS MAGGIE SAID AH'VE JIST ARRIVED FRAE ERSHIRE! AH CAME OAN THE BUS! NAW! SERIOUSLY! AH DID! AH CAME OAN THE BUS! THE AULD WIFIE SITTIN NEXT TAE ME WIS FUCKIN HORRIFIED! NAE WONDER! AH SHOT IT RIGHT OWER HER PEOPLE'S FRIEND! RIGHT OWER THE WEE WATERCOLOUR PICTURE O THE LARGS PENCIL! THE LARGS PENCIL! WHIT KINDA FUCKIN NATIONAL MONUMENT IS THAT? WE DEFEAT KING HAKON AND HIS MIGHTY VIKING WARRIORS TO WIN BACK THE HEBRIDES FOR SCOTLAND. HOW'LL WE COMMEMORATE THIS MIGHTY EVENT? AH KEN! WE'LL PIT A BIG FUCKIN PENCIL OAN THE SEASHORE! AND THE THING IS. SEE IF YE GO DOON THERE ON SETTERDAY RIGHT?*

I head for the bar and do all I can to prevent this verbal torture leaking its way through my ears. I order another dram and a pint then stand at the hatch with Sound Andy. We're able to have a low conversation without disturbing anybody. I'm on to my third pint at the hatch before Erchie brings his act to a close.

> *AND THEN FOR A LAUGH THEY GOT THE BUNG OOT THE RED-EYE BARREL AND WHEECHED HIS SKIDS AFF AND HAMMERED IT RIGHT INTAE HIS ERSEHOLE. HEE HEE HEE! JOHN WAYNE WALKED HAME THAT NIGHT LIKE THIS. BIG JOHN HAD THE LAST LAUGH BUT. YE SEE. LITTLE DID THAE GUYS KEN. MAKIN HIM WALK LIKE THAT? THEY MADE THE BIG GUY'S FUCKIN CAREER! AH'M ERCHIE SHANKS! THE BIG SPECKY BOAY IN THE ANORAK! SO WATCH YERSEL'S! AWRIGHT?! GOOD NIGHT!*

Give the big specky boay in the anorak his due he got a few hoots and a good round of applause. Personally I preferred Mystic Martin with his haunted crotchpiece. With Suzie Sparkle his sequinned assistant standing five feet away and moving her hand up and down to the Wurlitzer music. Mystic Martin's got this spangled apron on and a giant star on his head. As Suzie's hand moves up and down so does Mystic's apron around the crotch as though he's got this great big storker of a boaby that's under Suzie's control. All the while the Wurlitzer's playing and everybody's in knots. Then Mystic and Suzie chase each other round the stage like Hill's Angels with the big unseen boaby raising and lowering itself up and down under the apron. No hands and no strings attached how does he do it? They do a few daft tricks and I look around the room. Folk are rocking in their chairs or lying with heads on tables having a real good hoot. I wouldn't have been surprised to have seen clouds of steam rising out from under a table or two with folk pishing themselves *HECH!* Oops shouldnae do that laughing out loud in public there's a few folk in the café giving me some odd looks well excuse me. Then somewhere in there it was my turn on the stage and I got a Telecaster rigged up and gave it a few songs. Well received good plaudits man good plaudits. Thank you. Well thank YOU! Think I got back up there for a few more numbers later on but I'm drawing a blank. I remember having the guitar. Where did it all go wrong? Shouting pushing screaming the usual bar room confusion when something starts. Was there a blade in there? Christ that's put a sweat on me. Why. Why me Laird? Why this God given talent for getting caught in the middle of shit?

Put Shanks's Loco on slow steam and wander back through town in Sunday evening stillness. Across the empty tarmac plain of the shopping precinct car park. Great cathedral to the plastic deity. Under a bridge I go train rolling over thuds booms. Walking past clock towers with seized mechanisms each telling a different version of the hour. A massive cloud of starlings drifts across the windless sky. Pivoting and spiralling in on themselves in a whirlpool motion. The centre of the flock bursts free in an explosion of movement then they weave together again spinning around into another vortex. It's like God's up there playing with an invisible magnet behind the sky and the starlings are iron filings. God and his invisible magnet. Sorry. God and *His* invisible magnet. Past the glass façades of office towers redundant dockyard sheds stumbling along awkward roadsides with rounded boulders sunk in concrete. Walk on the road one driver toots here's a pair of digits for a rear-view ya bog-brained *ARSEHOLE!* Below a motorway ramp held aloft by giant concrete piles then along concrete pathways into a concrete world of multis and maisonettes with concrete paving and concrete play areas yes and even little concrete playthings like miniature concrete elephants to sit on and miniature concrete crocodiles I don't know maybe to play at being in a tropical concrete swamp and over there's little concrete toadstools for the wee concrete bairns to pretend they're in concrete fairyland and over there's the spot where the wee concrete lassie got hurted because her concrete mammy flung a concrete jeelie piece oot her twenty storey flat and knocked the wean shit-senseless. Ye cannae dae that missus. There's twenty thousand concrete weans'll testify tae that.

Along a road in shadow of tall tenements bus droning past. Not much life. The occasional Asian shop open a flicker of coloured lights from The Lucky Dip Amusement Arcade with its ancient fruit-machines. I mind them when I was a bairn. Ma let us play one yon day at the sea. She had to lift me up to reach the lever. I kept thinking all the different bits of fruit were going to come out the hole at the bottom. A few cherries and plums and maybe a sprig of grapes. What else would you get from a fruit-machine?

A few voices and a beery smell from the open door of the Blue Whale pub and a spot of wifie activity outside the Regency Bingo. Onward. I'm seeing there's a light glowing in the hall at the back of the Dragonchurch. Strange. There's a couple of cars parked outside too. One of the storm-doors is open and there's a light on in the hallway. First I'm thinking maybe it's the Order of the Orange the old Jaffa men getting it together for a wind recital. But organ music? That's organ music. Pass me the pipe and deerstalker Watson it's time for a Sherlock here a right good nebber.

Into the hallway. Through a set of heavy swing doors. Noise and light. There's a guy up front with flaky skin and a pale grey suit playing the organ hey it's a Bontempi a real farter! There's maybe twenty folk standing by their chairs giving it serious psalm-singing with hymnals outheld. This is The City of the Frozen Clocks so who's in a hurry? I pull up a chair at the back as the final sustained note of the organ lowers the congregation slowly back down into their seats. Then up onto the platform strides some geezer in a dog collar and a goatee beard on him. Good grief for a moment there I thought it was Mystic Martin again but it's definitely not him. Looks a lot like him. Mind you I can't quite see Mystic Martin out treading the boards with his Randy Magician act on a Saturday then in here preaching the gosp on a Sunday. You never know right enough. The Minister of the Gosp leads them off in prayer so it gives me a chance to have a wee look round. Well. This is all a bit. Hmm. Appalachian. I hope they don't wheel on a tartan shopping trolley filled with adders and expect us all to poke our hands around in it. Hup. Prayer's over.

> *FRIENDS. Friends of the congregation. I HAVE A VERY SPECIAL ANNOUNCEMENT TO MAKE. Having spoken to several of you before the service and listened to your concerns. And in the light of receiving further information on this matter from various sources. It has been drawn to my attention that there exists an establishment not far from our*

church where practices of a paganish and demonic nature are nightly being ritualised.

Oho! This is getting interesting.

Fronting itself as an establishment for the sale of alcoholic liquor. It is no secret that this shebeen of evil worship which revels in the themes of darkness and death

Hey! Whoa! Haud the bus meenister! Wahay! He's on about The Coffin here!

has become an initiation ground for the luring of teenagers and children into the dangerous pit of iniquity.

Hey! Extreme. Bollocks. I say baw-locks. Better no say anything. This mob are strange. Ho. Ho wait till I tell Maggie about this she'll have a total fuckin canary. Fuckin cheek though. Cheek. This is getting heavy. Lead weight heavy.

The tales I have heard of to date are of an extreme and diabolical nature involving satanic ritual and communal sexual perversion.

Haw! Wish I'd been there that night.

Having spoken to the police about this I have been angered by their indifferent response. Tonight is not a night for simple devotions. Let us rise together and demonstrate at the doors of this house. Let it be known that there are those of us in our city who will not tolerate such darkness on its doorstep. Friends! Collect your hats and coats! We shall combine to demonstrate our revulsion towards this unGodly establishment. Let it be known that He will bring a conflagration on their house and a great eternal torturing of their souls. We shall march as one on the threshold of this place.

Hell's bells. I'm out of HERE. I'll have to get to The Coff and warn Maggie she'll think I've gone stone raving mental altogether. That apart I'm choking for a pint and I don't want to have to break the holy picket line after sitting through their service what a brassneck that would be. There's a clattering and creaking of chair legs on the wooden floor as the crowd rises. I'm trying to get up and out and SHIT SHIT SHIT damn langcoat's caught under a chair leg aw the bloody thing's gone into a burst in the seam I've got to undo it now there's about ten of them in front of me queuing at the swing doors. Spilling out into the street and marching purposefully down the cobbles I'm in the centre of it. I open up the steam valve getting a bit of power into the shanks overtaking the crowd now striding a pace or two ahead. But suddenly there's one or two level with me and I can hear the rest of their steps begin to accelerate behind me bloody hell they must be thinking I'm the pace-setter here. I open up a touch more steam and they fall in behind I'm beginning to feel like I'm a fuckin *real* locomotive here with an invisible coupling that's dragging along a cargo of nutters. The hell with it I break into a slow trot. Next thing's a clatter of feet on the cobbles behind me I turn round and they're all running along holding onto lapels and hats bearing down like the Charge of the bloody Light Brigade. I can see the Holy Goat making his way up from the back like he's going for Olympic Gold. They must think I'm the zealot here. Number One God-Fanatic. Through the railway arch with the single glowing bulb echo of footfall. Now Goatee's caught up with me and running alongside.

Great encouragement young man! Spirit! Fortitude!

His words echo in the tunnel. I just turn and stare at him nodding even if I'd the breath I'd be lost for words. We're out into open space now and all I can see is this floating beardy head beside me with the landscape going past. Neck and neck for a photo finish. Of all the religious services I could have poked my big Sherlock neb into it had to be this one. For God's Jesus sake would you just leave me alone mister. Well excuse me for using the Gaffer's name in vain but this is. This is extreme. So for. For *Diddle's* sake leave me alone. Yes let's give Him/It/Her/The Supreme One let's give it a name that won't offend. *Diddle.* Now I'm sure there are millions of people across the world going about the worship of their own particular Diddle in a rational and plausible fashion but how trippy is this? Then again there are those who would plant a bomb in a 747 or mow down innocent tourists or throw incendiaries into busy pubs just to appease their own particular Diddle. Consign bairns to death camps or drain a squillion barrels of crude oil into a Gulf full of Diddle's innocent creatures as part of Diddle's divine vengeance. So I suppose a score of nutters scrambling down the cobbles to protest outside Maggie's death fun pub pales by comparison. But they've got it so wrong. I mean. The Coffin's nothing more than a cross between a Scottish Hallowe'en and a Karaoke night. I mean surely. Na. Ridiculous. And this whole scenario. This. Being caught up among cranks like this is symptomatic of my own existence. What I call The Life. The Life. It introduces you to worlds you wouldn't have guessed existed because you've never been close enough to know. Beyond the rim of the sanitised lavatory bowl of twenty-first century existence. No one chooses to know The Life. But to be there and live it is to realise that in every city there are different layers of humanity that co-exist unseen and side by side. Oh Mammy. *Deep.* Now I'm peching coughing slowing down and hear the collective breath and footfall of the others doing the same. There's hardly a breath in my lungs and a dizziness comes over I grab a lamppost with both hands and buckle over holding onto it. Drawing in gasps. Next thing. Next thing bloody Goatee Minister's leaning on my back and addressing his flock like I'm some kind of lectern. I'm too bedraggled to complain.

> *Friends! Let us tarry for a moment and collect ourselves. That is the establishment over there. Now we shall march in an orderly fashion and make our feelings known at their doors.*

The crowd heads towards the bar and there's no chance I can edge ahead of them now. We surround the Welcome To The City Of The

Dead door and The Goat starts up a chant.

Satan Out! Satan Out!

They all join in then he alternates it.

God In! God In!

Then.

God In! Satan Out!

Everybody.

GOD IN! SATAN OUT!
GOD IN! SATAN OUT!

Goat's at the front waving his bible.

PROFLIGATE SINNERS! REPENT WHILE YE CAN!

Now the doors are open with punters coming out for a look. Goat's thrusting the bible at them to the rhythm of the chant. There's a commotion in the doorway as out comes Mags in the vampire uniform.

Whit in the name is goin on here?

PROFLIGATE! PRACTISER OF NECROMANCY AND ALL THINGS PROFANE! REPENT WOMAN! REPENT!

Do me a favour! What is this the loony brigade?

WE KNOW ALL ABOUT YOU WOMAN. AND WHAT'S MORE GOD DOES TOO. WE'VE HEARD ALL ABOUT THE EVIL PROCEEDINGS IN THIS HOUSE.

Evil proceedings? This is a pub Mac. Drink. Live music. Ye know? Fun. Darts doms karaoke. Social events. Fancy dress optional. So you can either come inside for drinks and behave yerselves or otherwise take yer disciples off my doorway and go and have a miserable night somewhere else.

Aw naw. Maggie's clocked me. Whh. She's no letting on. Now there's faces up at the windows with folk standing on tables and chairs daft student bastards they've all begun waving their hands in the air and started a big PRAISE THE LORD and I WANNA BE SAVED and BROTHER this and AY-MEN that. It's turning into a total hoot but I still can't get by for a pint as Maggie storms back inside. The Goat starts up another chant then I notice this auld white-haired gadgie wandering along towards the bar.

The ould fella's got a shock of white hair and tough pinkish skin on him that looks like turnip hide. A grey raincoat. He walks with the bow-leggit gait of a man who's grafted at hard physical tasks all his days. He reaches the crowd when Goat steps forward and puts a hand against his shoulder.

Sir. We are demonstrating against the iniquitous goings-on here.

Whit?

The Beard pauses for a moment to compose his authority. No small fellow The Beard. Using the dark glower of his eyes and the breadth of his chest as an obstacle to the pub. His body language has changed from outraged militant evangelist to threatening and police-like. Now silence. One of those moments when you can suddenly feel a situation turn and there's an edge of danger in the air.

We are gathering to prevent any more custom from passing these doors.

Ah'm jist wantin a dram son. Ye'll hiv tae let me past.

If you must I would advise you to partake of your imbibition elsewhere other than this unGodly den.

A thoughtful look passed over the auldyin's face. He'd taken the meenister's point on board. It was a look that lasted just a few seconds but told of years of negotiation and compromise. With spouse employers family adversaries. A look that told the story of a lifetime. With fifty years' industry in his wiry little arm he easily prised the Goat's grip from his shoulder and moved him aside.

Away an take a fuck tae yersel son.

With that he was inside for his dram. I was thinking of just pushing them aside and going in myself but they'd maybe think I was leading by example again and storm in at my tail. There's a distant wail of sirens and OH YA DANCER Maggie's phoned the law! From the five ways comes the old mee-maw and blue flashing lights YES two squad cars and a van. They screech to a halt and the crowd swivel round as one. Hullo! With the holy heads turned I can duck through them unnoticed into the bar. I will explain Maggie honest but for God's sake would you just pour me a stout before I begin? Yes sir. That's the last time the Fach dons the old Sherlock gear and goes nebbing into a place of worship. Lemon Entry Watson. Lemon Entry.

* * * * * * * * * * * * * * * *

A couple of police officers have come in. They go downstairs and have a look in Golgotha's then come back up. They're having a talk with Maggie then question a couple of folk and have a laugh looking up at the Burke and Hare on the way out. I've found myself a stool at the upstairs bar where it's busy with an excited babble from all the crack that the mad meenister and his holy brigade've stirred up and folk are still laughing into their beers. Sound Andy's poured me a pint and I'm savouring it for all its worth. God bless the ale. Can you imagine life without it? Maggie looks over at me and shakes her head with a smile. A tad rueful. She's real busy behind that bar and says to wait behind until after the bell so that she can speak to me. Gad. What is this? Detention? Talk about putting off the evil hour she'll prob'ly give me hell for last night. It's only just gone nine so at least I've got a couple of hours suspended sentence. May as well enjoy it. She looks over towards me again from the lager tap. Maggie. Sometimes I think you can read my thoughts. You seem to know when I'm up or down. Even when I'm being haunted by the Brocken. The way you look at me when the glow's been on me it's as if you know. You're a good woman Maggie. Not bad looking for a vampire either. What would you think if I told you my story? That I live in a derelict Victorian station below the streets of Atlantis. Stumbling through the tunnel towards the safety of the womb and up the Wembley Eleven in the blackness with no light to guide me. Tried the torch but it was even worse faces coming out the walls and shadows between the ballast stones with things lurking. Think I prefer the floating skull. Living among the blackness and afraid of it. What would you think? Would you laugh? Cry? Care? Care that I live in dread of the light because I can see too much of myself in it? I just can't think straight anymore. Haunted by an aura that pours out of my skin in the tunnels. Now I've seen it under the lights of a subway carriage. Just off the right arm and thigh. One night on alcohol sends me into meltdown and I make a roaring cunt of myself. Malarkey. Parkie. Maybe Parkie'll send the polis down now. End up snibbed-up again. Where'll I go? Where? Could you guess that there was once a time when this big pale face of mines glowed from the bluster of mountain squalls? Working around the Saints. Fachie the barra man. God bless the barra and all the tools in her. Rakes shovels hammers the whole fuckin caboodle. Cutting the trees and building fences. Slabbing painting roading you name it. Living up at the Haven. Jesus man the Haven. I'll tell you what I'm going to do Maggie. Tomorrow. Tomorrow I'm hitting the road. Out of this town right out of it. Back to the Haven.

To burnt-out Knockhaven to pull myself out of the ashes. I've heard that one before. I pulled myself back onto the bridge eh? Somehow. What was the splash in the pool below? Can't answer that one. There was an east wind blowing. Chills. Can you hear me Mags? I know you can sense something from the way you look over at me whenever you're at the till. But how can I ever tell you all of this? Out loud I mean. I think you're the only human being I can tell. You can hear me Maggie. Yes. Somehow.

A crowd of eejits have got hold of a guitar and keep the evangelical theme going. Giving it big gospel welly with *I SAW THE LIGHT LORD I SAW THE LIGHT.*

All standing up and waving hands around on the Praise The Lord's it's turned into a right bampot hallelujah session. Little can Goat know the merriment he's stirred up with his Demons Out Demo at the door. Praise Cod as they say in the Western Isles. Yes. Praise Cod and bless his Sole. Now let us pray. Our Flounder. Which art in Herring. Halibut be thy name. Thy Ling will come. Thy will be done. In Oil. As it is in Batter. Give us this day our daily Breadcrumbs. And forgive us our Perch. As we forgive our Congers. Lead us not into Pollution. And deliver us from Eels. For thine is the Salmon. The Powen. And the Coalie. Forever. Amen. The Laird's prayer at the last fish supper nyahah!

I'm overhearing stuff about the Goat. An ex-evangeliser of the One True Faith who used to sell dodgy far-right literature outside Ibrox. Uncovering Popish plots I suppose and still trying to avenge Wishart's strangulation and burning back in 1546. Only now it seems the Goat's gone right round the fruit-loop and invented his own sect. All mystic healing and minority hatred. Gad. Talk about the shadow of the Beard.

Even down in Clydebank I never experienced much of the old religiosity. Ma never gave Kath and myself much of a church upbringing. Too busy with her art and the anti-bomb demos to bother with it. For Ma trying to get peace on Earth meant marching to the Holy Loch to yell slogans at the atomic Yankee menace. Na. It wasn't until I got shipped out to the cold sandstone mansion that the tenets of religion were spooned into this unwilling thrapple. And it wasn't just God either. Worse. It was Baden-Powell. Uncle Duncan's national hero. Jesus wept. He even named his own son after him. Fur fack's sake. Beat this. Baden-Powell MacNab.

There was no scout troop in the village but that didn't stop Dunc did it? Oh no. It was like religion. He found two versions of the Scriptures in the library room of the cold sandstone mansion. The Old Testament. *Scouting For Boys: A Handbook For Instruction In Good Citizenship.* The New Testament. *Rovering To Success: A Book Of Life-Sport For Young Men.* The camping expeditions to the Shannoch Woods. Thinking back on it now I sensed there was a kind of a discomfort or a fear on him when we were out there.

Dunc's attempts at tent-building were shabby but he'd always claim he'd done it deliberately wrong to give us something to improve on. Sending me to gather wood for the fire. Thumping me if the sticks weren't the right type or the correct shape. Duncan was always clobbering me. Hated the sight of me. Whatever the sins of my faither had been they'd come back to visit me via the twisted mind of his brother. What grave sin did you commit Da? It must have been something bad that ended up with me being brought up in the regime of Baden-Powell. Not that I dislike the outdoor life na na na it's not that. I've always had a love for the hills. It was just Dunc's version of it with rituals and prayers and flag-raising and empire games. Aye. Rituals. Some bloody rituals.

Lighting the fire. When Duncan had it configured according to the diagram in *Scouting For Boys* he recited the camp fire verse. Checking the contents as he paced round it before striking the match.

First a curl of birch bark as dry as it can be
Then some twigs of soft wood dead from off a tree
Last of all some pine knots to make a kettle foam
There's a fire to make you think you're sitting right at home

Generally it would gutter out after a minute or two. Then he would lose the plot and guddle a *Daily Express* out his rucksack to get it going blaming me for getting the wrong wood. When the fire was finally lit and the union flag up on a pole we did The Scout's War Dance. Duncan screaming.

Een-gonyama Een-gonyama. Invooboo!
Ya-Boh! Ya-Boh! Invooboo!
He is a lion!

And so we three cried back.

NO! HE IS BETTER THAN A LION!
HE IS A HIPPOPOTAMUS!

Duncan.

BE PREPARED!

Us.

ZING-A-ZING! BOM! BOM!

Banging our sticks down on the Bom Boms. Uncle Duncan didn't have a bugle but that didn't stop him did it? Fuckin root-toot-tootin root-toot-tootin. Bugling us to prayer. After prayers and rations came the game. Oh yes. The game. Keeping The Camp Secret. Secret? Hell's bells. We'd just Zing-a-Zing Bommed and root-toot-tooted half of the bloody Strath awake.

Myself and Baden were given a sheet to wear across our shoulders then he'd swathe each of our heads in a towel. One like a turban and the other like an Arab headdress. We were sent away miles on either side of the camp to stand by a trackside gate. If any strangers should happen by and enquire about the whereabouts of the camp it was our job to deceive them and send them in the wrong direction. We were to return when the sun set. The Camp Secret. Home in time for prayers.

The Chalice the Cross and the Sacred Word.
The Covenant the Sword and the Blood of the Lord.
The Family the Flag and the Glory of God.

Och Uncle Duncan. Twisted. Twisted. Twisted twisted twisted twisted twisted twisted.

Guiding light of the Gravy Star. My sweet blessed saviour. Shine down and give me the strength to make sense of this. Give me the energy to carry the load. Give me the courage to go back to the Haven just one last time to make peace with it. I can't find remorse for Uncle Duncan. He was cuckoo and cruel and I was the whipping post for his fury. Filthy! Church! Farter! Ho yes. And forgive me my own sins. Forgive me the church fart.

Looking back on it now I blame the household cuisine. But how was I to know that Auntie Mary's Saturday supper would have such a profound effect on the teachings of the Lord? Tripe and chapped neeps followed by stewed prunes. Then next morning a pre-church breakfast of porridge and eggs. It was hardly conditions to induce calm weather in the old intestinal zone eh? No sir. A storm was a-brewin.

Marching to church single file with Duncan at the head. He looked round to see me bent over with the pain in my gut and therefore Not Walking The Right Way. Poking me along the road with his staff until we were in view of the church.

Sitting on cold wooden pews that taught our buttocks humility. My gut felt like I'd eaten one of the Uncle's bowling balls. A great pocket of gas making its way down my intestines desperate to exhaust itself out the old smellyhole. I pressed myself hard into the pew in an attempt to suppress it as the church organ fired up and the congregation rose for the Twenty-Third Psalm. I went total limpet. Remaining seated clinging to the pew until Duncan grabbed me by the collar to hoist me out. The organ intro finished and the singing began. Duncan pulled harder as I gripped my fingers underneath whispering *No No*. He gave a yank and hauled me up. Talk about root-toot-toot. It certainly outdid Duncan's attempts at the old bugling. I reckon the fart lasted seven seconds. The Holy number. Its tune resounded out harmonising briefly with Mrs MacPherson's organ. A blanket of gas rippling up the inside of my pants like a hot flounder. The flounder swam up my shirt then out the back of my collar. Niffy effluvium. Silage sewage eggs tripe jobbies. Rancid. A real canary killer. A hymnal dropped to the floor. The Rev Thom with his Hitler moustache up there in the pulpit gesticulating furiously like he's trying to Nuremberg Rally the fart away. His voice hitting an unwanted falsetto on *pastures green*. Old Mrs MacPherson on the organ swivelling round in horror her spectacles shooting out on to the end of her nose. Then at the end of the service. Grips me by the back of the hair and marches me home like a thief to the gallows. Pulls the leather strop from the drawer. *HOW DARE YOU!* The mad bastard. Swinging it head height as I ducked and cowered.

> *How dare you boy! How dare you? How dare you PUMP IN CHURCH. FILTHY!*
>
> *AYAH!*
>
> *CHURCH!*
>
> *AYAH!*
>
> *PUMPER!*
>
> *AYAH!*
>
> *FILTHY CHURCH PUMPER!*
>
> *AYAH AYAH AYAH! AH! STOP!*
>
> *NO! CHURCH FARTER! FILTHY CHURCH PUMPER!*

Bringing the strop down on my back and arms he was screaming now high-pitched completely out of control.

> *FEELTHY! CHIRCH! PIMPER! CHIRCH FERTER! FEELTHY! BEAST!*

AAAH!

FEELTHY FEELTHY BEAST!

STOP STOP STOP!

NO! FEELTHY FEELTHY CHIRCH PIMPING BEAST! I'LL GIVE YOU CHIRCH! I'LL GIVE YOU PIMP! I'LL GIVE YOU SMELL!

I looked up at the psychotic glint in his eye. The cuckoos had finally chucked out the last of his brain cells and taken over the nest. I made a lunge for the window and managed to struggle out with the blows raining down on me. It was the first time I'd sought the overnight refuge of the gorge on my own. Sleeping under the lonesome pine with the whispering waters in the chasm far below. I managed to last out for three nights. It's anybody's guess whether he was worried or not. He didn't bother reporting it. I suppose Dunc didn't want it put about that things weren't all that hunky-dory at the cold sandstone mansion the twisted sick. At any rate the farting Antichrist made it back of his own accord. Poor Auntie Mary. Demented with worry. Good Gad youd've thought that old Misery Moustache would have been proud of me surviving three nights in the woods. Without having the Scout manuals with me too. Not that they would've done me much good. Na. It would be years before I discovered the old Scouting manuals to be of any practical use.

* * * * * * * * * * * * * * * *

een-gonyama! een-gonyama!

EEN-GONYAMA! EEN-GONYAMA!

ya-boh! ya-boh! invooboo!

YA-BOH! YA-BOH! INVOOBOO!

zing-a-zing!

ZING-A-ZING!

bom! bom!

BOM! BOM!

The Bull Bar in the grip of a Friday night riot. I'm on top of a table my youthful bumfluff sheen reflected in the light of the winter fire and a galaxy of candles. The langcoat trailing around my shins *Scouting For Boys* held out before me. The War Cry going down a storm with the mad Shanny team that was raised on the wild cry of Yawoo Yawoo. Sharleen with her green eyes like the sea. Turk with the battle-scars laughing and drinking. Harmless Deke pished his big bright red head floating in front of me. Like something you would see on *The Sky At Night*. Until a yawning crater opened on the surface.

It's your round MacNab! It's your fuckin round ya jube-jube!

I climbed down and pushed Planet Beetroot aside then went up to the bar to get the drinks. The pub was cookin. The Ancient Crawfords were at the mantelpiece playing their moothies. Big Chief Simpson at the bar. Back on the firewater again. In the full Native American headdress it would only be a matter of days before they carted him away again. Chief Simpson's forays into the non-institutionalised world of the Strath rarely lasted more than a week or two which he usually spent in the Bull Bar.

Frank Simpson claimed to be descended from the Blackfoot and this was actually true. I knew myself from reading about it in the old books. The MacNab Manuscripts in the cold sandstone mansion. Generations ago one of his distant forebears had travelled to the

New World and returned to the Strath with an Indian squaw. But it wasn't until middle-age when Frankie lost his manager's job at the mill and went kee-haw with the whisky that he began to take his ancestry seriously. Until *he heard the cuckoo call his name*. Back in the mill days Simpson'd earned something of a reputation as a strict manager. Firm but fair. The operators would often refer to him as the Big Chief and that too found its way into his consciousness. Now he lived inside a make-believe Red Indian world of Fifties Hollywood. You would always see Simpson getting excited when the schemie cry *Yawoo Shanny* went up. War cry of Woodend of Shannoch. Cul-de-sac of four-in-a-block harled houses with smoking lums ringed in a circle like *Wagon Train*. Ach. Nobody batted an eyelid at Simpson. Standing at the bar in his great feathered headdress that he'd found at an antiques fair in Stirling. He was a passive enough Indian and the worst he could do would be maybe to start up a dance. Na. People were left to be what they were Strath folk were good that way. A scarier figure was the Hen-Wife. Letting out the occasional cluck. But Bell would have to show her the door soon before she got out of control. There was one night she turned the bar upside down looking for her clutch of eggs. No joke. A song broke out and the whole bar joined in. Yawoo. Good memories. The Bull was cookin.

* * * * * * * * * * * * * * * *

Hold on to those moments. They can't take them away. Treasure those memories that all the Sherriff's Officers and creditors and sharks or any other low-life rifle-their-dead-granny's-corpse-for-a-fiver fortune-hunting fuckwits that thrive in this bold new world of car-poinding wheel-clamping asset-seizing wonder can't take away from you. The moments are yours. Covet them. I look around The Coffin Bar now and see them singing away to that guitar. Hoot City. Keep it going folks. Gie it laldy. They can take away our furniture. But they can never take our memories. Yawoo. Fuck them all.

Coffin crowd pressing in on top of me in the last half-hour rush for their drinks but as I sway back and forth I'm grasping tight onto the underside of the bar stool to hold on. Filthy church pumper. The problem is that Lantern Jaws has drifted over on the swaying crowd and washed up beside me like an unwanted piece of flotsam. What is it about Lantern Jaws that frightens me? Could be that he's tall ancient and gaunt looks like a drifter and wears a langcoat into the bargain? Maybe it's the ghost of Da. Could be. Da with his big gangster connections down in London. Two detectives at the Clydebank door telling Ma Da's deid. What *did* you look like? Maybe you *are* Lantern Jaws. Standing there yabbering to me about greyhound racing and the prevailing injustice of grocery prices. Everythin's a *floomin liberty so it is son.* Taught thin skin fretted with veins from cheekbone to jaw mister I'm sure your head's a Chinese lantern. For a moment I imagine somebody in the crowd unhinging a wee door at the back of his skull and blowing out the wick. His head falls into darkness and his voice fades away like a radio being switched off. Then again maybe old L-Jaws is looking at me and imagining *my* head to be a big neep lantern. Thinking about lifting the turnip slice off the top of it and blowing out the candle. Then going off round the room to find somebody with the civility to listen to him. No offence Lantern Man. I'm a bit *absorbed.* Please. Leave me alone. Please? It's just that I've been running a few things over in my mind today. Things I haven't thought about in a while. The Strath and the past and all that. Stories rattling past my eyes. Like opening a dusty old book and flicking through the pages. Used to love that. Delving into the old books.

By far and away I'd have to say the best feature of the years in the cold sandstone mansion was the books. The library gloomy and forgotten. One long window looking north to draw in a dim grey light. Out through pines and yews to the tussocked heights of the knowes. Long walnut shelves that sagged under the weight of a thousand dusty tomes. Duncan was never seen in here so it was a sanctuary for me. My own personal *Three Mile Girth.* Duncan himself had never got his eyes beyond Baden-Powell and the Holy Book. The Book of Dib-dib-dib and the Holy Bib-bib-bib. The Bib-bib-bibbity-bibble. The Word.

It's hard to credit that a nae-user like Da and a sad tube like Uncle Duncan were well-connected in the ancestry department. Right back to the founders of the Balshannoch United Cotton and Dyeing Company. But true. Our MacNabs were remnants of the first owners who'd sold the old mills on to the Buchanans. This was Duncan's inheritance. A cold sandstone mansion in High Drums with its thousand mouldy books. Praise be to Jehovah MacTavish that I was spared the rigours of Uncy Duncy's out-of-school educational programme. There was no easel desk for me. Great times they were those winter nights or dour drizzling Saturdays spent in the quiet of the library. Creaking open covers of volumes that released a musty odour of ancient print. The smell of wisdom.

The old MacNab Manuscripts taught me the story of the Strath that reached back over six hundred million years. How the Caledonian Mountains rose up from a great fracture in the earth's crust to create a chain of peaks the size of the Himalayas all the way from Norway through Alba and westward into the ocean far beyond Ireland. How it all cracked and eroded to let in the sea and how Dunreoch's volcano spewed up in boiling magma then froze into a mountain of molten rock. How the glacier gripped the high plateau for a hundred thousand moons then released its icy fingers to leave the deep gouge of the Strath. Then how the hunters came to slay the bears and the deer until there came the farmers of all those moons ago who left behind their cairns and skeletons and hut-circles. And the tribe with the knowledge of thermo-dynamics beyond our wildest comprehension. They'd melted together the great stones of the vitrified ramparts on Meikle Carnock. And how St Ronan came and blessed the ancient yew tree and how for three miles around it sanctuary was declared by the King of Scotia himself so that no man could be arrested within the *Three Mile Girth* no matter what crime he'd committed. The passage of the

Highland drovers with their thousands of cattle who'd stop off the night at the old change house to sluice down their bannocks with a mouthful of the local *uisge beatha.* The greatest horse and cattle fair in all Scotland was on top of Meikle Carnock and they came from everywhere from the Highlands from England and Ireland. And there were all the wild tales too. How the clansmen's swords came to be found in the black swirling Caldon and how folk disappeared on moonless nights on the knowes. How the great fissure through the solid rock of Dunreoch was caused by a swish of the Devil's tail. The story of how the conquering Douglas-Gilquhans came with their claim of noble family descent all the way back through every ancient classical civilisation to Adam himself. It was the last days of the Three Mile Girth when the Duggie-Gilquhans arrived. Burning disfiguring and hanging. The Douglas-Gilquhans had ordered the dragoons into the Weavers Row with their muskets blazing. Looking out from the Tower they'd seen the gallows ablaze and felt the spectre of the Bastille breathing down their necks. And there was a place for the MacNabs in their own chronicles. Bringing the mills to Balshannoch and a new influx of Irish and Scots to work there. BeJaz. The changes. Even in my own short lifetime there was the pulse of the mills and the smell of the distillery chimney back there in The Strath. Changed days my friend. Changed days.

EARTH CALLING FACHIE! EARTH CALLING FACHIE! IS THERE ANYBODY THERE? OVER!

Maggie!

By God Fach. Ye're miles away so ye are. You're awful distant.

Of course I'm distant. I'm from Drums.

What?

High Drums. St Ronans. Strathfinglas. Baw-nee Scatch-land.

Again?

Distant Drums. Where I come from. Away up yonder in the big Teuchie wilderness. Otherwise known to you worldly Lowlanders as Sheepshaggerland.

I gawp at Maggie with my jaw hanging loose and put on my glaikitest west Lowland voice.

Hu hu hu. Sheepshaggurs. Hu hu hu.

Whit? You're no pished again are ye Fach?

Na Maggie I'm just gibberin. Listen there's somethin I was needing tae talk to you about. About last night.

What about it?

Well. I'm sorry.

You're what?

I'm sorry.

There's a bit of a grin coming over Maggie's face. She goes over to the till to check something out with Andy. I take a look around. The bar's slowly clearing. Outside a drunken voice is still singing I SAW THE LIGHT. It's one of these songs of the moment that'll probably become a kind of theme tune in the pub for a while. Songs linked to events they're always the ones that endure. This is the kind of night when folk are reluctant to go home. When they've had a really nice time. They'll hang around outside for a while and chat under a lamppost. Who'll believe them at work tomorrow morning when they tell the story of the Holy Siege at The Coffin? There's only a handful of stragglers now I'm still on the bar stool and Maggie returns.

Fachie about last night.

Yeah?

You should get a medal.

Aye. The Rip-Roaring Cunt Award. Listen Mags I cannae really remember.

She grabs a hold of each ear tightly and for a sec I think she's about to header me. The world-renowned Glasgow Kiss. My twice-broken neb cowers in anticipation. Then her big blackened Goth lips zoom in on me and plant a lovely big smacker right on the chops.

Ya big darlin! Ye saved ma life!

Eh?

She's still got a hold of my ears and pushes me out then draws me in again for another big kiss.

Ye must remember surely. The guy wi the knife. The psycho. Ye flattened him. The bastard was gonnae stab me.

Flashback. There's a sudden picture of a crowd swaying around the middle of the lounge. I'm seeing it from the stage. There's blows flying but they all seem to be missing and shouts and screams and chairs getting knocked over. The crowd parts then draws back together again there's fists sticking out on the ends of arms it's pure cartoon. From behind the bar runs a lady vampire with flowing cape wielding a whisky bottle. She tries to part the crowd holding up the bottle *BREAK IT UP YA BASTARDS! NOW! ENOUGH!* It all seems to have calmed down and the Neddy invaders are being persuaded to leave by the Bohemian majority. They're all just about out the door and on the stairs with Maggie supervising when some wraith in a yellow jersey charges back in with a blade. His mate grapples him back and he's struggling to get at Maggie with the knife twitching. Screams and shouts. Panic. The telecaster's still round my neck. I'm fumbling at the jackplug hand trembling trying to get it free. I've got the shoulder strap off and making my way with the guitar across the room. Shaking. The Ned's broke loose and his mates've stormed off to leave him to it. He's advancing in on the vampire with the blade so I come up behind and give a big lumberjack swing with the telecaster that lands on his shoulder. His left knee crumples so I get in front of him and take a sideways swing then Hendrix him in the face and he flies back over a table. We're in the back of a speedy black hack holding the concussed body between us with streetlights flashing past. The yellow jersey's covered in blood. We dump him on the pavement outside the hospital. We're in the taxi going back the way there's two of us in it. Me and a vampire. We go downstairs into Golgotha's it's after hours and there's a handful of bodies round a table drinking speaking in hushed tones. I start drinking again. Doubles and pints.

Jesus Maggie. I'm shaking like a leaf just remembering it. I hope I've no done any permanent damage.

At least she's let go of my ears now. She's got us a pint of Guinness each and we both take a good draught out of them leaving frothy cream moustaches on our top lips. Maggie's face goes serious as she sooks the cream down off her lip.

Listen Fach. Phwhp. Ye did what ye had tae do. That skinny wee bastard could've killed me. He deserved what was comin to him.

Eh? Fuck him. It's the Fender Telecaster I'm worried about.

Mags lets out one of her shrieks. Sound Andy and the rest of the staff have gone off to while away the rest of the night in a club leaving us to it. We have another jar then Maggie's quizzing me about how I ended up in the Holy Siege. So I begin. Telling her about how I was starving and went for a meal at the Gravy Star. About the Dragonchurch service with the Bontempi fart-organ and the Charge of the Light Brigade. She's having a good hoot but she's noticed my scabby hands and the general state of me. So I do something I've never done before. I let someone in on the Camp Secret. The station. How I live in a black airless hole with pigeons for neighbours and a park full of beauty on the roof of my world. She's staring in disbelief. Maggie wants to know more about me but lets me tell it in my own time. I can't tell her about all the other stuff. Why should she know about the past? The present state of things seems about as much as she can take in for the moment. We go through the back and into the house behind the pub then Mags fills up the bath for me. Yes sir. A big hot soaking steaming bath. Oracle juice and nectar mhm even better than last night's scrotum and boaby dunk back home in the hot frothy bucket. I've left the jersey and baggy breeks and suspect underpants at the bathroom door and hallelujah I can hear that glorious Hotpoint sound as the togs get sloshed around in the washing machine ben the kitchen kadoosh kadoosh kadoosh kadoosh.

* * * * * * * * * * * * * * *

I'm lying on my side on the settee ben the living-room. Clean boy. It's maybe 3 am and only the occasional diesel drone of a speedy black hack going past. I've cast the blanket aside to let my skin breathe. Orange streetlight filters through the venetian blinds to make a tiger pattern down my big naked torso. I'm enjoying the moment. Just enough drink in me to keep away the worst of the nightmares and on an even keel but I'll stay awake just for a wee bit yet. The thought of St Ronans is beginning to weigh heavily. Maybe I should just leave it. Clear out of the station and try down the city for a hoose. Jesus a scheme house it can't be that difficult can it? So say I get one. A scheme house and then what? Would I still be buried in the Haven ashes? Loathing the ugly insides of myself from dawn till dusk. Can't believe Maggie was so upset to find out about the station situation. Can't believe there was a tear in her eye she only knows me from the bar but she's always liked me. You just never know what's out there. You just never know. Close eyes now. Striped pattern from the blinds. Diesel drone.

* * * * * * * * * * * * * * *

Mammy.

Go tae sleep wee man.

Mammy Kath says Da's a sailor on the sea. Then Mairead O'Donnel says that Da got ate by a whale and he's no coming back.

Mairead's just daft. She should mind her own business.

Mairead's a pant-pisher isn't she Mam?

Aye. A wee pant-pisher. A right wee dandelion.

Is Daddy a captain Ma? Kathleen says.

A captain? Ho aye. In fact. He's a admiral. Of all the ships on the seas.

Does he fight wi the pirates Ma?

Aye. And smugglers and storms and sea-serpents.

And whales tae?

No Farchar. Never you mind about whales.

Sing me the boat song Ma.

I'm lying with the covers pulled up to my chin. She holds out the picture with the matchstick person floating away to a strange horizon then sings.

Heel ya ho boys
Let her go boys
Swing her head round and altogether
In the windows
Where candles glow boys
We're sailing homeward to Mingulay

Wherever Ma was sailing to it wasn't Mingulay. Something had changed in her voice. She was sitting on the edge of the bed framed against the streetlit window of Glasgow Road. Somehow I remember lightning in the sky but I've maybe got it all mixed up. It could've been the flash of the welders' torches on the rising hull of the QE2 in John Brown's shipyard. Ma had stopped eating and was turning into the matchstick person. Her hair and nails were beginning to grow by then. I wasn't sure what it was about. The strange light had come into her eyes.

A bellyful of breakfast and fresh togs on my back yes mister this feels good. Not only that but the suspect underpants have withstood the trial of the washing machine and've been cleared by the jury. I'll maybe put them on probation to make sure they stay squeaky clean. Hech! Report in weekly before a bucket of Persil. She's a good sowel that Maggie the vampire wummin. That wasn't charity it was an act of friendship.

For all the rain that falls here on Atlantis there's sometimes a kind wind that blows in from the south-west. I'm breathing it in now. A braw zephyr coming over from the distant firth. White bundles of cloud drifting across bright blue. Oh Yooba Dooba I'm a Gulf Stream baby.

A moving sky frames the squat steeple of the Dragonchurch as I walk towards the five ways. You can smell the ocean on that wind. Just a hint but it's there with memories on it sea winds blowing in to stir awake an old city dream. Dreams of rigged ships returning with sugar and rum and African slaves for wealthy town merchants or gentry like the distant Douglas-Gilquhans. Or the old herring fleet. Packed to the gunnels with the silver darlings. Choking up the river from the Broomielaw to Bowling. Para Handy puffers with funnels spewing black smoke and men barking in Gaelic up at a riverside wharf. Giant liners. Sailing all the way from the quay of Yorkhill to quay of New York. It's hard to relate it all to this jungle of sprawling schemes and skyscrapers that spreads out across the hills from the ancient heart of the place. But this isn't Bergen or Antwerp. This is dark Atlantis. Where stone dragons snarl out from soot-eaten steeples and starlings scream the gospel from a shit-encrusted pulpit.

So this is morning eh? I'd forgotten what it's like. Traffic bustle and noise. Van deliveries and the exchange of pleasantries on shop doorways. Fur-boot wifies with tartan wheelie-bags meet on blowy corners. *Oh is that a fact Mrs McPhee?* Put the Shanks's on steady steam and stride on.

Time for a raid on the big Safeways at the top of Byres Road filling a trolley with the necessaries for the trip then wheel in towards the checkout lassie with a thrust of the legs and lying across the trolley with my feet up in the air behind me NYEEHOO! Loading the goods onto the conveyor. *Have ye got an ABC Card? Bleep peep bleep peep. That's one pound twenty-five the bananas. Bleep peep bleep peep. There's two twenty-two in yer oranges. Bleep peep bleep peep.* I fill up the plazzy bags then head down the park for the north mouth with the handles cutting into my fingers lifting the bags high above the bramble thorns in the gully as I carefully step down towards the portcullis.

No problems with the tunnel or the old Simpson Gemmel MacCreadie's now there's a fair flickering light glowing in the tilly ben the Waiting Room. Still that charred *Herald* lying around scary.

What to take with me and what to leave.

THINGS TO TAKE	THINGS TO LEAVE
Small kettle	Tilly lamp
Primus stove	Old blankets
Bottle of paraffin	Galvie buckets
Bivvy Bag	Guitar
Tea/sugar/dried milk	Books
All the food (checked)	Bedroll
Cutlery/pan	John Wayne poster
Torch/candles	Tacky ceramic leopard ornament
Handlines/hooks/weights	Brush
Farchar's Chap-Book & pens	Uncle Malky

Jesus how long have I been here? How many moons've passed over the splintered crag of Dunreoch since the day I jemmied the shackles? Can't honestly say. Start loading the big rucky with all the gear then swing it on to the shoulder. It weighs a ton so keep the torch in hand for the descent of the Wembley Eleven in case I end up arse over tits. Turn down the wick to let the tilly die then have a last look around the womb with the torch. The grate with its dusty grey ash. The twisted bedroll probably still damp from the sweats. The sweat'll dry in with all the ugly pictures from my dreams preserved in the blanket. A demonic version of the Turin Shroud. Hey! John Wayne! What you lookin at big man? Yeah. True grit. There's always a sad moment leaving a gaff no matter whether it's been the best or worst time of your life. Fuck it let's go. Just be thankful I didn't die in this fuckin place. Hell Hotel. Down the eleven steps with the big pack on the back. One hand on the rail and one holding the torch a white beam of light stabbing down through the dark. I'll leave the creaky unshackled in case anybody ever finds their way in here. A nice wee gaff if you don't mind the dark. But I'll be locking the portcullis to leave a wee challenge. And in case of nuclear attack of course.

Past the signal pylon then down the ramp off the platform and into the tunnel with me.

Out of the gully. The old railtrack here is a high ledge above the rippling Kelvin. Drop the load. Take out the jangle of keys from the langcoat then take a runny and a throw. My arm shoots out and lets go of the keys so they fly up into the air through the thin branches of the trees. They rise up glinting in the sunlight then drop towards the pool and spladoosh into the water. Yawoo! I've done it! Left the station at last. I run the image of the key-throwing moment over in my head a few times to savour it. Seeing my arm flick upwards the keys rising up and glint then dropping down into the pool. I run back an action replay in slow motion. The keys rise slowly up towards the sky. Slowly up towards the sky. Sunlight glint and dwell. Drop slowly down slowly down towards the pool. Landing with a splash and droplets of water sparkling in the light. Then replay it speeding it up this time so that the image of the keys splashing down recurs over and over like the tele-montage of a great goal at the World Cup GOAL GOAL GOAL YA FUCKIN DANCER GOAL!

Over the polished granite arch of Kirklee then along Garrioch Gate through the hole in the chainlink fence to cut past the Wyndford. Along the mud path towards a vision of failed post-war Scotland. Maisonettes and dull brown tenements absorbing the drabness of grey northern skies all the way from Dreghorn to Pittendreich. Calvin Homes. Winner of the Knox's Beard Design Award circa 1955. It's no more than we deserve. A predestined existence of daily toil with the hope of a few hours' overtime to shout in some extra Friday drinks in the Ram's Heid. Only now nobody's working. The floo'ers o the forest are discarded Superlager cans and crisp pokes and plazzy bags and the half-sunken carcass of a shopping trolley that litter an overgrown football field.

* * * * * * * * * * * * * * *

Hike up the brae towards Maryhill Road with its shiny new bingo hall and drive-through burger joint. Where is the match factory? The paint factory? The inland shipyard that launched its creations down the slip into a dock in the canal? The life and times of a local economy on Maryhill Cross exist only in the claik of reminiscing pensioners as they chat over the tops of their drams from within a haar of tobacco smoke. Or in the mouldy pages of the MacNab Manuscripts and mouldy memory cells of lay historians like the Fach. On the way past the Social there's a guy with a pram standing at the doorway with ink-marker graffiti on the wall behind him. The writing with the arrowheads on the stems of letters. Purple glint of a Superlager tin being tilted there's a carry-out at his feet next to the buggy.

FARKIE! HEY! BIG MAN!

Swivel round with the weight of the rucksack giving me a bit of extra spin. I'm a wee bit past the Social looking back and the boy's leaning out from the doorway with the can held behind him. There's no bells ringing but I better check it out. Blonde dyed straggly hair and a couple of jaggy broken teeth. Home-made Indian ink tattoos on the back of his hand. Eye glint. I've got him. Approaching Bernie Broon.

Farker ma man. How ye doin big chap?

Bernie eh? Bernie Broon?

I drop the rucky next to the wall of the Social. Take off the langcoat and lay it across to sit on top then start rolling a smoke. A thick-ee. Surprise surprise wee Bernie. Ex-neighbour from the days in the crazy flat at 7 Blane Gardens a rip-roaring time. There's a set of twins in the buggy.

I put a flame to the rollie fag to catch the crack with Bernie for a while. A reminisce about life and times in Mrs Cowan's B&B bedsits. Bern drains off his can then opens a fresh one for the both of us. Personally I'm not too keen on the Supers. Moon-juice if you ask me but I'm not wanting to be anti-social it's been a few years since I last saw the boy. There's a silence as we take a couple of pulls from the cans. Jee-zoss. Even after a couple of swigs there's a wee bit of disorientation. The people that brew this gear know the score all right. Know how to give a man a kick. Alcoholic heroin this.

Aye the Blane Gardens. Now there was a gaff. All kinds passed through that place. Made guys like Bernie seem normal. He was right enough though we'd some real good times down there. We used to jam with the guitars and have a few beers and a spliff. Bernie was no mean bass player either. We'd a whole band at one stage. As life and times go it was all pretty hunky-dee but the good times don't last forever as the man once said. Old Cowan put the eviction order on us and we occupied. Even managed to beat back the Security she sent in on us with their dogs. Maybe something to do with Bernie having a couple of Rottweilers to even up the score Hech! Sent the Security flying out the street with missiles pounding off their van what a hoot. Have to say I got a bit carried away in the excitement that time. Chasing the van clinging on to the back roaring like an eejit as it sped down Belmont Street. Met the polis wagon halfway up. MacNabbed. Cost me an appearance up in front of the Procurator Beako that one but we did a benefit gig to pay the fine.

So how the hell are ye Bernie? This must be The Broons is it?

Aye. Fuckin Hen an Joe. Whit aboot yersel? Ah see yer on the travels big man.

On the road mate. Is Colette the maw then?

Aw fuck aye. Me n' her've got four weans noo and a cooncil hoose doon the Valley. It's a wee bit mad but it's awright. They offered us wan away in Drumchapel but we held oot for the Valley.

Ye still bashin the auld bass?

Na. Mind you ah sometimes play a wee bit when ah've got the hoose tae maself but no very often.

Ye no workin then?

No any mair mate. Ah had a job for a year in a foondry away doon in Glengarnock. It was fuckin hard graft man. Thirteen oor shifts an two oors travellin.

Sounds a bit rough. Ye'd be coinin the overtime though eh?

Aye fuck aye the money wis good and I wis too tired tae spend it. Colette wis happy right enough.

D'ye get paid aff then?

Na. Jacked it.

Ye jacked it?

Aye. Lost ma temper mate. The guy that owned the firm tellt us we'd have tae work unpaid overtime tae clear the company debts and keep wirselves in a job. Fuckin hell man. Ah wis workin sixty-five oors a week and only getting paid for forty. We kept it goin for a couple a months knockin wur pans in tae try and save the place then big boss man fucks off tae the Seychelles on his honeymoon and swans intae work wan mornin in a sports car.

Dirty bastard. Whit happened? Did ye lose the rag and nut the cunt?

Na did I fuck. Ah walked intae his office and politely asked if he would pay me aff cause I couldnae stand it any longer. Travellin frae Maryhill tae Ayrshire. I wis fucked and skint. But the bastard jist stood there wi a big smirk on his coupon and told me I had nae choice. Laughed because I would get sin-dyed aff the dole if I chucked it. So I just walked oot man I couldnae stand the humiliation any longer. A few guys wanted tae back me up but maist o them were too scared for their joabs. Whit can ye dae aboot it? I got cut aff for three months. But whit can ye dae?

Bad crack Berno. I hope it all works out for ye anyway man.

Ach I'm minted Farkie man. Four weans and the hoose and that. Ah'll tell ye whit though. Ah sometimes still think aboot the old days doon at Blane Gerdens. Good times man. Whit about Cammy and Sharleen? Ye see much a them? Hey how's Ola?

I've no seen them for a while. Listen Bernie I've got tae go and catch a bus. Thanks a lot for the can I enjoyed that. All the best mate.

Ye look a bit doon on yer luck big man. You take care. Ach ye never know. We'll maybe win the Lottery on Saturday eh? Or if no maybe even next week eh? See ye later man.

Bern folds his empty can and throws it onto a muddy square in front of the Social. He takes the remaining Supers out the plazzy and puts them down the inside of the bairns' buggy then wheels off. I drain off the last few spits of mine then head towards the bus stop to drop the empty can in the basket. I'm needing to check the Swiftbus timetable anyway to see when the next bus is up north to the Strath. Bastardo! According to the notice on the pole the last one's away an hour ago which leaves me marooned in Maryhill with a large rucksack. Pish. I'd need some snips and a bar to get myself back into the station ballocks tae that. No way I'm bivvying down at the Nollie bank either so open up steam on Shanks's Loco and head northward towards the country.

The north. When you throw on a pack and start walking towards it there's a kind of magnet that pulls you towards the hills in the distance. The Wanderlust they used to sing about in the old music hall days. Hee-yooch. Sir Harry o' the Glens. Marching through the heather wi braggart in yer step. Kilt swirlin roon yer bare erse an sheep-ticks chomfin oan yer helmet.

Traffic on Maryhill Road grinds north and south. What's the hurry anyway? Where are we all going in such a rush? Drivers zig-zagging through traffic and farting on their horns at the first opportunity. Folk striding along the pavement with a determined set to their jaws then running to catch the wee green man *beep beep beep* like their fuckin life depended on it *beep beep beep*. High high above through a gap in tumbling clouds the tiny silver glint of a jet makes a thin white trail across blue space. The Shooman Race. Why this irresistible urge always to be running somewhere else? Chasing reaching catching chasing. Striving to reach the other side where the grass is always greener. In my own case my big legs striding northward. Heading for the Strath and the distant Haven. Stride on. Bad memories and the urge to purge.

From the canal locks and the site of the long-gone inland shipyard the lower expanse of the Clyde basin stretches away south-west to the low rolling volcanic heights of the Gleniffer Braes. In between's the Dawsholm incinerator and distant roofs and steeples and high-rise multi's. The broad view south-west from the canal lets in a big sky and makes a good weather window. There's still a gentle wind drifting in so I'll walk out of the town as far as I can before camping down for the night.

Along the old towpath towards the aqueduct. The Nollie drops foaming over lock gates into a long algae-filled channel where moorhens jerk across bright green scum. The aqueduct carries

Nollie waters high over the Kelvin on slender arches. Jouk off the bank and down steps to the walkway where the river churns into a powerful V-shaped weir. There's a couple of blokes out with the rods fishing in the pool under the weir hoping yesterday's storm's been enough to lift the river to let in a run of salmon. Hard to believe that only a few years ago the Kelvin was a stinking cess of sewage and dyes and oxides from outflows and factories and distant mines. Gone is the paint factory. But home is the *Salar* home from the sea. The impulses of some primeval programmed code sending it back to the river after a hundred year exile. All over Scotland and Ireland and Norway the salmon are disappearing into oblivion. Coming back in fewer numbers every year yet here it is in the Kelvin. Returning to fit together some long-lost piece of a genetic jigsaw. Yes. The salmon has returned. Navigating the murky current and submerged shopping trolleys and the occasional jettisoned settee from the Valley scheme. There can't be many rivers with a mystique like the Kelvin. Rising out of the Kilpatricks and the Campsies. Burns with names like Finglen and Luggie. Auldmurroch Allander and Auchnagree. Carrying their rippling moorland song to converge into the Kelvin and flow through wooded drumlins below high tenements and terraces right into the heart of dark Atlantis. The blue spark of a kingfisher and the odd black cormorant skulking on a branch. That's the Kelvin for you.

Upriver then across the old cart bridge to pick up the riverside path through the Garscube Policies. To the granite road bridge of Kilmardinny and into Suburbiana.

Soon I'll be over the Antonine line and into true Caledonia Land of the Picts. Just beyond the garden centre and the sports complex. I stop for a rollie smoke at a row of shops dropping the pack and laying over the langcoat for a bench. There's a postbox here so a few folk stop in their BMWs and Mercs to drop off mail and look down their big sniffy nebs at me against the wall. I hold out the cigarette in their direction with my fingers vee'd in an obvious salute while blowing out a big plume of smoke. Fuckin jube-jubes. Poash bastarts. *Oooh pess the meringues Missus MucWhirter I'm feeling oafy peckish the day. Oh thenk yoo very mich. And how's your boay Jason doing? I've heard he's doing well driving a fancy big motor these days. Got himself a nice wee joab in the film industry. Mind you fae whit I've heard his movies are aw cream eclairs and nuns fennies. But still. He's got a mervelous talent.* Nae joke. There was some eejit from this neck of the woods down in Blane Gardens did that. Filmed it in his room. The Cream Cake and The Carmelite Nun. Hey! Whit you lookin at mister? Bog-faced bastard. I am the Fach. I half-heartedly flick the burning stub of the rollie towards the red postbox and to my surprise it flies through the slot and inside. Time for a sharp exit.

There's a cross with a war monument. Bronze angel of mercy with outstretched wings twenty feet high she stands looking down over traffic queueing at the lights. Just beyond is the Antonius Bistro. From what I can gather it's a restaurant with a kind of period Roman theme to celebrate its position on the Antonine line. When the Romans ruled here eighteen hundred odd years ago. Wonder if they operate a menu to suit the size of your wallet in there. Maybe a Roman governor's menu which allows you to dine on fine foods and wines and spices from the distant corners of the empire. Then for the less well-off there's a Roman sentry's menu supposed to be typical of the scran that the guys ate while freezing their bollocks off up on the ramparts. Maybe lice and boiled shrew or something like that. Hech! And I suppose they've got some half nae-kit Pictish slaves on hands and knees bringing in the food on their backs to serve them.

On up the lang brae with its granite villas to the junction by the artificial ski slope then swing onto the Stockiemuir Road. What is it about skiing and golf that the nobs so wanted to institutionalise and claim as their own? I suppose that's one positive thing that you could say about the rancid fart that seeped out of Demoness Thatcher's crinkled auld anus. The stench of it was so overpowering that for a while it disorientated a lot of the institutionalised nobs. They got knocked out by it then regained consciousness to find themselves sharing an overcrowded golf course or ski slope with the aspiring hoi-polloi. The road heads north at Baljaffray under a canopy of tall oaks. This used to be the edge of the hinterland. Where you would consider yourself beyond city limits and into the country. But behold! The overpowering effects of that woman's howling fart were strong enough to fell mature woodlands and raze hedgerows and meadows to a bare muddy plain to make way for quality housing. A brickwork complex has risen up from the glaur. Signalling victory by raising the flapping standards of development companies on tall flagstaffs. Giving the streets an air of rustic charm with romantic pastoral handles like Poacher's Lair. What do they poach? Quails eggs in Chablis? Wouldn't fancy a poacher's chances trying to hide out in there. Duckin down frae the gamie behind a silver Merc or a conifer hedge. And especially not with the prying militia nebs of the Neighbourhood Watch poking through the blinds. Or maybe even the occasional Orwellian CCTV camera up on a lamppost there to guard over the gee-gaw baubles and nick-nacks of the nouveau nobs of Yah-Yah Land.

I'm into a rhythm now with Tweeville behind me and the open road beyond that heads out through fields and moorland. A good pace. The rucksack sitting square and comfy on the shoulders giving momentum. This puts me in mind of the old man I saw one time in the Strath walking out to the hills on his own. A winter's Sunday and Uncle Duncan marching us along the road to church in single file. Then a blue Swiftbus from the city pulled in at the stop beside the distillery and off steps the old lad in his woollen jersey and a canvas Bergen on his shoulders. A coiled blue rope on the back of it. He jouked the fence into a rime-frosted park then went striding out with a purposeful gait towards the crags of Dunreoch. Some old bod from the Smokestack. Great clouds of steam pumping from his mouth and nostrils expelling the fumes of industry out of his being. I remember thinking Duncan's Baden-Powellism would have had him praising the old bod's spirit but na.

Instead he starts fuming.

> *Damned fool. This is the Lord's day. God will punish men like him going where he shouldn't go. He will place a piece of ice under a rock. Then when the imbecile steps on it God will suddenly thaw the ice with the sun. The rock will collapse and send the fool crashing down on the Ugly Stones to his doom.*

> *Have you never climbed a mountain yourself Uncle Duncan?*

> *Of course I have! But never on a Sunday. I was among the first men to reach the summit of Ben Nevis.*

So I'm explaining how I'd read about the Victorian expeditions to the summit of the Ben which would only have made Duncan about a hundred flippin years old.

> *Silence boy! This is the Lord's day. Now hold your wheesht and march to church!*

HECH! The thought of the afternoon hymn session in the house standing around Aunt Mary's Hammond organ was enough incentive for escape. Coming back from the kirk I slipped out from the end of the marching ranks of the Junior Christian Soldiers and breenged into the woods. Fleeing down the path to St Ronans. Found Turk and Deke and told them about the old bod with the rucksack and the rope. We got together a rucksack of our own and filled it with cheese pieces and a flask of tea then whipped Mrs MacGruer's washing line off the poles and set out for the crags of Dunreoch. Man. That everyday object of a hill down the Strath. It took on the proportions of Everest as we walked in towards it. The winter sun. An amber orb hanging low in the sky. Making a dull red glow on the heather.

A great leaning crag angled high into the hillside. The beginning of the climb was straightforward with cracks and hollows in the rock face that somehow seemed to pull you upwards. Upwards and up. Cockin wur snooks at Newton. Upwards till we reached a narrow grassy shelf then sat down for a breather to scoff the pieces and the tea. It was surprising how breathless and shaky we were it had seemed easy until we'd stopped. Then we looked down. The moor spread below in miniature as a kestrel soared underneath. Loch Mhor with its wooded islets through a gap in the hills like a distant mirage. We'd gained hundreds of feet. Above the rock became sheer but a funnel rose inside it with some promising looking handholds. We clambered inside nearly to the top then hit an overhang a great vee of rock slipping out precariously from the crag. Turk got the rope out and put it round his shoulder then shimmied up clinging to the sides with his arms and knees then swung up at a heel of rock. He grabbed hold and pulled himself out of sight.

The clothes rope dropped dangling in front of us. Deke went first fastening it around his waist clambering to the heel before being hauled in by Turk. It dropped again and I shimmied up then got pulled up and over on to a flat bed of stone.

Looking down. Into a dark fissure dropping away to the Ugly Stanes. Standing silent. Shaking and exhilarated and feeling a bit invincible. The silence only lasted a minute or two until Turk filled his lungs and let go a blast.

> ***YAWOO! SHANNY YA BASS!***

The mountain echoing back.

> ***YAWOO SHANNY YA BASS!*** *YAWOO SHANNY YA BASS! SHANNY YAWOO YA BASS! YAWOO BASS YAWOO shanny ya woo bass shanny ya bass wooah wooah woo*

We were having a hoot shouting some filth into the echo then a different voice cried out from the bowels of the crag a big long *Hallooo.* We clambered along the spine of the rock slowly descending towards the hillside. It was an easier route down than the climb had been. Unseen voices rising and fading. We reached a path at the foot of the crag then followed it round inside the fissure as the voices became louder.

Giant glacier-rent slabs slanted out from the crag to let sunlight into a wide chamber. A crowd of people were sitting around a fire in the middle of it. A bright-coloured assortment of baggy jerseys and tartan shirts and woollen jackets and bonnets. They all seemed to be old folk maybe in their sixties or seventies then I spotted the old lad I'd seen getting off the Swiftbus at the distillery. They welcomed us into the throng and handed us cans of strong sweet scalding tea from the fire and corners of pies and pieces to munch on. We explained our climb up the big crag and the company were mightily impressed. We'd climbed a route called The Anvil which was only tackled by the most experienced climbers. As we dropped off the lower heather slopes of Dunreoch we looked back. A spiral of smoke was twisting out of the fissure and up into a dimming sky. A great rousing song echoing inside the mountain.

Years later when I was old enough to quaff Guinness I'd get on talking terms with the last remnants of the crew we met around the fire at Dunreoch. The River Finglas Bathing Club they called themselves from their annual custom of travelling out from the city to take a dip in the river on New Year's Day. I'd once witnessed this spectacle. At the Smiddy Pool a crowd of them in their great baggy trunks and period swimsuits and bathing-caps walked into the stream to hip height then plunged gamely into the Finny chill to swim to the far bank and back again. Upstream the Witches' Pool was reserved for folk who swam naked. An auld man and woman would walk scudders hand in hand to the water's edge reliving some romantic bygone memory. Folds of skin on the auldwife's body. The old man. His ancient whanger dangling from him like a dead branch from a withered stump. They'd walk in ankle-deep to the rim of the ledge halfway across the pool then dive. Dooking into the dark depths disappearing for a brief moment to surface with loud blowing breaths like whales and swim to the other side.

On Sunday nights the outdoor crowd were always in the Bull to catch a drink and exchange weekend stories before the last townward Swiftbus. Most of them were from the city and Saints was a kind of centre for them just far enough away and not too far that it couldn't be reached by bus in a day. They walked the high hills and backroads of their country. There was the old lad who used to row out to an island on Loch Mhor every Saturday to sleep out. It was all for a moment. Away from the workshop grind. To wake in the night and hear waves lapping on the shore. To open his eyes and look up at a shimmering canopy of cold northern stars.

* * * * * * * * * * * * * * * *

On the Stockie road cars flash north and south as the Shooman Race pursues its great ruinous agenda. Are these days lost to us forever? Stopping for moorland brews and exchanging the crack with fellow wanderers? But what happens when the Hydrocarbon Age comes to a close and coughs its last lead-fumed gasp into a poisoned twilight? The only travellers will be the Business Classes coming in from the Executive Sector to transact their global affairs. Suspended high above the wetlands whirring towards the city on George Bennie type railplanes. Shanks's locomotion for the rest of us. But we'll break free of the Schemeland Drone Sector perimeters and take to the high grounds we heard about in the old tales and songs and become the wandering clans once again. Sheltering in the remnants of the ancient conifer plantations. Stopping for a fire and sharing a moorland brew.

I let the Hilton Brae carry me down the long sloping road to the Allander brig with the wind among the langcoat and the pack bouncing on my shoulders. The wooden huts of Carbeth high on the shoulder of Craigallian Hill above the old coachmen's haunt of The Halfway Inn. The Allander gargles under the brig flowing away down towards Mugdock to meet the Kelvin. Upstream it winds high into the Kilpatrick Braes towards Duncolm and into the heart of the Saughen. Yes. The Kilpatricks. Saughen Brae and Loch Humphrey. Burns with names like Spardie Linn and Dirty Leven. Clydebank on the far side of the hills with its memories. We were out of the place years ago but there was still the Auntie Margaret and mad Aldo connection and the occasional weekends. I usually arrived early Friday evening and Uncle Conrad would take me and Aldo for a pre-supper pint. Wandering round old tenement bars with names like the Seven Seas and the Admiralty and the Cunard. Uncle Con'd say to us in his East European Scots. *C'moan in here boays and I'll buy yiz a nice pint.* Con was a gentle big lad and it was hard to believe in his young days he'd manned the barricades in the Budapest rising of 1956. We'd have a pint here and a pint there and usually end up in a corniced beer palace called Connelly's where men talked football and horse-racing and Irish politics. There was a raincoated midget of a man who seemed to follow you around every bar hawking discounted packs of razor blades. Out through Connelly's window was a crumbling black tenement where saplings sprouted from window ledges. The occasional glow of a 60-watt bulb in a window up there. Folk holding out till the end. The last days of Tamson Toon. Before the demolishers moved in to take away the town centre and the Singer's factory in one fell swoop. What's there now? They ripped out the ancient railway sidings and built this Finger-chicken Burger-lickin Big MacBeefy Dunkin-pizza French-fried donut bowling alley/multiplex cinema/shopping mall doodah Doodle Dandy kind of thing. Nae wonder old Walt requested to get his head severed from his corpse and stuck away in the freezer. He'll be brought back to life as this mad ice-box mutation thing with packets of frozen peas and oven chips sewn into his body. Lighting a big cigar and travelling the world to gloat over his cultural conquest.

Crumbling tenements and decrepit workshops. Smithereened by

the inevitable hammer of progress. Yet for all the improvements there's folk in Clydebank would tell you that a single blast of a fart from the Baroness's crinkled anus was more devastating than all the bombs dropped in the Luftwaffe's two night blitzkrieg of March 1941.

We'd sometimes walk along Glasgow Road past the gap-site where I'd lived until the night of the lightning storm. Going for our last pint of the evening in The Bisley Bar before heading back under the shadow of the giant United City Bakery to Auntie Margaret's. Conrad would always step into a wee shop called MacLelland's for his tobacco. A dark interior where a wall of dookets on one side held shiny tea-cans and mop-heads and firelighters and bunches of kindling. Behind the counter opposite were shelves of tobaccos and cigarettes. Senior Service. San-Toy Cheroots. Sweetie hatch at the far end with the Penny Tray. Mo-jos. Sour Cherries and Flying Saucers.

The Bisley Bar was on the corner of the Bisley Buildings. Multiple moons ago they used to have a shooting gallery in the basement there. And so called the Bisley. They sold a sour pish of a beer called Usher's and the gantry openly displayed the salubrious vintages of Lanliq and Eldorado. It was frequented by a table-load of card-playing flymen who called themselves the Bisley Boys and a Morning Star-touting communist called Bill. I once bought a *Soviet Weekly* from him that had a little colour supplement called the *Sputnik*. Man this communist Russia was some place. Full of cosmonauts and ballerinas. Bill must've developed a taste for yon Usher's pish because The Bisley was a lean market for him and his Kremlin journals. The pub convention was Glasgow Celtic and Irish Republicanism. It used to amuse me that a number of the Bisley Boys hailed from a nearby Catholic ghetto by the name of John Knox Street. I once mentioned this to one of them but the irony seemed to be lost on him. Ever mystified have I been by the history and religion thing. It seemed like you had to live a drinker's secular existence and not give a fuck about history or religion to be passionate about it. But then again. Maybe that's just it viewed through the eyes of a stranger. Article Number Five Hundred and Fifty-Three from the Fachie Book of Bollocks. Yes. The musings of a book-learned loner from the farthest neuks of Sheepshaggerland. Judge not lest ye be judged.

I always loved waking up in Auntie Margaret's on a Saturday morning and realising where I was. She'd come in with plates of toast and sausage and mugs of steaming tea. Aldo would put on *The Faithhealer*. He'd mixed a special version of it looping the synthesizer heartbeat at the start of the song so that it lasted ages. Uncle Conrad was a real fidget. He couldn't sit on his arse for five minutes except when he was in the pub relaxing. The small square of a garden in front of the house had a rockery and slabbed paving and a mock wishing-well painted bright green and yellow. The Anderson shelter in the back garden had a mini-lathe built from parts borrowed from the Singer's factory. Con would do any kind of job. He'd overheard *The Faithhealer* playing so for Aldo's birthday he knocked together a circuit of coloured lights in his room that pulsed with the synthesised heartbeat. On Saturday mornings me and Aldo'd sit under the flashing lights and plan out the day. Knocking the kit together the scran and the fishing tackle then head for the lochs and dams up in the Kilpatricks.

In slow fading light I'm walking a lonely stretch of the Stockiemuir Road. A few miles further and I'll find a spot to camp down. The wind gives out a gasp that sends a tussock tremor across the braes towards Clydebank ten moorland miles away. Whispering into the deepest folds of the hills to waken old memories. Memories of Aldo. Memories of Joe. Another Skeleton in my cupboard.

* * * * * * * * * * * * * * * *

Through that gap between the knolls. Up the hill beyond the roof of the filtering station. An October Saturday. We were working our shovels into the turf on the shores of a half-drained reservoir. I remember the logic. We reckoned if we stacked the peats on the scree of a windswept hill they'd dry into combustible fuel in time for the fishing season the next March. The Nissen bothy on the north shore was a remnant of the war years. It had an old iron stove in it that would consume anything once you'd put a hearty feed of embers into it.

It always surprised me that the Clydebank hinterland was only an hour's walk from schemeland. Beyond the Fyn Loch the hills opened out and rolled away towards the Highland faultline rising out of a low plain and reaching into the clouds. As we crossed Fynloch Hill with the wind in our faces I'd looked out to the furthest peaks to try and figure out where the Strath was. Away out there somewhere beyond Beinn Dearg. With the mind-eye I could see St Ronans in behind the mountains. The slate roofs and the narrow streets. The ruin of Gilquhan Tower and the mill and the obelisk. But all you could really see was the mountains. It was only because I knew it was there.

Along the shore from me Aldo was slicing his shovel down into the black peats.

Something was about to happen. Some momentous event. It was in the atmosphere. The gale had fallen and a pale yellow glow was on the loch. Red strands of cloud lay across the southern edges of the sky.

Ben Lomond rose beyond the stonework of the dam. The dimming sun had put a flame to the underside of a slow-drifting cloud as it passed across the Ben to make a smouldering volcano of it. Blue smoke was spiralling out from the fire we'd built on the shore for the brew-up. From the glen behind the dam a buzzard released a long lonely whistle then the wind gave out a gasp that sent a brief ripple across the loch and a burst of orange flame from the fire. I was raising my shovel to take the next down-swing then stopped to look at the sky. Columns of cloud standing like giant totems. Wind-sculpted into a thousand weird figures and faces. The shovel blade stabbed into the turf. I took a further three cuts to make a square then leaned back to prise the sod from the ground. The fibrous turf eased back. As I lifted it clear of the hole there was a face. Bone. Skull.

ALDO ALDO ALDO! FUCKSAKE ALDO LOOK! A SKULL!

We marked out an area around the body. Digging carefully in under ribcage spine pelvis arms legs then lifting it gingerly over to the grassy bank. On its arms were the black rotted remains of jacket sleeves. I stood on a rock and screamed.

THE NAVVY SKELETON! BEHOLD THE NAVVY SKELETON!

Aldo jumped onto the bank.

BEHOLD THE NAVVY SKELETON! THE GHOST OF MOLESKIN JOE!

All day we'd been finding artefacts from the navvy era. Clay pipes. Jeelie jars. Fragmented china plates. Printed pots from the Galloway Creamery. Whisky bottles and half whisky bottles. Bullet-shaped lemonade bottles with a trapped marble for the control of aeration. The wafer-thin sole of a tacketty boot.

Aldo was claiming we'd found the remains of Patrick MacGill's hero navvy. We sat on either side of him to have a think about it. We really didn't know what to do about bone-man. We couldn't just leave him there and we didn't want to put him back in the hole. Come December and all the rain he'd be back under the loch. Then Aldo had the big idea.

Hey Fach. Were we no considering headin over the hills for a bevvy in the Ettrick?

Aye.

So how about we take bone-man wae us? The poor fucker's been in the ground for years. HE MUST BE CHOKIN FOR A PINT!

Who can say why? It just seemed the right thing to do. And anyway. It was during a time when there was a bit of competition around to see who could pull off the daftest stunt. I was a man of sartorial adventure in those days. Splendidly attired in the top hat with the guinea fowl feather. Industrial safety spectacles and a pair of German stormtrooper's army surplus jackboots on me. The songs of the Sensational Alex Harvey Band were ever with us as I stood out on the shore and roared out Midnight Moses.

HEY!
HEY! HEY! HEY!
I SAID HEY!
HEY! HEY! HEY!
THEY CALL ME THE MIDNIGHT MOSES
EV'RYTHING I TOUCH IS COMING UP
RRRRRROSES…

Aldo was in a green tracksuit and a set of Conrad's outsize work-boots. He held his shovel into him like it was a Gibson SG wailing to accompany the Harvey lyric and pulling Maori warrior faces in an impersonation of guitar hero Cleminson.

We took turns carrying bone-man across the hills. Over the boglands. In fading glow past the Lily Loch under the whaleback mass of Duncolm. The acid stench of damp earth and rotting lilies was the perfect essence for the Procession of the Dead. Setting course for a few jars on the far side of the hills. Or towards the *sin gutter* as Uncle Duncan would say. Tramping the hills was ideal preparation for a night in the Ettrick. The floor had been worn into its own topography of bumps and hollows by generations of drinkers' boots. The Ettrick Bar. A half-circle of whisky-breathed old men sang around a coal fire. You pished into a dank crumbling urinal with a skootering flush-rail. No Shanks of Barrhead here. Voiding the bowels was beyond contemplation. Had you pointed your arsehole into the blackness of that shitpan your insides would have been sooked into a wormhole in a dark and distant galaxy. But the crack was good and Inverness Donald pulled a pint of heavy that would have brought a smack of the lips and a nod from Zeus himself.

The hill route consisted of a few loosely strewn grazing paths. Past a stone called Gilbert Scott until you reached Loch Humphrey and a farmtrack down to Old Kilpatrick. There was a cow's horn of a moon climbing into the sky. When we reached the top of the Haw Crag we looked down. For some reason town streetlights had failed to come on. The Ettrick under its derelict tenement was casting a hazy glow through stained glass windows into Dumbarton Road. Thanks to the darkness we reached the side of the pub unseen then dressed the bones in the top hat and a knee-length oilskin coat. We swung open the double doors and swayed in with Moleskin between us like three drunken buddies.

BEHOLD! BEHOLD THE NAVVY SKELETON!

Amid smoke and half-light dozens of faces peered round from pint glasses. Barmen craned to see over the heads of the crowd and faces swivelled round from seats. A shush fell over the whole room. Somewhere a glass fell to the floor and smashed. Then the place erupted. Cheers wheezes cackles.

It's the boys! It's the boys again! Another stupit fuckin joke!

We staggered round the bar to our spot in the far corner.

Hey son! Is that your granda?

Hiv ye got any spare ribs mate?

Ah'll bet that fella cannae haud his drink!

It was Moses/Red Sea as we moved through the crowd. Around the horseshoe curve of the bar towards Aldo's mates in the far corner.

A few of them were up on chairs to see what the commotion was. A couple of folk held to the bar and laughed their heads going up and down like nodding-donkey oilrigs.

We seated Joe on a bench against the wall with his arms rested on a table. The Saturday anglers were there. Intoxicated on whisky and the heady winds of distant Rannoch. One of them reached into his bag and pressed a cheese roll into a skeletal hand.

Ah'll gie him a chit. The boy looks starvin.

A lit Embassy Regal wedged into a gap in the teeth jutted from the skull. Being late October the whole thing was passing for a Hallowe'en jape. On whispered information only Aldo's company were made aware of the awful deathly truth. Bardic Bruce. Michty Sandy. Magic Gavin. Gary Two-Wigs. Astonished we'd dug out a corpse from the loch and carried it across the braes for a bevvy. Beat that. It sent me and Aldo right to the top of the Bampot Premier League.

When the bar closed we carried the skeleton onto the last bus. Stepping down at the Bisley Bar with Joe hoisted over my shoulder. Past the derelict Bank Cinema and the shadow of the giant United City Bakery. Into Whitecrook with death weighing heavily on me. We'd just about reached Uncle Conrad and Auntie Margaret's when a polis car drew up. MacNabbed. Serious snib-up Hall Street Hospitality. *Then the public prosecutor started prosecutin me. That man wanted to find out what was my pedigree.* We never did nothin. But we were. *Fraaaaa-aaaaaamed. Da ra ra Da ra ra Dar ra ra Da ra ra ra. Da ra.*

Dualt flows under the road into a deep wooded notch. Dark in here under the trees. Light finding its way through branches to shine in the pool under hissing falls. Dip kettle in water pours over the rim. Disturbance ripples out across the pool in tiny rolling waves reflecting the glow of a dying ember sky. Leaning over seeing the reflection of my gaunt head. Pebbles of red and quartz through my face. A halo of light around me from the afterglow of a setting sun. Somewhere a cloud of rooks flaps up in a great crawing squabble. You'd think they'd learn to live with each other after a few thousand years.

There's a wealth of kindling scattered around the place so I knock a fire together. Branches of oak and pine. Droning and sparking sending spikes of flame up and a warm woodsmoke incense into the chilling air. Nearby a mouse chirps out a frantic song wi panic in its breistie. Me the big intruder. You're not so far away my sma friend. Only a few feet. But you've nothing to fear from the Fach. *The best laid schemes o mice and men. Gang aft agley. And leave us nought but grief and pain. For promised joy.* The leafy roof trembles from the odd gasp of wind that brightens the ember glow of the fire and makes the kettle groan and creak as it rouses itself for the boil. Yabba dabba! Into the snug-bag beside the fireside with a mug of the hot sweet steaming stuff. Bivvy bag for an outer skin water-resistant am I yawoo. All Hail to the revolutionary breathable waterproof Fabbatex fabric.

Tired after the fifteen mile walk. Just lie back to look through dark boughs and branches at stars scattered across the sky. Blue glowing coals of creation. Sparks of the big bang. I wonder how many microcosmic universes I've destroyed with my own piece of combustion that dies down to red blinking embers. Tomorrow I can follow the Dualt and cross the Blane Valley and beyond to get myself back onto the north road and the Swiftbus route for St Ronans. There's a faint tinkling sound from the embers. The hissing falls. Eyelids heavy. Try to keep them open a wee while longer. Still a spot of tea in the mug. Kind of like big iron hatches wanting to drop down on rusty hinges. St Ronans. Sailing homeward. Dark fire-coals with fading red slits. Fire sleeping too. Close eyes now. Song of the Dualt. The river's song same as the wind in the branches. Where does one song begin and the other end? Ach aye this is the life. Ach.

The wind blows into the forest and kindles a flame out of the embers. It flickers away making light and shadow dance in front of my closed eyelids as I fade away. I'm seeing Ma framed in the window with the flash of welders' torches flickering against a Clydebank sky. Hair tumbling in a wild mane and fingernails four inches long. She'd sailed right over the horizon by then and her eyes were looking out across an endless sea. Waiting for the return of the fool Da. Imagining him trussed up in some dark London lane with his severed goolies in his mouth. *Mairead said Da got ate by a whale and he's no coming back.* So there was Rapunzel waiting for Jonah. Three floors up in a tenement. Kath found some biscuits in the press and we watched Ma from our bed. Looking up from the biscuits. Dressing ourselves in the morning. More biscuits for breakfast then unwashed off to school. The dreaded walk to the school gates in the gloomy shadow of the United Bakery. Then the ridicule. We were the ones with the dreaded affliction of the bugs.

Scabby-Heid Scabby-Heid! You've Got MacNab's Bu-uugs!

Scabby-Heid Scabby-Heid! Yer Maw's A Cow And Yer Daddy's Deid!

On the way to school I'd uprooted a stick from a hawthorn fence a kind of long triangular job with a sharp ridge down it. I held it behind my back as the taunting crowd surrounded us on the way through the gates. The biggest boy in the school stood in front of me dancing and pointing his finger into my chest to the rhythm of the chant.

Bugsy! Bugsy! Bugsy-Bugsy-Bugsy! Scabby-Heid! Scabby-Heid! Yer Maw's A Cuh!

I brought the stick down into his napper with a sickening thud. Silence. A few gasps and disbelieving *Aws* as he hit the ground with blood pouring from a gaping wound. Puir wee pet. Rushed to casualty with a Dunbartonshire County Council towel held into his scalp to stop the red flow. *Hands out boy! Both of them! Skelp skelp skelp! Skelp skelp skelp!* Six whacks of the tawse from auld McConkie. He kept it folded over his shoulder and whipped it out from the inside of his jacket with gunslinger menace. Wyatt Earp. Outlaws and varmints from the ages of five to eleven cowered in fear from the threat of that leather rod of vengeance. McConkie bifuck. What designation could you have in life but a tawse-wielding heidie with a name like yon? Did he enjoy it? You bet he did. Hands didn't thaw out till the next day. Kath and me decided we wouldn't go back. Sitting on the floor playing every day while Ma looked out the window. Auntie Margaret still down in London with the asylum-seeker Conrad otherwise it would never have happened.

Our room seemed to be frozen in still life while outside the world trundled on. Evenings on Glasgow Road were a great hour-long procession of buses cycles cars and motorcycles crawling slowly east and west as people made their way home from the workshops. Somewhere in the bustle the litanies of news-sellers rang out like the chants of phlegm-stricken Gaelic psalmists. *LATE FINE-ELL. CITI-ZEN FINE-ELL. EVE-NEENG CHIMES. EVE-NEENG CHIMES.*

We'd probably all have starved into wraiths like Ma if it hadn't been for old Nora Mochan bringing us suppers from Wallace's High Tide Chippy. Nora scrubbed us with carbolic in the jawbox sink then sat scraping a packed-tooth steel comb through our scalps with heads gripped in the vice of her knees. So much for MacNab's Bugs. When she was finished with us on her way out she would say to Ma. *Are you okay there Janet? Is there anything I can be getting you?* But Ma just gazed out into dreamspace. Nora's voice might as well have been the wind blowing. Whispering out across the Shanakeever heather of her native Connemara. Ma. And you a girl of Finlaggan.

Youd've thought maybe with your Islay heart youd've responded to the soft Irish tones of Nora instead of gazing out across that endless sea.

A windless summer came then a clammy smog descended as Clydeside air choked on its own stale breath. Kath and me had been fed and scrubbed clean by Nora and were in bed looking at Ma framed against the window. The sultry blackness intensifed the argon flashes from the shipyard that lit the window frame around her. Her hair a riot of knots and split ends. There came a bright flash that filled the room. Then another and then an explosion of thunder echoed across the town. There was the surge of rain then explosions and flashes that outshone the welders by a million. A gale blew out of nowhere and spewed a torrent of rain against the window. I looked up and Ma was still there. A burst of magnesium light. Then a deafening crack as the ceiling above us split in two and sent down an avalanche of slates and rubble. The bed tilted and began to slide down the floor. Smoke and dust and flames. A hand had me by the hair and was pulling me from the bed and there was this other hand that had Kath by the hair and we're being dragged along the floor.

> *Holy Mother of God! Blessed Mary! The Germans are back for us!*

Then Ma was with us and we were on a staircase where the walls on either side had collapsed and the rain was blowing in. There was smoke and blue flashing lights and torchlight coming towards us and shouting. Fire engines racing down the road towards the building. Ma was taken away in a car with Kath and I was taken to Nora's daughter's across the road. South Douglas Street. I remember. Pictures of Mary and Jesus with bright halos around their heads. Where did you go Ma? Where are you Kathleen? I heard years later that Ma got sent to Islay and took Kath with her. So where are you now? Where are you? All the years I thought you'd come back for me. The last time we were together we were escaping from a burning tenement. Huddling from the storm that had hurled a spiteful bolt of lightning at our house in its angry rage.

Angry rage. Angry rage. Forget angry rage. Sleep now. Listen to the burn and the wind. Listen for the border and find a way in.

* * * * * * * * * * * * * * * * *

The wind blows out of the gates of the day. The wind blows over the lonely of heart. Who *was* that again? Sounds Irish. Yeats I think. I always liked that. *The wind blows out of the gates of the day*. The sou'west wind's up bright and early with the dawn. A-blowin out of the gates of the day to shake and rattle the oak leaves of the Dualt. The bivvy bag's smeared with ash that's been picked up in the gust and I lean out into the rucko to pull forth the trusty Primus stove. All Hail To The Shining Gold Primus. Saviour of the Fach on many a night of purgatory in the dark pit of Botanic Station. Cleansing my soul with a decent cup of tea. Mighty Primus. Holy object and sacred relic. A Grail. Containing the droplets of Christ's paraffin. Made in Sweden. Stove of Scandinavian excellence. Now a Holy font as I work at the plunger to send a stream of lit fuel to the burner. Pumping pressurised paraffin up to the nozzle to send out a yellow-blue flame. Stroking harder and faster on the plunger to get a good roaring flame going I must be pumping even harder now than the legendary Minnie The Wife Pumper of graffiti fame. Onto it with the kettle. My elbow working faster than your man Minnie's oscillating arse. Rump pump rumpitty pump. Doing the rounds on the prison-widows of Drumchapel. *Aw. Gie's mair Minnie. Shag me. Aw. Ya beauty. Gie it tae me. Noo. Yes. Fuckin gie it tae me.* There's a grand flame on the stove now roaring blue. Jeez I can't believe it but I've got a bit of a storker on me now from the image of some gagged-out housewife getting a thorough boning from a promiscuous sleazeball in a dimly lit bedroom. I pinch my stiffened boaby and try turning it at ninety degrees to constrict it and soften it down a bit but it seems to be getting solider. Obviously I need to do some upper arm or boxing exercises. To draw away the blood and so on. That's a grand spot of tea and I scoff into a tin of sardines then bury the tin and pack up the rucksack with the stove and the snug-bag. The wanderlust is on me. Setting course for the north road and the Swiftbus route for Saints.

There was a Haven dream last night. Can't think about the Haven dream. Filling my mind with inane gibberish to deny it consideration of serious issues. *Serious issues? Who are ye kiddin? Fuck off Fach.* Naw. *You* fuck off. Naw. *You* fuck off. *Ach jist fuck off will ye?* Whit's the fuckin point of this anyway? Going back to the Strath and raking around in the ashes? *What's the fuckin point?* I told ye before. A hundred times. Told ye. Told ye told ye told ye told ye. Fuckin told ye. Move on. Got to get out of this. This. Got to get out of *this.* Can't move on until I let it go. Ach shit the tears.

Step out across the moor with the langcoat lifting in the wind. Picking up the tracks of an Argo that head in the right direction scoring across an open tract of bogland. Nowhere is it possible to escape the presence of mechanised man in the low hills now. A few years ago the only thing that would've got you across the moor here would be a decent pair of boots. High above an airliner leaves its own jet-stream tracks across an open tract of sky.

I was standing on the shores of a loch. A low burning sun sending amber light through bullrushes and spiked reeds. There was a cloud of blue dragonflies dancing around my head. Shimmering in the light and making a halo around me like the pictures of Mary and Jesus. I was walking round the loch towards a cabin on the far shore. My boots were sticking in the ground as though the bog was trying to hold me back from reaching the cabin. I came to a charred-out tree on the shore. All that was left of it was the trunk and two boughs forking out into a giant Y. A gaping black hole was at the base of it like an open mouth. In the fork of the boughs a giant heron was staring down as I walked past fearful of its spear-like bill. The heron uncoiled its neck but as it descended its head turned into a screaming baby's. A growling black dog emerged from the inside of the tree and was pacing towards me. I began wading backwards into the loch to get away from it. The loch had become covered in dead fish so thick I could hardly get through them. I plunged in and swam through the floating fish which were decomposing into thick mucus as I touched them. I knew I had to make the cabin on the far shore.

There was music coming from there. Dark deep cutting notes. Rising on the air until they became a flow like a current of sound. Now I wasn't swimming on the loch. I was swimming through the music.

Down a long field hitching a lift on gravity to get me to the roadside. I'm on the edge of the Highland faultline. Great peaks of rock and heather rising out of the moss reaching into the clouds. Mother Alba. Gazing down from a chair of ancient stone. Glowering with the wisdom of six hundred million years on her brow as the wind plucks her tousled hair of mountain grass. In rainfall she'll weep white foaming tears for all her wandering exiled bairns. As I walk in she looks down at my approaching tiny figure with a scowl and I acknowledge her disapproval.

Sweet Ola. You were the one who used to laugh at my moods and self-indulgence. There's nothing like the woman who knows you to occasionally make you feel inept and powerless. Reminding you not to take yourself quite so seriously. And I suppose it's maybe right enough. Us willie-danglers seem to be born with an agenda of taking on the world on our own terms. As if everything should bow to our wants. And then when things go pear-shaped we take it personal and lament as if Creation itself was some kind of an institution with a mission statement to throw banana skins under our very shoes. And I suppose when you look around yourself in places like this it can put things in perspective. When you look around here you realise you're nothing more than a blink of God's eternal eye.

At a farmhouse junction there's a wooden cabin of a bus shelter with a Swiftbus timetable pinned up. According to this there's a bus comes along at twenty past four so drop the load on the bench. By my reckoning it's maybe around three so I've got time for a brew with the primus and maybe have a scan at the Langcoat Annals to pass the time. Over in the field there's an old bath with a spigot on a post for watering the beasties. So it's over the fence and into the hoofprint glaur and under the spigot with the kettle and the old stove going on the bench in the wee bus shelter here to fire up a dandy brew to go with a bit of scran. Magnifico. Perfecto.

If I perch at the cabin entrance here I can look right down the long straight of road to see if the Swiftbus is coming. Haul the legendary folder out the bag well bless my stars but the old *Farchar's Chap-Book* is getting fair tatty these days. Put all the pages together that's the game. A life story in this thing. Almost. Some useful stuff here songs and the like. A wee piece about the Roman occupation and a good veggie curry recipe I'd forgot about that Lordy stone me there's the old fishing diary. Don't rightly know why I started this it was multi-moons back think I fancied putting together my personal MacNab Manuscript a compendium job. Carrying all the things you like in the one book instead of humphing a library around. There's *Twa Dugs* my old favourite. *'Twas in that place in Scotland's isle. That bears the name o auld King Coil.* Yawoo lookit there's all the old Bankies scores and league positions. Jazzus chasps but they've hit more highs and lows than the Fach here's them beating Celtic 3-2 in the Premier League there's victories against Aberdeen and Rangers and Hearts as well. Mister where did all the good times go? There's all my own shit too. I'll say this my handwriting was none too bad in the old days. *The Langcoat Annals: Travel Tales o a Towzie Transient.* The great unfinished.

Swiftbus engine revs from a roadway distance. Soaring the bend then gliding onto the straights towards me on wings of diesel. Coach livery is the emblem of a flying swift on a cream painted background. Stow the chap-book into the pack and haul out the load from the shelter then stick out an arm so's driver can see me well in advance. I've been dreading the prospect of seeing Turk at the wheel. Na. Turk never did the city run. He always worked the local routes but there's no saying things haven't changed since them days. The man might be dead for all I know. Might be making the maggot-offering under the green sward of the old kirkyard. Be merry my friends be merry.

Swiftbus pulls into the inshot braking hard sending a shower of gravel into the hawthorn hedge. Doors hiss and bang open. To reveal. The face of a stranger at the wheel.

Relief. Pay the fare. *Cheers mate.* Driver crunches into first pulls onto the road and takes off. I go shooting up the aisle with the pack on one shoulder like there's this invisible string tied round my waist wheeching me up the bus. Horizontal bungee BEDOING! That unseen puppet-master toying with me again. Like a Farchar on a Oompah Deedeelie! Oompah Deedeelie! String.

Three-quarters way up plump the rucky down onto the blue tartan seat then slump next to it. Plump and slump. Plump slump rumpitty pump. Rump pump pump. *Feelthychirchpimper.* A wee look around. One or two backpackers they'll be heading for the Drover's Way. They give me the nod acknowledging my status as a fellow rambler. Little can they know how different our quests. There's the ramblers heading away from the jungle of civilisation into the wild blue yonder to leave it all behind them for a while. Wish I could say the same for myself instead of hiking right back into the heart of my past. I have another discreet scan there's a few more passengers on the bus but nobody familiar. Fields and trees shoot by at a sickening speed as the driver gives it Big Welly Yahoo and we go into Warp Factor Ten. If he keeps this up we'll be in Saints by six o'clock and I'll be able to walk over to the Haven before it's pitch dark.

* * * * * * * * * * * * * * * *

Far across the Birchen Moss and climbing into the Gilquhan Pass where the Duggies used to defend their cattle from the Highland caterans. Dragging them up to the Gallows Knoll to dispense summary justice or just ripping out their throats on the spot. I look back to bid farewell to Nether Caledonia. In the movie-screen of the rear window the Lowland carse recedes then pans away out of sight as the bus pivots on a tight bend and the flank of a boulder-strewn mountain swings into view. I rest back into the seat and whirr the old mind-projector into life and run off a montage. A Duggie movie. Cue music. Wagner. Fade up the sound of pounding hoofbeat until it drowns the music. A small army of men on horseback are riding across endless dunes. Close in. The Saltire robes of Sir Douglas and his twenty lieges flap as they charge headlong into battle with swords glinting under a Palestine sun. Change scene. Close-up of a severed Arab's head in a jar of brine. Cue distant drumbeat and roaring crowd. Pull out. Inside a lamp-lit Scottish tower. The walls are decorated with shelf after shelf of severed Islamic heads in varying states of decay. Sir Archibald Duggie-Gilquhan is at the window dressed in nightshirt and nightcap screaming out.

> *THE SWINE HAVE SET THE GALLOWS AFLAME! ANARCHY! BLACKNEB ANARCHY! SEND IN THE COUNTY DRAGOONS! ORDER LOADED MUSKET AND CANNON! GOD SAVE THE KING!*

Zoom a half-mile to flame-lit faces in the amphitheatre hollow of Gallows Knoll. A man is standing before them.

> *WHAT WE PROCLAIM THE ADVANCE OF CIVILISATION THEY DENOUNCE AS TREASON! WE CALL FOR AN END TO WANT AND STARVATION AND THEY CALL IT SEDITION! WE SPEAK OF THE FRANCHISE AND THEY NAME IT REBELLION! NOW THEY WAIT SADDLED AND ARMED READY TO CUT YOU DOWN. LET US MEET THEM AT GILQUHAN'S HOUSE BEFORE THEY CRY SLAUGHTER ON ST RONANS. FRIENDS OF THE PEOPLE! LET US PROTECT OURSELVES! SCOTLAND FREE OR A DESERT!*

The torch-lit crowd surge forward on either side of the obelisk. The flames of their torches reflect on Finglas waters as the procession curves over the arch of the Smiddy Brig. They swarm into the parks of the estate smashing open the locks of animal cages sending a rabble of screaming monkeys before them and a rainbow cloud of tropical birds that disappear into dark branches above. When they reach the Tower there is only silence. Emptiness. Back in St Ronans gunfire rings out. Women and bairns are being slaughtered in their homes.

Daylight scene. A great wooden frame is being pulled into the village by the horses of the King's Guard. Behind it a cage with two ragged men inside. A black hooded figure takes them from the cage and leads them hand-bound to the frame. He places their heads in the prepared nooses then kicks their legs away. When the last twitch is out of them he cuts the corpses down and hacks off their heads then holds them aloft. Sir Archibald strides to the front of the crowd gesturing towards the hangman with the severed heads.

> *BEHOLD THE HEADS OF MACLEOD AND MACGRUER! HUNG ON THE HURDLE FOR THE PAIN OF THEIR TREACHERY!*

But the crowd roars back.

> *SHAME! INJUSTICE!*

Cut to the final scene. A white-suited man stands on a high hill surrounded by palm trees. Sound of surf on a shore far below. He is looking down on a sugar plantation. Close-up of his face. It is the man who incited the crowd at the Gallows Knoll. The man who led them to the Tower to leave St Ronans undefended.

Rivers of blood from the Jordan to the Finny. We are all of us puppets dancing to History's tune. I remember telling the Turk one night what I'd learned of his family history and how his great-great-great-grandfaither MacGruer had been a reluctant martyr and had got hung on the Hurdle and beheaded. On the way home from the

Bull Turk dug out a boulder and fired it through a window of the Institute and we ran down the Carnock Lane laughing. Revenge for 1820. And eight centuries on there were echoes of the Crusades too. Every Tuesday evening behind locked doors in the Gilquhan Institute. Knuckle-crunching Uncle Duncan Knight of the Shannoch Temple. I discovered his ceremonial gear one time in a wardrobe during a game of hide-and-seek when him and Auntie Mary had gone out for the day. The mace. A gold-painted crown on a stick ornamented with little gryphons and lions and unicorns. The apron. A mystical gadget bearing the insignia of a large human eye against a dark blue spangled with planets and stars. I tried it on parading up and down in front of the mirror with the mace held out before me then ducked under the bed when I heard a seeker's footsteps on the stairs. I must have lain under there a good half hour enjoying the strangeness of the costume until the game was a bogey and the man in the lobey had done his wee jobey and it was time to re-appear. Did you ever wonder about the whole secrecy of the Temple thing? The couthy sorcerers of Scotland? Business deals and comparing golf scores no doubt but what else? What else then Duncan eh? What else Duncan eh? EH? EH? EH? Try asking the Knights themselves. Na. They'd simply draw together and close ranks on you. Aye. And then the Knights'll be fair drawin in harumph harumph. Uncle Duncan. Some couthy sorcerer him. A man full of dark secrets if ever there was one.

Welly-man driver steps on the gas as we hit the long straight into Strathfinglas. I can see the sparkle of the Finny as it twists and flows down through the grazing parks with gorse on its banks. And there's Dunreoch rising out of the earth. King of mountains. Shoulders cloaked in trees and wearing his crown of shattered crags. Past the rusty Gilquhan gates then swinging round the hairpin to descend to the humpitty-backed Smiddy Brig and across the Finny. Past the old red phone box. Up the lang brae we go through High Drums whizzing past the cold sandstone mansion with my heart going as fast and erratic as the bus. No remorse for Duncan himself. Sorry Auntie Mary. Along the Shannoch Road then down the hill to stop in the Square. This is no movie. I'm stepping down from the Swiftbus. Looking at the obelisk that points a granite finger at the sky.

The brooding cyclops of the Gilquhan Institute frowns into the square. A triangular pediment with the town clock at its centre held aloft on sturdy Doric pillars. Ten past six. I'm amazed the old clock's still working. I thought it'd stopped ticking years ago. I look closer and see the Institute's had a facelift. Man. The whole stone-clean job. Hang on what's the business with a board up on the palings? Community events? Time for a Sherlock nebber here.

What's this Watson? There is a most unusual title on the Notice Board. St Ronans Community Collective? I've never heard of that before. What's it all about?

I'm a tad befuddled myself Holmes. Aerobics and the like according to the programme of events.

Jee-zuss. Get this Watson. Not only Aerobics but Tai-chi and Transcendental Meditation and the Alexander Technique and Crystal Healing too. But take note Doctor. This is Tuesday. Tuesday evenings were always Knight Night.

Evidently not any more Holmes. Unless the Holy Order has been transformed into the Holistic Order.

Somehow I can't see it Watson. Can't imagine those moustache-sporting mystical apron-wearers channelling their karmic vibes into a collective dolphin consciousness to dispense a dose of spritual healing all across the universe. No Doctor. There's been a major change here. With the facelift and all.

Good grief Holmes! Look up at the building. Up there! Even Gilquhan the XVIIth's biblical inscriptions have been re-painted into the stonework on either side of the ancient clock. Look!

JAMES II. 19

THOU BELIEVEST THAT THERE IS ONE GOD, THOU DOEST WELL, THE DEVILS ALSO BELIEVE, AND TREMBLE.

JAMES IV. 7

RESIST THE DEVIL, AND HE WILL FLEE FROM YOU.

REV. III. 16

BECAUSE THOU ART LUKEWARM, AND NEITHER COLD NOR HOT, I WILL SPUE THEE OUT OF MY MOUTH

REV. XX. 15

WHOSOEVER WAS NOT FOUND WRITTEN IN THE BOOK OF LIFE WAS CAST INTO THE LAKE OF FIRE.

REV. XXI.8

ALL LIARS SHALL HAVE THEIR PART IN THE LAKE WHICH BURNETH WITH FIRE AND BRIMSTONE.

REV. II. 10

BE THOU FAITHFUL UNTO DEATH, AND I WILL GIVE THEE A CROWN OF LIFE.

COR. V1. 9. 10

BE NOT DECEIVED, NEITHER FORNICATORS, NOR ADULTERERS, NOR THIEVES, NOR DRUNKARDS, SHALL INHERIT THE KINGDOM OF GOD.

Voices. The garble of a whole cathedral of maniacs speaking in tongues. Words to strike into your heart like swords. Stroll on MacNab.

Hell heaven hell heaven hell heaven hell heaven hell. Bad fires and horny deils or joy-kingdoms in fluffy clouds with big beardie God. So how much fear did those fire-breathing ministers of the dark centuries inflict on the people of the Strath? Those gospel-wallahs were nothing more than the yes-men of the Douglas-Gilquhans. Prior to their own signing of the Covenant the erstwhile Catholic Duggies had persecuted and burned the heretics of the reformed faith for fun. But as converts to the Congregation of Jesus Christ they rejoiced in the return of Jockie Knox from Europe and delighted in his persecution of Queen Mary. *That whore in her whoredom.* The now Proddie Duggie preachers had stood shoulder to shoulder with those other Godly ministers in the holy battlefields of Scotland where they had harangued the warring flock with their cry of *CHRIST AND NO QUARTER*! That great enlightenment! Church organs put to the hammer! Fiddlers charged with serenading Satan! Dancers frozen in mid-step! A shining new theological light cast in the flames of blazing cathedrals! And so the way of the Strath was to become the Calvinist way of Predestination. Preachers were chosen by feudal patronage until the eyes of God became the eyes of Gilquhan. The question of heaven or hell was a handy pre-packaged affair in those days. Saved or damned before you'd even been plucked from the womb. And so the peasantry found themselves burdened with an entire baggage of sin handed all the way down from Adam. And yet it was only the Duggies themselves who could claim ancestry back into those distant biblical times. The Gilquhan Book of Geneaology told of family descent reaching back to classical Greece and beyond. Down through kings and pharaohs of ancient Egypt to the dawn of the world and Adam Gilquhan of Eden himself. All the more curious that it should be the peasantry and not the Gilquhans who'd found themselves carrying the can for Eden and all the world's other transgressions to boot. And we think we've got it hard! Would you listen to us with all our complaining these days! The girning bairns of a new millennium. Complaining about the pressure in *our* lives! Parking problems and lengthy check-out queues. Responsibilities. Deadlines. Job insecurity. Fashion stress. Holiday stress. Road rage air rage. Retail therapy to ease the strain. Consumer lust and plastic spending. Loans. Mortgages. Overdrafts. What the fuck do you think it must have been like for the poor peasants of the Strath being in credit for all of the world's sin?

Crivvens! If only poor Calvin could have known how his teachings would become distorted by the likes of the Duggies. Maybe he would have thrown down his bible and hung up his cloak. Then charged his goblet with a decent drop of Beaujolais. Glugged it down and followed through with a belch and a ripping good fart. Cracking a joke with a Benedictine monk then spending out the rest of his days in pursuit of harmless amusement and the occasional game of skittles. The Improver Duggies had decided to glorify God through the ornamentation of their estate. Gardens follies gazeboes and sundials. It was with shadow-play in mind that one of them had commissioned a second obelisk on the great lawn in front of the Tower. When viewed from the ramparts at noon on midsummer's day it was designed to cast a long shadow which terminated exactly against the base of the St Ronans obelisk a half-mile distant. A wonder to be displayed among the visiting nobles of Europe. That and the jars containing the slowly-rotting remains of the Saracens' heads from the far-off days of the Holy Crusades.

* * * * * * * * * * * * * * *

I hadn't planned on it but all yon theology nonsense has given me a thirst for a pint. How could I walk past the Bull anyway? The best glass of stout on Planet Scotland. I'm not sure how I'll deal with Bell right enough or anyone else for that matter. Old wounds heal slowly. But what the hell man. I can't just walk past. Can I? The white gable-end of the Bull drawing nearer and a thousand memories fleeting through my mind. Life and laughter and tears. Even the quiet moments. Hours of contemplation and reflection sitting at that famous old bar with Bell singing softly to herself in the background.

Thumb presses down on the old metal pad and lifts the lever with a clunk. I take a deep breath and swing in the door over those ancient flagstones. Looking straight ahead towards the bar on the faraway wall. But it's not there.

All the old wooden booth seats have been ripped out and the snug has gone. There's a load of round copper-dent tables and slim chairs around the room which looks big and empty and I'm seeing that the bar's moved over to the left hand wall. How can it be? The faraway wall had the doorway through to the cottage. The fireplace has disappeared. There's a gas fire with sterile flames prancing around imitation logs. Crusties sitting at a table. Guys and women with the regulation dirty dreads or shaved-top and feathered-sides. None of them are Strathers I don't recognise them anyway. A couple of crustie dogs mooching around.

There's a bloke behind the bar in a white shirt with one hand leaning the other plunging tumblers into the glass-washer under the counter. He's noticed me just as I'm distracted by the whirling coloured lights of a puggy machine at the end of the bar. Did we win some fruit mammy?

Awlright mate? Wot would you loik?

Eh? Aye. Wh. Em. Guinness. Pint please.

The Guinness comes shooting out the pipe like foam from a fire extinguisher. Shirt-and-tie-man just keeps cowping it into the drip-tray until he gets a result.

There you go. Anyfingk else?

Wh. Aye. Em. Could ye gie's some criss there? Some tamatta criss please an a packet a saltit nuts. Ta.

Chee's moit.

Cheers man.

Gad. I feel like a bit of a jube-jube now for putting on the parliamo accent where did that come from? A kind of instinctive reaction to Essex man's brogue I suppose. Seems a pleasant enough bloke but what's happened here? What the fuck has happened here? Look at the state of the place. Who's castrated the Bull? The whole place has completely lost its balls. The bellowing muddy-hooved steam-breathing ground-pawing snottering ring-nosed shite-skittering Bull of a public bar has been replaced by this skinny rib-racked shorthorn heifer of a lounge with copper-dent tables and a puggy with whirling lights. I'm sooking back the cold gassy Guinness to wash down the salted peanuts when Steven walks in. Hell's bells. What'll I say to him? He creeps up to the bar like a fugitive and quietly orders his drink so it's definitely him. He'll spy me sooner or later. Poor Steven.

Years ago he went off to Glasgow to study dentistry. One night he's walking home and whack! Beat to pulp in the street a team of Neddy fuckers dancing on his head. Went to the city to study dentistry and ended up with his own teeth in his stomach. Filthy bastards. Less civilised than Gilquhan's monkeys. So Mister Darwin. How do you explain the Ned phenomenon? Steven got partially blinded from the attack and he wasn't allowed to finish his degree. The boy's confidence went altogether and he just came back to Saints to be with his folks. By the looks of things not much has changed with him. He eyes the crusties at the table and gives them a nod as he passes then sits at the table next to mine. He's given me a half-glance as he sits down but it's not registered with him. Looks like it's Fach's move. I lean across my table in his direction.

> *Steve. Hey. Steven. Are ye awright there?*
>
> *Aye how're ye doin man? Hey. Hey. HEY! Jesus Christ ah don't believe it! MACNAB! FARCHAR MACNAB! HA! Hell man I thought you were dead. Oh! Jeez-oh! THE MAD FACH IS STILL ALIVE!*

Only just I think Steven. Aye. But ye're right enough. I'm still alive anyway.

God save us Fach. Aw man! The wanderer returns.

Aye. Ye should've had the pipe band playin in the Square for me when I stepped off the bus.

Ach good tae see ye Fachie. It makes a change seeing a familiar face in here man I can tell ye.

Whit d'ye mean? Is everybody else barred or something?

Barred? For fuck's sake Farchar. There's nobody else left. Only me.

The last of the Mohicans eh?

Naw mate. Mair like the last of the Shanny.

But. Whit about Deke?

Deke? DEKE? Deke's been gone over a year now man. He went away to work in some farm up north somewhere. Laggan I think the name of the place was. Aye. Laggan. That was it.

Jesus. Deke's out of the Strath? I don't believe it man. What about Turk?

Turk? Turk's in Perth Fach. Working in some bus company office somewhere. Doing the schedules or something like that. He went through there to see what the job was like then a wee while later Joan and the kids went through as well. Sometimes he comes in on a Sunday with his folks and they have a bar lunch and go away again. But that's about it.

Look Steven I'm sorry about what happened between me and Sharleen. I suppose you must hate my fuckin guts now that you don't see much of her with her being in London and all. I don't expect any forgiveness.

Enough Farchar. It's water under the bridge. It's life. My wee nephew's yer fuckin double man. He really is. Wee Scott. I see him from time to time when Shar's home.

Aye well. There you go. Listen. What the fuck's going on with the bar here? Where's Bell?

Bell? For God's sake man. Bell's dead these past eighteen months.

Bell? Aw no. Aw no.

Aye. She took a heart attack while she was reaching up to pour whiskies for the old Crawfords. Died at the optic. A true barmaid to the last. We all thought maybe you'd turn up at the last minute for her funeral. Nobody knew where you were Fach. You never left an address man.

Aw no. Hell man I don't know what to say. Bell. Bell Bell Bell.

Aye.

Puh! Them old Crawfords eh? A foot in three centuries. They'll outlive us all.

Wise up. The Crawfords are dead man. Died within a few days of each other. They never saw the millennium.

Really? Shit. The Crawfords? Gad. And Bell too.

Under the sod now Fach mate. She'd a plot in the old kirkyaird.

Gad. What about Big Chief?

Him? Don't know mate. They shut down his reservation years ago. The big tepee on the hill. From what I heard most of the patients just wandered off. Care in the community and all that.

Care in the community my arse. He'll be sitting on a pavement in Edinburgh or Glasgow with a paper cup at his feet. And a blanket round him if he's lucky. Bastards.

God knows Fach. All I know is the likes of him and the Hen-Wife haven't been seen in a while.

They'll destroy us all yet Steven. All the ones that won't play the game. All us ones that can't turn a profit for them.

Aye well. I wouldn't know much about it man.

Anyway. I can't believe Bell's away.

Long away. God Fach I'm telling you. All the young Strathers are gone from the place now man. It's fast becoming the graveyard or the road south for anybody that belongs tae this place. You're wasting your time coming back unless it's just for a few bevvies. What are you doing here anyway?

Eh? Och just a kind of visit I suppose. Who's that team over there? There's a few of them eh? Where did they come from?

A few of them? There's a whole fuckin camp of them up the road. Four vans and a bus. Dogs and bairns and all. They seem okay. I've ended up there at parties a couple of times after the bar's closed but most of the locals hate the fuckin sight of them. There's one other guy's moved into the middle of the woods by himself in an old Bedford ambulance. He cuts about dressed like Jimi Hendrix. I tell you it's not the same village you left. Most of the houses have been bought up by white settlers. None of them are working but they've all got plenty money. Aye. Retired fuckin hippies man it's bizarre. They've even opened their own private school to teach their kids. Can you believe it Fach? A vegetarian primary school? And the kids get to call the teachers by their first names. There's one teacher there calls himself Zeeg. Zeeg! ZEEG! And there's this other buffoon there calls himself Rameses! Fuck man what kind of an education is that? Can you imagine it in our day Fach? Rameses? Vegefuckintarians? Christ! We had to eat greasy mince shipped to the place in urns by the County van. And that fuckin hot frogspawn of a pudding that they called tapioca. We used to get belted if we didn't eat the stuff it was fuckin torture man but at least we got a decent education. Then the nobs got this big Lottery grant to do up the Institute and they've turned it into a healing centre. Healing? Healing?! Can you believe it? Healing? There's fuck all wrong with them man! They've got more money than fuckin sense. And now that the travellers are turning up in the vans I'll bet half the property owners are absolutely fuckin horrified but they're not speaking out against it in case it makes them look unhip. I mean fair dos to the travellers they were good enough to invite me to their parties but to tell ye the truth man they're absolutely fuckin mingin. I mean there's a good river out there. The Finny. What's wrong with jumping in it and having a right good wash? It's no like they're genuine minkers or anything. These are educated people we're talking about here. Drop-outs. And who in their right mind would want to live in a disused fuckin ambulance?

I decline to tell Steven I've been living out my life in a derelict Victorian railway station under a city park. I'm listening to his ranting about the new-age invasion but deep inside I'm thinking about Auntie Bell and harbouring a tear for her. Bell. Not a real auntie of mines. Just Bell the barmaid. Oor auntie. Your auntie.

A'body's auntie. I ask Steven if he'd like another drink but he says he's to go home for his tea. So I wait until he's out the door then sling the pack onto the shoulder. Back out the old door into the Carnock Lane then over the stile and leg it across the swingpark to strike the track for the Haven. Here we go. This is it.

Everybody deserves to have a Haven in their heart. Some backwood or a riverside or a secret place where they feel at home. Somewhere you can visit or even just dream about to feel part of the land. You ask nothing of it. Only to go there sometimes and listen to the song-winds. I'm sure for Ma it was Islay. Distant memories of Finlaggan and Ballygrant. It was just that I had my Haven and I blew it.

The track cuts along the edge of the long hill for a good few miles. Running high above the Finglas until the river reaches the foot of the the hills where it splits into its five separate burns.

The Finny falls from the high high lands
Five flowing rivers five silver strands
Five witches' spells
And five wild songs
Five long fingers on a watery hand

The biggest burn of the five dog-legs north into the hills where the track follows it climbing alongside as the burn foams down in steps over smooth red slabs into rocky pools. Late summer and fading light. The patches of heather still have their purple flower but the grassy slopes are already brindled as tussocks and bracken show the first signs of the season's end. It gives the land a real depth. Up the stony track to reach the long moorland stretch as the road makes its way across the shallow gravel pools of the diminishing burn. The burn cuts away. Winding into the shadow of fallen rocks where rowans grow. Trees of legend. A long time ago in the days before Saint Ronan. Out of the far north there came a herd-boy named Fingal who passed here once a year droving his cows south with a stick of hazel in his hand. At the head of a broad green glen there stood a smoky old hovel where there lived five weird and hackit wifies. On each year that Fingal came by one of the witches would emerge from the hovel to try and put a jinx on him and his cattle. But each time Fingal would strike a stone in front of him with his hazel staff and the witch would be turned into a slithering adder. And each time Fingal would catch the adder in a bottle and carry it into the high hills where he would imprison it in a hole at the foot of a tree then place a boulder on top to stop it up. So every year the witches became less in number. Five and then four then three and two and finally one until after five years the fifth and final adder was imprisoned below a tree. So on the sixth year Fingal was able to pass peacefully through the glen on his travels south with the catttle without any trouble. But that year on Hallowe'en there rose out of the eastern sky the strangest and most powerful moon that anyone in the glen had ever seen. In their prisons below the trees the adders felt a great energy from it and heaved with all their might to turn the boulders aside and be set free. They slithered down from the hills and in their fury the five evil snakes met at the foot of the braes and writhed and conjoined into a terrible serpent called Conn Cheathach. Then Conn Cheathach brought terror to the broad glen killing and eating all the livestock. A fear and a cold dark chill descended there. The green pastures were turned to sickly grey. On the seventh year that Fingal went to come through the glen with his cattle he found his route barred by Conn Cheathach. He struck a rock before the serpent with his hazel branch to try and destroy it but the stick turned to dust in his hands. On his flight from Conn Cheathach Fingal followed a running fox. The fox led him to a hole in the ground and told Fingal to look in there. He reached down and found an old sword then he turned around and struck Conn Cheathach with it. With a blow of the sword the great serpent turned to water before Fingal's eyes and the grey withered glen was transformed back to a green pasture. The terrible coiling serpent had become a beautiful river with five silver streams at its head. A long time before the five haggard witches had been five beautiful sisters who had each in their turn fallen foul of a demon. The demon had assumed the shape of a king and promised them the earth in exchange for their virtue. Instead he took away their vigour and turned them one by one into the five haggard crones. So each of the five tumbling streams that converged into the Finny became the five wild songs of the sisters who had been set free at last and called down in all their sadness from the hills. And near the source of the five burns you will always find a rowan growing there. The tree where Fingal had imprisoned one of the five adders. So the river was named in Fingal's memory. And if you look at the River Finglas on a map you can see a long blue arm with the imprint of five skeletal fingers at the wrist. Five long fingers on a watery hand.

Near the road end through falling darkness I see the burn flowing down through tussocks from a glowing sheet of water. Lochan Cnoc a Habhain. A lochan a hill and a river. Knockhaven. The Haven man. The Haven.

The moon rises and I pick my way along the lochanside towards the steep hills at the far end. Away from the cabin. Turning I can see it still there. A flat grassy top looks high over the moonlit lochan. Black shapes among spiked grasses jutting out of the ground like the fangs of a prehistoric beast. Outline of charred timbers. Burned-out cabin against the night sky. Camp down here and wriggle into the bivvy bag and lie with a soft wind blowing through the grass around me. Tomorrow I'll begin to put it all together. Tomorrow. *Am maireach. Manyana.*

* * * * * * * * * * * * * * * *

The gates of the day blow open to let in a herd of white clouds that slowly graze across an expansive field of blue. I'm out of the bivvy bag and down to the shore. On the grassy bank of the lochan Primus flame roars up at a smoke-blacked kettle. Wind blowing in from the south rattling the tussocks. *Ach osnaich. Field of the sighing winds.* Song-winds. In brief harmony with one of the maidens' five wild songs as the sough of the falls rises up from where the burn drops away in foaming steps.

Upturn rocks here and there for worms to bait the lines. Weight them with chuckies then send them arcing out with a splash into the loch. The more fish I catch the longer I can stay in the Haven. It used to be great here walking round the loch with the old fly rod casting away. Ola up in the cabin there. She must've felt she was becoming something of a trout widow in those days. Looking out from the window and seeing MacNab's distant speck on the lochside lashing away with ten feet of fibre glass to send a March Brown and Cock y Bhondu out onto the water. Along the side of the lily beds where the big trout lay. Sometimes a swirl and kadoosh and yawoo! Two pound beauty leaping and turning as you hauled the speckled beastie to the bank. Poor fuckers. Lying there gasping till you chapped them on the head then into a plazzy bag with handfuls of sphaggy moss to keep them fresh. Divine scran though. Trout and tatties. Food of the Gods. Manna.

Oh yes. Paradise Regained. Let's ring the harp strings why don't we? What the fuck are you doing here? Who do you think you are? St Jerome? Come to live with the beasts of the plain and knocking a stone into your ribs to smash the devils out? St Farchar the Divine? Seeing some angel walking across the loch on pillars of fire to make you eat the Langcoat Annals?

Order. Order. I am here in the Haven because I reached it. Now because it is now. This is my choice. To lie on the banks of the lochan and watch giant white clouds scrape their way across endless blue. I am where I have to be. In a place where winds carry the long lost shouts of distant friends. From the Big Bang we were all of us born into the world. And just like the fragments of Creation that go forever exploding out then so do all our stories and dreams from the centre of ourselves. We try to gather them all into a sensible whole because we need to give everything a beginning and an end. To understand our place in time. I am here in the Haven. Throwing out lines and scrawling in the chap-book. Delving into the Langcoat Annals. It is only here among a million crazy memories and song-winds and creeping skies that I might have a chance of making any sense of this. I have to let myself spin at the same rate as the Earth. The wanderer is back. Travel Tales o a Towzie Transient. The great unfinished.

annals

I was announcing to Uncle Duncan that I was leaving the Academy. He was in a trendy mood that day. Sitting by the radiogram playing records a yellow v-neck sweater and a pair of brown slacks on him. He was the only man I ever knew who found it necessary to wear golf shoes in the house. Listening to Jim Reeves or Perry Como. Between slight nods of his head to 'the beat' Duncan took the trouble to turn down the volume for a minute to give his reaction to my momentous decision.

> *You are leaving the Academy of your own accord Farchar. I always knew you would amount to nothing. Baden will go to university and become a man of distinction. And what will become of you? You'll end up emptying bins or sweeping the roads if you're lucky I suppose. And don't for a moment think that you can leech a living off of me for the rest of your life. I wasn't born unto God's earth to support your indolence and alcoholism. I'll see you out of this house before long my lad. On your ear. As soon as you're sixteen years old.*

Alcoholism? Fur fack's sake! I'd only just developed a sheen of bumfluff on my chin that gave me the seniority to quaff a Friday jar in the Bull. After my decision I was enjoying a Guinness when somebody tapped me on the shoulder and pointed towards the window. There was Duncan with Baden and Edith on either side of him. Pointing through the glass at me like I was some kind of a specimen in Gilquhan's ancient zoo. *Tak tent Baden. Tak tent Edith. See how he grows into an alcoholic madman like his father.* It was one up for the Fach when I walked down to the Smiddy yard two days after leaving school. Scored an engineering apprenticeship and a tenner a week rental on a flat on the Smiddy Row to boot. Flats that today fetch five-figure sums on the property pages of the Hobnob's Gazette.

It was five past eight on the Smiddy's ancient clock when the chargehand Baxter led me into the gloom of the workshop. I followed him to the far end of the shop where we stopped at a long sturdy workbench. Baxter took down some files from a rack and laid them next to a vice. Then he pulled a piece of steel plate about the size of a slice of pan loaf from a scrap-pile under a mechanical saw. He threw the metal down on the bench with a clunk then handed me a tri-square.

> *Right Hector.*
>
> *It's Farchar.*
>
> *Eh?*
>
> *It's no Hector it's Farchar.*
>
> *Aye well anyway. I want ye tae file this square. Gie me two edges. Flat and square. Ah'll come back in a wee whilie tae see how you're getting on.*

I squeezed the steel-plate into the vice then set about it with a rough file. Working away until I had the saw marks out of it and a good-looking edge. I got my weight over the top of it and moved the file steadily back and fore. Then I took the medium file and worked at the high points. By twenty-five past eight I was taking the steel from the vice and holding it up to the light with the blade of the tri-square against it. Checking longways and crossways. With as much luck as judgement I'd got it bang-on. Flat as the Netherlands. Into the vice with the next edge up working fast and studiously. Filing it down and making it square to the first edge. By ten minutes to nine I'd cracked it. Both edges were flat and square to each other through ninety degrees. I stood next to the vice waiting for Baxter. By quarter past nine I was leaning with an elbow on the bench wondering where he'd got to. There was the occasional shout and whine of machinery from somewhere down in the workshop. When Baxter finally appeared at twenty-five past twelve I was sitting on the bench trying to stop my head rocking forward into a sleep.

How're ye getting on? Did ye manage it? I'll check it efter dinner.

The place fell silent as switches on the machines were dunted and the workmen disappeared. I went for a walk down to the Finny and watched the trout splashing in the Martyr's Pool. When I could hear voices up at the shed I went back and found Baxter at the front door with the tri-square against my work checking it to the light.

So ye came back Hector? I'm jist having a wee look at yer test-piece. No bad. No bad.

He stood for a moment in thought then went inside and climbed into blue oil-stained overalls. He ran his fingers through his silver hair then lit a cigarette.

Right Heck.

It's Farchar.

Right then follow me son.

We walked up the shop to a centre lathe. He handed me a piece of bar and a micrometer. He reached into his top pocket and pulled out a Regal packet ripping out the inside flap and doing a quick pencil sketch of a machined part with two diameters. 2.5 inches and 1.75 inches. *There ye go. Make the tolerance on the diameters five-thousandths of an inch. Plus or minus.* This time he stood behind me. I loaded the bar into the chuck then messed around with the machine feeds and speeds until I'd got a feel for it then carefully cut down the metal until I'd got the diameters to size. Baxter double-checked the sizes with the micrometer. He ran his fingers through his hair then turned on his heel and disappeared. He returned with a clean set of blue overalls in his hand and threw them towards me.

I've spoken tae Mister MacLeod. That's the boss of the firm. He says ye can start the day.

That's the way half the country used to score a career. I suppose you'd need an Honours in Quantum Physics for an apprenticeship like that now. Two days later I heard about the empty flat on Smiddy Row and returned to the sandstone mansion for my gear. The look on Dunc's face was a treat. Id've traded my left testicle for a camera that day. Click click click!

But. But you can't leave now. Where will you go? You are nothing but a child. Life is dangerous! You will starve! You will perish!

I'd taken a squad of buddies along with me and with all my gear collected in bundles we began the march down the Shannoch Road like a great desert caravan. Sharleen. Cammy. Turk. Deke. Doober. Craw. Sally. Herry Merry. Singing and hooting. Uncle Duncan had made his way to the gate and stared down the brae in silence. The teachings of Baden-Powell were echoing through my head. Be Prepared. Whistle And Smile. And Paddle Your Own Canoe. I threw my bundle down then turned around on the road waving my arms in the air with the langcoat flapping madly around my shins. Yelling my farewell at Uncle Duncan and the cold sandstone mansion.

EEN-GONYAMA! EEN-GONYAMA! YA-BOH! YA-BOH! INVOOBOO! LOOK AT ME NOW UNCLE DUNCAN! I AM A LION! NO! I AM BETTER THAN A LION! I AM A HIPPOPOTAMUS!

The hoots of my mates echoed into the trees as I turned around for a final verbal salvo.

ZING A BOM ZING A BOM! BOM ZINGA BOM ZINGA ZING!

ZING ZING ZINGA BIM BOM! ZING ZING ZINGA BIM BOM! BIM BIMMA ZINGA BIM ZINGA BIMMA ZING BOM! BOMMA ZINGA BIM! CHEERIO FOR EVER DUNCAN YA AULD FUCKIN BAW BAG YE!

Line number three. It's at a fair slant from where I left it. Moving slowly across the bottom of the loch. Lift it up slowly to head-height until it gives a slow jerk then haul it in hand over hand. Here's a fine fish on the line for you. Speckled brownie gold-belly of the pound-and-a-half variety. It'll make a fine pan-sizzle that one. Onto the shore with him then a dunt on the head over a rock and there'll be no more joogling from this fellow. I'll kindle a fire on the shingle strand with grey heather from the overhang and split the rowan bough that's hanging dead from the crag. The smell of the open fire and the trout cooking over it. Wind whispering through tussocks and the occasional brownie breaking the surface.

Looking back on the lost days. What is this thing called the past? Mind pictures. Memories. Moments. The personal home movie. And how close to the real thing is the picture we're left with in the end? This thing without substance. Ghosts that we hold on to for the rest of our living days. To cling to the past is futile. But to be without it is to have no history. And to have no history is unthinkable. The ghosts of our past are both the making of us and our undoing. They warm us with memory. Fool us with sentiment. Shame us with reminders of embarassing actions. Mock our failures and praise our deeds. They are the ghosts that drift out from our souls. We cast out a net and drag them back in to find them distorted by pulling against the current of time. But mister I tell you this. The Smiddy years were good years. Hector the apprentice. The name stuck. Working on pumps and turbines and engines. Real good crack with Bax and the rest of them. Sometimes in the workshop or sometimes out in the distillery or the hydro-stations. Until my fate was sealed by a Ugandan autocrat called Idi Amin and the last in line of the great noble family of the Duggie Go-whans.

The *Queen Euphemia* was a clapped out paddle-steamer that had lain rusting pierside on Loch Mhor for years until Gilquhan came home with his big idea. Douglas Douglas-Gilquhan of Gilquhan. Fleeing back from Uganda pleading injustice after your man Idi had seized his assets and put a few heavies on his tail. Shame it was for the Gilquhans and their kind. The colonial days were over. Time had eroded their fortune down to the odd parcel of land around the Strath and a sizeable house up near Drums. But the old ship the *Queen Euphemia* would prove to be the Gilquhan dynasty's very last throw of the commercial dice. Before Douglas Douglas the Umpteenth would scrape up the last of the sovereigns from the bottom of the family kist to blow them on the roulette tables of Edinburgh.

Gilquhan's idea was to reinstate the old ship back to her glory days then use it to ply the tourists up and down the loch. There were pictures of her in old sepia photos. Ghosting out of the mist on her great paddles with a crowd of Edwardian well-to-dos looking over her bows. Sure it was a grand idea of Gilquhan's but the old *Euphemia* herself was a bag of nails and Bax knew it. He'd surveyed the job then advised Gilquhan and Mister MacLeod at the Smiddy against it. But the Duggie-Duggie could talk money. He convinced MacLeod that he'd enough capital and so the job went ahead and we spent that spring and summer working on her. A fine job it was too. Putting lines off the shore for the trout while we were working then lousing off in the evening straight into the bar of the Beinn Mhor Hotel. Fridays we'd sometimes end up there till the death and the van would weave back to St Ronans with a stolen stuffed owl or some animal in it. A big fuckin moose-head once. They'd always end up dumped in the flat on the Smiddy Row until the place looked like a natural history museum. What a job. As the summer wore on the crack just got better. There was a well-known spot just off the pier. The folk that swam there were usually walkers on the Drover's Way. Sometimes young continental women stripping nadders then diving naked into the loch chill as cold rivulets ran over perfect skin and hard dark nipples. Our depraved engineers' boabies stood as tall and erect as the funnel on the *Queen Euphemia*. Jazzus I could've shagged a trout in those days I tell you.

But if the *Euphemia* job was the making of that summer she would prove to be the breaking of our livelihoods. MacLeod was unaware of the Gilquhan's chronic gambling addiction. He'd run up some serious casino debts and was in a bad way. There were rumours going round that the heavies were onto him. He was found splattered on the M8 below a high bridge near Glasgow Airport and the inquiry's verdict was suicide. Having left no issue this was the end of the line for the Douglas-Gilquhans. The last of that noble genealogy that had stretched all the way back through ancient Greece and Egypt to the Garden of Eden. The End. From Adam to tarmacadam. It was the end of the Smiddy too. The ancient Smiddy that had once shod the horses of Scottish kings. Who's to know how long it would have survived anyway? It was just around the time when the Demoness was bending over and building up a high pressure of noxious gases in her bowels. Pointing her crinkled anus north and preparing to blow Scottish engineering from the industrial horizon for ever. The gas would creep underground and blow the colliers out of their mines too. But my three years as Hector at the Smid were grand while they lasted. I'm a great believer in cause and effect. Had it not been for Idi Amin my life would have been different. And as for that noble family. They had terrorised Muslim warriors in the Crusades. Burned religious heretics on the stake and drowned and disfigured innocent women with the charge of witchcraft. They had hung innocent weavers on the hurdle and led mothers' sons to the slaughter in the name of Britannia's mighty empire. They had led men over the top of muddy trenches in the cruel murderous scientific war of a new century. They had been under the scrutiny of the British Secret Service throughout the Thirties and Forties then gone to Africa to recover their flagging fortunes. A thousand years of recorded history until the flame of their glory finally sputtered out. Their final act? To put the Fach and his mates out of a job and onto the dole queue. For this I am greatly honoured.

* * * * * * * * * * * * * * * * *

Those noxious fumes from Margaret Hilda's crinkly hole descended like an evil smog on the world. I was slinging a pack onto my back and stepping onto the Swiftbus. Sharleen boarded behind me and we sat together as the coach pulled out from the square onto the Shannoch Road. I suppose we must have looked really young then.

Where will you go Fach?

I don't know yet Shar. I'll try and get a job in Glasgow to set me up for the travelling. I really fancy the travelling you know. India maybe. Or even Brazil. I've heard that's some place.

A job? In Glasgow? What doing?

Machining and fitting. I've nearly got a trade. The place is full of factories.

From what I'm hearing they're all closing down.

Ach. Nae worries Sharbo. I always land on my feet.

What are you talking about? You've only ever had one job.

Aye. I suppose. But I've only ever looked for one.

Good luck to ye Farchar. Are you okay for cash?

Aye. I've got about fifty squid here.

Fifty squid? Ye'll need more than fifty squid. You can stay at our flat to get ye started if you like. But it's three lassies and there's only the floor. Have ye a sleeping bag?

Na. I usually just use this big coat.

The langcoat? Fach. When are ye going to get rid of that scabby auld coat?

Get rid of the langcoat? Are ye completely jubers woman? The langcoat is the key to the universe. The garment has power beyond all mortal reckoning. See how it enwraps me in its magical folds and shields me from the evils of the world. RESPECT THE MIGHTY COAT!

A few heads turned on the bus so I started clucking like a hen to give them something to think about. Sharleen was having a laugh and I watched her. Her red hair shaking as she struggled to suppress a hoot. She was framed by the window with fields hills and hedgerows shooting past as we headed towards the soot-blacked city that lay unseen in the distance.

Sharleen. My first sexual conquest. No. I fib. More like Farchar. Sharleen's first sexual conquest. Not that I'm calling Shar a slapper. It's just this old myth of libidinous young blades having their wicked way with chaste young maidens. Fiddlesticks I say sir. It was the other way around for me. One boring Tuesday towards the end of our school days Sharleen had suggested that we dog off a Maths lesson and go for a walk.

So we walked for a mile then sat behind a drystane wall in a park near the high wood. I'd no idea she'd designs on me. I'd seriously thought the purpose of our truancy behind the dyke had been purely for the sharing of an Embassy Regal. It wasn't long before Shar had us in a passionate snog and was helping my trembling hands find their way into the folds and curvatures of a new and enthralling landscape. She unbuttoned me then ran her hand down the front of my Wrangler Skinners. There was plenty of room inside there. I gulped in a sharp draught of breath as she clutched me thinking I was about to erupt on the spot. With great intuition she'd brought along a Rubber-Man. She unrolled it deftly onto the boaby. It was standing as solid as The Old Man of Hoy. We'd all our kit off by now then she guided me in and we rolled back and fore nae-kit in the long grass going to it hammer and tongues. I knew I wanted it to last but after about a minute I was beginning to tingle with an uncontrollable ecstasy. God I so wanted it to last. I so wanted it to last. I tried clenching the boaby muscles like you do to stop a pish in mid-flow if the aim's wrong and you want to re-direct it. The ecstasy eased and I never came but I began to feel myself soften a bit inside Sharleen. She was all over me. On top of me with gorgeous firm tits rolling across the top of my face. She rocked and rocked and I tried to catch them in my mouth like a Hallowe'en apple-douker. I ran my hands down her back feeling them glide over the curves of her arse and thought of the rolling knowes and the braes high above where we were. It was a good thought. I closed my eyes now and ran my hands all over her body picturing a journey across the hills with all their ridges and knolls and glens. I found myself stiffening again but still able to maintain a healthy thrust without getting carried away and spoiling the party. We rolled over and the picture of Sharleen's body became one with my vision of mountains and rivers. The mind-eye drifted over land on the wings of a falcon. Dropping swiftly on a green oak dell then rising away to the heights of Dunreoch. I had found a method. If I kept my mind on the landscape I could retain the passion and the stiffy without jiffing off too soon. We went to it for a while longer until I began to lose control. The vision of the landscape vanished as Shar rose up on her elbows and plead me with her eyes to give it to her harder. Her red Scottish hair fankling in my hands and dropping across her shoulders. My big white Highland arse thrusting up and doon as gleg as a squirrel until I could bear it no longer and let go. *UH! AW-MY-FUCKIN-GOD*. Spasm spitting ejaculation jiffing jolts jets of jissum into the johnnie juddering jarring clutching Sharleen's arse and releasing gasps of untrammelled joy. *SHARLEE-EEN! KEEP GOING FACHIE! SHARLEE-EEN! KEEP GOING! AH CANNAE AH AH AH*! Stillness. Breaths. I felt like I'd been pumped empty. The rubber man was half-full of my spunk so I crept out of Sharleen. Caution. Thumb and forefinger gripping the ring at the bottom of the johnnie back-stepping the boaby out like a soldier withdrawing from a building full of snipers. I unslid the rubber then threw it away into some foxgloves. We lay still in the long grass with me still on top. There was a skylark trilling in the sky. Sharleen asked me to fetch an Embassy Regal from the discarded clothing. I got onto my kness and reached over then let go a hoot. Sharleen sat up and we both looked out naked and hooted. We were surrounded by a circle of about forty cows that had congregated curiously then must've stood by in cud-chewing silence to witness the whole shebang. As we looked the whole crowd of them burst out mooing in a great bellowing racket.

It's not that I expected Sharleen to do the honourable thing and marry me after deflowering me or anything. But within a fortnight of The Shag Witnessed By The Forty Beasts she'd decided to go out with Cammy instead. A year later they got engaged and that was that. Now Sharleen had got a job in the city and you could be sure it wouldn't be long before Cammy would follow her there.

The Swiftbus droned through the douce villas of Bearsden on that drizzly Saturday afternoon then downhill into the industry-blackened slums of Maryhill. Sharleen was reading a paper so I looked out the window. Fractured rone pipes sent plumes of steam into the air from the backs of crumbling half-abandoned tenements. The sky seemed to darken as we descended further into it. From ground floor to top rusting Nissen sheets covered the windows of abandoned homes. In the occasional window there was the glow of a light or the flash of a television set. A cardiganed wifie peered out with her arms on the sill of a window. There were still spraypaint remnants of the gangs. The tenements. A dark matrix of decay. The abandoned homes were spent cells of an organism that had pulsed with the rhythms of daily life. A community that had greased the wheels of the world's richest empire. For the most part they were being decanted out to the concrete maisonettes and skyscrapers of distant schemeland. Yet still on Maryhill Road men birled cheerily from pubs. The Copper

Lamp. The Viking. The Caberfeidh. Knots of people chatted on street corners. Seen through Teuchie eyes the place had the air of a war zone where a cease-fire had been declared. The Swiftbus stopped in the drizzle of St George's Cross and I stepped down cautiously like Neil Armstrong. But before my feet landed on Planet Atlantis I was already questioning my choice of location for career advancement.

Even though I was dossing down on Shar's floor in Grant Street I knew there was next to no chance of us ever getting it together again. Still. The thought of it visited me most nights as I lay under the langcoat. I dreamed of running my tongue across the slope of her belly and down into the auburn grove. Then pictured her in sunlight by a riverside lying on a great flat rock with her legs apart. My tongue savouring the fruit. Red-haired and peach-like and Scottish. Who was I kidding? I was staying in a flat with three young women and there was as much chance of me getting my end away as there was of getting a job in the West of Scotland. I hauled myself back and fore across the city and out to places like Paisley and Cambuslang in search of factory work. Firm after firm was on the fold as thousands of skilled men watched the workshop gate close behind them for the final time and settled their arses into armchairs in anticipation of a long wait. What chance did I have? Didn't even finish my apprenticeship thanks to Idi Amin and the gambling Gilquhan. One night I pulled the langcoat over my head and shut out the picture of Sharleen from my mind. It was driving me demented. Forbye Cammy was a mate and heading for the city soon to be with Shar. So I put sex with Sharleen out of my mind. And thought instead of Brazil.

BRAZIL? You're off your fuckin head Fach. How much money have you got?

I've still got thirty squid.

Thirty squid? Thirty squid'll no get ye very far.

It'll get me tae London. I'll make a start there. Then work my way round the world.

Well I'll loan you twenty. Then you'll have fifty. But don't get carried away with all that money and go around the world twice.

You're a darleen Sharleen. I'll make a good start with fifty. I'll hitch everywhere to save the fare. Aye the idea of travellin's always appealed to me. See the world and all that. If I go round twice I'll make sure I stop off at Grant Street for a cup of tea. And to pay you back your twenty squid of course.

But why Brazil?

Why not? Why anywhere? The sun shines there.

I thought it might have something to do with gorgeous women.

Oh aye. That as well. Ma knob's been made redundant long enough now Shar. It's time he signed off the dole and went back to work.

He was working hard enough that day by the high wood.

HA! So he was. Right enough. So he was. HA!

I exaggerated the HAs when I realised I was starting to beam a wee bit. Sharleen had taken me totally by surprise. I never thought she'd mention the day by the high wood and the rampant shag. The only real shag of my life up until then if the truth be known. Outwith Herry Merry's obliging wanks and blow-jobs that had pacified my loins during the interim years and occasionally helped me to cut down on my bedtime boxing exercises. To draw away the blood and so on. I was a bit taken aback by my own beaming coupon too. Never really considered myself the blushing type. But then we both started laughing.

I've only got one thing to say to that Farchar.

What's that?

Moo!

Eh? Aw aye. Moo!

MOOOO!

Lifting the lid on long lost dreams. The fishing lines are still. Haul them in for a check change a worm here and there where the brownies've chewed without taking up on the hook. The baited lines curve out spladoosh in the rippling cool blue of reflected afternoon skies. Flash of red kestrel soars out from behind a hill with two ravens on his tail. Tagging and chasing like warplanes. They hit a blast of wind and curve upwards then speed off into a distant sky until the ravens return with victorious croaks. They'll be setting up the brandies tonight in the pilots' mess. Them and the rest of the crows. Silk-scarfs and leather jackets and chewing on fat cigars yarning off about the dogfight with the hawk. Away beyond the Highland faultline sky flattens out across the Lowland plains. Fire up the Primus and flame roars on the base of the kettle spouting vapour into the air then in with a handful of leaves the old char.

Tea pours dark red from the spout rich like a Provence wine. Provence wine pouring rich red from a bottle and filling a glass to the brim. *Merci beaucoup.* On a pavement café under a burning sun with the soft clunk of boules from the square and the low chat of straw-hatted men as they pace slowly around the game. Old men with dark craggy Mediterranean faces.

The bottle stopped pouring and I lifted the wine glass to my lips to let a welcome flow of alcohol pour over my throat. I pulled a battered Gitane from a packet then untwisted and pulled it to straighten it a bit before putting the tinder on it. The strong toasted scent of the Gitane wisped up as I drew on it then let go a plume into evening air. There was a raw hunger in me but the wine was gently easing it. Cheaper than food. The langcoat lay across my pack and I drew a chunk of bread from deep inside a pocket to dunk into the wine. I was down to maybe a hundred francs. It was an Irish busker in Paris who'd told me there was work down in the south. Selling doughnuts on the beaches. Who the fuck would want to eat doughnuts on a beach? The French of course. I knew I couldn't be far from the south coast now. I'd been travelling for days. The town I was sitting in was famous for the manufacture of smokers' pipes. There was mention of it on the *Bienvenue* sign at the town gates and I'd seen a tobacconist's window full of them all shapes and sizes. Magritte would have had a field day denying it.

There was a dark green wood to the far end of the square where the old men were bowling. I could hear distant voices now echoing through the trees with the odd shout and getting closer. From the wood bunches of young people began to appear walking into the village. They were mostly clad in shorts and T-shirts or girls in short summer dresses. The men at the game turned like old dogs wakened from sleep and peered towards the noisy intruders then waited for them to pass before casting the next bool. Suddenly the café was alive with voices.

What would you like Cosmo?

Get me a beer mate! Cheers!

Clive! Quick! Get on the football table!

Julie! Could you get me a Ricard? Fack's sake go on! It only costs about twenny pee!

It was like a sluice had opened upstream of a stagnant pool to send down a rippling babble of noise. More of them flowed into the café. English voices mostly. Before long there was a crowd around my table.

'Allo there mate. Are you looking for Daniel's?

Daniel's? Daniel who?

Daniel Auclaire. Le patron. The ice cream man. I thought maybe you was looking for a job as a vendeur. Down on the beach like. Sorry.

Na it's a'right. I came down lookin for work like. I haven't found a job since I left Scotland. Weeks ago man. What's this about ice cream?

Vendeuring mate. Sur la plage. Daniel makes the ice cream down in the factory and we take it away in the morning to sell it. Only he counts the cornets he gives us so that you can't sell any and keep the francs. Bastard. The money's crap unless you get a really good beach but he gives all them to the French vendeurs. The cunt. Still. Can't complain. You can eat as much ice cream as you want just so long as you don't use up the cornets. Just eat it out the scoop. Yeah. 'S a good laugh down here mate. You only get ten per cent of the money you earn but you can still make enough to get pissed every night.

Whaur dae ye's live?

In the forest mate. Daniel's got a heap of old tents. You just go and pick one up from 'im. Free of charge. See if you can find one with no holes in it. Keeps the mosquitoes out.

Yawoo. I strode to the bar and ordered a fresh cold beer then slung it down my neck and chewed off the last of the bread. I fired up a celebratory Gitane knowing I wouldn't have to be sparse with them. The English were looking at me like I was nuts for smoking the French fags. What the hell. When in France. Smoke the cheapest fags available. I took a drag then let go a plume with a sough of breath.

Aw man. Peace. Guidwill tae aw.

Yeah. Peace to you an all mate. Just be glad we're here and not back in England. Have you seen the papers? There's riots going on in every city. They're burning the place to the fucking ground man.

Giant willow above me in the night breeze. Waving long whispering garlands through Orion's distant blue coals. A bellyful of food and drink and the prospect of working on the beach. Langcoat wrapped around me for sleep. Dreaming of India and Brazil.

* * * * * * * * * * * * * * * *

Auclaire. I clocked the fly-eye on him right away. Big dug at his side everywhere he went. Even in the ice cream factory. Un thug. A ned's a ned. The world o'er and a that. He showed me where I should pitch a tent in the forest among a shanty of canvas then loaded me up with an ice cream box and drove me out to a place called La Croix Val Mer. A crowded tourist beach stretched away to a hill in the distance where villas stood on a rocky pine-clad terrace.

I turned round to ask Auclaire what I was supposed to be doing but he'd driven off. There was a child-like diagram on the front of the box with the prices. 1.50 Fr. next to the cornet with one scoop of ice. 2 Fr. for the double cornet. 2.50 for the doubler with the extra scoop on top. The trebler. The flavours were scrawled in ink marker. Framboise. Citron. Melon. Vanille. Chocolat. Café. Banane. The sun reflected fiercely from white burning sands. I strapped the box around me then set off among the sunbathers with scoop in hand. I felt a bit awkward at first stepping through them until I'd sold one or two then the Confidence Fairy kicked in. Suddenly I could shout in French.

Les Glaces! Les Glaces! Citron! Chocolat! Bana-nanana! Les Glaces Superbes! Vaneeeya! Frambwaaz! Meh-long! Get yer Tootsie Fruitsie! Les Glaces! Give yourself a treat! Get yer gums

> *around a big dripping dome-ended cornet! Fully flavoured! Yummity yum! Come and suck on the end o this! Les Glaces! Ici Les Glaces!*

My Barralandesque sales-pitch was scarcely understood among the multinational holidaymakers but the racket from it was attracting plenty of attention. Here and there a queue would form as I made my way down the beach quickly learning how to scoop and serve up an ice and somehow deal with the lingo and the money. *Une Glace? Quelle prix? Une franc cinquante? Certainement. Quel parfum madame? Citron? Allez merci!* The scoop was starting to make a considerable dent in each of the flavour boxes when a pair of gendarmes appeared either side and huckled me. They oxtered me into a van full of ice cream and doughnut sellers then shipped the lot of us down to the local clink. The gendarmes took us out into a square in the middle of the jail where they'd piled up all the merchandise. One of them yelled *Allez* then they set about a doughnut mountain with batons and boots. They opened a stank and hurled down all the ice cream. It was pure *Crackerjacques.* They had a few riot men on standby in case any of the vendeurs got tetchy about their stuff getting wasted. It was no skin off my nez. The cornets were blootered so I reckoned there was no record of what I'd sold and I could keep all the money. I could tell Auclaire I'd got huckled as soon as I stepped on the beach. Maybe better to let him have just a few francs to keep the scam tight. The gendarmes told me to sign a declaration to take back to Auclaire to let him know I'd witnessed his gear getting minced then the boy on the desk put me in the picture.

> *No Farcheur. It is not allowed you to come in France from Ecosse and sell ices creams here. The mens in the small shops on zis beach get very angry if you do zis. And so you must go back on Ecosse and sell ices creams there because here Auclaire he is bad man he is gangsteur. Maybee you go home and sell ices creams in Edeemboorg Castle or maybee for people who wants to watch for Loch Ness Monsteur. Maybee*

also you can play music for them on your bagpeeps? But now you must go away or we put you in jail. Maybe we take you to prison in Marseilles. There it is very hard.

Auclaire had us back on the beach armed with signed letters from the Mayor of Cogolin. Then followed weeks of ice cream selling and dodging gendarmes and irate café owners. But I was shifting the wares. It would have been pointless getting lifted before the end of the day when all the money was in. Then it was a pleasure to watch Monsieur Plod and his gendarme buddies trashing the ice cream box and pouring the last few meagre drips of les glaces down le stank. Les Fliques were obliged to hand you documentation that let your employer know his gear had been blootered. But it was only date-stamped without a note of the time of day which meant jingle-jangle in the sky-rocket and telling Auclaire the arrest had taken place in the morning when only a handful of pokey-hats had been sold. I opened an account with the Credit Lyonnaise bank down in Cogolin and started storing a few francs for the world trip. Auclaire le gangsteur knew I was on the pauchle but there was nothing he could do. No cornets. No record. He was beginning to dislike me.

At night the football table rattled and the pinball machines thumped and chinged above the babble of crack in Le Café Des Sports. Beer and wine and Ricard flowed like the Finny. A distant silver memory. There was a 40 Fr. menu in Chez Marie restaurant across the road which would have filled you twice over. I was glowing with it and the nourishment of the sun. I thought back on how I'd felt about losing the job at The Smiddy. The sense of loss. Not being able to crack with your buddies every day. Then getting a Swiftbus out of Saints to register with the dole and the boredom months of the postal signings. The flat at Smiddy Row had felt cold and empty during those endless days. Even the giant moose-head failed to cheer me up. Finally climbing aboard the Swiftbus with Sharleen then the disappointment of reaching the city in the valley. Dark Atlantis under a grey sea of drizzle. Now I was glowing. I remembered something that Baxter had shown me once in The Smiddy. He sparked up the oxy-acetylene gun and turned the flame on a piece of iron until it was white hot. Then he switched off the flame and we watched as the iron began to cool. Bright orange then all the way down through the red spectrum to a dull cherry glow. It had reached its original rust-coloured self when a moment later something happened. Without the aid of external heat the iron began to fire itself into a bright red glow again as the atoms within it reconstituted themselves into their original formation and sent out hot energy. Bax told me it was a process called Recalescence. I sat on the pavement and drank down a good measure of wine and felt myself glowing in the balmy night air of Provence. I was recalescent.

* * * * * * * * * * * * * * * *

Rattle of Haven tussocks. Ravens overhead chukk and rasp. They find a tunnel of wind then soar down it one by one. Pivot and tumble on the currents then re-group in the air like a team of mad acrobats waiting for applause.

One impetuous act and your life changes forever. A moment of drunken foolishness. If I hadn't peeled off my clothes and swung naked from a branch in some lantern-lit forest in southern France the course of my life would have flowed down a different path. No Berlin. No Knockhaven. No Botanic Station. No Gravy Star and no Journal Journeys. What are these singular moments that you look back on and reckon to be the point when the stream suddenly veers and carries you away in another direction? If I ever find the Amazonian butterfly that flapped its wings for me I'll hold a Zippo to it.

It was party night in the woods. Julie's birthday. A circle of fifty lanterns glowed. Burning inside cut-down Evian bottles that hung from trees on string. A discarded piano had been discovered in a back lane in Cogolin then trundled along a track through the woods to the camp. Tuneless chords were being banged out of it. Madness.

Somebody was hammering two sticks against an oil drum then a few more joined in beating it with their hands or clinking stones against bottles or anything they could find. The piano player started banging the keys to the drumbeat and soon the rhythm took hold and consumed the whole camp. The rhythm grew a life of its own as pots and kettles were found and struck. We swigged on strong red wine and tooted on joints and chillums of Morocco's finest. Ye olde Metaphysical Tobacco. The drumming patterns weaved this way and that until the rhythm would return to its original single beat with cries going up.

ULL! ULL! ULL! ULL! ULL! ULL!

A circle of faces in a glimmering pool of light. A forest under the spell of rhythm. I threw up a new challenge for the chant as every voice around me responded.

een-gonyama een-gonyama

EEN-GONYAMA! EEN-GONYAMA!

ya-boh! yaboh! invooboo!

YA-BOH! YA-BOH! INVOOBOO!

oomabwabba! oomabwabba! oomabwabba! oomabwabba!

OOMABWABBA! OOMABWABBA! OOMABWABBA! OOMABWABBA!

nee-nee-nee-nee-nee-nee-nee!

NEE-NEE-NEE-NEE-NEE-NEE-NEE!

Then I picked my moment.

Zing a Bom! Zing a Bom! Zing a Bom! Zing a Bom!

The volume was rising all the way through as we went pure tribal and I felt my heart pound and spine tingle with Strath pride and memory as the cry was returned from forty open throats.

ZING A BOM! ZING A BOM! ZING A BOM! ZING A BOM!

Daniel Auclaire's house was two hundred yards away. Just behind the ice cream factory. He rolled apart from his Vietnamese wife moaning *merde merde* then reached under his pillow. Night after night he'd been down to the camp to scream his disapproval at the noise usually just a cassette player going and a few drunk voices. This was *real* noise. Baden-Powell's hippopotamus cry from forty open throats. He fingered cold steel under his pillow then ran his fingers along the barrel until he felt the reassuring smoothness of the pistol's shiny wooden handle. Caressing it like touchstone. Strange an instrument that could cause mayhem and split bone and blood and noise and sorrow should have such a calming tactile effect. Then the gun began to speak. *Feel me Daniel. Run your fingers along my smooth curves. Yes. Slowly. That's it. Ah. Oui. Mhm. Je t'aime. Those bastards in the camp. For you they are making life hell. Fucking Anglais. You know they are screwing you of course Daniel. The beaches are busier this year than ever before and every night they come back with takings lower than expected. They are stealing from you. It is the only explanation. Then by night they make noise and drink until dawn with the money they steal from you. No sleep for us. And that tall one. The Ecossais. Him with the long coat who look like a scarecrow. Always getting arrested. How come he survive with no money at all? Let's go down in the forest now Daniel and we can give them a big fright. No need to kill any of them we can just laugh at their stupid faces when they look down their stupid English noses at you pointing me at them and then shit running down their legs. Maybe even fire me into the air and watch them jump and their whole bowels empty into their pants. Haw haw. Listen to them. What kind of a crazy noise is this? When was the last time you had a good night's sleep? And you hard working man of beezness. Fools and thieves. They make a clown out of you.*

Auclaire swung both legs out of bed dragging the pistol out from under the pillow then thrust his arms into a shirt and pulled on a pair of jeans with the shooter still in his grasp.

The rhythm had inspired a desire in me to remove clothing. In the heat of the Med nights I was usually shirtless under the langcoat anyway and removed it swung it round and round my head. I was in the centre of the ring and the crowd began to cheer.

FAWKWAH! FAWKWAH!

I was in my element as the boots and strides came off and so down to the skiddies.

Yawoo! Primeval disco! Zing a bom hey! Shanny ya bass!

Then the skiddies were off as I leapt up and down in the ring and willie-flapped freely like a clapper on a bell. There was a kind of laugh/cheer/laugh/cheer as I clambered into a tree and began swinging from a branch. Looking down on a circus of half-lit roaring faces swinging from side to side.

The scene below freeze-framed and fell silent. Then a high-pitched screaming French and every head turning towards it. Auclaire walked into the centre with the pistol held out in his right hand spitting out violent Gallic curses. He swung around with the gun pointed at the circle of heads. The crowd was transfixed with fear. I realised I was just above the light out of his view and gripped hard to the branch. Then he raised the gun above his head. There was a bang and a flash and the sound of ripping leaves as the bullet tore through the branches an inch or two away from me.

Who can account for the mechanics of the human body? It didn't happen immediately on the bang. Not quite. There was a second or two's delay. Then a sudden squirt of diarrhoeic shite escaped from me like a fulmar's spew from a sea crag. It descended in a brown string wavering and spinning slightly on the updraught. Glinting gold in candlelight as it fell. Then it landed square on the centre of Auclaire's head. He stood there in disbelief rubbing it out of his eyes.

Qu'est-ce qui se passe? Merde! MERDE!

He glared into the crowd suspecting it had been thrown across him rather than falling from a loosened sphincter somewhere in the foliage above. He held the shooter out in both hands and roared.

WHO MAKE THIS? QUI? QUI? VOUS? YOU THINK THIS FUNNY? Ih? IH?

Jerking the gun dangerously into a sea of faces. The crowd were anxiously staring at Daniel and too worried about his next move to look up at the dangling jobby-spurter and give the game away. But between the nerves and the shit-fright and the strain my arms and fingers could stand it no longer. I let go and fell down beside Auclaire. By the time my feet hit the ground I was off. Pure *Roadrunner*. He took up the chase and saw a great white arse charging through bushes and trees into the depths of the wood and came after me firing shots that tore through the foliage but I moved swiftly enough to gain distance from him and get away. I left the edge of the wood and into rows of grapevine that made their way up a long slope. Running on hard baked earth until I could run no more and lay down naked and wheezing. There came a distant voice from the edge of the wood.

Ecossais! A partir de maintenant you are feeneeshed! C'est terminé! TERMINÉ!

Lying on the baked earth the wheezing slowed as I gained breath. I was shaking. My whole frame began to convulse. Out of the quivering gasping frame came a laugh. And then a hoot. I began to chortle and rock as I lay there in the vines. Picturing my great white arse mounted on a plaque next to rhinos' and lions' heads above Auclaire's fireplace. I couldn't help it. I tell you. I just hooted. And hooted and hooted and hooted and laughed myself to sleep lying there scuddy in the Provence vines.

Julie and Cosmo found me next day and brought my gear to me. Shouting across the vines until we found each other. We walked into Cogolin and le Café Des Sports was full of ice cream refugees from the war-torn forest of the night before. Everybody was making plans for their next move.

Fuck this man. Oi'm going back to Ingiland. Thought I'd ea'n enough cash to make a trip to India but there's no way Oi'm working for that fucking lunatic Daniel for the rest of the summah. Oi've 'ad enough.

Wot the fack do you wanna go back to England fowah? They're buhning the place to the fucking ground man. Bristol. Brixton. Liverpool. Fatcha's policies are causing riots.

Ee-ah. Listen up! Oi reckon we should all gow to the police en masse and repo't 'im. Auclaire. Fucking 'ell. 'E could've killed us all. 'Specially Fawkwah. Wot d'you reckon Fawkwah?

Reckon? I reckon I'll be as far as I can out frae this fuckin place before nightfall. I'm still hearing Auclaire's parting words after he'd fired the bullets at me. C'est terminé. My French isnae so great but I reckon he means I'm either sacked or I'm dead. Maybe both. And fuck going to the gendarmes. Foreign law's a funny business. It's au revoir Cogolin for me.

Where'll you go?

Don't know guys. Brazil maybe. Eventually.

Oh well. Good luck mate.

I pulled on the pack and headed straight for the Credit Lyonnaise bank to draw out my couple of thousand francs of hard-earned ice cream money then climbed aboard a bus for Frejus where the nearest train station was. Someone'd mentioned there was a load of apple work in a fruit town called Cavaillon so I headed up there and trawled the markets and orchards looking for graft but there was an apple war on. The farmers were heading into town in the evening with cartloads of them and dumping them in the square in some kind of a price protest then heading back out to the country. The police were reacting by turning up an hour or two later and tear-gassing and clubbing bewildered café-goers who happened to be sitting ankle-deep in spilled apples. A collection of drifters from a riverside camp were constantly scouring the place with their hands out at the begging. There were one or two agony-buskers who would stand on a pile of broken glass on a street corner with hand held out. I'd found a hollow among some willows to sleep in at night and dossed down with the langcoat wrapped around me and a makeshift Uncle Malky gripped in the paws. Nightmare. There was a decisive *fuck this* voice from deep within so I slung on the pack and headed for the train station noticing a café with a 30 Fr. menu on the way and stepped in to fill the gut for a journey and there waiting for a meal with a bottle of red wine stuck between them on the table were Julie and Cosmo.

* * * * * * * * * * * * * * * *

I let go a whoop and the two faces turned then laughed. Julie and Cosmo they made a right pair. She was a Brighton babe with bottled blonde hair and Cosmo was this kind of renegade intellectual who had flunked Oxford then set off travelling. I think his faither was some top-dog quack in Harley Street. Cosmo'd a battered straw hat on him and let out a cry.

> *Oh no! The Naked Highlander! It's Primeval Disco Man!*

> *Aye. Very good. The naked bullet dodger. Phantom tree-shitter of the Cote D'Azure. At your service. How the fuck are yez?*

Julie and Cosmo were good crack and I liked them so I joined their table and found out the Cogolin forest had been cleared out by the gendarmes the day after I'd left. We were gassing away when I noticed an empty chair and a half-empty glass of red wine. I was on the point of asking who it belonged to when a dark-haired girl sat down. Cosmo's voice was soft London.

> *This is our friend she's from Scotland too. She turned up with her mate looking for work the day you scarpered.*

Cosmo was about to do the formals but I found myself jumping in.

> *Hi. Where ye from?*

> *Up north. My parents moved there last year. It's a bit off the beaten track you probably wouldn't know it.*

> *Where at?*

> *A place called Balshannoch.*

> *Balsha? Balshannoch? For the love o' goodness! I went to school in the place. I come from St Ronans. The Saints. High Drums to be exact! Hell's bells can you beat that?*

> *St Ronans? I've been in the Black Bull Inn there. Do you know it?*

> *Know it? I'm a fully-fledged member of Auntie Bell's Barmy Army. The Bull Brigade.*

> *I've only been in a couple of times. It seemed quite nice but there was this woman making hen noises.*

> *That was just the Hen-Wife. She gets a wee bit excited sometimes when she loses her eggs but she's harmless enough.*

Cosmo and Julie were looking at me like I'd just grown a set of horns. So I explained about the Hen-Wife then told them about Big Chief Simpson. But I realised I was rushing it because I wanted to get back to talking to the girl again. I was a wee bit nervous too I could tell because my jaw felt a bit tight. Her eyes were dark pools.

What brings you to France then?

Och. I fancied doing something a bit different this summer. We were travelling around Europe then somebody told us about the ice cream place.

What happened to your pal?

She went home when she heard about the gunman in the forest. Were you there when it happened yourself?

You could say that. I nearly took a bullet up the arse.

Oh well. So you must be the famous Farchar then?

That's right. I'll be Farchar then. And who'll you be?

I'll be Ola.

Ola?

Yeah. Ola.

That sounds nice. Kinda northern maybe?

My mother's from Orkney. Originally anyway. Dad's from Sutherland. What about yourself?

It's a bit of a long story. Clydebank first. Then the Saints. But I suppose I'm Hielan-blooded through and through. My mammy was from Islay and Da was a Strath man but he went to sea. They settled in Clydebank for some reason.

It's funny eh Farchar?

What is?

Sitting here drinking wine in France and talking about home. I suppose you think of it a bit differently when it's such a long way away. Home.

There was something about the way she dwelled on the word *home*. Something rushed through me that I'd never experienced before. It caught me unawares. A great wave of emotion and sitting there in the café I'd to take a deep breath to stop it rising up from inside me. It was a realisation. I suddenly knew then that I'd never really known the true feeling of home. Da's disappearance. Rapunzel. The lightning strike. Crazy Uncle Duncan and the cold sandstone mansion. The Smiddy Row. Atlantis Raintown and Cogolin. All these places. They had all just been stops on a journey. Maybe a journey that would never end and I'd just keep on going round and round and would never know the full meaning of the word that Ola had spoken so plainly and warmly. *Home.* The sound of it full of security and comfort. How many of us ever truly go home? I looked over at Ola's dark eyes like pools. Pools in the Caldon gorge where leaves drift down into the chasm to glide across the backs of the silver Atlantic beauties. Sure I loved the Strath and Saints and Dunreoch and the gorge and the Bull and all the crack that went with it. But I was never yet truly home. And world adventures were great. But to be home. That must be really something. I kicked myself out of the dwam as we ordered more and more and more red wine and started to have a real good hoot.

It was only small talk between us but that was what I first thought of Ola. The way she spoke words painted pictures for me. Eyes deeper than the pools of the Caldon gorge. Ola of the light. Ola of the wind and the sorrows and the rain.

We decided on Berlin. Nobody really knew why it just kind of sounded good. Fuckin good Lou Reed album too. We decided we'd all meet up at Checkpoint Charlie whenever we got there and that sounded even better. Julie and Cosmo hitched ahead with me and Ola behind. After half an hour they got a lift then the two of us an hour later and we were off. Lift followed wait followed lift with a beer in this village or a coffee in that city as we thumbed our way through day and night of a late continental summer.

Up to Lyons then Geneva. Along the side of a great blue lake that took you from fertile lowlands into the Swiss Highlands. Just like Loch Mhor straddling the boundary of the great Highland faultline. Over mountain passes with clean blue skies to industrial cities on the other side. North to Karlsruhe up through Germany. Five days' hitch across Europe with a girl I'd never met before who lived just a couple of miles along the Shanny road. We seemed easy in each other's company.

What is it you do Ola? At home I mean.

Nothing much just now. I was studying before.

Studying? Where? What doing?

Music. Violin. In the Royal Scottish.

Violin? That's brilliant.

Yeah violin and cello. Dad's a fiddler. I specialised in Gaelic fiddle music.

I didn't know there was any Gaelic fiddle music.

Oh yeah. Loads of Scottish music comes from Gaelic songs. People would learn the tunes on the fiddle. Then the song-collectors came and wrote music to them.

As we travelled through a strange land Ola told me more about the song-collectors. One of them had been a cattle-dealer called Fraser who'd doubled as a government spy. He went around the country mixing and drinking with the people and learning the Jacobite songs. Then he passed on information to the government about where the rebel strongholds were until it all ended in the awful slaughter after Culloden. But Fraser kept his store of songs and passed them down to his son who transposed them into classical violin music to try and make his fortune in the Walter Scott days. The young Fraser had sailed to Connacht as a King's man to wage war on the Gaels there in the name of Britannia and the One True Faith and took some of their music too. When he came home he drove the people from the land and replaced them with sheep. It was all around the time the dragoons had raided St Ronans and the informer's testimony had seen Turk's ancestor hung and beheaded. Ola had a bit of Gaelic from her Sutherland Da and sang in a clear ringing voice. I only had a smattering of the old language myself but the songs she sang by the autobahn reached inside and haunted me with pictures of ruins and desolate glens and sun-dappled lochans. Stories and music and eyes like the Caldon. Ola had it all.

Dark secrets and spying and opposing ideologies. We were heading towards East Germany. Slept by the roadside and talked and had a few laughs. Cooked our meals on a wee gas stove. Northwards and on up through West Germany and through Hannover to Wolfsburg on the edge of the Iron Curtain.

We caught our lift into the Eastern Bloc from a skinny long-haired specky hippy called Dedlev. He was driving a VW Beetle. An acoustic guitar on the front seat had this little ballerina doll stuck to the top of it. A wee figure about ten inches high with a white ballet dress was poised pirouette fashion fixed to the top of the soundbox. Don't ask me why. Dedlev told us he was making his way to West Berlin to marry the girl he loved.

When we got to the Iron Curtain it was fading twilight. We pulled up at the barrier. Four Red Army guards had the three of us out of the car and into this little cabin and they huddled round closely studying the ballerina on the guitar. They barked in German at Dedlev and to my surprise he started barking back at them so's not to take any shit. For a specky hippy in charge of a guitar with such ludicrous decoration he was obviously nobody's fool. The guards were pointing at me and Ola and firing questions at Dedlev and he pointed back and spoke firmly then the three of us got our passports back and clambered into the VW.

I looked back at the guards at the checkpoint bothy with their tired expressions and ill-fitting coats and caps. They were shabby imitations of pictures I'd seen of militarists in the *Sputnik* magazine Commie Bill had sold me back in the Bisley Bar. Bright coloured photos of stern men wearing layers of medals. They'd looked like the Commie General puppets on *Thunderbirds*. Icons of a Soviet Empire whose roads we now travelled along as we made our way through The Corridor to reach West Berlin. Capitalist island stranded in a Soviet sea. All we could see of the socialist world were the lights of the occasional high-rise flat or maisonette peering over the roadway. Land of concrete. Communist Cumbernauld.

* * * * * * * * * * * * * * * *

Dedlev dropped us in the centre of Berlin at midnight then we tried kipping down in the main railway station. Berlin Zoo. Fuckin appropriate. The place was full of barking primates. Nutter after screaming nutter approached us or just stood there a while and stared with strange menace. We were sitting with the packs behind us on a tiled wall.

Ola had fallen asleep on my shoulder when a madman pulled up on a silent motor scooter. It had no engine and he was in the saddle propelling it around the station with his foot scudding along the ground. He'd a mane of boggin frizzy hair that was collected in bunches with brightly coloured clothes pegs. He'd some of them clipped to his ears and one in each nostril and a stack of them stuck in his clarty beard. He'd a long tattered coat on him and so did I. Maybe that was the attraction. He sat there on the saddle of the stationary scooter and looked straight into my eyes. Channelling messages from the outland. Eyeballing me. Transmission of crazy signals picked up from some wormhole in the heart of a dark galaxy.

Something was about to happen. There was some kind of energy in the air and a trembling in my lower stomach. It felt like the time I'd raised my shovel on the shores of the reservoir and dug into the skeleton. Different scene. Same feeling. I tried to look away from the wild boggin man then realised I couldn't. I kept looking straight into him. The longer I looked the more familiar his strange look seemed to become. He was silent but somehow he was saying something from behind his eyes. Something I could understand without explaining in words. I broke away from the gaze for a few seconds to look at Ola but she was still asleep. I looked back at the decorated man on the scooter. Then it began. I blinked hard a couple of times thinking my tired vision was the cause of it. A glimmer of light was beginning to radiate from him. A sort of halo that surrounded the top half of his body. It burned brighter and brighter into a white glaring light as he gave me one last look then turned and foot-propelled the scooter back towards the main concourse of the station. There was a white flash of magnesium light across the concourse as he rolled out of sight to the far side of the station. I leapt on to my feet and roared.

HEY YOU! COME BACK HERE! HEY! YOU! MISTER!

Ola woke up in a panic striking her pockets to make sure nothing had been swiped.

What's happened? Did something happen Fach?

Ola! Fuck! This is weird! There was this tramp a minute ago a right minger. He was on a scooter. He was looking at me. There was this kind of a light shining out of him. Then there was a flash when he rode away.

It's only a dream Farchar. You must've nodded off and had a dream.

Naw. It wisnae a dream. It was real. He went that way. On his scooter.

Well funnily enough. I was having a weird dream myself. And then.

Then what?

Ach. Nothing. It was just a dream. Come on honey. This place is getting to us. It's full of mad vibes. Let's go before we end up as mental as the rest of them.

She saw I was affected and took me by the arm. We left the Zoo Bahnhof and walked into the balmy night air of Berlin. As soon as the U-Bahn started up in the morning we'd catch a train to Kochstrasse where Checkpoint Charlie was. Ola put her hand up to my brow which had chilled over with freezing sweat. I put my arms around her shoulders and we hugged close and I felt her draining the fear out of me and sending it away to a distant land. It was the first time we'd hugged and she felt so good.

Jesus Ola. That man. There was something on him. Maybe nobody else could see it but I could. A thing. A halo.

Christ on a bike? Or Simon Templar maybe.

Aye maybe. But. It wasn't a tin-foil halo like you'd get in a nativity play. It was more like light pouring out of his body. Something like that happened to me and two pals once up on the top of Dunreoch in the mist. Me and Deke and the Turk. There were big dark shadows above us that made the light around our bodies glow bright. Then when we came down from the hill and told some of these old rambler folk in the Bull about it they laughed and said it was only the Brocken Spectre. Something to do with the mist and the condition of the light. That's what scooter-man was like. In the middle of the station only much brighter.

So it was him then.

Who?

The Brocken Spectre himself. Did you not know the Brocken mountain was in Germany? He's come down off the mountain on his scooter to buy up all the clothes pegs in Berlin and take them back to the Brocken to hang out his washing. He hasn't done his laundry for years and that's why he's mingin. There. Simple. That's it explained.

Ye're mad woman.

Aye. And you're the one who's just seen an angel on a scooter.

We had a laugh then walked around and around the centre of the city using a half-bombed steeple for a landmark until daylight when the subway trains began to roll then made our way under the city from Zoo to Kochstrasse. As we walked towards Checkpoint Charlie Julie and Cosmo were reaching it from the other direction.

Farchar! Ola! We've found a gaff! We've found somewhere to stay for the four of us!

We grouped into a huddle then danced up and down for a wee bit. I looked up and saw a border checkpoint with cabins and barriers and razorwire in a gap in The Wall. There were warnings in German and French and English written on great wooden signs with American and French and British national flags printed on them. Behind the barriers and across a no-man's-land was a restricted view of the east with decrepit looking factories and high-rise blocks of towering concrete. Above it all soared a great slender concrete tower that reached into the sky where a giant orb rested on the top of it. Windows looked out from the centre of the orb and a huge antenna reached from the top of it high towards the passing clouds. The orb could easily have cast itself adrift from its great concrete stem and floated into the cosmos to become some massive pod on the cover of a Sci-Fi paperback.

The west side of the frontier was buzzing with traffic droning on all sides of us and a kiosk had just opened which was dispensing tins of morning beer to a raggle of boozy-looking Germans and clean-cut American servicemen gathered on the pavement. A giant building of glass and concrete where people moved behind windows and rattling printing presses carried the letters of a media empire on its façade. AXEL SPRINGER. Vandals had thrown tins of paint across the doorway and here and there it was spattered with the time-honoured Ⓐ symbol. Then Cosmo pointed over the wall at the great orb up on its stem.

See that thing there? That's the TV Tower. If you watch closely you'll notice the sphere slowly spinning round. There's supposed to be a restaurant inside it and it's Communism's showpiece. But wait until you see it at sunset! The guy who designed it was a secret Christian and he constructed it so that the setting sun would reflect against the windows of the orb to make this giant crucifix of light! Then he disappeared. Either a bullet in the head or Siberia!

Within a minute or two we were walking along a broad road which ran parallel to the wall. The busy street scene at the checkpoint gave way to dark derelict buildings and fields of rubble with a broad cracked street running through where only the occasional car droned to a roadway distance. There was the fragmented entrance of a blitzed railway station that had stood ruined since the allied assault on the Reichstag. I opened the mind-eye back through time and watched a group of Red Army soldiers celebrate beside their tank in the station's smoking ruins. Finding a bottle of schnapps in the rubble and performing a Russian folk dance.

We walked on past a tall square block which had a giant cartoon mural of Archie the Anarchist painted on the end wall. Archie was cloaked and had an evil grin on him. He was holding a round black comic-style bomb in his hand with a smoking fuse. Like Inspector Clouseau's *bimb*. The doorway to the building had bright coloured letters. KUKUK. Julie spoke in her Brighton voice.

That's the Cuckoo Squat. It's the biggest in Berlin. Somebody told us to try in there for somewhere to stay but there's no room. So we've found this other one.

We turned off Oranienstrasse into Lindenstrasse and I gaped down its gloomy corridor. To my left the street was closed off by The Wall standing twenty feet high and throwing a shadow halfway across an empty road. The Wall ran parallel with the street before turning at right-angles to make a dead end. The right-hand side of the street was dominated by a giant building that had been a fire station. From windows high in the brickwork banners were hanging with resistance messages and here and there a black flag with the white  . Even as a new arrival you could feel the air was charged with the electricity of political danger. Cosmo and Julie'd met a Bavarian anarchist called Tomas who'd happened by when they'd been waiting on us at Checkpoint Charlie then he'd shown them to a room for us at the fire station squat.

We climbed the staircase to the first floor and past toilets the size of the Kelvin Hall. Long urinal troughs lined the walls and dozens of washbasins yawned towards the back of the building that had once been the hive of Berlin's firefighters. Then we found our room on the first floor where two sets of bunks stood against opposite walls. To the front of the room a set of twin windows looked right over The Wall into the no-man's-land between West and East. A guard tower looked straight into the room. Two communist soldiers slouched with rifles on their backs.

I hadn't realised until then that our ideologies were separated not by one but by two Berlin walls. Between them was a garden of death. Rows of razorwire. Freshly planted mines. Fountains of triangular bullets that would shoot up and rip through human flesh and bone should anyone happen by to activate them. Should an escapee somehow manage to dance their way through this evilly designed It's-A-Knockout course there were still the guards in the tower to reckon with. Shoot to kill. I hung from the window and waved towards the guard tower and to my surprise one of them waved back. The Cold War was beginning to thaw.

Berlin sweated under sultry late summer heat. Hot sulphurous skies added to the intensity as day by day more armed police in their green uniforms made their presence obvious in the streets around the squats of Kreuzberg. They were waiting for the September go-ahead from the authorities that would allow them to charge the buildings and clear out the occupiers. Tomas had loaded his room with dozens of cobble stones for missiles. Pickshafts were freely available in hallways of the fire station like umbrellas in a stand.

Things cooled off in the evenings as the sun disappeared into a carbon monoxide smog. Around five o'clock the army of armed police would get loused off in time for their tea as the streets returned to normal again. No doubt one evening they'd catch us all by surprise. The Cuckoo Squat down the road had its own chamber orchestra so we used to go there sometimes and lug-in to a recital. Ola got up and played some tunes once and it was great. Jigs and reels and a slow air or two that would've brought a tear to a glass eye. She could play the classical stuff too. Then we got a loan of a violin and I got a hold of a guitar and we headed down the city. After a few bawling matches and slappy fights with angry German buskers over territory we finally found a good spot where we could turn in a few Deutschmarks without any bother from our rivals. We could both sing and built up a fair wee repertoire too. The old Scottish tunes like 'MacPherson's Farewell' or 'Bonnie Ship The Diamond' would always turn a head or two because they sounded that bit different. We played Clash and Rezillos too. And Loudie Wainwright was always a handy source for me on the guitar. Coins and notes and the occasional cigarette or lump of hash would find their way into the langcoat spread on the pavement.

We were cookin by gas as your granny might say. Julie found a job in an Irish bar. A real Irish bar. In the days before Irish bars became *Irish* bars. Cosmo'd somehow managed to argue his way on to the DDR welfare system and was reeling in a hefty Bundes-giro at the end of each week. For an Oxford Don he was a dab-hand at playing the system. Then to pull in extra Deutschmarks we sold our blood and plasma to the city hospital. Our pockets would momentarily expand until we'd blow it on mad weekend sessions.

We drank in the Rat Trap. Down in the gloom of Oranienstrasse between Turkish cafés. Through the doorway down to a dark cellar that had a photographic mural depicting a recently attempted presidential assassination. It was constructed in a series of images as you walked in. The first one showed Ronald Reagan stepping from a car. Then a commotion as he began to fall. Security men surrounding his body. By the time you reached the bar Reagan was on the deck with a bullet in his body and blood on the sidewalk. The club was awash with punks and there was the time I stood at the bar and said hello to Jayne County. Rubbing shoulders with the transsexual mighty.

Sometimes down in the city I'd see the man on the engineless scooter with his decoration of clothes pegs and I could see there was still a bit of light shining out of him. I began to notice it on a few other down-and-outs as well but the intensity on them was less. I kept it from Ola and the rest of them knowing they would only laugh at me. But the vagrant men or women who had the Brocken Spectre. Often they would gaze directly into my eyes. There was a look of understanding or familiarity in it that I couldn't put my finger on.

* * * * * * * * * * * * * * * *

Saturday afternoon and in the mood for my own company. I headed out on the forty-inch shanks across Berlin in the rain. Walking for miles. Along The Wall then down a long boulevard. Over an endless set of playing fields till I was below a towering grey structure finding a wooden door that led underneath. I walked towards the light at the far end of the narrow passage then out into a great concrete bowl. A grassy field was in the centre surrounded by an athletics track. The steps that led to the high platform were as steep as the heather slopes of Dunreoch. I stood there on the platform looking down on the arena and opened up the mind-eye. I felt the heat of the Olympic flame burning down from its torch above and heard the roaring *Zeig Heils* from forty thousand open throats directed at the place where I stood. Black swastikas on blood-red banners. Hitler was standing there in front of me saluting the crowd so I took a backstep and with all the passion in me swung a forceful right boot square into his racially-pure buttocks to send him rising four feet into the air then sprawling into the seating below. Oh but that a good boot up the arse could somehow find its way back some forty-odd years. Maybe it's a peculiarly Scottish thing that a swift toeing in the anal district is thought to be an act of teaching place and humility.

But ponder if the Fach's swinging size twelve could somehow have reached back through a channel in time and momentarily materialised to send wee Adolf up into the air then crashing down into the crowd below. Somebody in the crowd points and laughs and slowly at first it begins to spread around the stadium. Sniggers are suppressed in fear but it only makes it all the harder not to hoot out loud. The people are beginning to tremble and shake with hands held over their mouths as an embarrassed Adolf flails around in the seating. There is a lady in a fur coat. Pressure builds in her cheeks as they fill up with air. She can stand it no longer as a great farting rasp escapes from her pursed lips. Everyone around her begins to hoot. Soon the whole stadium is rocking in hysterics at Hitler's misfortune. His head flushes beetroot as he picks himself up and tries to compose himself on the platform wiping grime off with a leather-gloved hand. But even his security men around him have begun to break out in uncontrollable smirks and they turn aside and fold up. Ruination. Humiliation. Adolf sneaks out of the stadium and retreats to a shack high in the Alps never to be seen again. Lake fishing and log fires. A bit of landscape painting. Spending the rest of his days in silent contemplation. The world is spared. No Clydebank Blitz. No Leningrad siege. No Dresden hellfire. No Auschwitz and no Hiroshima. With a single boot I've aborted the Thousand Year Reich that was mutating and developing in the poisonous fluids of the fascist womb. Hitler had dropped his kegs to his ankles and climbed on top of a prostrate nation to waggle his wee hairy arse then duffed his load into an insecure and depressed industrial economy and the awful baby had begun to grow. But in the end there was only the triumph of Jesse Owens to stun the crowd. I stand and watch as the great black athlete breaks the tape to take gold. I find myself with a broad grin on me and the Fuehrer departing for the staircase in fury at Owens' victory. He takes a last glowering look at me up on the platform so I flick him the vee's.

Hey you! Gerrit up ye! Ya wee Nazi! Ya wee shite!

They were saying that Scotch whisky in the East was only about three squid a bottle. Just so long as you paid for it with dollars. The communist economy was hungry for western currency.

What you had to do was catch a U-Bahn to Friedrichstrasse where they sold the stuff in the station before you reached the checkpoint up in the concourse. It seemed discreet for only one of us to go so we cut the cards and the Fach drew a deuce. I donned Michael Caine's specs and the Harry Palmer raincoat then made my way to the station. Hand shaking as I paid the fare through the kiosk window then descended steps to the U-Bahn.

Standing on the empty eastbound platform for the first time. The carriage rolled in and spewed a load of passengers out on to the Kochstrasse platform then I stepped inside as the doors hissed and banged closed and we rolled down the dark tunnel into the Soviet empire. Fumbling a roll of dollars in a sweating hand. The train slowed and I waited for the light of Friedrichstrasse station.

The U-Bahn pulled up slowly at a platform where light shone down from a vent high above. A derelict booth with bricked-up windows stood in the middle of a concrete island littered with ancient rubbish and dust. The shaft of silver light made dim grey ghosts of two soldiers who paced up and down with rifles on their backs. The red stripe on their caps was a rude disturbance in a scene of total monochrome. One of the soldiers walked along looking in the carriage windows. He stopped to wipe grime from the glass and looked straight at me. I looked back. Fuck. He held the stare. I held my look. A gremlin was playing keepie-uppie with my heart but I had to stay cool. Thirty seconds passed like an hour. The soldier looked away then waved his hand towards the front of the train.

Carriage jolted and rolled into tunnel blackness with screeching wheels. I stepped out at Friedrichstrasse and found the bevvy kiosk in a tunnel at the top of the stair. A glum wifie in a pinafore stood in front of an array of bottles. Schnapps and voddie and kirsch and cognac. I scanned my eyes across them looking for the barley-bree while the wifie snapped at me. *Bitte? Ja?* My eyes eventually fell on a gold bottle with a red label. Striding across it was the dapper Johnnie Walker in his red tunic and top-hat and jodhpurs. Holding his monocle before him. I pointed up at Johnnie and nodded. The drink-wifie reached up and was about to pick a bottle from the shelf when I saw something that made my heart leap. I began bawling.

> *Nein! Nein! No Johnnie Walker! Nein missus! Nein Johnnie Walker! The other wan! Gie me the other wan!*

She looked puzzled and angry as I pointed furiously along the shelf. Then her hand rested on it. *Ja! Ja! That wan! Goot!* A bottle shaped like a whisky still banged down eye-level on the counter in front of me. A dark green label depicted the steep walls of a mossy gorge with a white foaming waterfall. Below the gorge was a quaint hand-drawn distillery with its pagoda tower and a screw of smoke rising from the chimney. The smoke made its way up the side of the picture to write a legend in scrolled letters on the sky above the waterfall. STRATHFINGLAS. Finest Scotch Whisky. I shouted up at the woman. *Svei! Svei! Gie me svei bottles missus!* She could see I was happy and a smile broke across her face as she placed down another bottle of the Finny dram. I handed over the American dollars and picked up the bottles and made for the platform with the forty-inch shanks on steady steam. The woman was leaning over the counter shouting after me and laughing.

> *Proust Schottlander! Goot whiskee! Trink! Trink!*

As I walked through the bustle of the East German station I could hear the falls roaring into the gorge a thousand miles away. The fear of being in the East alone left me as I spun on my heels and held both bottles up at the wifie and felt a roar rising from deep inside.

YAWOO! SHANNIE YA BASS!

She was cackling through broken teeth. The Cold War was definitely thawing.

* * * * * * * * * * * * * * * *

> *In the ancient Highland village of St Ronans they know a thing or two about making good whisky. And so they should they've been doing it for centuries. The mountain water which goes into making this uniquely flavoured dram sings its own legendary song. This is because the silver streams that converge into the River Finglas are said to be the love songs of five beautiful Highland maidens calling from the surrounding hills. This is the magic ingredient which will make you sing the praises of Strathfinglas. We're sure you'll agree. It's pure harmony.*

The return train rolled through the derelict station where the soldier had eyeballed me. I was having a laugh at the nonsense on the label then stuffed the bottles down my breeks in case the Western tax police were hanging around at Kochstrasse. Maidens' love songs ma erse. What about the haggard crones and the snakes and the death and the pestilence? The Finny dram was produced for the foreign market and it was seldom you could get your hands on it even in the Strath. The distillery had introduced security and punishment measures that the Stasi through the wall would have been proud of. Shoplifting in Tehran would be the better option.

In years to come the distillery's international owners would squeeze the last few drops of life-water from the copper stills before reducing the place to a field of rubble in the wee dark hours. Murdering a single malt in a single night. Berlin was my last ever taste of the Finny dram. We perished the two bottles of it in no time at all then I went through to the East bold as you like to bag another brace and we drank them too. We had a water fight in the washrooms then fell around singing for a bit then cut up a cardboard box and got hold of an ink marker to hold up messages for the guards across in the tower and watched them through a set of binoculars. The guards had a set of binoculars between them and read the signs and waved back. Then we hit on the idea of producing a play in front of the windows for the guards. Various subtitles were scrawled up on available cardboard. Signs with GUTTEN TAG! or ACHTUNG! or MEIN GOTT! or LIEBEFRAUMILCH! Displaying our sensitive understanding and command of the German language.

We got a hold of Tomas's stereo from the next room and hung the speakers out the window with Kraftwerk on full blast for the soundtrack. Then the play began. The action was mostly in a ludicrous mime style and was supposed to be this kind of a murder farce about a man going to his work while his wife's having an affair. So in one window you've got Cosmo in a set of overalls with a hammer and he's hammering away rhythmically like he's a human robot working at this invisible conveyor belt while Ola stands over supervising him with a clipboard and she's got this moustache drawn on her with the felt pen to make her look like a fascist gaffer. Then in the next window Julie appears in a black bra and pants and opens an invisible door to a man and it's me and I'm wearing a peaked cap and my trousers are half down. A sign is held up. GUTTEN TAG! She pours us both a drink and we hold up another sign. LIEBEFRAUMILCH! We look across at the guard tower and the soldiers are trying to wrestle the binoculars away from each other for a closer look at Julie's body. She disappears from their view between the windows and takes off the bra. Then she reappears in front of the window. ACHTUNG! The soldiers across the way are scrapping over their only set of regulation Red Army binoculars. Julie's in front of the window and starts to slip off the pants so's she's entirely in the naddy only Ola's ducked down and she's holding a piece of cardboard across Julie's fanny with VERBOTTEN! written on it. Then the workman comes home and appears in our window and finds me embracing his naked wife with my breeks half down so he begins robotically bashing me over the head with the hammer. I fall down dead and as I do so I grab the VERBOTTEN! card and Julie stands there with her fanny bared giving it a Hill's Angel pose. We all disappear by dropping down below the window for a curtain call then the four of us stand up naked and take a bow. The Army guards in the tower are still trying to yank the only set of binoculars in the tower from each other's grasp. We take a second bow and the two soldiers in the tower applaud and wave their arms for an encore. Ola and me do a naked duet with the fiddle and guitar with one of us in each window. End of show. In a few years time The Wall would come down for good. Somebody somewhere in the world today has that tiny fragment of concrete coloured red by a spray-painted message.

OLA I LOVE YOU
BONNIE STRATHFINGLAS FOREVER

Berlin. You broke my nose and took out two of my teeth when your policemen laid siege to our disused fire station home. But I bear you no grudge. Just remember my contribution. Forget Reagan. Forget Gorbachev. Forget Glasnost and Perestroika. Forget the SALT talks and the new world economy. For it was none of your global politics that brought down The Wall. No sir. It was us with our wonderful mime play. That's what we did that Berlin night as our heads birled with the Finny dram. We put the Cold War on permanent thaw. Changing the course of the world for the rest of its living days.

Only the croaking of frogs among spiked lochan reeds. There are three questions which my hand with its scrawling and darting pen strokes place before me in the chap-book page here in the dying light of the day.

1. Is there any point in writing this stuff down?

2. Will it make any difference to how I feel?

3. Who is ever going to read it anyway?

Ochone dear reader. I am at the pointless self-searching again. Och. Tilemma tillema. 'Tis when I am at the scribbling of the Annals that these questions do scour like chilling blizzards across the barren wasteland of my desolate bardic soul. I question my worth. This writing business. It is heaven and hell I tell you. My consciousness constantly wobbling on a fulcrum between self-loathing and Utopian smugness. Demands are made of my identity. What am I doing? Who do I think I am? Oft times they do rain down like hammer blows directed by a stern personal God in a boiler suit who is of the opinion that poetry is the domain of poofs or eighteenth-century ploughmen. *Writing? Poetry? How dare ye wield a pen when a spanner ye should wield?* And so I reply. But my great stern God. I entreat you. There is little work to be had these days. Heaven knows I've tried in the past. Application after application. The occasional failed interview. I'm out of it too long now. Out of work. Out of home. Out of life. And when you're out of it you're out of it. What do you suggest I do? There is only the writing to comfort me now. *Writing? Stick it up your jacksy my boy and leave such things to the Bard. Freedom and whisky and pastoral rumpy-pumpy. Haggis and neeps an' aw that. We can celebrate it once a year at the annual supper. The Round Table Bowel Challenge and such like. There is nothing like a half-digested animal's intestine to make a man's orifice wax lyrical. Now be out of here with your pen and your egotistical whimsy. Away with you now and find some work. Real work. Anything! There is employment to be had. Work a shovel. A lavatory brush. Direct a great train of supermarket trolleys across an endless car park. Try High Street leafleting. Remove your clothing to loud music and waggle your whanger at a lounge full of appreciative screaming menopausal drunken women for all I care but for goodness sake just get out of here and go back and join the working world. It might make you feel desperate but it can't make you feel any worse than you do when you're raking around in the past and writing down these bloody stories.*

But my pen scribbles on in defiance. Dragging me muddied and bruised through the existential mire to gaze out at the world through blinking mud-encrusted eyelids. *RIVET! I AM A FROG!*

for i
am a frog

hopping across worlds that
are stepping stones
on the starry pond of existence

from mercury to venus i leap
then poise
for a while
on earth
flicking out my tongue to catch a passing comet
and devour the knowledge
that burns with the light of all creation

and when i am ready i will go
hopping across mars jupiter saturn
to land
on uranus
(I will flick out my tongue on uranus too)

and when i reach Pluto i will make that final leap
into?...

Hech! Hech hech! Hech hech hech hech! Hech hech heeeeeech!

In fading light lochan glows pale yellow and shimmers in its cradle of dark mountains. The maidens' wild song drifts up then is lost among a sough of wind that sends a tussock tremor across lonely hills.

North-west the hawthorn stands beside the charred timbers of the Cabin. Scraping outstretched claws across the dying light of the sky. Big full yellow moon rising fast in the east. Decreasing in diameter but glowing brighter with blue-white light as she climbs. Auntie Phoebe. My Lunar Auntie. Your Lunar Auntie. A'body's Lunar Auntie. She sends a beam of light across the slow rippling waters as the last few fish of the day snap at heather moths that fall to the surface of the loch. *Sploosh.* Primus stove droning a low purr and pan-sizzle as I place another gutted trout flesh-first down on to the bubbling melted butter. Manna. The smell of it on the cold fresh air of night.

There was a night just like this one time when Ola had come down from the house and sat there on the bank for a while reading until the midges and the fading light made it impossible. We were talking about the future. The three of us. Me and Ola and the life inside her that would be born of music. I tied on a white fly to cast away for another hour or two then watched her making her way back to the cabin. She was maybe five months pregnant at the time. When she passed the bullrushes a whooper swan flapped then rose slowly over the waters climbing into the sky to fly past Venus glinting gold in the south.

She went her way homeward
with one star awake
as the swan in the evening
moved over the lake.

When Ola reached the house I watched the glow of the candle in the window then the light flare up as the Tilley lamp was fired. A few moments later a line of dark smoke screwed from the chimney and rose into a dimming sky.

I was thinking about what it was all going to be like when the bairn was born and the three of us playing together by the lochside. Ola's word echoed back at me from the first time we ever met in the café in France. *Home.* The Haven. Nothing more than an old wooden cabin and a good hike into the hills from St Ronans. It couldn't have been any closer. No wonder they say that a fool's eyes are at the end of the Earth. The cabin door was open. Ola began playing and her music drifted out. I could hear the dark song of the cello as I cast the line out over the water.

By the time we got back to Scotland the Rt. Hon. Lady's fart was gaining force. It had defied the rules of military engagement and blasted a torpedo from out between the cheeks of her arse to zip through the exclusion zone of South Atlantic waters and send a shipload of young Argentinian men to their awful death in a raging hell of burning steel. Gotcha. At home it had already flattened a few old industrial sites. But the wind of change from Thatcher's bowels was blowing in a new economic confidence. In dark Atlantis the gusts from it were blasting away ancient Smog Age grime from sandstone façades in the business heart of the city. Buildings were being reinstated to their former Victorian splendour and café society was replacing the old whisky howffs as PR men in shiny suits bandied around such fine words as *Renaissance.*

But if the stench of the fart was imparting a giddy euphoria on the suited men of the city centre its corrosive effects were already eating away at the fringes as more and more folk out in schemeland found themselves alienated from the brave new world of the service economy. Nascent consumerism. The fart was blowing away the pithead hoist and replacing it with the shopping mall. A consciousness nurtured on invention and production would be dazed and confused by it. Worse yet the fart's poisonous odours had aggravated the senses of police officers who charged down on striking miners with batons drawn like swords of the vengeful Gilquhans on their Holy Crusades. The Demoness herself would travel north and stand before the General Assembly of Meenisters on the Mound and attempt their conversion from Christianity to Mammonism. Through all of this the bywords were Confidence and Regeneration.

The soot-eaten tenements on Maryhill Road were gutted and primmed up as property and possession were heralded as the new shining path. But there were the heretic voices of ould fellars who spoke in low tones of caution. From within the shadows of gloomy pubs that had evaded the onrush of plastic pot plants and espresso machines. Between sips of flat afternoon beer and the occasional squint at a TV screen for a racing result. *It cannae last son. Daein away wi the engineerin an that. It's a house o cards. Ye cannae run an economy wi nae resources nor production. It's got nae substance tae it.* The old men's voices were little more than the forgotten whispers of a failed and archaic past as the City of London cracked open the champers and much of England's south-east congregated in their millions like hogs around a golden trough snorting after the scraps. The She-Farter called it the Trickledown Economy. The idea being that we would each of us get to drink from the giddy bowl of success. By gathering up in small cups the residue of Dom Perignon-scented urine that was trickling in droplets from under the cool shadows of a blue twin-set skirt. Oozing out of her prim middle-class fanny and down a varicosed leg.

Both Ola and myself knew it was pointless to be heading back to the Strath if we wanted to find work. The Mill and The Smiddy and all the rest of them were history now. So when we got back to Scotland and reached the city with its buildings clad in scaffolding and the streets filled with the noise of hissing sand-blast guns we phoned Sharleen and Cammy and found out there was a flat coming up for rent in their building. We caught a subway train for Kelvinbridge to become citizens of 7 Blane Gardens in the shiny new city. Yee ha! Welcome To Atlantis!

The crumbling townhouse stood on the edge of a steep bank that fell a hundred feet to the Kelvin and looked only a landslip away from obliteration. To the front a great wooden frame angled down onto the street to prevent the building falling forward. Grey paint hung in big flaking scabs. Weeping out green fluid that crept down walls like gangrene.

It was still daylight but as we walked towards the house we could see dull lights shining through grimy windows where mouldy drapes or blankets hung. On each door-pillar was the carved figure of a bearded elf looking down onto the street. The glum frown on them was a fitting reaction to their surroundings. The whole place appeared like a metaphor for what life here might be like. Scabby as fuck and without foundation. My finger reached out and pressed the doorbell then we heard a set of boots thundering down the stairs. The door flew open.

> *YAWOO FACH! YAWOO FACH'S WUMMAN! Come in. Come in!*

In truth the house turned out to be something of a sanctuary. A collecting-point for the driftwood of humanity. A landing stage for every kind of social misfit or headbanging jube-jube you could possibly hope to meet.

Fair play to Cammy and Shar though they'd got us the best gaff in the house. A self-contained job on the ground floor with a big sitting-room and a wee galley-kitchen with a tiny bedroom above it. Moons ago when the house was in its hey-day this had been the servants' quarters. It seemed a fair gesture on our buddies' part since they only had a bedsit on the first floor. They could've had first shout on the flat. We bought a carry-out and a new pipe and some big skins out of a head shop round the corner and fired up a celebration. Warmed the new gaff and swopped stories. Glasgow stories for Berlin stories. Sharleen had cultivated some nice grass and we grilled a load of it. By midnight Ola and me were on the uncontrollable yawns. We'd been hitching for days.

I realised Cammy and Shar's generosity had more to do with self-preservation than self-sacrifice not long after we'd turned in. The first notes of the trumpet began to ring out. A few toots first to get it warmed up. Then a long mournful trumpetting dirge. It floated out over back lanes and crumbling bin-sheds as cats swivelled with shining eyes. It rang through the walls of the house sending cockroaches crawling deep into black rotting crevices. I went to the door where the noise was coming from and found a sticker on it. CHRIST IS MY CASTLE. It certainly put me off chapping it. Grand. We were living next door to the nightshift trumpeter. The Jesus Basket they called him. It's no as if he was in a Sally Ann band or nothing. He was a soloist. Fuckin right he was.

The guy in the room at the front of the house was a young prostitute called Chris. Chris was providing services to a collection of businessmen and the occasional national celebrity. Up the stair Cammy and Shar shared the first landing with Alastair the Speed Dealer and a yellow-skinned cirrhotic alcoholic called Nathaniel. The next landing up had Timothy Hyphenated-Double-Barrel-Something-Or-Other. Yet another exile from Home Counties who professed to be some kind of a healer or a shaman. There seemed to be more and more tree-huggers finding their way up here. Maybe the magic magnet of Findhorn was slowly sooking them all north. Next door to Timothy was Sammy who'd been a convicted bankrobber. Before Sammy's brief career move into larceny he'd worked in a butcher's shop down in Partick. Now in his reform days Sam made a good wee sideline for himself producing meat in his bedsit. It must have been hell for a vegan mystic like Timothy seeing carcasses getting delivered to Sammy's door. Worse yet listening to the drone and clatter of those sausage-machines and haunch-slicers through the wall when trying to channel-in to the cosmic harmonies. Sammy had carcasses on hooks in there and I thanked the stars we didn't live above him. Across from Sammy was a sweet old widow-wifie called Miss Deans. Bernie Broon and

Colette and their two dogs were right at the top in the garret. The Crow's Nest we called it. They'd a system of gutters hanging from the ceiling on string that took rainwater back out the window where it belonged.

Old Mrs Cowan had us firmly by the balls. Every Friday a plazzy bag of groceries would appear hanging from the door-handle of each room. This constituted our meals and allowed Cowan a wide berth of tenants' rights as she could claim she was running a hotel business instead of rented rooms. Some beans and biscuits. Tins of hot dog sausages and a few tea bags. Hech! Talk about the Grosvenor man. All kinds of uninvited characters came wandering about the building too. You had to be sharp on a Friday to get your messages off the door-handle before some vagabond was off with them. Same by the letterbox on Giro day.

But aside from the Jesus Basket's nocturnal tooting our flat wasn't that bad. Before long Ola and me had trawled jumble-sales and Paddy's Market to get a hold of some good furniture that transformed the place. Even a harmonium. We'd wheeled it back three miles to the flat where it stood pride of place in the living-room. You could sit there and pump away on the pedals to send air up through the bellows then play out those deep harmonious notes on the keyboard. Even if you couldn't knock a tune out of it you could always recite some Ivor Cutler. Life In A Scotch Sitting Room.

Perched on top of a loaded skip we discovered our greatest household treasure. The Japanese Therapy Seat was a hefty steel square chair. Underneath the seat was an electric motor that drove a pulley system. Two steel rods held in slots stuck out from the backrest. These were driven by the pulley and travelled in an up-and-down motion. On the end of each rod was a miniature boxing glove. We wired up a plug and Ola wanted to go first. At first we were worried it would turn into an electric chair so we prodded it with things to make sure it didn't spark. Then Ola sat in. She turned the switch to start the motor and the chair whirred into life. The little boxing gloves moved slowly up and down the length of her spine punching away at it. Ola shrieked with laughter then reached down for the gearstick to move it to the next setting. The Japanese letters on the control panel must have read SLOW and FAST. The little boxing gloves suddenly sped up and punched their way up and down her back. Ola screamed as if she was on a ride at the shows. She reached down to move it to the next setting. VERY FAST. The little boxing gloves shot up and down the slots punching out so fast you could hardly see the movement as the floor vibrated with the motion of it. Ola fell out of the chair in tears then I had a go myself. But the Therapy Seat as it turned out was good for the bones and occasionally we'd get somebody at the door asking for a shot if the old back was giving then a spot of trouble.

As time passed Ola disentangled a tunnel of weeds and vines out on the terrace and made a garden for us perched high over the river. She freed a wooden gate at the edge of the precipice and discovered some old stone steps. We shovelled away decades of leaf-mould that lay on them working our way down. The steps wound their way down the sheer bank all the way to the river. We called it the Gateway and we'd start all our walks from there. Down into the steep glen. Walking for hours. Far away out of the city even to the oakwoods. Sitting on the Wishing Stone. Growing closer every day and dreaming a bright invincible future.

Sometimes out on the streets we'd see Alastair the Dealer. He was in a heavy state of paranoia looking back over each shoulder and walking swiftly from corner to corner. Alastair had devised a code for his customers to let them know when there was gear available. If you saw him walking around the streets wearing his shades and headband then this meant he'd no gear. Sans shades and headband would signal the good ship amphetamine was in. His paranoia was understandable. The Drug Squad in their wisdom had gone to his door with a battering ram and swept it clean away from the hinges. The problem was they'd gone a landing too high and taken away Miss Deans' door by mistake. The last we saw of her she was being stretchered into an ambulance with an oxygen mask over her face as an embarrassed detective stood on the steps of the house drumming his fingers on the handrail. Watching the paramedics bang close the doors then the ambulance sped out the street. There was a bit of explaining to do.

During the day we'd get a bit of revenge on the sleeping Jesus Basket when Bernie came down with the amp and the bass. Then we got a drummer and became Duma and started organising gigs in the town. Ola was playing her own music then but sometimes she'd join us on the cello and it added a forceful undercurrent. Bernie's energy on the bass drove through it to form the core that fused our diverse influences. My own vocals developed into a mucous growl as the seasons passed and the bronchial conditions of the flat set to work on the erosion of my throat and lungs. We needed the band sounding dark and edgy. Something that would live up to the name. Duma. Gatekeeper of Hell.

* * * * * * * * * * * * * * * *

It was only a chance scan in the *Herald* ads that gave us warning of old Cowan's intentions. That's when we saw the planning application for turning 7 Blane into a Granny Farm. We knew it'd only be a matter of time before the eviction notices came through the door. She must've deduced she could draw more money out of them than out of us. That she could wring out the wrinklies.

Realising we'd been pissed on more than Shanks of Barrhead we convened a meeting in our flat and everybody turned up. Even the JB carrying his basketwork rucksack with the home-made embroidery of the crucifixion in brightly-coloured wool. It was the first time I'd actually seen it. Calgary Hill was a lime-green affair. On the little figure up on the cross with his beard of brown strands were red threads of blood coming from hands and feet. I looked around at the people in the room. We were an unlikely alliance but we had solidarity. Everyone decided they wanted to stay. It was the only home we had. Better to have money spent repairing the place and making it liveable than casting people onto the street. We declared ourselves a rent-free zone and decided to occupy.

We won Round One when we sent the Security out of the street with missiles dinging off their van. *HECHITTY HECH! Then the public prosecutor started prosecutin me.* But we were pissing into the wind of course.

Round Two was a foregone conclusion when we were cleared out under police supervision and the building got shackled. Didn't even get back in for all our gear as we stood there out in the street with all we could carry. Ola with the cello and violin. Me with the big rucksack and my guitar. The harmonium and the Japanese Therapy Seat lost forever. The friends we'd made there too.

Mad barking dogs were echoing all round the Kelvin. Colette dragged the Rottweilers away as Bernie retreated with the bass and amp and police Alsatians strained at the leash. The rest of us went round the corner to a bar for a drink. Then a crowd of people representing years worth of payments of extortionate rents parted company and wandered off their separate ways into the unknown.

Making love. Lying together in the silence of the night. The window open. River Kelvin whispering up through the trees and the bell chiming through the dark from the University spire. Himalayan Balsam. Do you remember? Big blue flowers we used to pluck out of the riverbank. Vases full of them on the sideboard and in the fireplace. Only an old flat with damp walls but we made a world of it. Walking for hours. Through the Gateway and down the secret steps. Townland and Riverland. Borderland and Beyondland. We made the best of it Fach. Painted up the place and furnished it. Hung some pictures. A few books and a demented cat. We made a nice home there. I was writing my best music then. Himalayan Balsam. Do you remember it?

You were so far inside of yourself Fach. Sometimes I thought I'd never find a way in there. It took a bright flame but I think I got there. And what about you? Can you still carry a light for us? What did you think of when you were walking alone on the riverbank? Could you bear to think about us? Does denial put a cold chill on the back of your neck? Did you ever think there was something behind you?

Everything we did was an adventure. Going to the shops. We saw the Westbus coming down the boulevard and jumped on it instead. Got off at Loch Fyneside. Couldn't see the top of the tallest tree in Scotland for the mist. Mist drifting in from the Atlantic. Carrying in ghosts of warriors and saints and fishermen on the salty air you said. Old forgotten dreams of the west. Trawled the gantry in The Stagecoach Inn. Whisky tour of Scotland. From Glenkinchie up to Fettercairn. Glenlivet then west to the Ord. North to Scapa. Speed bonnie boat to Talisker then set sail south for Jura. Westering Home via Bruichladdich then tramp the Islay hills to Lagavulin. Drunk. Singing on the last city bus home. I was crazy enough to think it could always be like this. Adventures. Laughs. But I think it could have been.

You took me walks on Clydeside. Past derelict industrial sites and rotting piers. Ye were such a romantic Big Man so ye were. If we'd stayed there in the city. What would have come of it? Why did you do it to us Fach? Only blackened timbers and bad memories around this place. Wind coming down from Meikle Carnock to stir the ashes. Can you still hear me? Himalayan Balsam. I wrote a tune for us. Do you remember it?

We got a lease on Knockhaven after a chance meeting with Walter Ferguson in the Bull. Walter was after asking me what I was doing back in St Ronans so I gave him the gen about Ola and myself coming back to Scotland after Europe then about the evictions and all that.

The cabin at the Haven had been built as workers' lodgings for a massive forestry operation half a century back that was never to be. They'd mapped out the boundaries that would've draped an evergreen cloak from north of Knockhaven to the edge of the Birchen Moss. The Strath from end to end was to be roofed with a conifer thatch then the operations had begun with the building of the Haven bothy. A kind of solid looking Alpine gadget it was perched on a grass plateau above Lochan Cnoc a Habhain. Water was piped in from the burn. They'd put solid iron stoves into each of the rooms that were to serve as dormitories for the workers. Then they dumped a ton of coal to the side. The foresters had started on the first plantations in the hills behind the Haven. Ploughing and planting. But it had only extended a few miles when the whole operation came to an end. A dispute over land tenure followed by a national emergency when some angry geezer with a naff moustache had marched an army into Poland.

The upshot was that the forestry lads were needed elsewhere. So they loaded up the last of the gear on their Clydesdale horse and waved farewell to the Haven. All that remained was a wee bit plantation and a few tracks around the hills. A first-class bothy that would lie locked and a ton of coal that would remain unburned for several decades until yours truly bumped into Wattie Ferg in the Bull bar.

The land had gone back to the sheep grazing and so Strathfinglas was saved from suffocation. The grey stone tombs of the ancient farmers and the outline of their fields could still be seen in the heather behind the cabin as the wind blew down to send a ripple across the sapphire lochan. The five songs would sing out yet.

Then I scored a bit of land work. Freelance grafting. Cutting back trees and lining stone roads. Fencing. Hanging gates and the like.

Turk gave me a shot of his garden shed for a premises and I built up a good stock of gear as I went along. I was investigating the ruined stables at Gilquhan Tower one day and came across this ancient barrow. Iron wheels. Long oak handles and a flat deck. Yes mister. Potential. I heaved it over on its back and gave the wheels a spin and they ran as good as new can you beat that? By the time I got up the hill to Saints there was a line of tooting cars at my back urging me to get the fuck off the highway that they'd all been forking out their hard-earned cash on. I feigned a deaf lug and suppressed a hoot and just kept heaving the old barrow over the Finny's hump-backed bridge and all the way up to the Turk's house. You could have picked the man off the floor.

> *MacNab! Whit the fuck is that?*
>
> *That Mister MacGruer is my vehicle to success. Just think of the gear I can get on board this thing. Shovels. Shears. Rakes. Stanes. Cement. No more running a mile back to Turk's shed for a tool. This gadget'll carry everything I need. I can extend my operations with this.*
>
> *For fuck's sake Farchar. Can ye no just get yer drivin licence and buy a wee van like anybody else? It looks like somethin oot o a fuckin Constable picture. Have ye no heard o the Industrial Revolution? It was ower a hunner years ago. Ye're supposed tae be a gerdener no a flamin chimney sweep. For fuck's sake.*
>
> *So can I no keep it in your garage then?*
>
> *Christ. Aye a right then.*

I suspected Turk would get interested in the barra and he did. He was a mechanic at heart and liked studying how things were constructed and how they ran. We ended up stripping the wood back and putting a clear varnish on it. We sanded down all the wee finicky balusters along the side of the deck and gave them a lick of red paint. When I was away home at the Haven over the weekend Turk buffed a century's rust from the wheels until there was a shine on them again which he coated over with Hammerite. We cleaned out the bearings and gave them a dollop of lithium grease until they ran even smoother. Smooth as the wind. The barra was ready. So I'd go around the place from job to job pushing the barra. The job man.

What the hell. There had been a plague of mock Victorian sweetie barrows in the shopping malls of Atlantis that had become a kind of symbol of new enterprise. Women in striped smocks and Yes Mar'm bunnets were selling choice confectionery to the punters. You could get a government grant for that kind of thing. So who was to stop the honest Fach from wheeling his implements from one gentleman's mansion to the next? Certainly not the abusive drivers in their horseless carriages who would yell obscenities out their windows at this hindrance to their progress on the highway. No. Be off with you sir and your ear-splitting motorised vehicle. Or I shall insert my three-rowed wired brush into your anus and deal you a vigorous cleaning out my good fellow.

But tell me this. All those mock Victorian sweetie barrows. What ever happened to them?

Then Ola picked up a job as a home-help around St Ronans which basically meant brewing up tea and listening to yarns of the likes of the ancient Crawfords for a few mornings a week. Ferguson sold us an old jeep that could ferry us bang-clatter between the Haven and the foot of the hills where the track reached the main road. Perfect. You could spit into the village from there and wouldn't need a driving licence. I bought a mountain bike and we were complete. Jobs. Transport. A gaff in the hills with a loch to the front and a ton of coals to the side. The Haven.

At night we'd sit in the front room with the iron stove glowing red from burning logs and coals. The stovepipe lum had a draw on it that droned like a skyful of WW2 bombers. We'd carted furniture off the barra onto the jeep then drove up from the village. Ola and me would be snugged up on the settee with only the hiss of the tilly and drone of the stovepipe and the sigh of the wind blowing through the hills.

Sometimes a greenshank would cry into the night or you'd hear a fox barking. I used to like stopping off from reading and just listening to the drone of the lum. The mind-eye would fill the sky with Luftwaffe bombers swarming down from the north. Away above the lochan. Black shapes blotting out the stars and droning south with a cargo that would rain flame and death on the industrial West. Night after night. Ola would say *What are you thinking about?* Then I'd talk about how the lum drone made me think of the warplanes flying to the Blitz and what it must have been like in the towns. The Crawfords said you could see the flashes in the sky seventy miles away. Then Ola said I was obsessed with the past. What was the good of thinking of it now? I said I thought it was important to remember. Then she said *What about Iraq*? We were starving a million bairns to death for the sake of a stabilised oil price that allowed us to go on investing in Philippine sweat shops where women worked themselves to death. To make the boots and jerseys that we were wearing ourselves. So what was the point of dwelling on the bombs that had landed on our doorstep half a century ago? She was good at hooking me. But Ola's comments only made me dwell all the more. Had it really come to this? That the glint of the baubles of consumerism had blinded us to a mass cruelty of our own doing? What was the truth anyway? Maybe all just dark secrets and opposing ideologies like it had always been. One thing was sure. The country we once knew was fast becoming a bourgeois superstate. Where ordinary people would sweat out mortgage concerns to the symphony of a thousand electric mowers humming on the evening air. Keeping up suburban appearances certainly meant more work for Fach with the barra. What harm starving a few thousand Ai-rab bairns to death just so long as the economy was stable? Anger was futile anyway. It only dissolves to impotence in a fast-turning world whose only worry is consumption. A Big MacBeefy followed by a Big MacShite then your guts are empty ready for the next Big

MacBeefy. So what do you do? You opt out. Opt out how? We were all part of this money-grubbing machine that stimulated itself on emergent industries like wheel-clamping and the sales of Belgian confectionery. I myself had become a champion of enterprise. So you shut off from it eventually. And defect into the silence. Sit back and listen to the drone of the lum.

* * * * * * * * * * * * * * * *

I'd be up out of bed and climbing aboard the trusty bike as dawn was painting red streaks across a cold blue sky. Uncle Duncan often used to quote Baden-Powell's great maxim on cycling and it would come to mind as I pedalled down the track.

With your little steel steed between your knees
You can go wherever you jolly well please.

Uncle Duncan was never seen on a bike himself but would always quote Baden's rhyme whenever he saw someone else on one. Usually from the seat of his car. My little steel steed went bouncing down the hill-track that descends to St Ronans as I veered around potholes and boulders and gulped in big lungfuls of cold morning air. Ever wary of the dangers of crossbar and saddle in such haphazard cycling terrain.

With your little steel steed between your knees
Be mindful of those testicles – please.

Sometimes if I'd set off late Ola would pass me on the jeep and go bang-clattering away down the brae with her hand waving from the window.

The chill Finny waters rippled under a tunnel of mist that followed the river's course to the end of the Strath as far as the eye could see. In places the vapour reached out in strands into fields and woods then dissolved in curling wisps as the sun eased itself over the top of the knowes to breathe warmth into the morning air. And looking back you could follow the five burns with their sleeves of mist smoking their way into the hills. Five long fingers. Before I reached Turk's I would have my day planned out. Pushing the barra to where I needed to go. Maybe it would be shearing back a bank of brambles or rebuilding a timber bridge in some woodland garden. With each passing week my shoulders became stronger and I glowed with the energy of sun and light. I became capable of putting in a good day's work without tiring too much and with a bit of method I was able to plan weeks in advance as order after order came in and I found myself even having to start a book to keep track of it. Champion of Enterprise. The orders would usually come from somebody stopping me on the road or turning up at Turk's shed. Once or twice Uncle Duncan passed me on the road and I'd give him a big wave and he'd briefly glimpse down at his moustache then drive on with eyes fixed dead ahead.

At the end of the day I'd garage the barra at Turk's then pedal home on the bike. Heaving up the long stony brae to the summit then through the pass to the Haven. Smoke twisting from the stovepipe lum.

Ola. We explored every neuk of the Haven and lived its stories. Within a mile's radius of the cabin the story reached back a hundred thousand moons. When winds shook branches against a night sky and the flames of the hunter's fire trembled to the cry of the wolf. There was the langcairn. A mound of grey boulders with its vault of ancient skeletons. Remains of hut circles where the Bronze Age township had stood and the crannog on the lochan. Melted stone ramparts on the top of the brae. Legacy of the warrior-scientists of Meikle Carnock. There were the remains of the black houses. Crofters who had scratched a living on this land for endless generations until the last of them had left in the Thirties when the forestry plan came. Their methods had barely changed in the sixty thousand moons since those mouldering skeletons sleeping below the langcairn had turned the first soil with their ploughshares of bone.

The forestry buy-out and the brief use of the bothy by the foresters and now us. Ola and Fach. We were guardians of the Haven. We hauled trout from the lochan and cooked them on the red hot iron plate of the stove. We climbed to the top of Meikle Carnock and swam in the deepest pools of the burn. We both loved sex in the open air so hauled off our gear and made love when and wherever we felt like it. We were without contraception and relying on withdrawal. The old interruptus. I was barely making it. With a gasp and a groan and a spurt spurt spurt. We made love on so many patches of grass the juice of my orgasms was beginning to rival the cuckoo-spit. Let's face it. It was only a matter of time.

* * * * * * * * * * * * * * * *

Candlelight and low drone of the stovepipe. I'd just come out of Ola as we lay naked on the cabin floor. We were full of the afterglow as I reached over for the tin to roll us a cigarette with a liquorice paper and a pinch of baccy.

Fachie. I'm a bit worried.

Worried? What is there to worry over?

It's late.

Na. It's barely past twelve.

No ya tube. The period. I'm late.

You're late? How late?

Not sure. Few days. Maybe more.

Hmm.

What?

I said hmm.

What do you think?

Hmm.

Is that all you can say?

Hmm?

I remember the snipes drumming. The eerie hum of wind rushing through their feathers as they flitted over the moss. The fire had dreedled away. Only a low purr from its pulsing embers. Ola was looking straight at me.

What do you think we should do?

Maybe we should get one of those gadgets. The test kit.

I already got one today.

You already got one?

Aye. Bought one down in the village.

You haven't done it? Haven't pished on it yet then?

No. Not yet.

Well. Better do it next pish Ola. Just to be sure.

I'll do it now.

Okay.

Somehow I knew before she came back. Or thought I did anyway. The purring embers quietened to a faint hiss and you could hear the sounds from all around the lochan clear in the night now. Croaking frogs and the pipe of greenshanks and screeching herons. We were into the heart of spring and all nature was getting it together for the mighty seasonal shag. We had become so much a part of the Haven it felt like an omen.

Well?

Farchar.

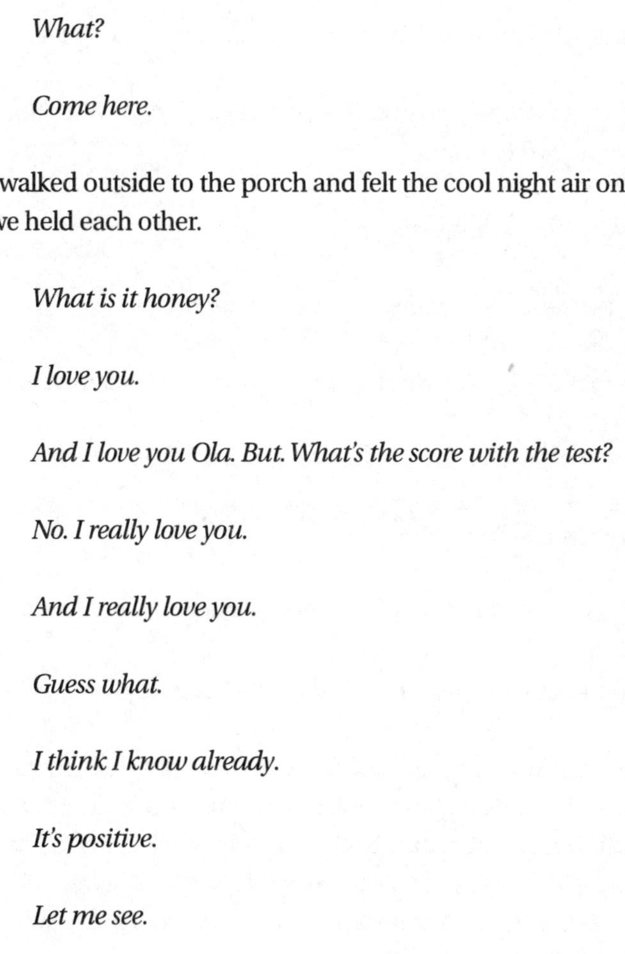

What?

Come here.

We walked outside to the porch and felt the cool night air on our skins as we held each other.

What is it honey?

I love you.

And I love you Ola. But. What's the score with the test?

No. I really love you.

And I really love you.

Guess what.

I think I know already.

It's positive.

Let me see.

See? See the wee blue stripes?

I'll hold it to the light.

I went into the cabin and went to the candle to study the result. Three blue stripes.

See?

Good Gad.

Where are you going Farchar?

There's a bottle of Islay Mist in the press. If I don't have one I'm going to fall over.

Make mines a large one.

Are you sure you're allowed? In your condition?

For fuck's sake. Just do it. Pour me one. Ta. Here's to us Fach.

My bonnie sweetheart. Here's to us.

Here's to the three of us.

Oh my God. The three of us. What a thought.

Good Gad. Good Gad Good Gad Good Gad.

When we went away on the Swiftbus to have the scan done the midwife traced the date back as near she could and I was ecstatic. It had to be that day. It could only be that day. The week before it Ola had gone to stay with her folks and the week following it I'd gone out on a job away down at Birchen and stayed over a few days. There was only that day. The day in the middle.

* * * * * * * * * * * * * * * * * *

The morning Ola came back from the visit to her Ma's I'd been out casting on the lochan when I heard her music coming from the cabin. Fiddle music. Some Highland slow air drifting over the waters. I'd already a couple of trout on the bank and walked up to the house with them then we fired them up on the hotplate and had a good-sized Islay Mist.

After we'd finished Ola played some more music then laid down her fiddle on the settee. We'd missed each other. We had a long snog the kind that takes the breath out of you then we rolled off the settee onto the floor.

Ola was on top of me and had me pinned down. She moved her hand down and undid me then she slipped her top off. I could see Ola had the gag too her nipples were like bullets. I kept trying to sit up or turn over but she kept pinning me back down until she had all my gear off then stood over me with her foot on my chest and took off her tight jeans. I was totally helpless lying on the floorboards and groaning by now and she was having a laugh at me. I looked to heaven and thanked God almighty. The Great One responded in my favour as Ola ran her tongue down my stomach then slipped her lips over the top of me. I drew in a loud gasping breath then pulled her thighs back towards me and slid my tongue into wonderland. But Ola didn't let it last too long. She was still in control. She rolled around then I felt her slide over me. Ola was on top thrusting down on me. I brought my knees up to make a backrest of my thighs and she leaned far back into them as she pounded down on me. I could see she still had a smile in her eyes. And then it happened. She shifted her weight angling herself towards the settee then grabbed hold of the fiddle and bow. As she bounced naked up and down on me she put the fiddle to her shoulder then struck the bow over the strings and began a tune. I looked up at God again. Trout whisky shagging and music it had to be heaven. She played a slow air and wriggled over me to the sensual movement of the tune. The music drifted into a strathspey and the pace quickened a little as her belly and hips thrust down over the top of the hugely swollen boaby. Then she broke into a reel. A real good Scottish reel. Her gorgeous body thrusting up and down on me in four-four time as she played. Quickening quickening. Then I realised something and began to hoot. I hooted and hooted and hooted. A beautiful woman had me on the floor and was fucking me and serenading me with native Highland melodies. But no. It wasn't that. It was the realisation that all the way through it I had been tapping my foot on the floor. Which just goes to show. No matter what. You can never stop a Scotsman tapping his foot to the good old music of the fiddle.

She played on until we both came and the tune began breaking up. Holy shit. What a noise it must have been. Between the discordant music and the screams of us. I looked up at the window expecting to see the roe deer and the snipes and the frogs and the foxes and the swans and all the creatures from around the Haven looking in to see what the hell was going on. Yawoo. I tell you. At that very moment there was little in the world that would have surprised me.

I was cycling down the brae singing to the skies. BeJaz. The Fach to be a da? This bairn would truly be born of music. I was even thinking about turning up at the cold sandstone mansion and telling Unc Dunc and Auntie Mary about my imminent faitherhood but I was able to contain myself. The wee cratur was due early next year so I might as well enjoy it before the real work began.

I spent the day clearing cress out of a ditch then made my way back to the shed. Turk came home in his busman's uniform and gave me a big handshake that had more to it than any of these half-arsed sentimental Thespy hugs that have become the order of the day. When the weekend came me and Ola made our way down to the Bull and everybody was rooting for us. Bell leaned over the counter and planted a slobbery peck on me. Turk offered to put us up that night and for the first time in years a full-on hoolie with all the old brigade got under way in the bar. Everybody was there. Even Deke straight off the farm in a Hawaiian shirt and shades. I was returning to the table with a tray of drinks and couldn't resist it.

een-gonyama een-gonyama!

To my pleasant surprise back came the return.

EEN-GONYAMA! EEN-GONYAMA!
YA-BOH! YA BOH! INVOOBOO!
ZING A ZING! BOM BOM!
HE IS A LION! NO! HE IS BETTER THAN A LION!
HE IS A HIPPOPOTAMUS!

A circle of faces roaring out. There's nothing to compare when the crack takes hold of a crowd. It's like a fire. As the night passed the drinks came faster and the noise got even louder. No. There's nothing like it.

* * * * * * * * * * * * * * * *

I worked on with the barra. Late summer and the land turning dark again. Ola began to grow. September rains and great runs of salmon leaping from the Martyr's Pool. Jolting through the black channels of the gorge or upwards into the five songs as far from the sea as a salmon can go. Brackens withered and dried into brown crisp ferns. The baby began to move inside Ola. Screeching jays blue and crimson spread their wings to follow the courses of the burns from one sparse grove of rowans to the next feeding on bright red berries as the last of the leaves fell from the trees. Dropping in silent flurries of red and gold to lie among yellowing tussocks. Soon the frost would come and the skies would be busy with geese.

I filled bags with berries and hauled a few salmon from the river. The cabin smelled like a Bordeaux winery as the berries fermented in big buckets with sugar and yeast. Under dark tumbling clouds I caught the last of the season's trout from the lochan. Lurking at the burn mouth or among the lilies.

At night Ola's belly became a punch-bag as the wee cratur thrust out with all his might. We used to say he'd a fiddle in there and it was his elbows banging against the sides. Ola and me prepared the place for winter. We went out with the hatchet to the groves and I shouldered home dead boughs of rowan and alder for logs to add to the diminishing supply of coals. We moved the bed into the front room now and would only need to burn the one stove.

We waited for the cold to arrive but the clammy back-end days prevailed. There was still no hint of frost. Only mist and rain and dense muggy air. Still. We made fires in the stove if only to keep out the damp and send out a red glow to cheer the darkness. It seemed the winter cold would never come. There was still plenty of work to be done with the old Gilquhan barra and I was out all the time clearing leaves from lawns and ditches or maybe cutting back trees and brambles here or there through grey days of rain. The wee cratur kept hitting out at Ola's belly. Keen to start his gig in creation's big concert.

There was one day I was working at a big garden in Drums when I noticed some auld biddy pacing around at the gate. An auldwife happed inside a coat and a headscarf. I looked over towards her and she half-waved but then she made to turn away. I was thinking it was somebody looking to have their garden done so I strode up the road then caught up with her. Inside the headscarf was Auntie Mary. I couldn't believe how old she looked.

> *I'm not supposed to be here Farchar son. You know what your Uncle's like. But I saw you working here yesterday and I've got a wee something I've been meaning to give you. I've heard your good news.*

She reached inside her coat and pulled out a plazzy bag. She pushed it into my hand and was gone.

I reached into the bag and guddled out a tiny baby's cardigan. The regulation Auntie's knitted job. Poor Auntie Mary. I could picture her making it in secret from Unc Duncan hiding it down the side of a chair.

At the same time as I was reaching into the bag some invisible hand was reaching down my throat into my chest ready to tear out my heart. Somehow the tiny knitted garment had brought a surge of memories out of the past. Then I knew what it was. A monochrome picture flashed into my mind. An old photo of Ma balancing me on her knee and I'm wearing a cardy on my wee fat body identical to the one Aunt Mary's just given me. Kath to one side of us and we're on some west coast pier. It must have been a holiday and we're waiting for the steamer. The sun beating down and the three of us laughing and me only a year old. I suppose it must've been Da who'd taken the picture. In a flash everything came back. Kath. Ma. The lightning bolt and burning tenement. I went to the back of the Drums house and split some logs for a while to use up a bit of energy and maybe take the emotion out of me. No matter how hard I swung I couldn't seem to purge it.

December and still no sign of the frost.

Don't get me wrong. I was over the moon at the prospect of the wee cratur. But midwinter had set in and taken a grip of my mood. The Haven seemed to be under a perpetual shadow with low tumbling clouds and soft winds carrying in bank after bank of dark drizzling mist. It became difficult to lever yourself out of bed in the mornings. The old memories were weighing heavily on me. I still didn't know where Kath and Ma were. For years I'd tried to get the story from Uncle Duncan and Auntie Mary. Twilight was setting in by three o'clock. You hoped for a gale or a storm anything with a bit of energy in it that would bring life to the burns and open up the sky to let the light in again. Then a good solid frost. Clear and bright with stars at night. I withdrew into a darkness inside of myself as the drizzling mist came floating in day after day.

Even descending from the hills into St Ronans didn't take you out of the mist. The smoke of chimneys dropped under their weight into windless streets and became one with the fog. Trees stood black like shadows. Gaunt with silver droplets hanging from branches and boughs.

The glow of Bell's fire drew people around it by late afternoon. I'd louse off early and go for a few jars. But the talk of the place was dull or forced. It would be better if we'd just listened to the tick of the clock and the dull sparks from the fire and said nothing at all.

Aye Fachie son.

Aye.

Winter eh?

Aye. Winter.

Misty isn't it?

Aye. It's fairly misty.

Dark too. Gettin dark gey early these days eh?

Aye.

Did ye notice yesterday? It was dark at half past three.

Aye. I noticed.

Dreich stuff eh?

Aye. Dreich.

Still. Never mind Farchar. It'll no be long till Christmas.

Don't remind me man. If there's one thing I hate it's bloody Christmas.

Oh aye. Christmas. Awful depressing right enough.

Nightmare.

Kind of stressful time Christmas eh?

Aye. Supposed to be something to do with raised expectation followed by acute disappointment. They start the baw rolling in October now. Building it up with month after month o shite on the radio and TV and in the shops. Christmas this and Christmas that. Then it passes in one Godawful day and everybody's skint and miserable. Loada fuckin shite.

Dreich stuff eh?

Aye.

Still. There's always the New Year.

Thank fuck for that.

Aye. Ye're right enough.

Aye.

Aye.

The clock ticks on and the fire phuts half-heartedly sending a puff of smoke up the lum into the darkening mist outside. How can you hold onto your sanity at a time like this? I cycled up the brae in a black haar occasionally sprawling off when the front wheel dropped into a pothole or dunted into tussocks at the side of the track. My arms tired as I split a few logs and loaded the fire then put a flame to it. I heard the rattle of the old jeep then looked out to see headlights casting giant halos in the mist as Ola carefully navigated through the pass along the flat muddying track to the road end. We hugged and I knelt down and felt the knocks and kicks of the life growing inside her. It sent a wave of emotion through me and I went outside for a cry.

When Ola went to bed I sat for a while in the firelight. I woke in the blackness with the fire dulled to its last ember. Still half sleeping I felt a burning pain around my left elbow and put my hand across to massage it. A strange vibration like an electric shock went into my hand as it reached the centre of the pain. I looked down then blinked my eyes in disbelief. There it was. Maybe an inch out from my left arm a thin strand of glowing light. I stood up and the glow went with me. I jolted the arm about from side to side. The glow moved from side to side. I whirled the arm round like a propeller and the glow whirled round leaving a trail. I went to bed for two days and said nothing about it. Two days of darkness. Said nothing at all.

For God's sake Farchar why are you like this? Talk to me. Please.

Ola was sitting on the bed. I just wanted to bear it out. To lie still until the feeling passed like the mist surely would when the wind rose again. Her words pierced into me.

Is it me? Is it something I've done? What's wrong?

I don't know.

You must know something. No secrets remember?

Just leave it Ola. Please. It's old stuff. Clydebank stuff.

Then tell me. Surely you can tell me.

Can we just leave it? It'll pass.

When are you getting out of your bed? It's not doing you any good.

Light. I need light.

Light? You won't get any light lying there. Go for a walk.

There's no light outside. I need light. I'll feel better when there's a bit of light.

For heaven's sake Fachie do you think this is easy for me? I've been carrying this kicking lump around for eight months. Try strapping a sack of tatties round your belly. Then swallow a Tasmanian devil and you might just begin to know what it's like. I haven't even had a drink or a cigarette since the night we did the test.

I'm sorry Oley.

Ola was right of course. She'd been carting the wee jiving cratur around all this time and getting driven out of her wits with night cramp and heartburn. Surviving a hormone storm. She kissed me on the brow then went over to the cello. She drew the bow over the strings and the bass notes went into the pit of my stomach. Ola was playing Himalayan Balsam. The music she'd written for us. Babbie must have heard it too as she held the cello close into her. The dark song of it vibrated through the cabin. I let the music drift through my mind. Nourishing me. Cleaning me out. Filling me with the memories of Ola and all the good times we'd had.

* * * * * * * * * * * * * * * *

On Christmas Eve I walked over the hill with the bow-saw and took down a fir tree. It was double the size of the house so I had to cut it in half then dragged it back to the cabin. We put it in a corner of the room then Ola began decorating it with Stewart tartan bows. It was looking right dandy. I'm not much of a one for guns except on certain occasions so I'd borrowed Turk's air rifle out the shed and headed down to St Ronans wood.

I sat motionless with the gun ready happed up in the langcoat. Puffing on a rollie and waiting for a wee bit of movement. After a while I had two phezzies in the bag and away back up the hill. Cock and a hen. Being a bit of a pheasant plucker and a pheasant plucker's son I whipped off the heads then cleaned out the guts and stripped the feathers holding a candle underneath to burn off any stalks or downy bits. For a hoot I placed the two pheasants heads on the ends of branches on the Christmas tree. Who needs fairies or baubles?

We marinated the phezzies in a pot of nouveau elderberry wine and cooked up a rabbit stew then went to bed. Cuisine par excellence. On Christmas morning the Haven smelt like you could have floated on its aromatic waves all the way to gastronomic Nirvana. Scrumdiddlietumptuous. I'd lit fires in every stove in the house and the tang of coal and woodsmoke drifted in an out of the food smells. Incense to blessed St. Bridget. Patron Saint of the family hearth. The phezzies were cooking away inside the main iron stove and pans of tatties spat and sizzled on the hotplate. A witches' cauldron of broth sent out clouds of delicious steam. At midday we heard the drone of an engine as Turk and Joan with their two boys and Deke sharing the back seat rolled into the misty Haven.

We sat round the table and got fired into the solstice scran while the two boys forgot all about their new toys and chased each other around the rooms with the pheasants' heads. I still had a bit of the dark mood on me but being occupied and getting a bit of crack was keeping me out of myself. I'd checked my body in the darkness the past few nights and the glow had definitely waned. What was I worried about? So I didn't know what it was. Or maybe I was hallucinating. Something to do with the effects of midwinter darkness on the mind. So what about the electric shock I'd got from my own elbow? I thought back to the glowing man in Berlin. The boggin man in the Zoo Bahnhof and the other derelicts I'd seen with the light glowing out of them. Deke pulled me out of the dwam with a request for a song and pushed a guitar into my lap. I threw back an Islay Mist and fingered a few chords then began to sing. Thinking to myself as I sang. Ach. Christmas. It's never that bad once you get to the actual day.

* * * * * * * * * * * * * * * *

It's the Hogmanay Fach. Why don't you go down the Bull for a few pints and come home at closing time? I'm not feeling up to it myself. Anyway Bell'll close sharp tonight. If you take the jeep you'll easy be home before the New Year. It'll do you good to see your pals for a while.

But will you be okay?

Sure. I'll be fine.

We had the radio going good style hooked up to a car battery. They were playing out the year's tunes up until midnight. I was quite enjoying sitting there with a few beers and a smoke and the voice of the lum droning underneath the music. Reflecting on times gone by. Old New Years the ones we used to have back in the city at Blane Gardens. The five day party. I always did have the capacity to drink for a few days without pausing for breath when the mood was on me. The Ne'erday was generally the time. At the end of that New Year me and Cammy and Sharleen and Ola had gone out on to Belmont Bridge. Under the big crown-shaped sandstone steeple of the Kelvin Church. Chucked over the Christmas tree with all the decorations still on it then laughed spladoosh as it hit the pool and rocked and twisted away down the brown spate. Then the evictions and the Battle of Blane Gardens. The move to the Haven. Working the barra and turning my wee fortune. A season of alfresco shagging. The greatest musical recital in the world ever and now a baby growing in Ola. Jeeze. And to think my life was only just beginning.

For a moment I really felt like just staying put by the iron stove and waiting for the midnight dram. Then again there was sure to be a bit of crack down in the bar. The option of the Bull was doing tug-o-war with the fireside beers and radio option. The Bull gave a final heave on the rope and the fireside team sprawled over defeated on the turf. I stood up.

Okay then. I'll away down for a while. We can always go visiting in a day or two when you're feeling a wee bit better.

I put the keys in the jeep's ignition and started the bang-clatter engine. Ola was standing at the door. She walked pregnantly out on to the porch and the door swung behind her shutting out the light from inside the house. I blinked hard then screwed in my eyes and blinked again. It couldn't be. A faint strand of light surrounded her body as she waved. I looked away then back again but she'd opened the door to go back in and stood in the glow of the house. I rolled down the window.

Ola! Are you okay?

Aye!

Sure?

Sure! I'm fine!

Bye bye! Take care! I'll be back before the year's out!

Toot on the horn and I was away. Rolling down the track. The jeep rocking and dipping through potholes. Keeping my eyes out of the darkness. Gazing hard on the headlight beam.

Thumb pressed down clunk on the old iron pad. The door swung open to a galaxy of bousie heads. Somehow they looked like cartoon drawings of planets. You know the kind? A benign looking man-on-the-moon. A red-faced sun with a solemn expression. Angry Mars. Wistful Venus. The Bull was packed. A galaxy of planet heads in a firmament of bar-room light. Bound in harmony of low conversation. Slowly revolving this way then that to speak to their cronies with pints or drams in their hands. I stood in the doorway for a moment to take in the vision of the drinking planets then guided myself through the drunken constellation to the bar. BeJaz! Even old Auntie Bell had a good drink in her and was hooting away as she delivered drams and pints over the counter to outstretched hands. The Ancient Crawfords were at the corner table and had started up some tunes with a melodeon and a mouth organ. On the table beside the harmonica-playing Crawford was a set of false teeth he'd obviously spurned as a hindrance to the moothie music. A standing crowd gathered round them tapping feet and letting out the occasional hooch. The tune ended to a smattering of applause. The melodeon played on. Drifting in to the next tune as the toothless Crawford laid the harmonica down on the table beside his wallies and he swiftly knocked back a dram. Then he *shtarted shinging.*

For theeshe are my mountainshhh
And theeshe are my glenshhh
The dayshh of my sssshildhood
Shhall know me again
No landsshhh ever claimed me
Though far I did rooo-am...
For theesshe are my moun-tainssshhh
And I'm coming home

Everyone watched the toothless Crawford belting out the song. Without the dentures to keep his features in check his face just about closed up altogether. It seemed like the point of his chin would reach the peak of his bunnet until he opened his gob to release a cascade of saliva as he belted out the next line of the old music hall favourite. Folk who had put down their drinks on the table were hastily retrieving them lest they should get an extra charge of water in their dram. The entire bar was avoiding eye contact in case a hoot should escape and spread across the room. Like the Berlin Olympics it would have taken just one person to crack. The song ended to cheers and applause when a roar cut through it.

Fach! Ya mad drunken jobby!

Deke was in the Hawaiian and shades with a pint in one hand and a double in the other.

Drunk? Deke! I'm stony sober man.

Whit? Bell! Emergency! A pint of Guinness and a large Islay Mist!

The smoky Hebridean nectar hit the spot then I sluiced back the Guinness and ordered up more drinks for Deke and myself. The Bull was going into lunar orbit and it would have been pointless trying to stay sensible in company like this. A fiddle had joined in with the melodeon and moothie as the old tunes competed with the roar of conversation. Half past eight. Three and a half hours to go.

* * * * * * * * * * * * * * * *

The old inn windows were steamed up and running with condensation when a bright flash reflected into them. Headlight glare shining directly in from the square. Whatever it was it must have been a fairly big vehicle as it was taking a few manoeuvres to reverse into a parking space. I said to Deke. *What the hell's this? A coach party?* We craned our heads towards the window at the distorted picture through rivulets of moisture. The bus was jerking back and fore attempting to park then a door opened and it began spewing out bunches of people as it jolted from side to side. They all seemed to be holding hefty plazzy carry-out bags staggering out into the middle of the square holding on to each other. The odd shout could be heard. Eventually a figure fell from the bus then tottered to the front of the crowd slanting under the weight of his carrier bag. He pointed with his free hand towards the Bull then the crowd surged forward as they came towards us. The door banged open and they streamed in.

Hey Missus! Missus! Gie's a fuckin pint! A pint o' anythin!

Some of them were still swigging from cans as they jostled their way to the bar and screamed out their orders. One of them fired up the jukebox as the KLF vied with a jig being played by the makeshift band in the corner. A whole busload. It seemed to be young guys mostly a few lassies too. I was leaning on a shelf when the figure who had fallen from the bus and pointed the rest of them towards the Bull came reeling forward.

Farchar! Ma main man! How's it goin mate?

I gave him a coupon scan. A few straggles of hair fell over the front of his face from a lurid green quiff. Nose rings and a mouth-stud. He'd on a scabby brown leather pilot's jacket with a few names of bands dabbed on in Tippex. Waltzers. Y-Fire. The Spanners. REEZ. He tilted a cider can to his mouth and I looked hard to see if I could put a name to the face. Blankitty blank. Must have been somebody I'd met in a bar back in the West End days. Maybe from the Halt or the Carnarvon. He drew the can away and some of it dribbled down his chin as he handed it to one of his buddies. He put his arm round me.

Hey! Listen up ya bastards! This is the guy I've been telling yez about on the bus out. And I havenae seen im for fuckin yonks! This is the greatest guy I've ever met in ma life. The maddest guy in St Ronans. The maddest guy in the world! This is my big brother. Fachie!

Wh. Wh. What? Baden?

He landed a fake slow-motion punch in the middle of my chest.

Of course it's Baden. Of course it's fuckin Baden! Farchar! Ma man.

Well blow me down. Baden? I hadn't seen him since I'd quit the cold sandstone mansion all those years ago. Maybe since the night Uncle Duncan had brought him and Edith to the window of the Bull to show them a specimen of drunken degeneracy. Father son and daughter had been dressed in matching duffel coats and sheepskin gloves on that occasion. How times change.

Baden. What are you doing? Who are all these people?

We've come out for the New Year. It's my pals from the Uni.

The Uni?

Aye! I'm at the Caley now! We're all mechanical engineers.

That's great. You brought them here on a bus?

Aye. We hired a bus. Cool eh?

Where willl they all stay?

Stay? They can stay in the house man. It'll be pure Madsville.

You're taking a busload of drunks back to first-foot Uncle

Duncan and Auntie Mary?

Eh? Naw naw ma man. Uncle Du. Ah mean ma mum and dad. They won this winter holiday thing. Mum sent away to a competition in the Sunday Mail *and she won. They're away to Madeira. They'll no be back till the sixth of January. Mega eh?*

Aye. Mega right enough. What about Edith?

Edith?

Aye. Your sister? Edith. What if she tells?

Edith's away. She'll never know. Anyway Fach. I'm no giving a fuck anyway. Okay ma man! Wahay!

Baden fell headlong into a crowd of his pals then they formed into a rugby scrum and began trying to heave each other back and fore in the middle of the room pushing people aside knocking over tables spilling drinks knocking glasses to the paved floor. Nobody in the bar seemed to care. Quarter past ten. It seemed most of the Strath was there. All the celebrities too. The Crawfords. Deke. Big Chief and the Hen-Wife. For a moment I wondered how Ola was doing when somebody thrust a guitar at me.

Go on Farchar son. Gie's a song!

I hit D minor and launched into Minnie The Moocher. By the end of the first chorus the whole bar was roaring out

HI DEE HI DEE HI DEE HI!

There is such a thing as a parallel universe. A place where things move at a different rate. Believe me. In the past I've known myself to hang around the Haven maybe going for a walk or a cast or just sitting around the porch of the cabin playing a few tunes. Time seems extended. Clouds scraping their way across that endless sky.

Likewise with the drink the same process can be reversed when time contracts. With the passing of these last few years I've since come to diagnose myself as what might be called a binge alcoholic. There have been times when I've started out on a session and the days have rattled past without my even noticing them. Thinking it's all passed in the span of a day. The parallel universe. This isn't a denial thing and not necessarily when I've been in a state of oblivion either. Sometimes more like being carried along on a tide of euphoria. But if a man is to suffer a bit of depression and the occasional mild hallucination in this life then it is vital that he holds on to each moment of joy as it passes. Clinging to the flotsam of the shipwreck to keep you afloat. Thus can my selfishness be justified. Cheaply but philosophically.

Well folks that was the story 'bout Minnie the Moocher
She was a no good hoochie-coocher
She was the roughest the toughest frail
But Minnie had a heart as big as a whale

hi dee hi dee hi dee hi...

HI DEE HI DEE HI DEE HI!

ho dee ho dee ho dee ho...

HO DEE HO DEE HO DEE HO!

hee dee hee dee hee dee hee...

HEE DEE HEE DEE HEE DEE HEE!

hi dee hi dee hi dee hoooooaaaa...

HI DEE HI DEE HI DEE HOOOOOAAAA...

Student eejits were doing the bouncy-bouncy to the chorus and the Ancient Crawfords waved their walking sticks in the air. The Hogmananny hootenanny was full-on now as they called for one song after another. Deke raised his glass to the throng.

We might be a bunch o miserable bastards! But at least we know how tae enjoy wirselves!

A redhead craned out from the crowd and planted a kiss on me. Hell's Bells! It's Sharleen! Sharleen ma darleen! I passed on the guitar and we hugged.

Shar! Ya beauty! Where's Cammy?

He's no coming home Fach. We had an argy-bargy last night

and he pissed off in the cream puff. He's decided to take in the Ne'erday with some pals in Glasgow. Eejit. There's no way I'm spending the New Year down there on my own. The telly's the same old Scottish shite every year. I caught the last bus out this afternoon.

Grand!

Where's Ola?

She's no coming down she's no feeling up to it. Usually goes to her bed early these days. In fact she'll probably be sleeping by now.

God Fach would you look at the time. It's almost the New Year. I thought the bar would be closed by now.

So did I Shar. So did I.

We gauged it by the bar clock. A hush descended as the clock reached the final minute before midnight. Every pair of eyes in the bar was on that clock. As the second hand hit ten-to a big count down was chanted out.

TEN! NINE! EIGHT!

People reached down fumbling their drams at the ready.

FIVE! FOUR!

The volume rose.

THREE! TWO! ONE! ......ROOOO-AAAAR!

The toothless Crawford had his pipes ready and fired into a reel. The whole bar hugged together and danced up and down on the spot. I stood up on a table with my dram holding it to the light and said quietly. *Here's to everybody I've ever known.* I tilted the dram then rejoined the hooly. Bell let it go on and on. Drinks were being handed over the bar rapid-style until at some point she dang the bell for closing time. God knows when. The party was beginning to fizzle a wee bit as people got into their jackets when Baden stood up on the bar.

> *Everbody on the bus! Everybody! On the fucking bus! It's party time!*

The Bull punters spilled out into the square then made their way onto the bus. A flurry of snow had begun and was swirling down over the square. The first of the winter.

More and more people were cramming onto the bus. Every seat was taken and the gangway was crammed then more folk got on and bellied along the tops of people's heads above the seats. I'd managed to squeeze myself onto a seat with two people already on it and Sharleen knelt on top of me. I took the sole of a Doc Marten in the face as more bodies panther-crawled past. There was an upside down face beside me as some eejit dangled like a gibbon from the luggage rack. A mad rabble screaming and swearing and laughing until the driver started up the engine and the whole bus cheered out with one voice like bairns going on an annual picnic as we wheeled out onto the road. Baden was somewhere near the front screaming out directions.

> *Take a left driver! Yes! That's it ma man! Cool!*

It felt strange as the driver swung the bus off the Shannoch Road down into the gravel drive of the cold sandstone mansion. First time I'd been here in years. A scraping and cracking as the bus pushed its way through a tunnel of branches.

> *Ha ha! Don't worry driver! Fuck the trees! Keep going! Cool!*

The bus pulled up at the house then the crowd emptied out. Baden was at the front ushering everybody inside. I paused at the door.

Are you sure about this Baden?

What?

Did you not clear this with Uncle Duncan before he left for Madeira?

Fuck him Fachie. Fuck HIM! Come on dude! Party!

I went inside thinking maybe I'd better hang around for a while just to keep an eye on things. The bus passengers had emptied into the living-room. Two of the students were at Uncle Duncan's radiogram and had lifted the lid to look around inside for records.

Here man! Check this! Val Doonican!

Fuck's sake. What's this? Ken Dodd?

As they searched through the albums they were discarding them by skiting them in mid-air across the living-room. Each skite was getting more vigorous as they made their way through the collection until the flying records were banging into the opposite wall.

Des O' Connor? Fuck off!
Skite!

Perry Como ma arse!
Skite!

Jim Ree-eeeves. Get tae fuck!
Skite!

Baden was doubled up laughing in the middle of the room. Screaming out in his ridiculous and obviously recently adopted Glasgow accent.

Hahaha! Whit a blast! Ma Da's records are shite man!

I was on the verge of calling a stop to it when the humour of the situation struck me. Poor Baden. The boy was just letting go of a lifetime's repression and he was entitled to it. Just a bit of crack with his pals. What the hell if a few Val Doonican records were going to get scratched as they got ejected out the radiogram like clay pigeons. Let him have his fun and his newly found expression of Weegie-speak. No wonder he went a bit daft when he got to Glasgow with twenty years of Duncan for a father. Duncan'd always insisted that Baden would study divinity to become a minister and that Edith would become a nurse. Ach good on you Baden. Have your release son. You're right enough. Fuck old Duncan. Fuck him. Fuck HIM.

A bottle of tequilla came towards me and I took a hefty swig. Then a joint. Then a can. A tequilla. A can. A whisky. A joint. One of the student engineers pulled a portable CD player from a rucksack and got it going. A bit of dancing and people moving from room to room. I'd bought a sizeable carry-out from Bell. The whole downstairs level of the house seemed to be stacked with drink.

The only thing that concerned me now was the presence of a couple of minky neds from The Close. The McDougalls. Sinky and Bud. Sinky was the worst of them and had a bit of a menacing presence due mainly to a complete lack of neck. His head sat square on top of his shoulders giving him the appearance of one of the earlier models of *homo sapiens* on the evolutionary scale. But I think Sinky's glower was worse than his bite. One day I'd left Turk's shed unlocked then come back for something and caught him raking around my gear. Laying some tools to one side that he'd obviously decided for his own. I lost the place and offered to kick his arse the length and breadth of Strathfinglas. Sinky wasn't long in reversing out of the place but he found time to hang around the gate and mouth a few threats. So I told him I'd be letting Turk MacGruer know he'd been on his property and the effect was magic. Sinky disappeared. Your man Turk would have kicked Sinky the length of the Strath and further with a single boot. My worry was that the McDougalls would find the students a bit beyond their comprehension and might start lashing out. Surely not. It was the New Year. Nobody fights at the New Year.

* * * * * * * * * * * * * * * *

It started in the kitchen. The usual thing. Banging and rumbling feet and screaming. Shit. I sprang off the living-room sofa. A crowd of Baden's pals were trying to restrain him as he reached out slapping away trying to connect with the McDougalls. Sinky was cornered trying to fend him off with a vodka bottle. Bud for some reason was standing in the doorway with his hands gripping hard to the bottom of his jersey. He had it tucked up to his chin with some kind of a bundle crammed inside the front of it. Baden saw me and stopped swinging then started pointing.

> *FACH! FACH! THAT PAIR A CUNTS! AH CAUGHT THEM IN THE FREEZER. NICKIN MA MUM AND DAD'S BUTCHER MEAT! AH'LL FUCKIN KILL THEM!*

I grabbed the bottle out of Sinky's hand. The best thing would be to get rid of Bud and Sinky as quietly as possible. I sent Baden out the room to try and restore a bit of order. I couldn't see Bud but Sinky was still hanging around.

> *Okay Sinky. Enough's enough. Just fuck off and take your brother with you. If ye don't fuck off I'm callin the law. So just fuck right off. Now.*

Sinky skulked towards the front door when Sharleen came birling out of the living-room with a bong in one hand and a can in the other.

> *What's this I'm hearing McDougall? Thievin wee shite! Stealing people's food? Away back tae yer ain neck of the woods. Ha Ha!*

Get it? NECK of the woods. Ya NECKLESS cunt!

Sharleen got hammered onto the carpet. Lying with her hand across her mouth and blood trickling through. A tingling sensation went through me. It seemed to rise up from the soles of my feet. Red blotches were swirling in front of my eyes and a kind of metallic taste came into my mouth. I felt weak and powerful at the same instant as the adrenalin put a shudder through me. I sprung forward and let one go. Sinky was a few inches smaller than me and the punch smacked into the middle of his forehead. He was still up but stunned so I let fly with a forty-inch shank that caught him in the side of the ribs and he sprawled towards the door. I tried to direct the blows so that he would keep flying in the direction of the front door. He stayed on his feet and managed to reverse out backing on to the lawn. I didn't advance any further and stayed put in the doorway. Bud was in the middle of the drive with the bundle of meat from the freezer still happed inside his jersey. You could see steam rising from it and the moisture making its way through the cloth. Sinky staggered over towards Bud then Baden came outside and joined me on the doorstep. There was a fair smattering of snow coming down now.

Hey. Fach. Some cool pugilistics there ma man. Hittin a woman eh? That showed the bastards. Hey! Haud on man! Check it out! That dirty bastard Bud's still got the meat!

They were backing out the drive. Then Baden let go with the insult that had rallied the McDougall brothers to fisticuffs throughout their long suffering schooldays. It was something they seldom heard in their later years but was obviously still capable of hitting a raw nerve.

HEY! MINKY SINKY! BUD THE FUD!

Even with Sinky nursing his wounds they both swivelled round.

GIVE ME THAT BUTCHER MEAT BACK! RIGHT NOW!

Sellophane parcels with rock-solid frozen mince and square-slice sausage came flying out of the air like missiles. Baden and me were ducking for cover as a bunch of links smashed through glazing on the porch then a lump of liver took out the living-room window. Baden's pals spilled out of the house and fired a salvo of beer cans and bottles and bits of Aunt Mary's rockery towards the McDougalls. One or two rocks came hurling back once they'd run out of meat but we managed to overcome them with our superior firepower as they retreated out of the drive and legged it up the Shannoch Road under a volley of sticks and stones and lumps of earth. I was hooting uncontrollably now and couldn't resist it. I ran up the road after them then let go with my last brick and a cackle and a roar coming out of me reminiscent of days long past.

> *YAWOO! SHANNY YA BASS! SHA-NEEEEE!*

Baden and myself went into Dunc's garage and had a laugh pulling out a board and covering over the smashed pane on the living-room window. The snow was getting thicker.

We headed inside. The party was back on full tilt after the victory as music and songs and screams and cackles and shouts blared out. I found Sharleen and gave her a hug to make sure she was alright. Then I ran a bath to take the grime off me. I left the water running then nipped downstairs to grab hold of a bottle of whisky to take into the bath. I could hear Baden ben the sitting-room reliving the battle with his mates.

> *Did ye see the size a that fuckin brick ah threw? It jist missed tae. Heh. Ah telt yez big Fachie was fuckin mental. Ah telt yez din't ah? Din't ah? Din't ah fuckin tell yez? Din't ah?*

Back into the bathroom. Silence and steam. The taps had stopped running. Sharleen was in the bath.

So I got in the bath. I suppose it was a kind of comfort thing after the fight. Sharleen was still a bit shaky and so was I. We had a drink and soaped one another up a bit until the old whangly-dangly was getting fair rigid. I put my hand down and shampoo'd Shar's red pubes. We were both really drunk and the prospect of an aquatic shag was getting dangerously close. It was thwarted by banging at the door then somebody flying through it pinging the snib off. There was a queue of pishers as Shar and Me got dried then dressed ourselves. Sharleen looked at me and laughed and we let out a moo.

Then came the whine of a two-stroke engine and my heart sank. Some eejit had gone out to the garage and found a moped and was whizzing through the downstairs rooms on it. I could hear Baden's laugh screeching out.

Nahahahaha! Fuckin Easy Rider!

I ran down. Things were getting bad. Baden was sitting at the Hammond organ in the hall. The one we used to gather round for hymns on a Sunday afternoon. Aye and he was playing it all right. With a hammer held in each hand. Smashing into the keys until the organ sounded like it was yelling in pain with each blow. I tried to stop him but couldn't get near for fear of a backswing taking my head off. Next keys and bits were flying off as the keyboard began to disintegrate. One of his mates was on top dancing until there was a crack and half of him disappeared inside it. Half-man half-organ. You don't see that every day. Baden had climbed aboard a roller-coaster of hysteria and now it was going so fast there was no stopping it. I was about to punch him when I heard a roar coming from upstairs. Aw naw. At the top of the broad curving stairs. A bunch of them had overturned a wardrobe and dragged it from a bedroom. Four bodies were sitting up inside it with the doors propped open as the rest of them pushed their giant sledge to the edge of the stair. *ONE! TWO! THREE!*

They let go as the wardrobe trundled forward then picked up speed and came flying down the staircase banging into the floor at the bottom. The riders fell out in hysterics then started dragging it back upstairs. Baden leapt in the air.

Nahahaha! Ah want a shot! Ah want a shot!

It was out of my hands now. What could I possibly do? The only thing that would've stopped them was a machine gun. The flying meat and the broken windows had lit the fuse for an explosion of destruction. The world of inhibition was a universe away. I took a slug of whisky and lit a cigarette then opened a can. Cheer followed cheer as the wardrobe and its passengers went clattering down the stairs again and again. Then came a louder cheer and I went out for a look. The idiot on the moped was at the top of the stair preparing for a cresta-run. He opened the throttle and jolted forward. The front wheel went over the first step then the bike flipped over and sent him somersaulting down the stairs. Baden was out front now cheering dressed in Uncle Duncan's Sacred Temple apron with the stellar insignia. I was just thinking things couldn't get worse. They did.

The noise moved outside now and Baden had them gathered in the snow. He'd taken out Duncan's best set of golf clubs. I watched as he pulled the clubs out of the bag one by one and bent them over his knee then tried firing them through the air like boomerangs. I headed through to the kitchen. There was a knee-trembler going on against the wall with the lassie's arms outstretched gripping on a shelf knocking cups off cup hooks and sending them smashing to the deck.

The hour was striking eight. This I remember because two idiots were waiting beside the cuckoo clock in the hall waiting to punch the cuckoo as it came out. By the seventh cuckoo the clock fell to the floor smashed to pieces. The two of them stood laughing then walked away. There was a dull whirr and a click as the tiny wooden bird appeared in slow motion and gave out its very last cuckoo and lay dead on the end of its spring.

The living-room was Paddy's Market meets Hiroshima. Snoring corpses lay across the wreckage of furniture and shattered ornaments. The needle on the radiogram was sending out a regular *cladunk...cladunk.* I lifted the album off the turntable and looked around for its cover. The Steele Combo. Five guys in white crimplene trousers and wide-open shirts sported hairy chests and medallions. Posing like psychedelic haddies on the steps of some baronial castle in Aberdeenshire. I put the album back in the cover and had a scan at the sleeve notes. *We in Scotland can be justly proud of the Steele Combo and the music they have made so popular at dance halls throughout the north. We would like to extend our thanks to their manager Wee Sandy Meldrum who always makes sure the lads arrive at the dances on time.* Grooveball city. Cheesecloth heaven. Those were the days my friend right enough. I started picking up any albums I could find sticking them in their covers. There were still a few days to go before Auntie Mary got home. Surely something could be done to minimise the intensity of her impending cardiac. I made my way through to the next room and found Baden sitting in the wreckage of an armchair with a bottle of whisky in his hand. Sobbing and laughing at the same time. I sat on the floor and pulled the bottle out of his grasp.

Jesus Baden. You let it get out of control. You've done it now.

Ach that's all right Farchar. Don't let it worry you.

Worry? Auntie Mary's going to die when she sees this lot.

It's all right Fach. Everything went according to the plan. Even better if the truth be known.

What? I'm not following you.

Fuck it Farchar. Don't you think I planned this? The busload of punters to the house. The place getting wrecked. It went like a dream. When my old man gets back he'll probably try and get me the jail for this. I'm no worried a shite Fachie. Honest I'm no. The job's done now.

The job? For heaven's sake Baden. Are you telling me you hired Bud the Fud and Minky Sinky to start a riot?

Na. That was just a bit of luck.

Your poor mother.

Well. If she drops down dead at least she'll be rid of that bastard Dad.

Baden. You're not making sense. You're not making sense at all. The place is wrecked. What the fuck's the point of all this?

I'll tell you what the point is Fach. I've been planning revenge on that old bastard for most of my life.

Revenge?

Aye. Sweet revenge. Revenge for me. For you even. And especially for Edith.

Edith?

Edith couldnae make it tonight. Ye know why? I'll tell you why. Because Edith's in the mental hospital Farchar. In Glasgow. In Gartnavel Royal. She's ill. Really ill. Clinical depression. And I know why. I know exactly why.

Tell me Baden. I want to know.

It all begins a long time ago Farchar. You were there. At least you weren't far away.

I was?

Aye. Do you remember my Dad's expeditions to the Shannoch Woods?

Of course I remember. The empire games.

What else do you remember Fach?

What else? I don't know. The bird impression contests stick in my memory right enough.

What else?

The disguises! I remember the disguises! The silly old cunt used to drape you and me in sheets and a towel head dress. We were supposed to be foreigners and stand guard either side of the camp to act as a foil in case any intruders came.

Did you never get lonely standing there Fach?

Na I don't suppose I did. I had a handline planked that I used to bait up and fish a pool in the Caldon. No way I was going to stand beside a path on my tod doing nothing for three or four hours.

So you broke the camp pledge?

Of course I did. All that crap your Da used to tell us about how we would be cheating God and our countrymen if we didn't protect the Camp Secret. Even when I was a wee boy I realised your old man was a total frying-pan.

More than you'll ever know Fach. And do you want to know what the Camp Secret really was?

I think I remember this. The Chalice the Cross and the Secret Word. The Covenant the Sword and the Blood of the Lord. The Family the Flag and the Glory of God. Protect them from danger and cover your tracks. Sometimes he used to sit at the camp fire and tell us about how he hid from the Japanese in the jungles of Burma.

Aye. If he managed to get the camp fire lit. Burma my arse. My old man spent the war checking auld wifies in the Close for leaving a light on during the blackouts. They kept him in his job at the Mill right through the whole war.

Aye. Where he managed to spin more war stories than uniforms.

The Family the Flag and the Glory of God. Protect them from danger and cover your tracks. Or the enemy will bring his vengeance and burn you in your sleep forever. It used to terrify me Fach. But when my faither would send us out on guard duty at the camp I used to get lonely. Awful lonely. Scared even. Used to imagine I could hear voices on the wind. Then one time I sneaked back to the camp. That's right Fach. I broke the pledge and went back. You know what I saw man? You want to know what I saw?

Where is this going Baden?

I'll tell you what I saw. I sneaked up on the tent. I looked through the front flap in the canvas. It was my Da. Our great patrol leader. He had Edith pinned down. He had Edith. He had. He had Edith. He had Edith. He had. Oh my God Farchar. I've never spoken about this before. Oh Jesus Fachie. I'm sorry man. I'm sorry.

The tears were rolling out of his eyes. He started to jolt with the emotion.

Fuck's sake Baden. Are you sure about all of this?

Am I sure? Of course I'm fuckin sure. Just like I'm sure the old bastard used to fuck around with me. Jesus Christ. We were only children. Sweet Jesus Christ. What about you Fachie? Did he never?

Eh? No. Jesus. No.

There were four of them in the end Fach. Dirty evil old bastards. Influential people. I think they were all members of The Temple. It used to go on in a back room of the Institute. Behind a locked door.

Fuck's sake. Jesus. We should get the law onto this.

How do you prove it? They used to take us there one at a time. Right up until we were about thirteen. Edith's a mess. Total mess. She took really ill about a year ago. She's tried to take her life twice. I'm the only person that's been to visit her since she went into hospital. Dad and Mum are denying there's anything wrong. Mum doesn't know the truth anyway. About Dad and his cronies fiddling around with us.

The foundations of the world I knew were crumbling around me. I'd always considered there had been an order to my existence. Okay so maybe not an order of the ordinary sort. My father's disappearance. Ma's breakdown and the burning building. Growing up in St Ronans. Going abroad. Life in the Haven. It was all bound together by confusion but it was a kind of chaos I could live with. The things Baden had told me in the last few minutes had shattered everything. A sickness was brewing inside me. There was a black shape sitting over Baden and for the first time in my life I felt the tangible presence of evil. I could say that I wanted to cry or shit or maybe spew like they always do in the TV dramas but it wasn't like that. Only this dark empty feeling. Sure there was nothing lost between Duncan and myself but for the life of me I'd never have expected this. Christ. My own father's brother? There was nothing of value any more. Nothing would ever be the same. Nothing.

But Jesus what could I do? I had the sweetest girl in the world waiting up the hill for me and my wee cratur growing inside her. Life was waiting for me. I picked myself up to leave then tottered sideways and fell crashing into a glass-fronted display cabinet. The room swirled and I closed my eyes.

I awoke nestled in a pile of shattered glass then looked myself up and down for cuts. I had the magnetic sensation on the top of my head. The sensation that follows a bout of rampant over-indulgence. Like there's this invisible magnet poised just above your head sooking all the matter out of your brain. Music was playing in the next room and voices drifted through. I was still clutching the bottle of whisky.

I'd had a dream about Uncle Duncan and his three co-perverts. They were dressed in their stellar aprons and were hovering over Edith as she lay anaesthetised and helpless on an operating table. They prodded at her naked body with different implements that they picked up from a surgeon's tray then Uncle Duncan selected a razor blade. He held her wrist over a steel bucket then drew the razor blade across. The blood began to pour out into the bucket and as it poured down foaming it made the noise of the Caldon rushing over rocks. I stood over the bucket of blood and cast in a baited handline. Then I'd woke to the sound of crinkling glass. Lying in shards around my head and shoulders as I stirred from the dream. I felt myself up and down for cuts then sat upright and gave myself a shake to try and get the dream out of my system. Like a dog shaking water from its coat. I took a swig out the bottle then found a can of lager. January the First. I think. All over Scotland people would be reaching out for a bottle or a can to take the sting out of the hangover and start again. I felt I needed it more than anybody else. Or maybe it was January the Second. Who knows? I was in the parallel universe.

Ben the living-room the party was kicking in again. After a few cans I was feeling okay and had a word with Baden in the kitchen and everything was dandy. He was feeling much better after telling me what happened at the camp all those years ago. He had no remorse about wrecking the mansion. The Swiftbus would be running again in a couple of days after the New Year break and him and his daft student cronies would head back to the city before Duncan and Mary got home. Half of St Ronans had been in the house so it would only be a matter of time before Duncan found out who had been responsible for trashing the place. Fuck Duncan.

So it began all over again. The wardrobe sleigh runs and the attempted moped rides down the staircase. I even had a shot myself and everybody cheered. In the greatest tradition of Scottish male hypocrisy I allowed myself a shagging from Sharleen. It was a braw shag. She had me in my old bedroom and I thought there was something quite sexy about that. It was only a New Year fuck. What the hell? The world was falling apart anyway. With the exception of the Battle of the Frozen Meat I don't recall seeing the outside world once during the whole New Year session the curtains in every room were drawn. Any time the Guilt Fairy started nipping at my ear I would reach down for the bottle. This was my very last fling. I was an expectant Da. It was the New Year. Surely Ola would forgive me. When the drinking was over it would be into January for real and I could start the year with a fresh optimism.

* * * * * * * * * * * * * * * * *

When we left the cold sandstone mansion the white light of day was blinding our eyes. I walked up the Shannoch Road with the procession of would-be engineers and saw them to the square to catch the Swiftbus back to Atlantis. Baden had a squint at the timetable. There was an hour to spare and a screw of smoke was climbing its way out of the Bull chimney. It's always a treat to drink a pint after days on the canned beer. The atmosphere in the pub was a wee bit edgy as the seriousness of the last few days began to kick in. I suppose folk were beginning to worry about the prospect of charges being pressed. After a couple of pints it eased off and the tunes on the jukebox made the atmosphere good again. I drank a third pint to put me on an even keel then bade my farewells.

Walking up to the jeep I wondered how long it would take Ola to forgive me and start speaking to me again. A day? A week? Never? I'd left her stranded up there but there'd been plenty of food and fuel and stuff in the house. Walking through the swingpark at the back of the village I noticed how mild it was. Almost like summer. There was a real balmy atmosphere as the sun forced its way through spent rainclouds. The old global warming. Some day there would be no seasons at all. I got to the jeep and tried to start it but it wouldn't turn over. Only a dull click from the ignition. So I slammed the door shut and began the long walk up the brae gaining height on the strath below me.

All over Strathfinglas rivers were roaring. Burns foamed down from the hills filling up culverts and spilling out across the track. Far below the Finny had burst its banks and was sending brown muddied swirls out into the parks. I could see the main road away south was under siege and the distant blue blink of a fire engine. The whole place echoed to the sough of rushing waters. I wiped sweat from my brow. The oozing alcohol combined with the effort of the walk uphill in the balmy warmth had me soaking from head to foot.

The five songs were in full voice and it became impossible to walk the road dry-shod as ditches and burns flowed out across it. I reached the track's end looking hard at the top of the chimney to see if I could see the familiar twist of smoke. As I walked on there were moments when I swore I could see it. It was only an impression on my mind. There was no need for a fire today anyway. It was sweltering. The ground below me squelched as I made my way across the tussocks to the house.

I clumped on to the porch sure I would stir Ola then pushed the door in to a dull grey light. I held my breath not knowing what to expect. A scream of abuse. A rebuff. A crack on the head. I walked into the living-room. The stove cold with a sprinkling of cold white ash around it on the floor. The radio still hooked up to the car battery and a tiny distant voice coming out of it. Looked around the room. Nobody there. Opened the window. Ola was gone. I'd finally blown it. I turned around to make my way outside to the porch and think about things. Then I saw her in the bed in the corner. Her shape under the cover. Lifted the quilt. The mattress a mess of blood and bits. Ola clutching a tiny wee baby boy in the palms of her hands. A naked wee boy coated in white grease and blood and trails of congealed afterbirth. A petrified stare in Ola's dark eyes. Both of them still. Stark still.

I tottered away from the cabin seeing the land before me tilting through a blur of tears and disbelief. My steps were unsteady and breaths came short and sharp as I began to run down the track. When I reached the top of the brae where the road drops away I put my weight forward and let myself get pulled downhill with my legs responding of their own accord. I must have looked like a puppet broken loose of its strings. Then back up to the Haven in the police Land Rover staring out at the foaming rivers as we passed.

Again and again the officers asked me the same question. How could I have done it? Leaving a pregnant girl stranded in the coldest weather and worst snow storms in recorded history. I sat there in genuine dumbness. Either they were trying to fuck with my head or they knew something that I didn't. And they did. Which was this. The temperature in Strathfinglas on the 31st December had plummeted from plus nine degrees to minus twenty-two degrees in the space of only a few hours. For three solid days Siberian winds had carried in blizzard after blizzard of blinding snow. At the end of the third day the temperature had soared from minus twenty-two degrees to plus fourteen. Cloud after cloud of torrential rain had washed away the snow in a single night. I'd missed it all during my stay at the sandstone mansion. Ola and the premature wee baby didn't have a chance. The police took away their bodies and I sat there and looked out the window at a desolation of flattened grasses on the brown soaking lands.

How long did I sit there? Night followed day. By night the light poured incandescent out of my body as I watched it through a blur of tears. Day followed night. I looked up and saw a great twisting pillar of black cloud that stood on top of Meikle Carnock reaching miles into the sky. It made its way downhill in a solid body until it reached the lochan. It moved across ripping waters from the surface of the lochan carrying them high into the air in a terrifying vortex. It came towards me and shook the cabin like a leaf in a gale with boards creaking and banging before the tornado released its grip to advance northwards. A deafening crack then a flash as a bolt of lightning came searing out of the clouds and struck the ground in front of the cabin sizzling the wet grasses. Is there such a thing as a vengeful God? I don't know. You tell me.

As the days passed I was collapsing with hunger then began nibbling at food. A tin of sardines first. Some cold beans. Then managed to light the fire. Dull red glow in the nest of the grate filling the whole stove up with log after log and shovel after shovel of coal until it was crammed. It began to take and sent out raging flames and smoke and the lum roared like some awful beast lurking out in the darkness of the hills.

When the fire dropped I banked it up with more wood and coal to let it rage again. Sat in the flashes of it with all the whisky I could find at my feet. Drank the whisky. Somewhere in there I fell into a deep confused sleep. Woke up with smoke burning my nose and my feet stinging with awful pain. The floorboards of the cabin were ablaze. My boots had melted onto my feet and the bottom half of my trousers had flames climbing up them. The smoke cutting into my throat and lungs like knives. Fell to the floor to get below the smoke and began to crawl along the burning floor for the door. Put my hand forward. I reached up and touched something. Ola's cello on its stand. The wood beginning to crack and blister and throw out trails of smoke. Reached the front door making a run for the lochan feet stinging with awful pain. I ran into the chill waters then looked back at the cabin behind me. Dull orange flashes behind the windows and a plume of black fumes rising into the sky. Light began to flicker across the lochan.

> *ALL LIARS SHALL HAVE THEIR PART IN THE LAKE WHICH BURNETH WITH FIRE AND BRIMSTONE.*

There was a bang and a shower of sparks as the roof lifted then the flames of the blazing cabin lit up the whole Haven and as far as the crags of the Meikle Carnock. Then I saw it. Bounding over the tussocks. Caught in the flashing light of the blazing cabin. A black hoodie figure caught in the flickering light running from the track's end and out of the Haven.

* * * * * * * * * * * * * * * *

Moonlight found its way through dust-clung windows and picked out the silent machinery of the production halls. The sound of the Finny water in the tunnel underneath the mill sent up irregular breaths like the serpent being disturbed in its sleep. The occasional clinks and plashes of back-currents and eddies found their way into my sleep. Echoing off the tunnel wall to send up a garble of voices like a whole cathedral of maniacs speaking in tongues. Somehow I could understand the message of it.

> *BECAUSE THOU ART LUKEWARM, AND NEITHER COLD NOR HOT, I WILL SPUE THEE OUT OF MY MOUTH.*

> *WHOSOEVER WAS NOT FOUND WRITTEN IN THE BOOK OF LIFE WAS CAST INTO THE LAKE OF FIRE.*

> *NEITHER FORNICATORS, NOR ADULTERERS, NOR THIEVES, NOR DRUNKARDS, SHALL INHERIT THE KINGDOM OF GOD.*

I was surrounded by demons spitting Revelations at me as Ola played her burning cello. The dream would always end with the black running figure in the hood charging out of the Haven. Waking with a start to look up at the great frozen looms of the textile machines which still held thread in some of their reels.

It had only taken a few years for the courtyards of the redundant mill to be reclaimed by willow bushes. Forcing their way up through cracked paving and rusting railway lines. I'd come out of the building on my sticks and pushed my way through the bushes towards the Shannoch Road. The rucksack on me and heading for Balshannoch to get some supplies out the mini-market. Leaning on the two sticks I must've looked like a cross-country skier. Hobbling on the blistered pus of my scalded feet.

I was making my way back along the hedgerowed road when a Swiftbus pulled to a juddering stop just ahead of me. The door hissed and banged open then Turk stepped down in his busman's uniform. He was shaking with rage and it wasn't a pretty sight.

Where the fuck have you been? We've been worried sick.

Sorry mate. Couldnae handle it. I'll maybe see you around eh?

Like fuck ye will.

He grabbed hold of me and lifted me into the bus then dropped me in a seat at the front. I looked up the bus and thirty glaikit faces looked back. Bags of shopping and a couple of dogs. Turk drove up the road then pulled into the Woodend scheme and drew up outside his house. He took me in then put the kettle on.

We sat for a while with a cup of tea and Turk told me I could stay with him and Joan. He went through and ran a bath then made sure I got into it. I shut the bathroom door.

Right Fachie son. I've left some clean gear for you outside the door. I'll see ye later. I better get back tae the passengers.

* * * * * * * * * * * * * * * *

My feet swelled until new skin made them work again. I feared sleep and I feared the waking day. Every night my dreams were visited by the running man. The hoodie. It was always the same way I would see him. Running splashing in the flashing light of the blazing cabin. Charging through the tussocks to the track's end. The Avenging Angel. He would get me yet. I kept it to myself. If I ventured out of the house I would always have an uneasy feeling of being watched.

When springtime came Turk got a hold of me and made me promise I'd go out to the fishing on the first day of the season. Saying it'd be good for me. When it finally arrived there were heavy rains around and the conditions were good. Turk couldn't come because of the driving. He kitted me up with a rod and a jaiket and a cheese piece then made sure I was out the door with him when he left for the bus depot with rain falling out of the dawning sky. Turk looked up and was nodding his head.

Well Fach it's lookin good. Wish I was comin with ye instead o this shite.

I was after the springers. The salmon. They weren't as numerous as the autumn fish but they were usually wild and silver and lively glowing bright with the cold winter seas of Greenland. I fished my way upriver past the Martyr's Pool then fished the confluence of the black swirling Caldon. There was no sign of any springers yet so I made my way into the gorge to have a cast after the trout. It was more sheltered from the rain in there under the curving mossy walls of the precipice.

I climbed down to a good spot where the Caldon drops over a sandstone ledge foaming down into a deep black pool and you can stand and let the flies drift down the stream. I fished away hauling wee brownies out and the diversion was good. It was time to come to terms with the paranoia. The Avenging Angel thing. It was purely a symptom of guilt. The burning coals in the stove must have spilled out and put a spark to the cabin while I was sleeping and that was that. So I'd seen that hoodie man. Aye and I'd heard Revelations too as I stood up to my knees in the lochan. Out of my head on whisky and hunger and emotion.

As for Ola and the wee cratur I'd have to live with that for the rest of my days. It was good standing there with the sound of the rushing waters echoing against the walls of the gorge soothing a bit of reason back into my mind. It was going to take years to deal with this big fuck-up. That was my cross. I'd have to bear it. The Caldon fell down foaming into the pool sending up bubbles that reflected the gloomy walls of the gorge and a crack of gleaming sky. The bubbles broke away from the body of foam under the falls transporting tiny photographs of the gorge that drifted away down the pool. I could see my own reflection in them too. Standing dark with the fishing rod pointing down. I followed my image as it spun away downstream on a bubble then it popped and I disappeared. I let my spirit find its way into the secret place where the sough of the flowing waters meets the sound of the wind in the trees. Where does the sound of the water end and the sound of the trees begin? There must be a way in.

A deafening explosion. Crack and a shower of water and sandstone shrapnel blows up in front of me into my face and eyes. I spin backwards into a soft bed of leaf mould holding my face. For a second I thought I was blind. When the blotches clear before my eyes there's a dark hooded figure standing over me. It took a few seconds for the picture to unblur. To come into focus. I could recognise the face inside the shadow of a hood. Craggy features with pitted skin. Bright cold eyes and a grey moustache. I focused in closer on the face. Uncle Duncan in a snorkel parka.

He was standing in the slow of the stream pointing the shotgun straight at my head. I watched him pull the trigger and felt a weird sense of calm knowing I was about to die. A split-second of peace that I've never felt in my life before or since. He let go with the shotgun then the kick of it sent him spinning. I'm up on my feet. BeJaz. Some hoodie executioner him he'd missed from three feet. I knew both barrels were spent and he'd need time to reload. It was straightforward enough then. He started backing off until he reached the ledge and I caught him a good clatter on the side of the head.

Give me the gun ya stupid auld bastard! Gie's it now!

I grabbed the butt and yanked it from him. My hearing began to recover from the bangs. A dull ringing in my ears subsided then the hiss of falling waters rose like the volume of a TV being turned up. I filled the muscles of my right arm with tension and adrenalin ready to break bones if I had too. The shanks were pulsing.

So it was you ya old fuck! It was you that tried tae roast me up there in the Haven.

Please Farchar. Take mercy! This is all Baden's fault. He's been spreading these. These horrible lies about me. I know what he's told you. He bribed me with…with lies so that I wouldn't press charges after what happened at the house at New Year. And he told me you were in on it too.

Lies ma arse! What about Edith?

You mustn't believe them Farchar. Baden and Edith are living in a web of lies. It's because they've gone to Glasgow and become drug addicts. It's warped their minds. They'll kill me with their lies. I want it to stop. I want it all to stop now.

Shut up ya old pervy cunt! You've tried tae kill me!

Oh God no! If this gets out. Oh God no I'll be finished.

If what gets out? What is there to fear if it's not true? I'll tell ye ya shite. There's nothing to fear. Absolutely nothing. Every day I open my eyes I walk and talk guilt. I know what it's like. Every waking hour. I breathe the fuckin stuff. And I can see it in your eyes. I can feel it glowing out of you now. I can see it glowing! I can fuckin see it! I CAN FUCKIN SEE IT GLOWING! I CAN FUCKIN SEE IT! SEE IT! SEE IT! SEE IT! GLOWING!

Farchar please! Don't hurt me.

Hurt ye? I'll fuckin kill ye! I'll kill you now. Ya bastard.

Reality check. When I said to Uncle Duncan *I'll kill ye* it was merely a figure of speech. Okay so the rage was on me. But I'd no intention of killing him at all. Though he clearly believed I was going to. He shouted over the noise of the rushing burn.

Merciful God help me! I didn't mean to hurt anyone. I didn't mean to do it. Please stop. Things got out of control. I didn't want the other men to get involved but they found out and blackmailed me.

The others? Ye mean the three auld pervy cunts at the Institute? Ya filthy bastards. Ya dirty fuck.

It was blackmail Farchar.

What about the tent at Shanny woods? I'll give ye Camp Secret ya bastard.

I couldn't help it. God help me I couldn't stop it.

You've fucked up everything! You're an even worse man than me! And d'ye know somethin? I'd no intention of telling anybody anything. For Aunt Mary's sake. And Baden and Edith. But you go and try and kill me? Oh I'm going to expose you. I'm going to expose you now.

No Farchar please. This is a family matter.

Family? Ya sick. Ya fuckin.

I took the gun in both hands then whooshed it dangerously through the air in front of his face. God he was pathetic. Backing off towards the falls till he could go no further. So pathetic I found myself suppressing a hoot. Standing there cowering on the edge of the waterfall in the green wellies and blue snorkel parka with the furry hood up. Begging for mercy and forgiveness and redemption and all the usual shite. It was hard to believe this was a murderous sex beast. The running man who had plagued my nightmares for the last three months. Whimpering like an idiot. Shaking like a rabbit with the myx. In truth I didn't know what to do. I could've easily scrambled out the gorge and away. I doubt he'd ever come after me again. In truth I was beginning to enjoy the moment then swung the gun an inch or two over the top of his head.

I'll give you family! Now repeat after me.

What?

I said repeat after me. The Family!

Eh?

Say it! The Family!

The…The Family.

The Flag!

The Flag.

And the Glory of God!

And the Glory of God.

The Family the Flag and the Glory of God!

The Family the Flag and the Glory of God!

THE FAMILY THE FLAG AND THE GLORY OF GOD!

WHOOSH! WHOOSH!

NOW DANCE! LIKE THIS! THE FAMILY THE FLAG AND THE GLORY OF GOD! DANCE!

The Family the Flag and the Glory of God! The Family the Flag and the Glory of God! The Family the Flag and the Glory of God!

Unmissable. Him in the parka dancing in the burn chanting the camp pledge.

You know what I'm going to do Duncan? You've covered your tracks long enough. I'm going to put posters up in the village. With your photograph on it and telling people the truth. The whole world's going to know what you are. You'll be lucky to get out of the Strath in one piece.

Please Farchar no. Remember my kindness. What I did for you.

You? You sat in your fuckin mansion with your money while

my mother raised us in a single end. Scraping her pennies together to feed me and Kathy. She went mental with the strain of it. And you stood by all those years and watched it happen? Ya dirty bastard!

Remember Farchar. It was me who took you in. Who fostered you.

Aye. And just as well I was a tough bairn or you might have had yer wicked way wi me.

Please Farchar. If you agree to keep this quiet. I'll make sure you get paid.

That was it. He was really nipping my head now. I decided it was time for a bit more sport.

Fuck you! How about I take you down to the village square right now? Then I'll tie you tae the obelisk and make a public announcement.

No. Please. Think of your Aunt Mary.

Naw! You think about Aunt Mary! Then I'll drive ye like an animal through the place. The church first. Then the golf club. The school. The Institute. Gather round everybody! Hurry Hurry! Get a stick and poke the paedo!

No!

Yes! Let's go! Let's make a start now!

Please.

Lead on MacDuff!

Please! No!

Move it! Let's go tell the world about pervy Uncle Duncan.

God forgive me. Please. God forgive me.

Duncan stepped back then jumped off the sandstone shelf into the black swirling pool. With the parka and wellies on he dropped under fast. The current was strong enough to drag him down the gorge. I threw the gun over the falls. Clambered down the bank shimmying at a crazy instinctive speed to the far end where the burn dropped away to the next deep pool. I reached up the bank and grabbed hold of a long branch ripping it through grass and moss to free it. Duncan had surfaced and looked into my eyes as he floated towards me. *UNCLE DUNCAN! GRAB THE STICK!* I cast it out in front of him. He gripped on to it then swirled round. The speeding current gathered inside his wellies trying to drag him away. He held on to the stick and righted himself to make an attempt to reach the bank. Then he looked up and let go. You could see in his eyes it was a conscious decision. The Caldon pulled him over the falls rushing him away down the quickening current. His two arms stuck out as he bobbed down the deep channel of the dammed-up pool. As the two arms reached the dam they spun around then disappeared as the river pulled him under. Dragging his body down a hundred feet of pipe to stick against the motionless rusting blades of the ancient turbine. I clambered down and out the mouth of the gorge. Running over the bank where the storm washed the elephant out of the soil all those moons ago.

I ran and ran and ran. Jouking fences and gates till I reached the road. Breath wheezing in long desperate gasps. I got to the road and began running towards the phone box at the far side of the hump-back brig. The soles of my boots hit the tarmac with a steady rhythm. Badum Dum Badumpa. Badum Dum Badumpa. As I pounded on a mantra found its way into my head that fitted exactly with the beat of the boots. Something from days long past.

Badum Dum Badumpa. Filthy Church Pumper. Badum Dum Badumpa. Filthy Church Pumper.

Running over the brig to the old red GPO phone box. I lifted the phone from the receiver and heard the hum of the dialling tone. Then I stopped. What was the point? A thousand tons of water would have poured over him by now. Who would believe my version of it? I had a moment of clarity. This was the way it should be. Sure for a time Auntie Mary would wonder where he was but in the long run she'd be free. Baden and Edith would always be his prisoners but at least he was gone in the physical sense. It was over. The Camp Secret was mines now.

I leant there on the cold metal shelf of the phone box gasping in lungfuls of air. Rain beating on the thick glass and running down the insides of the windows to collect in little puddles on the worn concrete floor. My ears pounded with the mantra. From the lashing I'd received for releasing a waft of fart gas in the kirk. That day I'd seen the glint of madness in Duncan's eyes as he came flailing down towards me with the leather strop. Filthy Church Pumper. Filthy Church Pumper. Filthy Church Pumper. FILTHY CHURCH PUMPER.

When they laid Ola and the wee cratur in the ground wee Scott was already beginning to grow inside Sharleen. As the song goes. It takes a worried man. So Sharleen quit for London and that was that. I didn't show face at the funeral. How could I have? Ola's Ma and Da. So now it's time for my own wee service here. In the best way I can. I've only missed it by a few years.

I look at the charred timbers of the Haven up there above the shore of the lochan. I've made two wreaths out of heather and the white flowers of waterlilies and make my way up the hill. Big tumbling clouds in a giant sky. I reach the remains of the cabin and walk among the charred timbers with a wreath in each hand.

> *There's no point in saying sorry. I've said it a million times. I knew I'd make it back some day. I'll always carry the both of you in my heart. Can you forgive me enough to let me do that? I tried to join you one night on Belmont Bridge. Can't explain that. Anyway. I'm here now. Maybe we all are. I miss you both.*

I kiss the wreaths and lay them in the ashes then walk away. So that's how it was.

There's no point in thinking about how it might have been. Ola and me and the wee cratur. Born of music. Living in family bliss. It's done now. Back down to the lochan and stay just a wee while longer at the Haven. That's all it should take. Yes. Indeedy. Just a wee while longer.

daniels

After I moonlighted from Turk's and reached Atlantis East End I had an old buddy down there called Jimmy Campbell and we used to go drinking. Our gaff was this big lodging house up on Duke Street called the Great Eastern Hotel. I remember the time Jimmy started telling me his story and I could see his light glowing. It was a different light from mine. A dull glow. Like a fire dying down.

Jimmy had found his way west via the Scottish prison system. He'd gone into his first job in a Dundee creamery when he was fourteen then his mother got diagnosed with the cancer. It was a neighbour told them that butter was a treatment for easing the cancer. He got caught with a block of it under his cap on the way out of the creamery so they put him in the court then sent him for a term on a borstal ship called the *Unicorn*. They made good use of the inmates in those days. Working them to the bone in the hulls of that ship away out in the cold grey waters of the Firth of Tay. He was timid and shaky and well-mannered. Found himself in The Life at an early age I suppose. When he was a young man he married his first sweetheart but she died within the year. His second wife nagged him right to the edge. Nagged him so far he'd strangled on her neck until her last breath then let go. Hard to believe such a slight wee polite man could do a thing like that.

I was struggling a bit in those days. Thought I could drown it. Pouring the bevvy down me like the water going down the pipe into Duncan's grave. You can tell you're struggling when you're seeing gargoyles coming out of buildings where they shouldn't be. Mine and Jimmy's was a fleeting association but I suppose it was a telling one because his story got me around to considering quite a few things.

Jimmy's last job had been as a watchie looking after the river-dredgers down at Rothesay Dock. I told him I'd known the place as a bairn and this surprised him. Belied my Teuchie accent I suppose. But the memory of the dock was vivid and I remembered they used to berth those dredgers on the north side of it. Painted dark blue and cream in the regulation colours of the river. Hopper Number 25 the Lennox. Or Number 28 the Blythswood with its big gantry of rotating buckets. The other side of the dock was where all the commercial stuff came in. Great long ships getting coals clawed out of their insides that the cranes droppped thundering into trucks before a locomotive would haul them off to the giant power station at Yoker. Standing high on railway banks of clinker we'd watched them. Me and Kath. Puffing on tarry Portuguese cigarettes cadged from the sailors off a sulphur boat.

They've no need for the dredgers Farchar. There's no the same activity down there now. The Port Authority's likely sent them to the breaker's yard by now. And why shouldn't they? To keep somebody in a watchie job? Things move on. The old place round about us was a living endorsement of that. All kinds of things happen. There was probably a time when some crowd of redundant monks had sat right on the spot where me and Jimmy were. Mulling into their habits over pots of ale. What the fuck would they do with the rest of their lives now the cathedral was sacked? Yes. They'd all flowed through this place at one time or another when the job was over. Scots and Highland and Irish. Polish and Russian and Lithuanian too.

Jimmy died on a Sunday afternoon. Sitting on the edge of my bed he was about to put a lit match to the end of a cigarette. His arm only reached halfway when his heart gave in he never got to light the smoke. He just hit the floor. There wasn't a breath in him and that was that. I went and reported it and the authorities organised his going-away in a Corporation cremmy in some housing scheme away up in the north of the city. Four of us were sitting on the pews staring at the coffin. Three other lads from the lodgings had made it along too.

For a moment I reckoned I could maybe see the last bit of light coming out of the top of the coffin but maybe no. I'd just come out the brightness into this dingy light. Four geezers in top hats had carried the box in and laid it up on the plinth then bowed and made their exit. They let it sit there long enough to allow us a few parting thoughts then these crimson curtains opened and it trundled away down the rollers towards the fire. It was all a bit gaudy and fairground-attraction. I was waiting for one of the top-hat men to leap out grinning and strike a few bars on a Wurlitzer as the box rolled away through the curtains. That was Jimmy off now anyway.

We all knew one another but we shuffled around outside at the gate and shook hands awkwardly not really knowing what to say. Clouds of steam were pouring out of our mouths into cold bright morning air.

Are ye comin for a drink wae us Farchar son?

I said no thanks and left them there and made my way towards the canal path that would carry me above the road and down towards the city centre. I don't think the lads would've been too surprised at me not going with them. I didn't really associate much with any of them. Campbell had been the exception. Even then all I really did was listen. Some of them called me The Quiet Man and I liked that. John Wayne eh?

The nerves were still jangling a bit from Jimmy's collapse and there was an empty feeling going through me. I passed a rotting lock gate with foam pouring through and thought I could hear the scriptures hissing in the churning water. Something drew me to the edge of the canal. There was something down there. Down under the scummy weeds where eels slithered through sunken garbage and dead puppies and discarded TVs. I gave myself a jolt and continued down the towpath.

At the canal-end they were gutting a dilapidated granary to transform into prestige flats. A grim-looking wharfside building had lain empty for generations. Beside it to the north was Possil with all its woes and dereliction. Directly behind to the east was a hill crowned with electricity pylons and giant transformers. The tall chimney of a processing plant spewed down a perpetual yeasty stench. Underneath to the south was a roadway canyon ten lanes broad where one of Europe's busiest motorways belched clouds of lead into a choking atmosphere. To the west the stagnant canal sat under the nose of the building. But the development would be a roaring success and the flats here would go for a song. It was all about audacity. The triumph of the bold over the unlikely. All that and sophisticated surveillance equipment.

Any fool could see the world had changed. It was property or nothing. But if there was one thing thinking about Jimmy's story taught me as I walked towards the heart of Atlantis it was this. He'd made his exit with a fiver in his wallet and a half-tin of tobacco in his jacket pocket. The sum total of his estate. And what'll the rest of us have when we go anyway? They'll lay us on a slab and strip us naked. The property we once thought we owned'll be divvied up among some shower of squabbling relatives. Tearing the last will and testament to shreds like a flock of corbies at a road-splattered rabbit. And if they don't get you somebody will. Yes. There was only one possession common to us all that we ever really owned in this world. Wee Jimmy had been keen to share his with me before going on that final journey to the Land Beyond the Crimson Curtains. The one and only possession we can truly call our own. And that is. Our story.

When I got to London Road I had a couple of drinks to get the funeral out of me. They collared me as I was making my way past the Green. Two officers sat me on an old graveyard wall then radio'd for a van. MacGrabbed. Carted and snibbed.

First I'm thinking it's just a sweep-up until they came down to the cell for me and took me upstairs to the Hospitality Suite. We were sitting in total silence. Inspector Daniels with his arms folded. Sitting across the table from me. He had one of those *I know exactly what's going on inside your head son* expressions on him. Like instead of looking at me he's looking at this screen in my eyes that's telling a story. Tilting his head this way and that as though he's following images and smiling wryly and nodding every so often. Thus I'm supposed to conclude that he can visualise my crime as it re-runs itself in movietone inside my mind. Then I begin to *crack.* Fuck's sake. You're invincible Daniels. I can hear Inspector Taggart now. *Hey. Jere's been a kidney washed up on the banks o the River Finglas. We've done a DNA check. It's been idjentified as your uncle. I happen tae think this is a murdjur. Come oan sonny. Did joo do jis murdjur?* If there's one thing the Fach's good at it's sending his mind to a remote place. The land where the rush of the waters meets the song of the wind among the trees. Daniels was trying hard to find his way in there. Through all the vines and thorns and swamps that made up the topography of my past.

> *Funny how death seems tae follow you about is it no?*
>
> *Pardon?*

He lashed out with the regulation hefty slap on the side of the head. I've had worse.

> *Don't come the funny man wi me. I said. Funny how death seems tae follow you about. Is it no?*
>
> *I heard you but I don't understand.*

You know what I'm sayin? I'm sayin Jimmy Campbell for a start.

Jimmy Campbell? I'm just back from the man's funeral.

And how did he die?

He'd a heart attack. It was me that reported it.

So I heard. You're a funny customer you are ye no?

Naw. No really.

Oh I'd say you were a funny customer. Killed yer fuckin bird and yer wean did ye no?

I went on a New Year bevvy and neglected to look after my lassie's needs. She was pregnant and went into labour early. They were up in the hills at Strathfinglas.

Aye. Fuckin killed them eh?

They were frozen to death.

Fuckin wean killer eh?

Ask the Procurator Fiscal. There's a death report.

Fuckin funny cunt. Lassie killer. Fuckin wean killer.

Am I gettin charged wi something?

I'll ask the questions here ya fuckin big eejit. What's your relationship with Duncan MacNab?

He's my uncle. He was my foster parent as well.

WAS?

Aye. I don't take much to do with him now.

And how long has he been missing?

Missing? I don't know. Didnae know he was missing.

There's something no right wi you son. I know all about you. You've got previous have ye no?

Eh? Aye. Nothin much. Just a couple of daft breaches in Glasgow. I got in an affray at an eviction once.

Oh I've got mair than that in front of me here. Ten days remand? You and your cousin. In possession of human remains. Carrying a corpse aboot the streets in Clydebank. Know what I think? I think you're a fuckin freak son.

That? It was just an auld skeleton. We found it in the peat up the OK hills. We only got a wee breach for it a thirty quid fine.

Fuckin weirdo. Remanded in custody for carrying a corpse in the streets?

They snibbed us in Longrigend until some Professor up in Glasgow Uni did tests on it. The thing was ancient. A lot aulder than me anyway.

And what were ye doin' taking it back tae yer cousin's?

Ah don't know really. Use it as a kind of ornament I suppose.

An orn? An o-ornament?

I don't know. It was years ago. A conversation-piece or somethin.

Cheeky bastard! You killed yer bird and yer wee wean and ye carried human remains through the streets in Clydebank. You're fuckin warped son that's ma opinion. And what did ye do wi yer uncle then? Eh?

There was something holding me together and when they took me back to the cell I realised what it was. I hadn't killed Duncan. He'd taken the leap from the sandstone shelf then I'd given him the option of grabbing the branch and getting ashore. Okay so I could've phoned to get him out of the pipe. Fuck that. Theyd've sent divers into the gorge and come up with the shotgun. So I left him down there in the turbine among all the river debris with a million gallons of water pouring through him every day. Plucking at his decaying skin until he looked like one of Gilquhan's Islamic heads in a jar. His organs would be eel fodder by now. A skeleton in a parka. But it was a guilt-free conscience that was keeping me clear-minded. All I had to do was keep my mouth shut or they'd rap me for it. So maybe his top lip and moustache had popped up at some riverside picnic. But Daniels was certainly being vague. That was it. I would brass it.

Day after day the Inspector was deaving me with the same question. Where was I on the First of March last year? Jazzus. How was I supposed to remember that? My mind was fucked. I was just an auld wine-riddled jakey now. Dredging the gutters of darkest Atlantis. My head was full of blanks. Blankitty blank. Blankitty blank blankitty blank blankitty blank. Supermatch game. Hech! Hech hech hech! Hech hech hech hech HECH!

What exactly was your relationship with Duncan MacNab?

Uncle and foster parent.

I'll ask again. What. Exactly. Was your relationship with Duncan MacNab?

Just what I told you.

What exactly do you stand to gain on the death of Duncan MacNab?

Eh? Nothing I know of.

Sure?

Sure.

That's no what I've got in front of me here. He owes you does he not? You know there's a will.

I don't know that Inspector.

Oh I think you do.

Fur fack's sake. The cruel uncle and the inheritance. He'd worked me into a Dickens novel now. If there was a will it was the first I'd heard of it.

Have you ever heard of a man who goes by the name Lord Scobie?

Whoops. Decoy. Red herring. Banana skin. Step over it. Then Daniels threw a photograph down on the desk. If it was a banana skin it was a clever one. Photo of a refined looking gadgie in tweeds.

Look closely. Do you know. Or have you ever seen. This man?

I have never seen this man.

Another two photos came down in front of me. Old guys again and dapper looking.

Well?

I can honestly say. That I don't know these men.

Sure?

Sure.

Tell me somethin. If you saw Lord Scobie walking along Argyle Street. What would you say to him?

Something went through my head along the lines of *if he said to me will ye have a dram I'd reply aye man that's my hobby.* I kept the button on it of course.

I'll ask you again Farchar son. You can confide in me. How did you get on with Duncan MacNab?

To tell the truth. For all the years I spent under his roof we never got to know one another.

Sure?

Aye sure.

Did he ever touch you?

What?

I'll make myself plain. Cranky stuff. Stoat the baw.

Pardon?

Noncey poncey.

I'm not with you.

Come on son you know what I'm saying. Square peg in the round hole. Sneakin in the boys' gate.

I'm sorry Mister Daniels. I haven't a clue what you're.

For fuck's sake son. Did he sexually abuse you?

Naw. For fuck's sake naw. No at all.

Have you ever heard of an organisation called The Chalice the Cross and the Secret Word?

This time I wobbled. He felt a wee twitch on the end of his line. He folded his arms on the table and started viewing into my eyes again. I shook my head. Logical denial I could cope with. Lying might be another kettle of haddock altogether. I was still this side of the truth. I had never heard of an *organisation* called The Chalice the Cross and the Secret Word. He was bound to ask me about Baden and Edith next. Daniels kept staring. I looked back. Then something began to happen. The Inspector's form was changing. A shabby greatcoat found its way over his shoulders. A military cap with a red stripe appeared on his head. There was a submachine gun in his hands as he stared hard into my eyes through the grimy window of a U-Bahn carriage from the platform of a derelict station. I was only going to Friedrichstrasse for a bottle of whisky but if I cracked I'd end up in a Siberian death camp. Brassing it out for the sake of a cheap dram. If I could manage the Red Army I could manage Daniels. Surely. He lit a cigarette and the uniform faded away as he fumbled with the photographs again. He put them face down then turned them over one by one like he was dealing Black Jack.

Him?

No Sir.

Him?

No Inspector.

Him?

No Mister Daniels.

They took me away in the dark blue wagon then snibbed me up in Barlinnie and that was the last I saw of the Inspector. I was there for thirty-six days waiting on some kind of charge. Every day I waited for a result. Daniels unsnibbing the door with a grin on him like a big cat. They'd found a bit of Duncan. They'd dated the death. Somebody had heard the shotgun. Somebody had witnessed me running to the phone box.

On the thirty-seventh morning I was led from my cell and out the front door. Not a word was spoken.

Outside the jail there was only the groan of traffic plying east and west on the M8 as I unbundled the langcoat. I put the langcoat on me then palmed up and down the sides and had a fumble about to ensure all the trusty possessions were still present and correct. Bingo. I rolled up a smoke and lit it then looked back at the high security fence and the featureless grimy sandstone halls of the jail. Between the interrogation and the Bar-L I'd been in custody for a total forty days without charge. No explanation. Nothing. I opened up steam on the forty-inch shanks and headed townward. Then I started on some drinking. Serious drinking. The Brocken Spectre was burning bright on me in those days. I could see it on some of my buddies too. What the hell. It doesn't necessarily make you a bad person. There were ones down there who would've shared their last smoke with you.

* * * * * * * * * * * * * * * *

Made my way west one day trawling for old memories. Realised I couldn't handle it any more and stood on the Belmont Brig. Right by the spot where we flung off the Christmas tree. Kelvin rippling far below. Ribbon of light under the gloom of the trees. I climbed up on the parapet. Out I went. OUT OUT OUT I went.

What the hell happened that day? I made the leap then drifted outside of myself and saw my body fly out across the water. I was standing on the parapet watching it go down. Then back up I came. Crashing into myself knocking me sprawling down on to the pavement. Swear I heard a splash in the pool far below. People were passing. Looking then walking away. An old wifie stopped. *Are ye awright son?* I was shaking and crying and holding onto the bridge then I stumbled up and walked away. There was an east wind blowing. Chills. Cold numbing chills. I felt weightless. Something had drifted out of me. Knew one day I'd have to find it again.

When I reached the Gallowgate the east wind had got angrier and spat flurries of sleet between the buildings. The orange streetlights flickered into life. The lights that make a blurry subsea world of this dark Atlantis. Buses and cars groaning in and out of the city centre beneath the soot-blackened unicorn of the Tolbooth. I bought some wine and cider paid for it through an iron grille and sat shivering in a cobbled pend until the warmth of the alcohol found its way through me. I fell asleep don't know how long. When I woke the shanks were frozen numb with wet sleet lying on them so I eased myself up and made my way into the street.

The café under the disused rail bridge sent out a welcome light. The lady in there treated me just like a regular customer. I'll never forget that. I managed to slurp down a soup then she brought over a mug of hot sweet scalding tea. I looked around me.

All around the walls were little home-made decorations fashioned like five-pointed stars and covered with different-coloured shiny foil. Each star had a legend on it written in ink-marker advertising the fare of the café. There was one with CHIPS. Another with BEANS. COFFEE. STEAK PIE. And PEAS. A car passed under the bridge and for a second its headlights caught the inside wall of the café and the light reflected against one of the stars. A wee star shining just for me. I knew I had to get out of this. There was one star shining for me. The Gravy Star.

I reckon whatever it was that hit the pool below Belmont Brig dragged itself from the river and took on a life of its own. A double of me in a langcoat of algae and slime dripping with water and smelling like the Kelvin. One day we'll meet up and shake hands and have a real good crack about our different adventures. As for me. I left the café of the Gravy Star that night. I started getting paranoid about Daniels' men. Jouking into closes every time I saw a uniform or a car. I dossed out in the pend then next day headed back up the West End. I remembered the tunnel I'd discovered with Ola years ago when we'd been out walking away back in the Blane Gardens days. Found it again but it was all shackled up. No entry. Until later that day. Then along came a man with some snips and a bar. Some snips and a bar ha HA!

I'm watching the wind sweep over Lochan Cnoc a Habhain and stowing all the gear into the trusty pack and throwing it on to my back. Strolling away with the Haven receding behind me. I'd reckoned on a grand march back into St Ronans. I'd stroll past the Bull and deek in the window for a last final look before stepping aboard the Swiftbus. But there'd be no plastic fittings or sterile gas fires or tables of bored crusties. Instead I'd look through the window at another time. In the dim light I'd see us all there. Letting rip with our mental chants and songs and old Bell laughing away at the far side of the counter. But to different paths. There's still a couple of days' food left. If I strike out across Meikle Carnock I can miss St Ronans altogether then cross the Strath and over the southern hills and find my way through the glens all the way back to Atlantis.

With each step I can feel the life coming back to me. Over rocks and heather and tracks and ancient drove roads for mile after mile. I walk under the stars then doss down for an hour or two in the shelter of an ancient tomb. I'm up marching with the dawn until I march into the great mountainous sweep of Loch Katrine and pick up the track that follows the route of the stone tunnel carrying water all the way to the city in the unseen distance. Through pipes and syphons and filters that strain off all the unwanted matter that lies under the murky shadows of Katrine. After all. You never know what's down there eh?

The aqueduct crosses the deep cut of the Duchray. This is a place of magic where three centuries ago the Reverend Robert Kirk disappeared into the Secret Commonwealth of the faeries. *Lured by their faery tunes and dances and laments that would draw a tear from a corpse.* Kirk's writings combined the rites of wizards and seers with biblical quotations and it got me thinking about all the unknown things and about my Brocken Spectre. Who knows what it is? I only know it's there for real. But just like one day the Gilquhans were trying and condemning innocent women for burning haystacks twenty miles away there might be a simple explanation. Chemical combustion in the case of the burning stacks. But why does the Brocken flare up when it does? Good question my friend. As for the incident on Belmont Brig. Somebody or something still wants me around.

I'm marching on with relentless pace over hill and moorland. Breaking away from the aqueduct route and through a grove of conifers to the heights of Bad Ochainaich where herds of deer run and the Muir Park Loch glints like a blue gem far below. Down into the village of Drymen then southward on the Stockiemuir Road. I veer off the road to strike the old potholed track that'll complete the last memory and final leg of the journey. Following the course of the Burn O Crooks where it twists down foaming through little mossy chasms as it drops from the moorland.

I'm on the wee grassy knoll perched above the Burn O Crooks. Getting a good fire together. Heather heart in smouldering forge. This is as good a place as any to put a flame to the Annals and end the story for good. Cremate the chap-book and the past. Might as well. Onto a different path now. I take out the bulging folder and poise with it over the flames. But then I find. That I just can't bring myself to do it. So I stow it back in the pack then fill the can and brew a hot sweet bellyful of tea and chomp down the very last of the scran that'll see me to the other side of the hills.

The forty-inch shanks stride on with all their great power away up the glen to the loch where we dug the skeleton out of the turf all those moons ago and that we did time for. Then uphill to the Lily Loch and over by Fynloch Hill. Along the shores of Loch Humphrey then pick up the track past the Black Linn. Walking off the braes with the Annals still in the bag. The great unfinished.

I break off from the track that leads downhill from the Black Linn. Across the Linden dam then find a path to the gully that leads down Connalton. Walking down the big field the lights of Central Scotland have come on and the whole of the valley is glowing like embers. The Clyde flows through the heart of it then passes below into the broadening firth reflecting the rising moon. As night darkens the constellations of scattered towns take on discernible shapes against the blackness of the land. The light show. Down the other side of the firth Port Glasgow becomes a camel. A hump of glistening streetlights and a long neck and head. Above Bishopton a kestrel hovers with curved wings. Far to the east an isolated curve of lights is a train heading towards the city. Then moving lights flash below me as the giant shadow of a 747 drops down to the airport runway with its strip of lights far beyond. The whole broad valley glints. A great gigantic carnival.

How it all changes in half a lifetime. She-farter in her dotage now. Appearing every now and then to release a half-hearted *pimp.* Crawling out of the black rotten woodwork of her heart to condone political mass murder in Chile. Eengonyama. She is a hippopotamus. The Auchentorlie burn flows down into blackness in a gloomy tunnel a hundred feet below the West Highway where cars and trucks thunder between Dumbarton and the city. I pass under the road then pick up the Loch Lomond cycle track and stride into Bowling. Jouking off the track at the Manse Road and down into the Bay Inn for a beer.

This is a good place and I'll sit here a while with a cold beer in front of me dreaming about what's to come next. The past will never be done and dusted. Maybe I'll never deal with it. But at least I've had a wee try. And I'll try and get all that political shit out of my head too. Futile. And my obsession with the industrial past. Well. Maybe for a day or two anyway Hech! I know I'll have a place to stay tonight and for as long as I like because Maggie's told me so. Maggie the gorgeous vampire and her Coffin Bar. The Coffin Bar with all its undead and sci-fi anoraks and Goth throwbacks. Aye. Hang out with some normal people for a change. At eleven o'clock I'll head along to Bowling station and catch the last electric train back into the city. Past Bowling Harbour with its sunken skeletal wrecks in the mud. Where ships of the world would pass through Scotland between the Atlantic and the North Sea. Oops. There I go already.

Then I'm hearing a conversation at the bar that they're opening up the canal again. For pleasure boats some big tourist project for the new century. Upriver they'll be turning the old yards and factory sites into a giant marina and hotels.

New times ahead for MacNab my friend. The millennium and all that shite. But for now I'll just sit here a while with a pint or two and dream. Yes. I know I'm an unusual figure sitting in my langcoat with my tall gaunt frame. Every so often somebody at the bar turns around and has a wee look at me. But they seem like friendly folk here and none too fazed. And I can feel myself begin to glow. Not with the Brocken but with the wind and the light of the sun from the last few days I've spent out on the land. Hey mister. You at the bar. Turn around and look at me again. Go on. Tell me. What do you see? Yawoo. I am the Fach. I am the glowing man.

Publishing May 2001

The Dark Ship
Anne MacLeod
This vast literary saga celebrates love, music and poetry in a finely woven story that reflects the complex past of a community on a Scottish island.
1-903238-27-7
£9.99

Dead Letter House
Drew Campbell
Suspend your disbelief for a bizarre trip into the surreal. On a twenty mile walk home a young man explores time and space and discovers his own heaven and hell.
1-903238-29-3
£7.99

The Gravy Star
Hamish MacDonald
One man's hike from post-industrial urban sprawl to lost love and a burnt-out rural idyll.
'A moving and often funny portrait ... of the profound relationship between Glasgow and the wild land to its north.' James Robertson, author of *The Fanatic*.
1-903238-26-9
£9.99

Strange Faith
Graeme Williamson
This haunting novel tells the story of a young man torn between past allegiances and the promise of a new life.
'Calmly compelling, strangely engaging.' Dilys Rose
1-903238-28-5
£9.99

About 11:9

Supported by the Scottish Arts Council National Lottery Fund and partnership funding, 11:9 publish the work of writers both unknown and established, living and working in Scotland or from a Scottish background.
11:9's brief is to publish contemporary literary novels, and is actively searching for new talent. If you wish to submit work send an introductory letter, a brief synopsis of your novel, a biographical note about yourself and two typed sample chapters to: Editorial Administrator, 11:9, Neil Wilson Publishing Ltd, Suite 303a, The Pentagon Centre, 36 Washington Street, Glasgow, G3 8AZ. Details are also available from our website at **www.11-9.co.uk.**

If you would like to be added to a mailing list about future publications, either register on our website or send your name and address to 11:9, Neil Wilson Publishing Ltd, Suite 303a, The Pentagon Centre, 36 Washington Street, Glasgow, G3 8AZ.

11:9 refers to 11 September 1997 when the Scottish people voted to re-establish their parliament in Edinburgh.

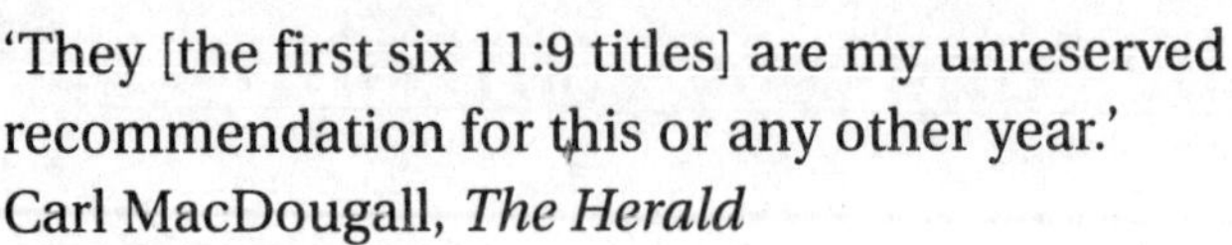

'They [the first six 11:9 titles] are my unreserved recommendation for this or any other year.'
Carl MacDougall, *The Herald*

Hi Bonnybrig 1-903238-16-1
Shug Hanlan
'Imagine Kurt Vonnegut after one too many vodka and Irn Brus and you're halfway there.'
Sunday Herald

Rousseau Moon 1-903238-15-3
David Cameron
'The most interesting and promising debut for many years. [The prose has] a quality of verbal alchemy by which it transmutes the base matter of common experience into something like gold.'
Robert Nye, *The Scotsman*

The Tin Man 1-903238-11-0
Martin Shannon
'Funny and heartfelt, Shannon's is an uncommonly authentic voice that suggests an engaging new talent.'
The Guardian and *Guardian Unlimited*

Life Drawing 1-903238-13-7
Linda Cracknell
'*Life Drawing* brilliantly illuminates the contradictions of its narrator's self image ... Linda Cracknell brings female experience hauntingly to life.'
The Scotsman

Occasional Demons 1-903238-12-9
Raymond Soltysek
'a bruising collection ... Potent, seductive, darkly amusing tales that leave you exhausted by their very intensity.'
Sunday Herald

The Wolfclaw Chronicles 1-903238-10-2
Tom Bryan
'Tom Bryan's pedigree as a poet and all round littérateur shines through in *The Wolfclaw Chronicles* – while reading this his first novel you constantly sense a steady hand on the tiller ... a playful and empassioned novel.'
The Scotsman

Already available from bookshops and the 11:9 website: www.11:9.co.uk